TENEBROUS TALES

A STITCHED SMILE ANTHOLOGY

© 2019
STITCHED SMILE PUBLICATIONS
ISBN: 978-1-945263-97-2

Stitched Smile Publications books may be purchased for educational, business or sales promotional use. For information please email vasquez@stitchedsmilepublications.com

Cover Design by Darque Halo Designs

Table of Contents

GHOSTS OF MEMORY

(night terrors part 1)

BY JASON MORTON

The thunder crashes,
The room explodes in shadows,
The wind rattles the window with intensity only seen when gods
are mad.
The screams echo,
Is this real?
A truth I am terrified to find out.
Mommy crying,
Daddy laughing,
Piss stained sheets chaffing my skin.
The ending of a dream,
But all so real,
I awake in a scream.
Ready for my lungs to burst,
The rain is falling,
And the thunder crashes.
I cower beneath the sheets,

Afraid to face this again,
The light burst in seconds of illumination.
A face gazes back,
Smiling with blood-stained, razor blade teeth,
Another flash the face is gone.
 Mommy crying,
Daddy laughing,
Piss stained sheets chaffing me.
A blast so loud,
It echoes off the walls,
A thump as something hits the floor.
Boots scraping,
Dragging something behind it,
Coming closer.
Nearing me,
Instilling a dark fear in me,
Shadows dance as the door opens.
Cowering in fear I look up,
Eyes pop open,
Lost in mid screech.
The Terror killing me,
The rain falling,
The thunder crashes.
It seems I've lived this before,
I try the lights, but they won't work,
The end of another dream slowly evaporating from my mind.
A new form of shadows moving along the wall,
A giant man with a giant knife,
Standing above me.
With a gleeful laugh,
Ready to kill me,
And I scream.
Oh, how I scream,

Will this be it?
The window breaks.
Glass falls in storms of fragmented sanity,
I pray, I scream, I cry,
The giant above me disappears.
Gone with the glass from my window,
I hear Mommy's cries turning to screams,
Daddy's voice rising with evil intent.
The violence inside him stronger than any storm,
Darker than any dark,
Smash, crash, then a loud pop.
The screams stopped,
Everything silent and still,
A dragging of something heavy.
A dull sound like blade hitting the bone,
The storm outside echoes with crashes and explosive laughter,
I close my eyes; the flash of the storm wakes me up.
All is eerie and oddly quiet,
The night is over, everything destroyed,
It was years ago that everything changed.
When my mom was killed and my dad went insane,
Now that storm is history.
But there is a storm inside,
It haunts me every night,
The dreams of terror haunt me.
They will never end,
They are my ghosts of memory,
My visions of insanity.
One day I will be strong enough to leave this place,
One day they will let me sleep without restraints,
Until then I'll remember that day.

BORN POLITICIAN

By Peter Molnar

"Something's come up, John."

Carter Neulander stood a full foot taller than Dr. John Teller, and his barrel chest was more widened ribcage than muscle bulk. Neulander was still dressed despite the lateness of the hour, nearly 1:00 a.m., in a charcoal pinstripe suit and a red tie the billionaire always wore longer than the buckle of his belt for some reason. Dr. Teller wanted so many times to fix the damned thing but thought better of it. *How the fuck is it I know how to knot a tie better than my boss—the Carter Neulander of Neulander Pharmaceuticals, Incorporated? I'm a veterinarian, and I know how to tie a tie better than this hump!*

Carter Neulander laid a hand on the senior veterinarian's shoulder and smiled with little laugh lines stitched across his temples. "Our little exotic in Cage Seven? I need you to put it down. Painless. Above all else, *painless*. Do you understand?"

"Cage Seven?" Dr. Teller felt his heart between his teeth, pulsing and copper-tasting. He thought of the photograph in his wallet, the one he'd cut out of an old *Vogue* magazine. He always

9

wondered what Neulander would do if he ever found out the veterinarian carried around a clipped photograph of the billionaire's wife, dead from suicide a little over a year ago. *A beauty! Fragile. Drifting, yes! But beyond lovely!* "Are you serious?"

"As the Big Casino, John. Within the hour. I want it done tonight. That and the burial. By morning, I want it to be as if it never existed."

Dr. Teller gnashed his teeth at Neulander's word choice. *It.*

*   *   *

Portia Neulander reached her father's estate while he was consulting with the wildlife reserve veterinarian. The Bradford Reserve (named after Portia's late grandfather) housed nearly fifteen rare, exotic, and endangered species of birds and mammals. It occupied two-thirds of the palatial estate on Long Island.

The estate's servant, an old man named Duke, escorted her up into her father's study with a slow, belabored step. When he was younger, he used to give Portia horsey rides all around the east wing of the mansion. Of late, Duke had retreated into something of a sullen soul as the years fled by. He barely managed more than the cursory "How are you?" as they wound their way up the stairwell to the second floor. Before he left her, the old man flung his long arms around Portia and gave her a hug. She felt the pinprick of tears at the corners of her eyes and blinked them back. Long ago, Duke would prattle on and on to her about one day opening a cheesesteak shop in downtown Manhattan to rival the joints in South Philly. No mention of that for as long as she could remember.

Her father always kept his study colder than the rest of the house. It was where he spent most of his time. He called it his *war room,* and she only recently found herself there more and more after he appointed her Chief Overseer of his Exploratory Committee. Father was seriously considering a run for president.

The numbers Portia and her team gathered from a cross-section polling of voting-age Americans in red and blue states yielded results that inspired the whole team. They would be enough to nudge her father out of mere consideration and into the realm of making a formal announcement.

Still, Father sounded flustered on the phone earlier. *Scared, even?* Portia decided that wasn't it. *Just jitters. He wants to run. This will lift his spirits!*

"We have to talk," her father said over his cell, rousing her out of bed at half past midnight. "It has to be now. I'll see you soon."

Her father didn't make requests; his were words the equivalent of a Papal Bull.

Portia checked her watch and swept her eyes about the study. Father's *War Room* smelled of varnish and cigarette smoke. This was where he snuck his butts. Even after his bypass, he couldn't kick the habit. Portia was a gym rat when she wasn't working. Her lithe body and washboard stomach were proof positive of the healthy addiction.

The walls were lined in hundreds of book spines, a good number of them old and leather-bound. A few thrillers by Harlan Coben and Michael Savage peeked out among the more priceless volumes, the newer hardcovers' spines cheery and colorful in contrast to their stuffy neighbors. Sconces glowed low between each bookcase, casting subtle yellow bands down the oil paintings hung beneath them. Four of the five oil paintings in the study depicted different lines of the feline family. A mountain lion standing on a tall bluff, staring off menacingly into the sunset. A jaguar charging through the green, leafy lush of a rainforest. A cougar stalking a pronghorn antelope across a barren desert, legs in furious mid-pump. Here a leopard. There a—

"Bitch," Portia hissed, as her gaze fell upon the largest painting hanging behind her father's cherry desk. It showed a woman in her early fifties, with ash blonde hair piled high atop her head and sprayed heavily to hold the height. She sat in a red velvet-lined chair with a high gold-caste back that rose well above the bun of her hair. A throne. *Bitch!* Her thin, white fingers grasped the gold knobs of the armrests as if for dear life. She wore a canary yellow evening gown, a string of fat white pearls at her porcelain throat. No cleavage. Portia remembered her flat as a rail with a body thin and straight as a spike in heels. *Those eyes.* Emerald green. Pinprick pupils. An aquiline nose ran down towards a sliver of bloodless lips set into a snarl, which passed for a smile among those who had known her and a hex to those who had only ever seen her image spilled across the tabloids.

I'm glad you're dead. I don't know what my father was thinking. He had his own money. His own notoriety. You were nothing but a wicked stepmother descended from a Disney movie screen.

Daniella Devereaux-Neulander.

Heiress to the Devereaux coffee fortune.

A socialite whose death produced as much fodder for endless media speculation as her addiction to plastic surgery. An addiction that swelled in severity over time. A nip here. Tuck there. Millions of dollars poured into a boundless venture that soon turned to madness imprinted upon the face she had originally been trying to "improve" upon. Portia had her theories about what Daniella was trying to achieve with the surgeries. The tabloids soon validated her suspicions by running article after article with headlines like:

Daniella Devereaux-Neulander: "The Cat Lady."

Devereaux: "My husband loves the way I look!"

And Portia's personal favorite:

Journey into the Heart of a Socialite's Madness: "The Cat Lady's" Descent.

Portia's father always held a rich fascination for the feline species. He even had a tabby that ran around the mansion like she owned the place. Millie. A gift for Portia when she turned twelve; although, the cat had latched onto her father almost immediately. Portia lost interest soon after. Millie was still around, but her advanced age restricted her to the first floor. The tabby's legs couldn't carry her up the stairs anymore. Her father never could explain what his fascination stemmed from. He called them "beautiful hunters." "Stalking temptresses." "Art in motion." Portia chalked it up to her father's respect for anything or anyone who downed their enemies with a sly and stalking approach.

The heavy wooden door sighed open, and Carter Neulander came charging in. His breathing was labored, the knot of his tie yanked to the side, away from his bull throat.

"Beautiful Portia," he said, as she rose from her leather wingback chair and opened her arms for her father's trademark bear hug. "I'm glad you could get away. What did you tell Nicholas?"

"I told my *husband* you called, and it was important. That was all he needed. Honestly, Dad."

Carter held his daughter at arm's length and studied her with a small, doting grin. "Let me look at you," he said. "I mean, really have a look at what a lovely, intelligent young woman you've grown into."

This isn't like him. He doesn't say things like that. Portia immediately thought the worst. She envisioned X-rays with a shadow on them. Her father shrunken and wasting away in a hospital bed from lung cancer or an inoperable tumor.

"You okay, Dad?" Portia couldn't help herself, though she suspected he would not like the question.

He nodded, released her, and crossed the office to the tallboy against the wall, where a decanter of brandy and two snifters awaited his indulgence. "Drink?"

"It's late."

He poured out two fingers each anyhow. He handed her a snifter, waved her down into her wingback again, and claimed the other one arranged in front of his desk.

She fully expected him to take a seat across the desk from her, and when he did not, her alarm mounted all the more. She envisioned him in a sleek black casket, his arms folded over his heart with a green and white carnation pinned to the breast pocket of his burial shroud, a charcoal gray Armani suit. A shiver traipsed up and down her spine. She took a sip of her brandy.

This seemed to please her father, her partaking. He raised his glass and took a mouthful of his own firewater.

Portia dove in. "I've got good news about our polling—"

Carter raised his hand, closed his eyes like he was suddenly in great pain. "Hold on to that until I'm finished."

"Are you all right, Dad?"

"There's that question again," he said, wincing and adjusting himself. "Why don't we leave that one alone for now as well?"

He's not going to answer it. He never would.

Portia nodded. "All right. What's going on?"

Carter sat there for a moment staring off into space, as if he didn't understand the question. Then, he fished his hand down into his pants pocket and brought out a small folded slip of yellow legal pad paper. He handed it to his daughter, curled both hands around the snifter. "I'm being blackmailed."

Portia unfolded the paper, scanned it, and folded it back up. "Is there a magic decoder ring to go with this?"

Carter snapped his fingers, and she handed it back to him. He smoothed it out across one knee. He looked at it once more and raised his squinty green eyes to meet his daughter's expectant gaze. "It makes perfect sense. To me."

"Well, what does it mean?"

"The paper. The doctor's name written there."

"Who is he?"

He seemed to consider his answer beforehand. He taste tested it. "Private physician. Works out of New Delhi where he services an exclusive list of clients. Yes, I know him, and I gave him my business. A curious task, but he barely batted an eyelash when I told him what I wanted him to do. He did not demand any hush money when I had him sign a non-disclosure statement regarding his work. Of course, he had permission from the patient to perform the work. She was—I can't say she was of sound mind—but she was clear and lucid about her intentions. She wanted the procedure—*procedures*—performed. Both of us wanted it."

"She? *Who* is *she*, Dad?"

Carter Neulander swallowed the rest of his brandy, stood up, and stretched his arms outward. A wide wingspan for a man. He went and filled his glass once more, three fingers the second time out. Then, angling his body towards his daughter, Carter said, "Your late stepmother. She would do anything for me. To make me happy. So I would desire her. She also suffered from a rather severe form of *body dysmorphia*. She did not see herself in the mirror as you or I saw her. The general public. The cameras. Towards the end, she saw something entirely different. And we both agreed the only way to cure her of this discrepancy of self was to match up what she saw in the mirror to what she actually looked like."

"What did she see in the mirror?"

"It's my fault," sighed Carter, returning to his seat and collapsing into it. "My damned obsession became hers. Tenfold."

"Dad? *What did she see when she looked in the mirror?*"

"A cat," Carter said. He leaned forward and looked her dead in the eyes. "Like the ones on these walls. So … the name of the doctor written on that piece of paper, which was at some point slipped into my suit jacket during the day today? He saw to our request, and he did what we asked of him. Your stepmother was surgically transformed into … a member of the feline species. A mountain lion, to be exact. From head to toe. Someone close to me knows, and they are blackmailing your ole dad."

"Is that why she committed suicide?" Portia bolted forward in her seat.

"No-no-no," Carter said, waving his snifter in the air. "She's not dead. Let me explain. But understand, Portia, this will make you one of those in the know. The Indian doctor wouldn't do this. He'd only be incriminating himself. The surgeries he performed would most certainly come under fire as inhumane. A form of torture, even! Then, there is the part I played. There is your stepmother, but she's not talking. She wouldn't, even if she had the means to speak. Can't say who else would want to do battle with me. If they know me well enough to have access to an inside pocket of my suit coat, then they know I *could* and I *would* destroy them beyond reason. They know what I can do. What I've done."

"Tell me, Dad," Portia said. Despite her father's bold talk, there was still a visible palsy in the hand holding his brandy snifter. "Just … tell me everything."

Carter began.

*   *   *

When Dr. Teller finished, he pulled his khaki pants back up around his waist, zipped his fly, and fastened his belt.

He watched the animal lower its hindquarters back down to the ground of its caged enclosure. Its back legs were longer than the front ones, resulting in its flank being raised higher than its head and shoulders while crawling on all fours. It retreated into the far left corner of the enclosure. The animal's limbs quivered under strain, and its front paws grasped the turf to hold itself upright.

"I've found a team of physicians who can reverse *most* of this," he told her. "They're asking for an exorbitant amount of money, of course, but they don't know who you are—who you *were*—just yet. I'll tell them when all the preparations have been secured. Once payment is made, I'll take you out of here, and we'll travel to their facilities. No one will stop us. Carter Neulander can't afford to. He'll pay when I name our price. Right now, he's probably pulling his hair out trying to hash out who the hell figured it all out. Who has the balls to blackmail the likes of Carter-*fucking*-Neulander, right?"

Dr. Teller had known what the animal housed in Cage Number 7 was, or rather *who* it was, for a little over a year. The timeline of Daniella Devereaux's suicide (when she "walked into the Adriatic Ocean, her cargo pants packed with big, heavy stones and sewn shut") preceded the new arrival of the animal in Cage Number 7 by only three weeks. After the empty-coffin funeral for his wife, Neulander, distraught and tearful, made one of his regular business getaways across the globe and returned with this creature in his Learjet's cargo bay.

What Neulander failed to understand was the animal retained the watchful, stoic stare of Daniella Devereaux's emerald eyes. The unmistakable reticence shown through them and revealed the astute human consciousness behind them.

Dr. Teller spent more time with the new arrival than anyone else on staff. He'd also developed a powerful infatuation with Neulander's "dead" wife in life and before her "demise." Teller masturbated to a *Vogue* magazine cutout of her three times a day on average. It was no wonder he recognized her stare, the woman behind the oval, feline pupils of her eyes. His lustful obsession, come home to him in another form.

Needing rescue.

He secretly ordered a blood test. The results confirmed his suspicions.

"I told you we'd get him, Daniella. I know you never wanted this, but he's going to try to spin the whole thing. He's going to portray you as a nutcase. Don't worry. I'll be your voice, at least until they can restore your vocal cords. I promise."

Neulander often returned from his trips abroad with new and exotic animals. There were all manner of African cats, as well as other endangered species, that stalked their cages or enclosures all day and slept in fits and starts through the night, conjuring in their dreams the high plains and natural lushness of vegetation and bloody hunts.

"Hey," he said, advancing on her. "What's wrong?" Palms out, he hunkered down before her.

No tears. Unblinking eyes. *She's crying on the inside. One more thing he made sure she couldn't do if she needed it. To fucking emote!*

"Daniella. What we do together? It's not wrong. You know that, right?"

The animal dropped her head and spread her oddly shaped paws along her matted white-furred belly.

"I've always loved you. Why else would I go to all this trouble to free you?"

No movement. The animal held her pose, seemingly defeated.

"What do you want?" Dr. Teller asked. "Tell me?"

So the creature lunged at him and ripped Dr. Teller's throat out.

*   *   *

Carter Neulander explained: "Your stepmother was very ill. She had a warped self-image, and I don't use the word *warped* for lack of a better one. But it wasn't always that way, Portia. I know you can remember the good times we had together as a family early on. The vacations to San Trope. The wintering at the Pocono cabin. Christmases. Glorious trees rounded with all those gifts, many of which your stepmother handpicked for you throughout the year. She loved you like her blood, Portia. I know you resented her. Perhaps you thought of her as cold. But she was merely … misunderstood. This … condition … this *body dysmorphia* was not the first symptom of instability she exhibited. Her mental illness manifested itself as paranoia before anything else. She saw cameras watching her from every darkened ceiling corner. I had to replace at least twelve different iPhones for her because she smashed them all, insistent someone was watching her through her screen. She was certain … she was … terrified something was going to happen to *me*. We kept a nurse on staff, as well as a psychologist. Your stepmother attended daily sessions with her psychologist. The nurse saw to it she took her daily medicine without fail. Four tablets, twice daily. Nothing worked. As it was explained to me by her psychologist Doctor Lowenstein, Daniella was tragically resistant to any and all forms of medication.

"Then, she started to see herself in a far different light than any of us could have planned for.

"One night, she called me in hysterics. This was around nine in the evening, the time she performed her nightly ablutions and went to bed. I was in-flight on the way to Michigan to meet for late night drinks with some clients. She sounded so unhinged it was a wonder she possessed the presence of mind to use her cell phone. She said there was someone staring out at her from the mirror in the master bathroom. In retrospect, I might have said something else to comfort her, but how could I have known? I told Daniella she was seeing *herself* in the mirror, no one else. She fell silent. I thought she'd hung up. The next thing she said was what marked the beginning of what would become her own personal downward spiral.

"'I've become my spirit animal!' she told me. 'Oh my God, I'm a mountain lion! I'm one of your *goddam* cats! And you're going to hunt me *if I'm not careful*. Don't come home!' she begged me. 'Don't come home. You're going to hunt me. You're going to kill me and *mount my head in your office! You stay away from me!'* I was shocked to the core, Portia, to say the very least. I immediately phoned her nurse, commanded her to administer a Xanax to Daniella and to sit up with her for the remainder of the night. I was afraid she would hurt herself if left alone, and I couldn't exactly turn the jet around.

"When I arrived home the following day, I saw she had come into this office and taken all the paintings off the walls. All of them, including the one of her behind the desk. She was in a weakened state when I looked in on her, curled up in bed. She had the nurse call on her extended family members several times. What I can tell you about them is they did not disappoint in behaving like the bastards they always were. They were jealous of her fortune. Her father cut the rest of them out of his will. I heard it had something to do with a family fistfight in the Hamptons, an embarrassingly public one resulting in the Devereauxs being asked to leave the country club where they were about to tee off. Her three brothers each told her nurse Daniella was 'reaping what she had sown.' Vile human beings. You missed the worst of it, Portia. Judging by the look on your face, you had no idea about any of this."

"I—I didn't," Portia said. She glanced up at the portrait of her stepmother, only this time the sight of it summoned a profound sense of pity rather than boiling blood and rage. This was a woman who had never shown her warmth. All this time, Portia could only assume it was the woman's way, that the heiress was merely fulfilling the stereotype of her title by holding everyone at arm's length if you were family, and further away if you were not. Portia remembered the venomous things her stepmother said to her, especially during her awkward teenage years when she could have used the kind words of a mother figure in her life. Painful breakups were met with derision from Daniella Devereaux ("No one will ever want to make you or marry you unless you spread the money around, little girl, so get used to heartache!"). That was what Daniella called Portia growing up, whenever she addressed her: *little girl.* Portia nearly cracked under the pressure at seventeen. For years, she had been praying to her long dead mother for guidance, for some sign she would come out the other side of it all unscathed. Her mother never answered, at least in any way Portia would have recognized. But Portia did persevere, despite her stepmother's cruelty. "I had no idea. I just thought she was—"

"Evil?" Neulander suggested, wryly. "That was never the case. In our more private moments, she confided in me how horrible she felt about the way she treated you. She wanted to help it, to stop her abuse. Every time she tried to open her mouth with a kindness towards you, it was like a *devil* would rear up and push itself to the front of her mind, and she'd have no choice but to scold you. Hurt you. Widen the distance between the two of you. That's how she explained it to me."

There was one time. Isolated, which made it all the more memorable. Portia was a few months shy of her twenty-first birthday. She had come down the main hall and was approaching the top of the winding stairwell. The hall interconnected all ten upstairs rooms. Portia found Daniella lingering at the top of the stairs. She was still wearing her crème silken bathrobe. Her hair looked like it hadn't seen a detangling comb in days, and the black, ominous caking of black eyeliner ringed her eyes so deeply, it looked like it had not been washed away by the spray of a shower in just as long. She did not look drunk. She was not wavering. But Daniella Devereaux locked eyes with Portia the moment she came into view, as if her stepmother had been waiting there for her. Daniella's eyelids were pinched. Swollen. "Come here, little girl,"

Daniella beckoned. Portia checked her watch, fully prepared to charge past the woman and insist she was late for an appointment. But something stalled Portia. "Yes?" Portia asked, her tone tolerant and impatient at the same time. "Little girl, I don't know how to … I don't … know how to … I …" It was almost like Daniella was a machine running out of gas. She gave up, rushed past Portia, and shut herself up in the master bedroom at the end of the hallway. The slam of the door echoed like the door to a tomb. To this day, Portia wondered what the end of Daniella's sentence could have been, her complete thought.

Maybe, 'I don't know how to be kind to you?'

Carter Neulander frowned over the rim of his snifter and leaned forward. "She became suicidal. The more her inner circle negated what she insisted upon, that she was *changing*, the worse she felt about herself, and the more hopeless she became. I would try to change the subject whenever mention of her facial distortion cropped up in conversation. But eventually, every conversation I had with your stepmother became about her *alleged* morphing into a … it still sounds like a bad joke … a—a *fucking* mountain lion, for God's sake!

"Daniella took to wandering around the house in her robe and her ratty slippers. You'd barely know she was there in the room with you until she suddenly announced her presence with things like, 'It has to match! Why doesn't it match! Who ever heard of a mirror telling lies?' She was referring, of course, to the fact that what she saw in the mirror, the horror of her transformation, was nothing anyone else could see, and she desperately *needed* for her *mirror* to match what those around her saw. I was afraid to leave her alone, you see. This isn't to say my business affairs were not in the most capable of hands, but you know me, Portia! I'm not comfortable with leaving it all to the *help*. I was due in Buenos Aires for a convention, and I was the keynote speaker at the event. It wasn't like I could have backed out, even though I knew Daniella was worse than she'd ever been. She wouldn't leave the house. Agoraphobia set in. Sank its filthy claws into her. I left for the convention.

"While I was giving my speech thousands of miles away, your stepmother swallowed fifteen Xanax and chased it was a fifth of bourbon."

"Oh God, Dad!" Portia said, arming her wet eyes. "Why didn't you tell me?"

Neulander held up his hand, pushed on. "What came next was my idea. My. *Brilliant.* Idea." He set his drink down on the gleaming cherry end table beside his wingback and netted his hands across his knees. "I kept thinking about what she needed. By this time, her reputation was already damaged beyond repair. She had been labeled an unstable recluse in the tradition of Howard Hughes by the press, and there would be no coming back from that. She did not wish to leave the house. She did not want to be seen by people, and, ultimately, she communicated she would be happy with only myself as her company. She said I 'calmed her.' But, our relationship suffered during this ordeal. We weren't …" Carter paused, glancing at his daughter furtively. "We stopped being intimate. She wanted to. I couldn't … *perform.* Don't look at me like that! Let's not make this any weirder than it needs to be. You're a big girl, Portia."

"I'm not looking at you *any* way, Dad," Portia said. "But … what was *your idea*? Why are you being blackmailed?"

"I started researching doctors who could—and I know how this is going to sound, Portia—who could somehow match Daniella's vision of herself in the mirror with the one people see who would have contact with her, as profoundly limited as that became. I was careful not to involve anyone in this research. There was no paper trail of any kind. I did not relegate the task to any of my assistants. I handled it personally. I found Doctor Kumal Singh of New Delhi, but not by simply typing my questions into Google."

He paused, his light eyes narrowing with something of guilt. "I delved into the depths, as they say. I scoured the Dark Net, as it's called.

"I found Doctor Singh's contact information on one of the sites listed there. He runs a small, exclusive practice. Small staff comprised exclusively of close family. I purchased a burner phone and called him. Again, there could be no middleman here. Now, I want you to hear me when I tell you this. *Really understand me.* I discussed this with Daniella *before* I moved forward with any arrangements. She *wanted* to do this. To have to look in the mirror and see what no one else in the world sees is a crippling thing, and that is what she told me. Since neither I nor her therapist could convince her of her delusions, she and I decided it would be better for her to match what she saw in the mirror. Now, Portia, I did *not* try to hard sell her on this. In fact, I undersold the option, but Daniella wanted the surgery. So, we discussed further what would need to be done if the surgeries should prove a failure. She told me if it was a failure, and what was done could not be undone, she would want to be put out of her misery."

"Oh God, Dad," Portia said, rising and crossing the study towards the black, gaping mouth of its dormant hearth. "I think I understand now."

Carter sat there, staring off into space for so long his eyeballs dried up. He remembered to blink, set down his snifter, and raked his sandpaper-colored hair up and back from his forehead. He was a big man but crumpled up like a discarded sheet of paper right then. "The work she had done prior, to her face … it was nothing compared to what she wanted. The widening of the eyes and their slant at the corners. Those dreadful contact lenses she insisted on wearing that transformed her eyes into that of a cat's. The stretching of her mouth further up her cheeks so they touched the indents of her jaw bones. The incessant darkening of her skin to a bronze color in the tanning bed she made me buy for her. Pinching of the nose. Pink pigment injected just beneath the rugged cartilage of her nose. The paparazzi managed to get some shots off when she would stand by a window or peek her head out. 'The Cat Lady.' That's what they started calling her once the pictures circulated. In the days leading up to the procedure in New Delhi, your stepmother threw herself into her new role. She shaved her head of every blonde lock. She left a fine peach fuzz where it had been. I was extremely disturbed by what she was turning into. What she would ultimately become."

Portia looked at him, long and lingering. It was written all over his face. *You were frightened? Come on, Dad! Admit it, for once in your life! Show some humanity!*

"Doctor Singh secured the corpses of a pair of mountain lions. They were already on ice when we arrived there at his private clinic. The night before she would begin her transformation, we shared a long conversation of the soul where she again insisted if she looked *far worse* than a monster, I would have Doctor Singh deliver her a lethal injection. And if he wouldn't do that, I would have someone suffocate her." He paused, shook his head forlornly. "I knew I couldn't do it. I would have to figure something else out.

"You would be wondering how your stepmother passed for a such an animal and garnered no suspicion. Let me tell you, it was no doubt a painful process for her. I don't recall exactly when it was, at what stage of the transformation, but Doctor Singh suggested her voice box be removed. He told me she often awoke from her anesthesia screaming in agony. It got to the point she blew out one of the chords themselves, and that would have required a separate procedure. Her voice turned soft and gravelly, like a heavy smoker's voice in their final years."

Right then, Carter looked at his snifter like he couldn't remember how it ended up in his hand, let alone emptied. "You're going to have a hard time with this, but understand I was acting in her best interest at all times. I never lost sight of the ultimate goal, which was to match her appearance to the mirror. I didn't consult her about having her voice box removed. I simply heeded Doctor Singh's advice. I suppose a part of me understood the doctor was looking to protect himself from prosecution further down the road, and what better way to secure this than to rob the patient of her ability to speak. That's not why I allowed him to do it. My conscience was clear. I simply wanted her to fall back into her mind, and I thought taking away the ability to scream or to voice her exquisite pain would keep her locked into the physical torment of the surgeries. The doctor told me the vocal cords could absolutely be restored later down the road."

Portia sighed, dropped her gaze to the hardwood floor. "I don't believe that for a second. Not for one goddam second! You were invested in her silence. What did you think? She'd keep her mouth shut about what the two of you did to her once it came clear you were acting completely opposite of her *best interests*? I'm not an idiot, Dad! I'm disgusted!"

Carter stood with a grunt and approached the tallboy once more. He filled his snifter to its brim and turned towards Portia. A bit of the old, familiar malice glinted in his eyes. His nostrils flared, mouth a bloodless pair of white slugs. "Are you finished?" he asked, one salt-and-pepper eyebrow arching upward as he pulled a deep swallow of his nightcap.

"Are you?"

He winced at the burn of the drink in his chest. Then Carter Neulander laughed, quick and dirty. "Not by a mile, young lady," he said. "I have to purge, and by Christ, you *will* bear witness to my confession. If you're going to judge your ole dad, you're no better than my most unworthy adversary. Which side do you want to come down on in this? Decide now, or you can get the hell out. I'll see you in the breadlines before I announce my intention to run for the presidency. What'll it be?"

Portia tasted ash on her tongue and could have gagged. Nevertheless, she gave a quick, cursory nod. *I want him to finish it. I want to know all of it. He hasn't talked to me like this since prep school. Threats? You'd threaten your confidant?*

Carter gazed out the window into the dark void of night, framed by the pane like a fathomless black acrylic painting. "Doctor Singh worked swiftly once Daniella lost the ability to speak. I suspect he wanted to have done with all of it. He sawed off Daniella's legs at the knee and transplanted the legs of one of the mountain lions at the joint. He severed Daniella's hands at the wrists and attached the other mountain lion's paws to her arms. The sutures were monstrous, black thread stitched so thickly into the flesh she looked like she was wearing black manacles at the points of amputation. The doctor administered what he called 'the mother of all antibiotics' to allow for the bonding of the two tissues together. I was certain her body would reject the limbs, but ... it did not. Christ, it was almost as if her body welcomed the disproportion! Daniella would come to, and Doctor Singh would explain to her what was *new* about her. What he'd done while she was under. He showed Daniella her *new legs*. Her *new paws*. Her eyes watered and bulged. Her mouth flopped open and closed like a fish out of water. But I would sit with her after the doctor left and caress her. The panic left her eyes. I had that power. Believe what you want."

"I didn't say anything," Portia said.

"You didn't have to. It's written all over your face. I feel like I've got your mother in here judging me. Condemning me to hell. You look so much like her. It's almost too much right now." Carter paused, sniffed at the air. It did not appear to bother him as it did her. "The doctor grafted the mountain lion's fur all over her body. I want you to imagine the painstaking, time-consuming efforts it took to achieve this. To graft every last goddam strand of fur into your stepmother's skin until her whole body was covered in it. Her smooth, alabaster skin was completely concealed.

"Once they covered her in fur—"

"You insist *this* was what she wanted?"

Portia cried out when Carter smashed his snifter on the hardwood floor, his jowls blazing red. The back of his dress shirt split down the back, producing a sound like an unexpected fart. When he straightened, the look in his eyes terrified Portia. She glanced at the door, mentally measuring out the steps to the exit and whether she could make an escape faster than he could lunge at her. *I don't know this man. I have no idea who he is.*

"You're not going anywhere until I'm finished, Portia!"

Five wide strides ... maybe ...

That's when Carter Neulander moved towards the door to the study and placed himself in front of it. He folded his fat arms across his wide breast, a sentry. "You're sickened? Are you? I still loved her! Even then, I still loved her!" His eyes adopted a thousand-yard stare. "Then, they caged her. For two months, they trained her how to walk on all fours. To use her new limbs. Through the use of torture and reward. It did not come easy. It was never meant to. None of this was. That's the point! But, after a while, Daniella ceased to exist. She walked—stalked, I should say—like a deadly predator. She paced back and forth behind the bars of her cage, contemplating something I could never know.

"The first time I saw her down on all fours, I vomited. For hours. Dry-heaving. Terrible pains. I thought I'd bust the stents in my heart they put in over at Mercy Medical after my bypass surgery. I decided ... and it was no easy determination ... I decided I would not visit her again at the Singh Clinic. I decided I would stay away. Instead ... I set to work on something else."

Portia's mouth was a desert, her tongue stuck to the palate. She had to peel it away to speak. "That's when you started laying the groundwork for what would be my poor, *troubled* stepmother's upcoming suicide. The story. You started planting the seeds. And, congratulations, you sonofabitch! The world ate it right out of your hand! Your bullshit lies to cover up your sick decisions! Bravo, Dad!"

"They did," he said. "That's always been my strong suit."

"I   can   see   that."

"Deception. Sleight of hand."

"You're a born politician," she said.

*   *   *

Duke Worrell, the Neulander's butler, stopped what he was doing when he heard the sound of a baby crying just outside the window above the kitchen sink. He never had any children of his own, but Duke was godfather to his younger sister's daughter, now a mouthy sixteen-year-old. He remembered Cynthia was colicky as a baby. He'd been on the phone with his sister, and Duke could hear the little infant screaming in what sounded more like one of those New Year's Eve blowhorns than a child. *Weh-weh-wehhhhh!* Hearing his goddaughter all those years ago, crying and carrying on over the phone, did not rattle him nearly as much as the sound he heard coming from outside.

The screaming child he swore he heard tapped each and every button of his spine, like a xylophone. He was prepping tomorrow night's meal, a spicy twist on the traditional chicken divan dish. His hands were slick with raw chicken slime. He stood there in the low-lit kitchen, listening to the savage mewling.

Then a wretched, piercing *screeeeeeeee* ripped its way across the entire first floor.

Screeeeeeeeeeeeee!

"Dammit to hell," Duke said, and flung the cut of raw chicken down onto the cutting board. "How did that old cat get out *again*? How the hell does she *do* it?" Millie the Tabby had become more the thorn in Duke's side the last couple of months. She kept finding her way outdoors. Somehow. Mr. Neulander couldn't have cared less when Duke expressed his concern. What had Neulander said, with a brandish of his dismissive hand?

"Survival of the fittest. She'll win out."

Millie was a house cat and had been her whole life. Yet, she found some kind of covert exit by which she came and went. Duke must have searched the entire Neulander mansion for eight hours for any openings. Damned if he discovered anything other than they had a cockroach infestation in the laundry area.

"I should let you die out there! It would serve you right! I got work to do!"

It's Portia's cat, my man. You can't just leave it out there to become some feral animal's dessert. She loves that cat. As for never having any kids, Portia is the closest you ever came to loving someone like a daughter.

The cat let loose a long peal of torment.

Duke clutched his carving knife with the blade down, his hand curled around its black handle. He booked it through the hallway to the glass doors that opened onto the expansive oak deck.

"If I end up in the middle of a catfight, Mr. Neulander's going to *have* to pay me way more for my trouble. This is above and beyond!"

He slunk along, holding close to the mansion's rear stucco wall like it was home base offering protection. Spotlights positioned along the gutter splashed their ethereal white glow across the deck, converging into a rich sphere of light that fell strategically across the row of reclining chairs and table. Another spotlight lit up the side yard, and Duke was thankful for this. He descended the stairwell leading off the porch and emptying out into the sprawling expanse of grass, still green and thick despite the chilly fall temperatures. He stepped into the damp grass and discovered, to his dismay, he had a hole in his left shoe. The black sock beneath the patent leather sole *squished* and *squashed* with his every footfall. He bit his lip and trudged along, knife raised before him.

"Millie?" he whispered, his voice an irritated hiss. "Millie? Come on now! I don't have time for this shit—"

Rou-screee-screeee-rah-rou-

"Millie!" It sounded like one of the battling animals was rending the flesh off the other. "*Millie!*"

Duke broke free of the spotlight's spray, forging into the darkness. The change was disconcerting, and, suddenly, he heard his heart in his ears, a steady bass drum that hurt his eyes with every thud.

Screee-rou-rou-ROU!

It was coming from a row of tall arborvitae bushes, each a half-foot taller than Duke. In the dark of the waning fingernail moon, they looked like a line of dreadful shadow giants with their arms at their sides and pointed skulls aimed up at the slowly swirling heavens. He squeezed the knife handle and wondered if he'd have the *stuff* to stab a living thing if it came down to it. *One way to find out.* Duke surged forward; breath trapped in his lungs.

Something wet and warm struck him in the face.

His mouth was hanging open.

Fur bits stuck to his lips. Clung to his tongue.

Duke gagged, swabbing at his mouth.

He stepped into something soft, but sturdy enough. "Jesus Christ!"

The ruined remains of Millie the Tabby lay at his feet. The cat's stomach cavity was hollowed out. Splintered curves of bone jutted out of the jagged opening. The cat's eyes stared blankly up at the canopy of stars as if searching in vain for the Big Dipper.

"Oh dammit-*dammit!*" Clumsily, Duke stooped to gather up the cat.

He never heard a thing.

He knew nothing more once it landed on his back.

*   *   *

"So," Portia spoke, after a swollen time of silence, "you stopped visiting her. What you're *really* telling me is you abandoned her when it became too much to bear. I never thought I'd say this, but I feel sorry for that dreadful woman. As a matter of fact, could it be she wasn't so terrible? That it was you I ought to have dreaded all along?"

Carter smirked, eyes squinty and lips disappearing into his face like his mouth was a sinkhole. "You can't be serious, Portia. Don't be ridiculous. I've never given you any reason to dread me. I've given you every damn thing you ever wanted. Would you forsake your fortune in life? If that's the case, I could break your bank accounts. A few phone calls, and you'd be ruined."

"Yet, you would have me keep your secret?" Portia asked. "This isn't exactly warming me towards that possibility."

"Possibility?" Carter slammed the flat of his palm against his desk. "*Possibility?*" He stood to full height and felt for his tie. He calmly buttoned up his shirt to his throat and tightened his tie around his neck.

Portia saw him do this time and time again when cameras appeared without warning, but never in the privacy of a closed-door meeting with his daughter or any other member of his staff. *This must be his reset.*

"You never let me finish. I ceased visiting with her until after the funeral. I kept away from where she was being kept because I didn't want to raise any sort of suspicions. But, thinking back, no one could possibly have connected the dots. There would have been no reason to even try. For all intents and purposes, Daniella Devereaux-Neulander was in the ether. A month after we buried her empty coffin in Albertson, I started visiting with her again. After all, she was close at hand."

"Wait a minute," Portia said. "*Close at hand?* What does that mean? Where have you been keeping her?"

Carter raised his tired eyes to her. There was no light in them. It was as if he'd died right in front of her and somehow managed to remain standing while his eyeballs glazed over. "Come on, Portia. I'm sure you can figure out the answer to this one. Once you figure it out, we can get started with how I'm going to cover any and all possible tracks."

"You … you're not honestly still thinking of running?"

"Are you joking, Portia? Of course I'm going to run."

That's when someone or something threw their full weight at the door to the study.

Once.

Twice.

Thrice.

"Dad?" She nearly ran to him when the thing behind the door raged out loud.

Rou-rou-rourourou-ROU!

Portia watched the blood drain from her father's face. Every bash and strike rattled the door in such a way the heavy coat of varnish soaked into the wood's pores shimmered like glistening icicles. Portia stood there, staring at the heavy door shifting within its jamb and straining against its wrought iron hinges. She saw without hearing, thought without feeling. She barely heard her father shouting at her. He might have been cursing her. Might have been calling her to him so he could protect her.

How was I blind to this? All my life? You hear stories of denial every day, but you never think it's you until … well, there's a reckoning outside your door.

"—behind me, Portia! Come on! Get *behind* me! Behind the desk!"

"What are you going to do, Dad?" Portia asked, her voice an echo of an echo in her head. "*Kill* her?"

"It!" Carter cried. "I'm going to keep *it* from tearing you apart!" He moved behind his desk and dropped to his knees.

Portia knew he kept a firearm locked in one of the drawers, and up until that moment thought it as absurd as it was paranoid. When she turned her head, her neck moving on what felt like a rusted swivel, she saw her father slapping a magazine up into a sizeable handgun with the flat of his palm. It made a sick, bone-crunching sound.

"Get your *ass* over here, Portia!

"I'll be right there," she said.

Portia strode to the door, reached out with one palsied hand to grasp the doorknob.

"*What are you doing, you idiot?*" Carter exploded.

She felt the gun suddenly aimed at her head. It did not surprise her.

"You and your wife need to talk," she said. "I'm opening the door."

*   *   *

Bostwick loved a big bowl of coffee ice cream when he watched television at night. He enjoyed putting his feet up on the ottoman arranged before his easy chair, tilting his head back, and simply sinking into the plush. The cold of the dessert tickled his back molars. One of them probably needed filling, but it just so happened Bostwick feared the dentist. A gun in your face? In your mouth? Even up your ass? *Yeah, fucking try it! You just try it!* He didn't fancy himself Dirty Harry. Clint Eastwood's character played fast and loose with the law in all those movies, but he and Bostwick were worlds apart.

Bostwick was a fixer. Dirty Harry had a *line*.

Me? Michael Bartleson calls me on a burner phone down the street from his law offices, places his order, and I fill it. I'm a short-order guy. The relaxer in a world of kinky curls. Bartleson called him a few months back, woke him up. The lawyer prick most certainly was *not* at his office or anywhere near it, unless he was still banging his secretary in the off-hours. Bostwick wasn't sore at him. He figured it would be good, whatever it was. Pressing. *At 3 a.m.? Sheeeit!* An hour later, the night electric with the coming dawn, Bostwick was gliding his classic El Camino up the long meandering driveway that sidled up alongside the front door to The Big Man's pad.

Not a pad, exactly. A palatial estate, to be exact.

Michael Bartleson met him outside the open front door, led him inside the wide, whitewashed foyer. Crystal and silver winked at Bostwick like dirty women from every corner as he followed the short, greasy lawyer up the winding stairwell. Bostwick couldn't take his eyes off the ever-widening bald spot at the crown of the lawyer's tan, freckled head. The skin was peeling from a recent sunburn. It would have been ballsy to suggest Bartleson look into some plugs. Still, a man needs hair. Bostwick thought so. Then again, a man with long black hair pinned up into a fat bun behind his head could afford to hold fast to such firm beliefs.

"So, this is strictly *show* then?" Bostwick said, following up behind Bartleson, until they came upon the second floor landing. "No *tell*?"

"I wouldn't even know what to tell you about this," Bartleson said. "I can't believe it myself. The Big Man has more skeletons than any of us ever could have guessed. Makes my job harder. Makes a guy like you richer. Follow me."

Oh ... the skeletons.

One human, with a bullet wound in the side of her head the size of a softball. *She'll never be hot again.* Bostwick would never be able to pleasure himself to her image on cable news either, not after the way he found her sprawled in the middle of the study with half her face ripped away to clean bone.

One, *not so human.*

"What am I looking at here?" Bostwick asked, down on his haunches beside the monstrosity lying face-up before him.

Bostwick remembered how cool The Big Man was about the whole thing. It might as well have been a call in the dead of night to run on over to Albertson to clean up some spilled milk. He had never spoken directly to The Big Man before that night. He'd only ever seen him on the same forty-five-inch flat-screen he was watching the nightly news on with a bowl of ice cream in his lap. In the study, The Big Man proved to Bostwick what little regard he had for a lowly *fixer. I'm guessing that's why Bartleson kept the two of us apart and acted the middleman all this time. The Big Man's a prick. A man of few words and an insufferable prick.*

"Clean it up." The Big Man said the words, then made his way out of the study, dumping a handgun he'd been holding onto the floor beside Bostwick. He stepped over the body of his daughter without so much as a backward glance and disappeared into some other wing of the sprawling mansion.

The thing was, Bostwick thought at first glance it was going to be a cakewalk.

Until the lawyer tossed a few wild cards into the equation. "I walked the grounds. You got another body down in the wildlife reserve. The head vet. He was ripped apart. Some kind of animal. *That* kind of animal, to be exact. And … no sign of the butler, but Big Man says he sometimes sleeps in town. Gets laid. I got a call into the cathouses he frequents. No one's picking up. Busy time of night, I'm assuming. I'll keep trying."

"You do that."

"What are you going to do?"

"You never asked before," Bostwick said, his hands itching to touch the beast. *What would it feel like?* He imagined it would *feel* like a lion, even though its flank was wider and more pronounced. The back legs more extended. Bostwick figured when the thing walked upright, its ass was up in the air above its head. A human making like a cat—

"I'm asking now." Bartleson said.

Bostwick told him.

So, fast-forward to the ice cream. The ottoman. The calm, peaceful warrior lounging before his flickering tv screen.

All the cable news channels were running with the announcement.

He went with the local New York City network. The cable channels would only add their spin to the whole thing. Bostwick wanted to hear the *motherfucker* say the words. The words this *lowlife fixer* made possible. Provided for in what Bostwick considered to be a damned crafty way.

The Big Man always had a serious hard-on about wild cats. Bostwick never asked where it came from. There were just some things you let ride. Bostwick imagined it didn't have to *make sense*. Not everything has to make sense. If everything made sense, there'd be no need for religion. The things that don't *make sense* are usually explained by rubber-stamping it with one simple solution: *God*. So God must have put the obsession in The Big Man's head he would love, revere, and downright worship the feline in all its forms. His wildlife reserve housed all manner of wild cats. Only one of each, though. The Big Man knew not to be greedy. One panther. One puma. One bobcat. A jaguar. Something called an ocelot.

The thing Bostwick had to dispose of and incinerate at an abandoned factory (somewhere on Long Island) was neither cat nor human.

Somewhere in between.

Bostwick was okay with never knowing. Less to cop to if things got heavy.

Bostwick watched as, on the television, the news cameras jumped to coverage of the live event he'd been waiting for. He saw a sea of waving hands at the bottom of the screen. The Big Man never failed to fill every "room" to capacity, no matter how big the space, when he made a speech or even so much as a short statement. The guy was a rock star without the music. Always had been. This was no exception. A podium stood on an elevated stage above the hands, and a row of American and New York state flags flanked the blue curtain backdrop. The newscaster sounded like a guy with a painful hard-on, his voice exuberant and nearly breathless as he announced the arrival of The Big Man on site.

I'm still shocked he let us gun down two of his most treasured cats to cover up the crime scene. It really was the only way to explain any of it. A faulty lock on one of the enclosures that housed two of the wild cats. An attack on the vet that resulted in a near decapitation and a complete disembowelment. Then, a break-in through the back double-glass doors. I shattered the panes myself in such a way it'd look like the work of wild animals lunging at the panes. The confrontation in the study. Accidental shooting of that piece-of-ass daughter of his. The two big cats laid out on the floor of the study with a bullet in each of their brains. Flesh from the vet and Portia under their fingernails. Open and shut.

The Big Man crossed the stage, shaking a number of outstretched hands on the way. A plastered-on smile of blinding pearly whites. A spray-on tan. Long tie, hanging low enough to touch the guy's balls if he were standing there naked.

Then, the words Bostwick was waiting for. The Big Man raised his hand above the adoring crowd like the Pope bestowing a blessing. The newscaster fell silent, as did much of the crowd. And The Big Man stepped into the silence as confidently as you please.

"Big moment for this country, ladies and gentleman," Carter Neulander said, his voice strong and vibrant. Not the voice belonging to a grieving parent.

No sir. Not at all.

"I'm here because I want to announce tonight, I will be running for president in this upcoming election! We're going to take this country back!"

The crowd exploded.

Bostwick shook his head. "You're welcome. Prick."

He took a big heaping spoonful of his ice cream, lost his appetite, dumped the rest down the drain, and padded off to an early bed.

BODA NEGRA

By H.R. Arswyd

(for Lisa)

Renowned Spanish doctor Pedro Orosoco Salazar was many things, but he was not a doctor, tuberculosis specialist, radiologist, apothecary, massage therapist, or dentist; although, he plied all those professions. Come to that, he was not even Doctor Pedro Orosoco Salazar, nor Spanish. He had been born in Mexico as Miguel Reyes, and what medical training he actually had was as a mortician's assistant. To his credit he was very good at that, and he possessed an innate artistic gift for transforming cold clay into a remarkably lifelike simulacra of the deceased. He was also a consummate liar with an actor's flair for a role, a natural hauteur, and cultivated mannerisms calculated to provide "corroborative detail, intended to give artistic verisimilitude," as the saying went. His Spanish had a stage intonation, masquerading as being from Spain which was extremely convincing to the peons and peasants, less so with the more urbane or educated. His English faded in and out of accents as required by the needs of the moment; although, thanks to a lot of time over the border in Texas and New Mexico he could speak it as well as any native-born Texan cowhand or roughneck.

He had style down as well: with jet black hair swept regally back from his high forehead, a van Dyke beard, and long, waxed mustache, that might have inspired Salvador Dali, both also jet black. That he did *not* look 52, his true age, was due to his cosmetic skills, a naturally good complexion and a robust constitution. He was always elegantly attired in expensive clothing, which he had obtained over the years by robbing only the best-dressed corpses of their final raiment. So, although he was none of the things he professed to be, he by God looked the part, and as he had learned, that was more than half the battle.

At the moment, he was plying his various trades in the desolate West Texas boomtown of Monahans. Oil had been discovered in the vicinity just a few months back, and workers flocked into the area, along with everything that trailed in their wake. For a medical con man on the run from the families of a couple of recently deceased "patients" in Juarez, it was a perfect opportunity to slip across the border for a while until things cooled down. It was a tradition stretching back nearly a century: villains, desperadoes, con men, and ne'er-do-wells from both sides of the border regularly slipped to the other side when the heat was on, cynically using the international boundary to avoid a reckoning, and relying on the venality and incompetence which flourished to a legendary degree on the southern side.

With the sudden population boom of roustabouts and roughnecks, replete with the dangers inherent in the work and the inevitable hard play that went along with it, the arrival of Doctor Pedro Orosoco Salazar filled a desperate need, and he was soon doing a booming business in pills, potions, stitches, casts, pulled teeth, and the occasional corpse.

It was late October of 1926, when the family of Clyde Jedson moved to town. Clyde was an out-of-work roughneck whose family was barely scraping by on the kindness of neighbors and family, so the opening of the Hendrick oil field seemed like the path to salvation. He loaded up the battered truck with what few possessions they had and headed for Monahans, Texas. Someone had even painted "Texas or Bust" on the doors of the truck, a grim joke given the well-known mutual antagonism between Okies and Texans.

Clyde's diminutive wife Emma had been through a very difficult delivery of twin boys a few months back. Between taking care of them, Clyde, and their oldest, a thirteen-year-old girl name Helen, she had never really recovered or regained her strength.

It was hoped this move to the hot, arid west Texas desert would be especially helpful for Helen Jedson. She had been diagnosed with tuberculosis when she was ten years old and was frail at the best of times. Despite her illness, she was an unfailingly sweet and gentle soul, and her condition gave her a certain airy otherworldliness that sometimes verged on the angelic, especially when the sun caught the halo of her long, strawberry blonde hair just so. She was just coming into womanhood and showed every sign of being a real beauty—provided the Lord or the consumption didn't take her first.

Once they finally got to where they were going, Clyde had no trouble finding work on the first day, which allowed them to move into a one bedroom clapboard house in the rough and tumble part of town where most of the other roughnecks resided. It was a real improvement from the squatters shack they had been forced to live in after Clyde had lost his job however. Clyde, Emma, and the twins all slept in the one bedroom, while Helen made her bed on a dilapidated old sofa in the parlor.

Despite the rough and tumble boomtown character of the place, there was a school and an actual truant officer who made sure it was occupied to capacity. So, soon after getting settled, Helen found herself being forced to go to school for the first time in her life. She hated it. She was not stupid, but her environment fostered neither the interest, nor the desire for education, and as a result she was far behind those her own age. Being uneducated, poor white trash, she understood. But being confronted with it on a daily basis, sometimes brutally, did nothing to instill a love of learning in her. Her mother could read some, enough to read parts of the Bible to them every day, albeit haltingly, and she could do basics sums, and that was considered all that was required.

They were devout Methodists, attending services every Sunday. Clyde's people were Pentecostals, and they did not look kindly on him for changing over to his wife's faith, which they held to be too soft and sinful. Secretly, Clyde often felt the same way and thus was more rigorous and zealous in his devotions to make up for the weakness. A simple and devout man, he worked hard, prayed hard, and partook of none of the dubious delights of the flesh so readily on offer twenty-four hours a day which constituted the "other" route to riches in a boomtown.

Their simple, unsophisticated faith in the Lord's plan gave them a rugged strength and endurance to cope with a lifetime of want, tragedy and sorrow. When Helen had her periodic tuberculosis episodes, the laying on of hands was always the preferred treatment, both by inclination, and by financial constraint.

For the first few weeks, things seemed to be steadily improving in the Jedson household, and the pinched looked of want and malnutrition began to fade with the regular meals they could now afford thanks to Clyde's paycheck. Emma even bought some calico and made new dresses for Helen and herself. Then Helen had an episode.

It was a cold Sunday in January. The small congregation was singing the hymn "Jesus, Lord, We Look to Thee," when Helen started coughing. Probably because the air was not only extremely dry in this desert climate, but warm and sooty from the heater in the little chapel, she couldn't stop, and soon she was coughing up blood all over her newly sewn dress. The little congregation immediately began praying for her, and there was a laying on of hands, but to little apparent effect. Someone suggested she be taken to a doctor they knew of, a Spanish gentleman who seemed to be very erudite, although that was the not the descriptive term used in the discussion. So, Helen was carried to the truck and driven to Doctor Pedro Orosoco Salazar.

The building he was using had belonged to the former undertaker who had died some time before. It was an old two-story affair with a pair of false front façades. On one side the words "Funeral Parlor" were painted a faded black in the florid script of a bygone age. On the opposite side, facing the next street over, Salazar had "Doctor-Dentist" painted on that façade in clinical white. The building was divided into two rooms on the ground floor the larger on the Funeral Parlor side, the smaller being the clinic. In between was a small kitchen on one side, and on the other a larger area where bodies were embalmed and stored in a walk-in ice box. People used whichever side they required. Someone had called ahead and when the Jedsons arrived, Dr. Salazar was waiting at the door for them when they pulled up.

The moment Helen stepped unsteadily from the truck, his heart caught in his throat, her naturally pale skin was even paler, and somehow her big eyes were even bigger, full of a desperate terror that aroused in him a burning desire to protect her. Her waifish slenderness and her hair, blazing in the sunlight, kindled a fire in him, one that was only stoked by the shocking stains of garish crimson that trailed from her chin and down her budding bust, standing out all the more starkly against the fresh, crisp white calico. She stood coatless and shivering. Her father rushed around the front of the trunk and wrapped a burly, protective arm around her as he helped her walk, an action which cause the doctor a sudden and irrational burst of jealously which made him flush with anger momentarily.

As they walked toward him, he took a deep breath and began softly humming an old tune. He couldn't remember the name of the tune, and only remembered fragments of the words, but he liked it. It soothed him, and that was all that mattered. It was a coping mechanism he developed over the years to detach and calm himself in moments of extreme stress, like being confronted by the upset family members of a dead patient or angry local officials or fear-crazed peasants convinced he was a sorcerer—or, on a few occasions, outraged parents. He quickly shoved this last from his mind as he watched Helen walking weakly toward him, leaning on her father.

Her father looked up at him and spoke, "Sir, Doctor sir, my little girl is sickly with the consumption. One of the congregation told me you was a good man and could help her."

Helen looked up at Salazar, fear and trust in her eyes, and his knees buckled slightly, causing him to sag against the doorway for a moment and he fought to say something.

"I … I will do whatever I can to help, of course. Please!" he said gesturing, "Please come in!" He reached out to help and took her arm; a tingling frisson shot through his hand as his fingers gently brushed her skin for the first time, and he had to bite back a groan.

Once inside he had her sit on the exam table while her father stood close at hand, and it was a terrible struggle to keep his hands from shaking. "I'm, I'm sorry it is so cold in here," he said by way of explanation. "I was not expecting a patient today."

"We're just grateful that you can see us, ain't we, honey?" Clyde said, and Helen nodded and gave a weak smile.

"I, I need to examine the patient," Salazar said, his voice husky with suppressed excitement, which he masked with a slight cough. *Control yourself! You have got to control yourself! Take things slow and easy; don't rush them!* he screamed inside his head. He reached to the side and began to pull a screen across for privacy, but Clyde put a hand on his forearm, stopping him.

"Doctor, sir, we ain't got much money, and that's the truth. If you could see yer way clear to extendin' some credit, I give ya my word you will be paid in full, if you'll just gimme some time."

Salazar's heart was thumping in his ears, and he felt flushed but with supreme control he managed to keep his hand from shaking and his voice from quaking as he gently removed Clyde's hand from his forearm. With all the calmness he could command, he said, "My dear sir, there will be no charge to you for my service."

Clyde suddenly drew himself up and puffed out his chest, "I ain't askin' for no charity, mister. I always pay my debts. I ain't no tramp," he said, anger at the edges of his voice.

Salazar quickly changed his tack, eager to gain the man's trust and gratitude. He turned on all the assumed "old world charm" he could imitate and gave a slight bow. "You misunderstand me sir! I have no wish to give any offense! When one of your congregation called and asked if I could see your daughter, notwithstanding it being the Lord's Day, I felt it my duty as a good Christian to do what I think Christ Jesus would have me do on his day and aid the sick. My statement was certainly no reflection on your honor, sir, I assure you, it is merely my wish to do a good deed on our Lord's holy day. Please, forgive my unintended offense." Salazar extended his hand and smiled warmly.

Clyde wasn't exactly sure what to make of the "high-falutin'" speech, but he understood the man's religious sincerity and took Salazar's soft, delicate hand in his own calloused, thick, strong one and looked him dead in the eye. "I didn't mean to come over all touchy and all, sir. I 'preciate yer words and what yer doin' for my girl. Thank you. Thank you, and God bless you, sir."

"What is your name, friend?" Salazar asked.

"Clyde Jedson, sir."

"Well, Clyde, would you like a cup of coffee? I have just brewed a pot, and I bet you could use some to take the chill off."

"I'd be most obliged, thank you."

Salazar motioned toward a closed door at the back of the room. "It's just straight through there, Clyde. Help yourself. I will take a few moments to examine your daughter, then we will see what we can do to help you."

Clyde nodded once and made to tip the hat he was not wearing. "Thank you kindly, sir. I'll do that. Helen? Now you do what this fine doctor says, hear? He is gonna make you all better, honey." He nodded to Salazar and disappeared through the door into the kitchen.

The door closed, and Salazar let out a sigh of relief then turned toward Helen, extending his hand. "I am Doctor Pedro

Orosoco Salazar, Miss Helen, it is a pleasure to make your acquaintance," he said, kissing her hand.

Helen stared at him goggle-eyed, having no experience at all with fancy manners of any kind, especially foreign. She snatched back her hand as if she had been stung and gazed at it for moment before replying, "Pleasure to meet ya, Doctor; I'm sure."

Salazar fought down his desire, even as his eyes devoured her. He felt weak, light-headed, and hot. His tongue involuntarily peeked out and moistened his dry lips as he struggled to contain himself.

"Now, Miss Helen," he said, his voice thick; he cleared his throat. "Now, let us see if we can help you, yes? Please … disrobe, if you would be so kind."

Helen stared at him blankly.

"Dearest Miss, if you would be so kind as to remove your dress so that I might better examine you," Salazar said, reaching a tentative hand toward her, shakily.

"Do as he says, girl." Clyde's voice crashed like thunder in Salazar's ears, and he started and gave a little yelp. Clyde was standing in the doorway holding a cup of coffee. Salazar hurriedly pulled the screen around behind the exam table for propriety's sake so that Clyde would not see his daughter undressing; although, Salazar still had a peripheral vision of Helen.

Embarrassed, Helen cautiously began to unbutton the blood-soaked dress then slid it down past her shoulders, pulling out her arms and stepping out of it. She hung it on a hook on the screen before sitting back on the exam table in her chemise, holding herself and shivering, with cold, embarrassment, and fear. Her head down she mumbled, "Ok, Doctor."

Salazar turned and audibly caught his breath, chewing his lower lip, which made the pointed ends of his moustache twitch like the antennae of a searching insect. He reached his hands toward her and carefully touched her throat, his desire seething inside him like a boiling pot. He probed gently along either side of her windpipe as he had seen real physicians do, then along her exquisite jawline, slowly working back toward her ears.

She shivered and shuddered more, gasping and wheezing.

He was so very, very tempted to lay his head against her chest to listen to her heart, to feel the warmth of her and smell her skin, but he fought down the temptation and reached into a drawer on the table, extracting a stethoscope.

He put in the earpieces and touched the diaphragm to her bare skin, below her throat. She gasped with the coldness, and he saw her small nipples harden beneath the flimsy cloth. Her breathing sounded like dead winter leaves in a breeze. Fighting desperately to focus, he did what he had seen done, moving it about and listening, but keeping it well above the neckline of her chemise.

After what he considered an appropriate amount of time, he withdrew the device and took out the earpieces, formulated a serious and wise aspect onto his face as he returned the instrument to its drawer. He clicked his tongue and hemmed a few times for emphasis, even going so far as to cup his chin for a moment while he gazed at her.

Inside, however, he was a raging turmoil of desperate desire and passion, his inner voice all but shouting at him to notice her eyes, her lips, her flawless skin, and luxuriant hair and, and …

He had to do something, say something, *anything* before he gave way completely!

"Yes," he said, his voice again thick and immediate with desire. "Yes, it is a very serious case."

Say something! Do something! DO it NOW! The voice in his head was almost hysterical. *You are acting strangely; her father will notice! Act like a doctor!* He cleared his throat.

"Yes, well ... I think I might be able to help you, Miss Helen."

For the first time she smiled, and he about collapsed from the sheer beauty of it; the child-like trust that beamed from her face was almost more than he could stand.

"So," he said, "I will go prepare an elixir which I would like you to take which will help that cough. Please wait here for me."

Helen nodded. Salazar walked purposefully through another door, closing it behind him. He leaned against the wall and panted, mopping his forehead with the kerchief from his breast pocket, muttering "I must be patient, I must be calm!" He pulled himself together and went to a closet and rummaged, pulling out a beautiful, black velvet dress in an older style, along with a long coat. He held them up and passed a critical eye over them. "Yes ... yes, those should fit perfectly!" he murmured.

He lay the clothing aside and went to a small table upon which were scattered vials, bottles, retorts, and assorted small wooden boxes. He took a clean blue glass bottle and into it added thirty drops of laudanum, some powdered ginger root, dried lemon zest, and a dollop of honey, before topping up the bottle with brandy. Capping the bottle, he shook it vigorously then slipped it into the pocket of his jacket, carefully picked up the dress and coat and returned to his "patient."

He strode purposefully into the room, nodding at Clyde, but motioning for him to stay where he was. He turned the corner of the screen, and Helen was still sitting as he had left her, her arms wrapped around her shoulders as she shivered. Salazar held out the dress to her.

"Please, Miss Helen. Please, you would do me a great honor if you would take this dress and wear it. It is warmer than the one you wore today. Besides, that one is now ruined with the bloodstains. I know how terribly difficult they are to remove, I assure you."

Helen stared at the elegant, if slightly old-fashioned, dress and reached a hand tentatively toward it, stroking the fabric. "It's soooo soft!" she whispered.

"It is velvet, Miss Helen. Please!" he added holding it toward her, then turned his back.

Helen slipped it on, and it fit perfectly, as Salazar knew it would. He bit his lower lip again as he looked at her, and Clyde came over.

"Doctor, sir, I can't let you give the girl a thing like that! It must cost a fortune!" he said.

"My dear friend, think nothing of it. Sometimes patients leave things," he said cryptically. "In any case it is not something I have any use for, and Miss Helen's dress is ruined. It is also very thin for this cold weather. As a doctor, I insist she wear something warmer." he passed Helen the long, elegant coat. "It is for her health, Clyde. She must stay warm if she is to recover." Before Clyde could say anything by way of an objection, Salazar withdrew the bottle from his pocket and handed it to him. "Give her a spoonful of this every night, and every time she begins to cough. It will help reduce the coughing and help her to rest. Please come back in a few days so that I can check on her progress, okay?"

Clyde took the bottle and stared at it for a moment, then turned his gaze to Salazar, "Doctor, you are a fine and good Christian man; God bless you, and thank you for all you done for my girl. Don't know how I can ever repay you."

Salazar waved theatrically. "Think nothing of it, sir. As I said, it is my Christian duty to help, is it not? What would our savior have me do?"

Once again Clyde extended his big, powerful, rough hand and took Salazar's delicately manicured one, squeezing it, unintentionally, to the point of pain. "Thank you again, sir. I'll be sure she gets her tonic and stays warm."

"And bring her back, please. Yes?"

Clyde nodded. "Come on girl, let's get you home. Tell the doctor thank you!"

Once more the fragile smile bloomed on her as her big eyes settled on Salazar's. "Thank you for all your kindness, sir. I'm most terrible obliged to you!"

"Think nothing of it, dear Miss," Salazar replied, even as he felt himself swaying and a sweat coming over him.

Clyde led her to the door, and Salazar fought to keep his knees from trembling as he walked them out and to the truck. He waved as they drove off then turned and slowly walked back in, closing and locking the door behind him before leaning back and groaning loudly.

"Holy Mary, Mother of God!" he moaned, his left hand gripping his aching manhood through his trousers. Then he saw the dress still on the hook. Helen's crisp, white calico, the front stained with drying blood. He staggered toward it and tenderly removed it from the hook, burying his face in it and slowly, deliberately and in ecstasy, inhaled her, his delicate nose savoring the complex bouquet of her under the metallic sting of the blood.

Cradling it gently in his arms, he made his way upstairs to his rooms, softly humming.

As requested, Clyde brought Helen back the following week, and once again Salazar examined her, and once again the experience nearly killed him with desire. However, he convinced Clyde Helen should come in once a week so he could monitor her, and refill her "prescription." Salazar had to constantly monitor himself and check himself from acting too cloying and fawning. He worked hard to project a deeply caring dedication to Helen's well-being.

He longed to take her in his arms, to kiss those tender young lips, explore her firm young body with a religious passion, to make her his, and cure her tragic illness with his devotion and love. To wait on her hand and foot, slavishly, and just bask in the effulgence of her beauty in eternal, sacred bliss.

During a "checkup" a few days before Easter, Clyde asked to speak with Salazar privately. Salazar readily consented and led Clyde to his little office.

Clyde looked somewhat embarrassed and spoke haltingly, "Sir, you are such a good man, such a good Christian man, and you have done so much for my girl," he began.

"My dear man, think nothing of it!" Salazar gushed.

"Well, sir, I know you are a highly educated and refined foreign gentleman, and all, but, my wife and I would take it real kindly if you could see your way to having dinner with our family on Easter Sunday, to celebrate our Lord's resurrection, sir … if, you don't got other plans, of course. We ain't rich, as you know, and the fare ain't gonna be the sort of high on the hog eating a man like you is used to, but we would be honored if you'd join us, sir," Clyde said. He was embarrassed at his poverty and lack of education, but his gratitude was genuine and heartfelt, and Salazar was strangely moved at this big man's sincerity.

"I would be honored, sir, very honored. Thank you," he said and threw in a deep and flourishing bow for good measure.

Sunday came, and Salazar arrived for the meal. The Jedsons were almost painfully solicitous and attentive to him, and they had gone all out with their meager resources to provide a feast worthy of both their Lord Jesus and their honored guest. By way of entertainment there was hymn singing. Salazar knew none of the songs but, having an ear for music, was able to hum along in a fine tenor, nicely pitched above Clyde's powerful bass.

Over some spectacular buttermilk pecan pie and coffee they talked about the importance of music, and Salazar saw an opening, which he immediately took.

"I have read in some medical journals that some sounds, some songs, can have curative powers. Science is not sure exactly how it works, maybe it is the vibrations effects on the body, or maybe the sounds stimulate the release of chemicals in the body, but there does seem to be some direct effect between music and health," he said.

"Oh, I believe it!" Emma said, nodding her head in sincerity. "The Bible is full of examples of the Lord working his wonders through sound! Think of Joshua and the trumpets at Jericho! Land sakes! And the Bible tells us to make a joyful noise unto the Lord, too."

Clyde nodded in agreement. "And I always find great comfort in our hymns, always calms my spirit and soothes my soul, yessir."

"And what do you think, Miss Helen?" Salazar asked with a deference and politeness that seemed a bit too indulgent.

"Well, I … I love music. I think it is one of God's greatest gifts to man," she said, lowering her head with shyness, but peeking up at Salazar through the veil of her hair.

"Exactly! A gift from God! How beautifully put, Miss Helen!" Salazar praised. She blushed prettily. Emma rose and asked if anyone wanted more coffee. "Yes, please!" Salazar said, passing her his cup and saucer. "Thank you!"

Clyde also passed her his cup and took out his pipe, which he thoughtfully packed in the sudden silence.

Salazar affected a look of deep contemplation, as if he were considering deep and profound things, tenting his fingers beneath his chin and staring downward, almost in an attitude of prayer. When Emma returned with his cup and saucer, he started as if wakened from a reverie. "Ah, thank you so much, madame! You are too kind!"

Emma smiled and blushed slightly at his attention, "Oh, it was my pleasure, Doctor."

He slipped her a playful wink and took a sip of his coffee before placing the cup and saucer on the table. "I was just thinking, perhaps you do not know, but I am rather musical. I play the organ, actually. In fact, my other practice, with the funeral parlor, I play the music for the viewings and family get togethers there. Well, all this talk of music started me thinking. The organ is a very special instrument, as I'm sure you know. You can feel the sounds very clearly throughout your body when you hear an organ. Anyway, I was thinking that perhaps we might try some organ music therapy with Miss Helen? I know the organ is small and not as large or powerful as a church organ, but the space is also smaller," he said, carefully framing his pitch from the standpoint of "pure science" while once again offering his services as a good Christian gentleman.

Emma reached across and patted his forearm, "Doctor, you have been so good to us, to our girl. We sure wouldn't want to put you out any more than we already done," she said. Clyde nodded through a cloud of pipe smoke.

"It would be no trouble at all, I assure you, madame! Besides, I could certainly use the practice! Let us try one hour a week for a few weeks and see what happens, shall we?"

The following Saturday Clyde brought Helen in to try organ therapy. After the usual cursory exam. He presented her with a thin, gauze smock. Helen looked embarrassed and Salazar sought to assuage her concerns.

"You see, I have been reading more on sound therapy, and it is of the greatest importance that nothing interferes with the natural purity of the sound waves. So, any clothing will distort and muffle the sound and could limit the effectiveness of the treatment. There must be minimal barriers between your body and the sound, Miss Helen, and no clothing should constrict the flow of sound energy, that would not be helpful," he said. Now that he was speaking it aloud, it sounded better and more convincing than he had thought it would.

Helen stole a glance at her father, who nodded and said, "He's the doctor, honey, and you been doing better thanks to him. Best do as he says."

"When you have changed, just come through this door here. We will wait for you there," Salazar said with his best doctor smile.

He took a cup of coffee for himself and offered one to Clyde, who took it gratefully and they adjourned to the viewing parlor on the Funeral Home side of the building. It was hung with dark burgundy velvet tapestries and draperies. In the middle of a raised dais adjoining the wall was a marble bier, now draped in black velvet and in the corner to its right was a small pump organ.

Clyde looked a little dubious at his first glance, but Salazar hastened to allay his concerns. "I know it is a little, shall we say, 'peculiar,' but I assure you this is the best arrangement. Besides, the organ is here, and I don't believe the effects would be nearly as beneficial if the sound were to pass through the walls first, you understand."

Clyde nodded and sank down into one of the plush chairs usually reserved for immediate family of the deceased. Salazar seated himself at the organ, his back to the room and the bier, and opened a book of simplified organ devotionals. In common with many church organs, this one, too, had a mirror attached to the side of the frame to allow the organist to observe cues from whoever was conducting the service. Salazar carefully adjusted it until the bier's reflection filled the mirror, his hands shaking badly.

Get hold of yourself, man! Stay calm! Everything you do takes you one step closer to those soft, young thighs ... do not wreck this! Remember what happened in Monterey! he told himself.

The door set in the paneling silently swung open, and Helen cautiously entered. Salazar fought the aching urge to turn and look at her and instead, in a thick voice that was barely above a whisper, instructed her to lay on bier, on her back, with her arms crossed over her chest. His eyes were locked on the mirror as her lithe form, backlit so the smock was nearly transparent, did as instructed. He felt his swollen member pulse and quiver and suddenly release in his trousers, and he bit his lips together, hard, tasting blood.

Once she had settled herself she whispered, "Okay, I guess I'm ready."

Salazar fought to speak in as normal a voice as he could muster. "Very good," he said, "Now Miss Helen, just relax and try to think of peaceful, happy thoughts."

His feet began pumping the pedals which compressed and sent the air into the pipes, and he began playing, shakily at first, a simplified arrangement of the "Meditation" from "Thais" by Massenet.

As the time wore on, the slimy ejaculate in his trousers grew cold and sticky and uncomfortable, especially so with the constant pedal pumping motion required to give breath to the organ. To add to his discomfort, he was getting a headache from the constant refocusing between the mirror and the sheet music before him. At times his playing faltered when he could barely tear his gaze away from Helen's reflection.

After forty-five minutes or so, he had to stop. Clyde had fallen asleep in his chair, and Helen had floated into a hypnogogic state of extreme relaxation. She appeared lifeless, her perfect beauty preserved forever as she lay on the bier.

Salazar discreetly cleared his throat, awakening both Clyde and Helen, and he pronounced treatment complete for the day. He had a moment of panic when he slid off the organ bench, afraid the state of his trousers would be embarrassingly evident, but he noticed with relief his white smock coat provided ample covering.

He instructed Helen to go change, telling her they would join her shortly and invited Clyde into the other room for another cup of coffee.

"I'm sorry I feel asleep while you was playing, it was mighty soothing, for a fact," he said.

Salazar forced a smile through his aching lips. "Then I accomplished my goal, Clyde. I truly hope it has done Miss Helen some good."

"I'm sure it has, I feel like a new man myself," Clyde responded.

They went into the other room, where Helen was putting on her shoes.

"And how do you feel, Miss Helen?" Salazar asked.

"I feel real calm and peaceful, sir. And sorta real rested," she replied.

"Good! Good! Well, only time will tell if the treatment is of any help. I pray it does you good, truly."

"Thank you again, Doctor, sir, I do feel better right now."

"Well, let us try a few more sessions and see where we stand. I shall expect you next week, same time, sound good?"

"We'll be here, won't we, girl?" Clyde said.

"Have a safe week, do not hesitate to call on me if you need anything. Promise?"

"Sure, and thanks again," Clyde said, escorting Helen out and waving behind him.

He waited until they were out of sight and carefully collected the smock she had worn, her warmth still lingering in the thin, gauze fabric as he pressed his face into it. His loins began tingling again, only now the sensation was unpleasant because of his earlier accident. He rushed upstairs and drew a bath, and while it was filling, tenderly lay the smock on the other side of his large bed, opposite the bloodstained dress Helen had worn on her first visit. After soaking in the hot water for what seemed like ages, he emerged dried himself thoroughly, then lay nude on his bed, between the dress and the smock and let himself drift away into a wonderland of carnal delights with Helen. Gradually he fell to sleep, a look of ecstatic bliss on his face.

As the weeks went by and spring displaced the cold weather, Helen's condition appeared to gradually improve. It was undoubtedly due to the improved diet and living conditions, and the drier climate, but to the Jedson family, and especially Helen, there was only one obvious cause: the ministrations of the kindly doctor, his weekly organ sessions, and dedication to her wellbeing. He had come to a solution for his own embarrassing problem, which had happened twice more during organ sessions; he began taking himself in hand, so to speak, before Helen arrived for her "treatments." However, the passing of time and the gradual familiarity with Helen did nothing to tarnish his desire for her, in fact it had the opposite effect, which was why he was certain she was, in fact, the one, true love of his life, for whom he would do and risk everything.

Salazar continued his "practice": setting breaks, stitching up cuts, and pulling the odd tooth. He even indulged in his funerary artistry on two occasions. In the intervals, he began reading as much medical material as he could find in the desperate hope of actually understanding real medicine and finding a way to cure his beloved. If only he could save her, he *knew* Clyde would be honored and humbled to give him her hand in marriage, then she would be his, *his!* legally and in the eyes of God, unlike what had happened the other times.

Helen had another episode of coughing up blood during the Fourth of July festivities which appeared to be miraculously cured by a special procedure Salazar invented on the spur of the moment, using his embalming aspirator to suck the fluid out of her lungs, followed by more of his "elixir." He travelled back to the house with Clyde and Helen in order to stay with her during the night to make sure she did not start bleeding again, although he was worried that if she did, he would be unable to do anything about it.

Clyde invited him out onto the porch for a cup of coffee, and they watched the fireworks in the distance, neither saying anything for a time.

Eventually Clyde said, "You been so good to our girl, sir. My family sure appreciates everything you done.

But I got to ask you, do you think she is ever gonna be well? I mean, I know the consumption is a pretty bad condition, but I hear tell some folks live for a long time with it, but others it takes pretty fast."

Salazar tensed; he could feel an opportunity here, a way to fulfill the desire that was daily burning him from the inside out. *Be careful! Slowly, slowly!* He told himself. He took a sip of his coffee, desperately wishing it was brandy, but knowing Clyde was teetotal. In the distance a flowering burst of bright green bloomed, followed a couple of seconds later by the hollow *boom* of the explosion.

"It's hard to say, Clyde. These things are complicated. I think that if I could provide constant supervision and keep a close watch on her condition, we could improve her odds ..." He trailed off, but every nerve and sense was keyed up judging the effect of his words on Clyde.

Clyde said nothing, just nodded slightly, and packed his pipe. He lit it and smoked for a while, rocking gently. Salazar continued to discretely watch him, but kept his own mouth shut. There was a triple burst of red, white, and blue fireworks, and Clyde said, "Well, we just ain't got the money for that kind of care. I can't take her in every day what with work, and Emma has her hands full with the twins. Not sure how we could arrange that. Besides, your clinic is fair small, it ain't got but the two beds. Can't ask you to give up part of your livelihood that way. No sir, that wouldn't be right." He tamped the pipe, and its orange glow underlit his features, brow knit in thought.

Salazar's mind was racing, he could hear his heart pounding in his ears and was grateful it was dark so Clyde wouldn't see how flushed he was and the sweat pouring down his face. *Go easy! Play it natural and calm! Don't make this into something big, or he'll suspect.* "There ... there might be another way, Clyde. I've been thinking ..."

Clyde said nothing, and Salazar had a feeling that Clyde already had an inkling of what he was about to say. "Look, during the time I've got to know you and your family while caring for Helen, I have come to be very fond of you all … and especially of Helen."

Clyde nodded, but continued to watch the fireworks display.

"What I am trying to say is, Clyde, I could take better care of Helen if she were with me all the time, not exactly as a patient I mean."

"You askin' to marry my little girl? That it?"

"Well, yes. Yes, I am. I know I am older, but I would give her as good a life as I could. I have a decent career here, and I would be able to devote myself to easing her condition."

Clyde was still slowly rocking, smoking, and watching the fireworks. His face betrayed no emotion. "She's only thirteen years old, you know that?"

"I know she is young, but, in my culture beautiful young women marry young, often to older men who can provide for them better than suitors closer to their age."

Clyde shot his head around, and his voice was clipped. "Well sir, in *my* culture thirteen is awful young to marry. I appreciate you got a more worldly view of these things and all, but I can't say as I cotton much to the notion. Anyway, I got to talk this over with Emma if you're serious about askin' for Helen's hand. It ain't that I ain't grateful for all you done, ain't that at all, but this is a real big thing you're askin,' real big. Need time to think this over, talk to Emma and all." He turned his face back forward and drew on his pipe, "I think Helen's gonna stay sleepin'. Might be best if you go for now, no offense meant. You took me by surprise with this, and I need some time, understand?"

Salazar nodded, stood, and extended his hand. Clyde kept staring out at the fireworks and just nodded.

Salazar walked the two-odd miles back to his place, lost in thought. The streets were full of revelry and drunken exuberance, but he skirted the crowds, occasionally returning a wave or greeting with his best olde-world charm. He found he was humming that song again, and once again wondered what it was, and then wondered why he couldn't remember the title. He was sure it had words but he couldn't remember them either. It was something from his past, from when he was young maybe. It was in a dark, minor key with a strange, shifting cadence and, to his ear, it sounded very old, maybe an old folk song. He stopped worrying about it and walked along to the rhythm while the tune kept floating around in the back of his head, and he thought about what had happened.

He let himself in, poured a big tot of brandy, and climbed the stairs. He drank off the brandy in one long pull and collapsed onto the bed, between the blood-soaked dress and the gauze smock, and sobbed himself to sleep in frustration and desperation.

Two days later the weekly "organ therapy" session was supposed to happen. Salazar paced and checked his watch as the allotted time came, then passed with no Helen. He became concerned after fifteen minutes and truly alarmed after half an hour. Unsure of what to do, he continued to pace and mutter to himself with increasing hysteria, both the length and frequency of his stride increasing as his panic grew.

What am I going to do? What if I never see her again? No, that cannot happen! Do I call Clyde? No, he doesn't have a phone. Drive over to his house? And say what? That I am checking up on a missed doctor appointment? No, he will never accept that. Oh

Jesus! What if I never see her again? Oh God, I want her, I LOVE HER! I have to have her! We are meant to be together!

He worked himself into such state that he finally collapsed into a chair, sobbing with deep, soul-wracking howls of despair. When he had cried himself out, he slowly got to his feet and shuffled to the cabinet where he kept the brandy. He started steadily drinking until his mood began to change.

It'll work out; I can get her back. This is just temporary. Clyde is a reasonable man, and he is bound to see that I am a better match for his daughter than he could ever hope to get, given his circumstances. I just need to give him time to think things through; I'm sure he will see reason and the sense of my proposal, especially after everything I have done for him AND for her! Especially for her! I've saved her life at least twice! She is doing so much better now thanks to my efforts!

He dispensed with the glass and took a long pull straight from the bottle. Somewhere between his unstable emotional state and his rapidly spiking blood alcohol content he lost sight of the reality he was *not* a real doctor and had no idea what he was doing in his attempts to treat Helen for an untreatable and inevitably fatal disease. The panic gave way to anger.

But that isn't the point! That isn't what matters! What matters is all the time and effort I've spent! Surely, I'm owed some consideration for everything I've done! Who does Clyde think he is, keeping us apart? Why does he think I am doing all this? We were meant to be together! I'm the only one that can keep her safe and healthy, and Clyde is stopping me! I've got to get her out of there! Then she'll understand this all for the best because I love her!

Drunk as he was, he began fumbling for his car keys. He was going to stage a heroic rescue of the fragile, delicate, and possibly dying love of his life from her wicked father who was keeping her locked up to keep them apart. It was like the old stories he had heard as a boy, or maybe one of the plays he had seen or been in during his short theatrical career—he couldn't remember which through the brandied brain fog, and it didn't matter now anyway. What mattered now was rescuing his damsel in distress. He took one last, long pull at the bottle and theatrically threw it against the far wall, then spun dramatically on his heel to storm out and ride to the rescue.

The dramatic spin was what undid him. His balance and equilibrium were pretty much theoretical at this point, and the hardwood floor was well waxed and slippery. The heel turn became something more akin to an ice skating spin, and he completed nearly three complete rotations before crashing sideways into a row of chairs, one of which malevolently entangled his ankles. After lashing out his legs, cursing and struggling frantically, he lay back for a moment to catch his breath, and passed out.

When he finally awoke the next day, he looked and felt like he belonged right where he was, in a mortuary. He sat up slowly, and groaned, pausing for rest before attempting to scale the summit of getting to his feet. Once he was finally able to stand, he staggered upstairs and took a long, hot bath, sweating out remains of the brandy.

An hour later he was dressed and drinking strong, black coffee while contemplating his situation. Although still semi dull-witted, and aching, he felt strangely light and tranquil, which is often the aftermath of a stress-induced emotional meltdown and alcohol fueled tantrum. He was calm about Helen and knew what he had to do: go and formally present himself to Clyde and Emma and officially declare his interest and intentions. It was the only honorable thing to do. She was different; this wasn't like the other times, and the notion someone could see his passion for Helen as anything other than the purest love and devotion, angered and sickened him. The one thing he was more certain of than ever before was she was meant to be his, forever, and nothing could stand in the way of that destiny.

He finished the coffee and was just starting another pot when a woman came staggering in helped by three children.

"Doctor, Doctor! Ya gotta help mamma!" the biggest one cried out, "The baby's a-comin'!"

Delivering children was something Salazar could do, as long as there were no serious complications, and he quickly ushered her in and got her on the examination table. The dregs of his hangover and his obsession for Helen were forcibly pushed aside by the crisis at hand. He lost track of time as he worked steadily and with concentration. Eventually he helped bring a new, fragile life into the world.

It was this vision that held him through the rest of the day as he cared for the new mother and her infant and the three other ragamuffins until the father arrived in a lather, straight from a rig, reeking of sweat and oil in equal measure, both of which liberally oozed and puddled onto the floor. After checking on his wife and son, he slapped Salazar on the back with a blow that nearly floored him while pumping his hand as if he were trying to pull up oil from the bottom of the Permian Basin.

"Thanks, Doc! Thanks so much for takin' care of her and my new boy! I 'preciate it like you can't imagine!" He reached into his filthy jeans and withdrew a vile leather wallet that was degraded to an almost gelatinous mass and pried it open, "How much I owe ya?"

"Oh, there's no need for that now," Salazar replied. "We can settle up later."

This comment earned him another staggering thump on the back, "God bless ya, Doc, God bless ya! You got any kids of your own?"

"No, sadly," Salazar responded, *not that I know of,* he added silently to himself. Then an epiphany struck him: *I want children with her, I'm not too old! Plenty of men my age are fathers. I want to see her holding my son, nursing him!*

Almost as if he read Salazar's thoughts, the new father said kindly, "A man should have children, they are the joy of his life, makes all the struggle worthwhile. You ain't too old! Find yerself a good woman and have a family, Doc."

Salazar nodded and smiled, and realized he was blushing. "That's … that's good advice, friend. Thank you."

The proud father insisted on taking the family home with him, new mother and baby included, despite Salazar's protestations. By the time they were all bundled off, it was late. Salazar locked up and headed to bed, where he gently cuddled the blood soaked dress and whispered softly to it about motherhood and babies, and cried himself to sleep, the despair and longing in him an aching void sucking him down like a portal of Hell.

In the morning, he made up his mind to go see Clyde and Emma on the coming Sunday. In the meantime, he would contrive to walk or drive past the school around three each afternoon on the chance he might catch a glimpse of his beloved. As three o'clock rolled around, he casually took a stroll down by the school, but across the street as he didn't want to arouse any suspicions or let her see him. He paused and lit a cigar, watching through the rising smoke, and caught a glimpse of Helen, tall and pale, withdrawn and seemingly friendless. His heart leapt into his throat, and he broke out in a sweat at this merest glance of her. He walked briskly back to his abode, smoking furiously in a futile effort to calm his passion.

He continued his afternoon walks all week and was rewarded every time with a glimpse of his beloved until Friday rolled around. As he had done all week, he sauntered down the street across from the school and stopped and lit a cigar next to a tree behind which he could dodge if spotted. He stood casually, pretending to take his ease, but his eyes never left the door of the school. Children of all ages spilled out in a riot of shouting and laughter as they scampered off toward home or play, but Helen did not emerge. At first, he was not too concerned; perhaps she was finishing an assignment or was being forced to stay after for some disciplinary reason. But by the time he tossed the butt of his spent cigar into gutter, she still had not come out. He drew out his big, gold pocket watch, which he had acquired from the corpse of a banker in Monterey shortly before his unplanned and precipitous departure from that city; it was now twenty after three. Glancing up he saw someone leave the building, locking it behind him.

The panic hit him like a thunderbolt, and he ran all the way back to his clinic. Rushing inside, he hurriedly mixed up another batch of elixir, grabbed his bag, and climbed into his car, roaring the engine as he sped off down the street. As he drove, dodging through traffic like a madman, it never occurred to him to think of what he would say when he got there. He pulled up in a welter of dust and, grabbing his bag, bolted for the door.

Emma, hearing the racket of his arrival, had already opened the door and was standing in front of the screen door when he reached the wooden steps. He stopped and looked up at her, she looked worried and scared and was actually wringing her hands.

Oh God, what do I say? I can't tell Emma I've been spying on her daughter and noticed she wasn't in school today! How am I gonna explain myself? What do I say now?

He was spared by Emma slowly pushing open the door and saying, "It's real bad. Clyde said I wasn't to bother ya, on account of everything you already done for us, and for her, but … Lord Jesus! I don't know what to do! Clyde ain't home from work yet, and I don't 'spect him for a couple more hours at least."

Salazar bustled inside, giving Emma a sympathetic smile and saying, "Never you worry; what matters is Helen. She is all that matters. Let me see if I can help. Where is she?"

Emma led him to where Helen lay, apparently unconscious. Blood in various stages of coagulation stained the coverlet over her, and fresh rivulets were oozing from the corners of her mouth. She wheezed with every rattling breath. When Salazar listened through his stethoscope, it was far, far worse; the crackling, hissing, and popping reminded him of the sound of a range fire scorching and devouring its way across a desert hillside.

Helen abruptly coughed, and a geyser of blood, effluvia, and lung tissue erupted onto Salazar and the old blanket in which she was swaddled. He took the damp compress from her forehead and gently wiped her mouth and face, then smoothed back her hair before handing the now bloodied compress back to Emma. He noticed his hands were shaking.

"I will do what I can," he said, trying to sound calm and reassuring while within himself the panic and terror ran riot. He tried to give her a sip of his elixir, but this caused another fit of coughing and another eruption of blood and tissue. Digging into his bag he withdrew the pump and tube he had fashioned and, with infinite care, slowly fed the tube down her throat and into her windpipe. He guided the tube as gently as he could into what he hoped was a lung and began pumping out bright, red blood and chunks of tissue. It was the only thing he could think of to do.

In the back of his mind something was screaming at him that he did not know what he was doing and her worsened condition was his fault, and if she died, it would because of him. He struggled to keep a semblance of calm as he worked the pump and fought down the howling voices in his head.

Again and again he emptied the receptacle of its contents while time lost all meaning. When next he was aware, the room was getting dark for the sun was halfway down, casting a golden light and long shadows through the room. Helen appeared to be breathing easier, although she was still unconscious, and the dying sunlight caught her hair, turning it into a fiery halo. He finally paused for a moment, took off his spectacles and wiped his face with the kerchief he drew from the top pocket of his suit. The sweat of his endeavors, his panic, and his internal struggle had carved deep rivulets into the carefully applied makeup he habitually wore to look younger, and vast patches of it now came away onto the kerchief. He hurriedly re-stowed it, then, as he put his glasses back on, looked up and was astonished to see Clyde standing in the doorway, one arm around Emma, holding her tight against him. Clyde's face was a perfect mask of despair, and unchecked tears were coursing down his deeply weathered visage, carving two paths through the grime. Emma's face was pressed against his chest, and her tiny frame shook with muffled sobs.

Salazar was torn between being found out as a fraud, a sleazy con man who's unslaked lust for a thirteen-year-old girl had spurred him to such outrageous recklessness, and his horror that this beautiful child-woman he knew he loved with a holy purity might actually be taken from him by the unremitting claw of death.

Salazar struggled to find his voice, "I … I am doing what I can. She seems to be resting easier now," he said. His guilt grabbed his tongue before he could stop it. "We need to get her to a hospital," he blurted out. To his own ears, ringing with culpability, he sounded panicked, desperate and responsible, hardly the tone to instill confidence.

Clyde gently moved Emma aside and stepped toward Salazar, placing a grubby, powerful hand on his shoulder and giving it a firm squeeze. "Ain't no hospital for a hundred miles I been told. 'Sides, with night comin' on ain't no easy way to make that drive no how, even if we knew where we was a-goin.' You taken real good care of her so far, and me and Emma, we put our faith in the Lord, and our trust in you." He knelt and Emma knelt beside him, clasping his hand, and Clyde prayed.

As he did so, Salazar bowed his head in reverent devotion, genuinely thankful he had been spared a reckoning, and even more grateful for the simple-minded trust of Clyde and Emma. At the same time, he too was offering his own heartfelt pleading for some sort of divine intercession because he knew without it, his darling Helen would no longer be, and to his mortification, there was not a damned thing he could do about it, and he knew it.

Clyde concluded his prayer, and Salazar joined Emma in a hushed "Amen."

"I will stay with her during the crisis," Salazar said. "There is nothing anyone can do now. It is in God's hands," he added, eagerly keying into the religious tone.

Emma added another "Amen," and Clyde nodded.

The twin boys were howling, and Salazar realized he had no idea how long it had been going on, but the sudden swell in volume served to break the spell.

Clyde said, "Best see to the boys, Emma."

Daubing her eyes on her apron she nodded and went to comfort them.

"You look like you could do with some coffee, sir. How 'bout I brew up a pot?" Clyde said to Salazar.

"That would be most appreciated, thank you."

The night wore on, and Salazar stayed with Helen, refusing Clyde's offers to take over so he could get some sleep. He sat next to her by the dim light of a turned-down kerosene lantern, occasionally listening to her ragged breathing and checking her faint pulse. As the night progressed, both steadily diminished, and Salazar's exhaustion—enhanced by his gut-wrenching fear and crushing sense of guilt—gradually took its toll on him.

As he blearily stared at Helen's face, the brown streaks of dried and crusted blood spoiling its smooth, pale perfection, he slowly and gently took her hand; in his heart he prayed to her.

I am so sorry, my love! This is my fault because I failed to cure you. Please know how sorry I am and how very, very much I love and adore you. You are the most perfect woman in the world, and I know in my soul we were meant to be together forever! Please, PLEASE forgive me!

Salazar started slightly when he perceived her hand squeezing his lightly.

I should have done more to save you, but I let my pride interfere. Helen, my dearest, most beautiful, sweetest, most perfect girl! I love you! Please, please come through this so that we can be together forever. Let my love give you strength! Don't leave me!

She was glowing softly in the dim light, her hair a burnished halo again as it had appeared at sunset. He saw her eyelids begin to move and then flicker, finally opening. Her bright, gleaming eyes fairly shone with adoration, and he felt them pierce him to the core, filling him with such a warmth of love a frisson rushed over him. He felt her squeeze his hand again, ever so softly. He watched as her lips began to move slowly, struggling against the sheen of dried blood. He could barely perceive the susurration and cautiously leaned forward, the intense sensations of her breath and voice so immediately against his ear causing him to shudder with ecstasy. He strained to catch every intonation, every sound, every particle of what she was saying, her breath enfolding him in its flowery perfume.

I love you, my love. Forever and ever. We must never be apart. Stay with me always, and I will be with you forever.

He stayed leaning with his ear against her mouth to catch the slightest sound, but there was none. He felt her squeeze his hand gently once more.

He suddenly felt himself falling and jolted upright, staring about him in confusion for a moment before remembering where he was. The dim light of the lantern was lower now, guttering an unearthly blue, and he cautiously twisted the knob, raising the wick and illumination.

He saw Helen staring wild-eyed up at the ceiling, her mouth a silent scream and her face a frozen rictus of abject terror. A sickly-sweet metallic reek from her lips vied with the noxious vapors of excreta in a miasma that was the pall of death.

He sat staring for a while, knowing her soul was no longer in her body, but also comprehending the reality of what had happened; she *had* come to him! She *had* sworn her love! She *had* sworn to be with him forever! And gradually, as the sky began to slowly lighten with false dawn, he made up his mind what he must do.

He reached over slowly and extinguished the lantern and just sat there, feeling very old and very tired, but with a deep, secret thrill growing and unfolding within like a hidden flame, warming his soul and banishing both fatigue and sadness. He was so lost in thought he didn't hear Clyde walk up behind him. Clyde let out a gasp, and Salazar turned and looked up at him, then back at Helen's body. He hurriedly pulled the old blanket up over her tragic face and mumbled, "I am sorry, Clyde, so very, very sorry. You shouldn't have seen her like that."

Clyde placed a hand on his shoulder. "I'm sure you did all you could for her," he said softly. He sniffed and added, "And I know you loved her, too. This'll be real hard on Emma. Real hard. Hard on all of us, but it's the will of the Lord, so we must bear up and take comfort in his wisdom."

Salazar nodded and automatically added an "Amen," then patted Clyde's hand. He knew what he had to do. "Clyde, let me do one last thing for her. Let me prepare her for burial." He slowly stood and turned, looking Clyde in the eye, man to man. "Let me do that for her. It is something I am very, very good at. As a final gift to her, as a way of showing my devotion to her and my respect for you and Emma. Please, Clyde, let me do this."

Clyde looked at him for a long minute, then nodded, extending his hand, which Salazar grasped, and they shook hands firmly, eye to eye, as men.

"You're a good, good man. God bless you." Clyde said. "I don't want Emma seein' her like this. Wouldn't be right, not with her in the state she's already in."

"Is she still asleep?" Salazar asked.

Clyde nodded. "She cried and cried a long, long time last night, and I think she finally cried herself out a couple hours ago. I hope the boys let her sleep."

"Let's carry her out to my car now, then," Salazar responded, and began tightening the old blanket securely around the stinking bundle.

They carefully and quietly carried Helen's body out and placed her in the back of Salazar's car.

"Thank you for letting me do this, truly," Salazar said.

"Thank you for all you done."

"I will let you know about arrangements once things are prepared. The finest of everything, and don't worry yourself about costs. There won't be any. It is the least I can do."

Clyde just nodded, the numbness starting to sink in. He waved mechanically at Salazar's retreating car, then turned and slowly climbed the stairs and went to tell his wife their oldest child, their only daughter, the apple of their eye, was no more.

Despite his exhaustion, Salazar felt a sense of elation. Although Helen's body and soul had parted company, her soul had spoken to him, had told him she loved him, and how they could be together. He pulled his car up to the undertaker's side of his building and gently took Helen's corpse in his arms, she weighed almost nothing it seemed. He carried her into the tile-lined room and carefully laid her on the chipped, old, embalming table. The fatigue and stress made his hands shake as he was tenderly unwrapping her. He discarded the befouled old blanket.

He knew there was plenty to do to prepare for this greatest act of adoration he could perform, and he was determined to not rush, and to make no mistakes. He would get a good night's sleep before he began. As he contemplated her, he knew, however, he could not leave her like this, smeared with the vile remains of her failed, frail form. He softly washed her face, clearing away all the dried blood and the rime of sweat that had begun to show at her hairline, closing her eyes and mouth. Covering her with a fresh, clean, sheet, he worked his trembling hands beneath it and removed her soiled undergarments.

"Forgive me, my love, but I must do this. You do not deserve to lie in blood and shit all night, love of my heart. So please bear with me, angel," he said softly as he worked.

He then carefully washed her, again under the sheet, not daring to look at her naked body in his highly agitated state. Throughout the procedure his hands shook so much he could barely hold the sponge, dropping it a few times. He kept working until the water that sluiced toward the drain below her feet appeared clear. He replaced the now soaking wet and lightly soiled sheet with a fresh one, and kissed her forehead. "There, my love! All done for tonight. You were a very good girl. Tomorrow I will start on making you immortal my darling. Rest well."

He went up to his room and chastely put the blood-soaked dress and the light shift Helen had worn for her organ treatments away. He realized they were no longer necessary. He slept a deep sleep where he was once again with the girl he loved in a moment of exquisite, perfect bliss. When the morning sunlight streamed onto his face he awoke reluctantly, not willing to leave Helen's spirit and come back to the mundanity of earthly life and the inevitable task he must now perform, but she had told him how to keep her with him and how they could be together, so he knew he had no real choice.

Her body had moved and shifted during the night as rigor mortis set in, and the lividity showed what little remained of her blood had settled as well. He straightened her body, smoothing the sheet which covered her, and then smoothed her hair. He went to his supply room and came back with armloads of things, including a bolt of white, oiled silk.

As he was setting up his things, he spoke to Helen in a hushed, confidential tone.

"First we are going to give you another bath to remove whatever may have been missed last night. Then we will remove the rest of your blood. I have to use a large needle for that, but don't be scared, my darling; you won't feel a thing, and I will take very good care of you, my love."

He stepped over to the embalming table and formally, in his official capacity of an undertaker, pulled back the sheet and saw, for the first time, Helen's nude body. He clutched the edge of the table as his knees buckled despite his best efforts. "My God, my love, you are so beautiful!" he muttered as his eyes scoured over her. They stopped momentarily on her pudenda, and he frowned; there was already a layer of fine hair there.

"We have to fix that," he muttered, and feeling strangely embarrassed, he gently covered Helen's face so she wouldn't have to see what was about to happen. He tenderly washed her whole body down again, using perfumed soap this time, carefully kneading her muscles to restore some mobility. Once he had finish bathing her, he worked up a foaming bowl of lather and, softly and lovingly spreading her milk-white thighs, gently brushed the soap over her pristine mound. "I know it tickles my dear, but we will soon have this disgusting hair gone. It's not your fault, I know it happens, sadly, but I will take care of it for you." So saying, he began to shave her with the greatest possible caution, removing every last pubic hair and leaving the delicate skin bare, smooth, and flawless. He gazed at his handiwork a moment after dabbing away the last vestiges of soap with warm towel. Unable to resist, he glanced to his left, then his right and leaned forward, planting a quick, light kiss on the now hairless region, "Soon, soon my love you will know all the joys," he whispered, before resuming a more upright pose.

He attached the pump mechanism and inserted the large trocar and let the machine do its work, draining the last of her blood and fluids. He then flipped the switch and the machine began pumping embalming fluid into her. Once the procedure was completed and the machine disconnected, Salazar arranged a series of large metal dishes on the counter behind him.

He peeled back the cloth covering her face and addressed her. "My darling, I told you I would make you immortal so that we could be together always, but the procedure is long and unpleasant. Please don't watch as I work. I swear to you, on the love I bear you, that the results will be worth it. You are beyond feeling any of this pain, but please don't watch me." He kissed her lips softly, patted her hair and pulled the cloth back over her lifeless face.

He made one long, expert Y-shaped incision, carefully avoiding damaging her budding breasts and began his work. He expertly removed each organ in turn, placing it in one of the metal dishes, working slowly and methodically, careful to avoid letting the bowels, stomach, or bladder leak any contents into her visceral cavity. After taking out the lungs, he removed her heart with a holy awe and set it aside for special handling later.

As he worked, he could not help but recall the others he had loved, and how his passion for them had made him an object of scorn, loathing, and disgust in the eyes of those who could not understand his desperate desire for a love that was different, but no less passionate or consuming. All the sacrifices he made for the others, Lupe in Monterrey, Marie in Tamaulipas, and, worst of all, Sara in Matamoros. Her family had nearly killed him when she had told them how he touched her. Worse even than the beating was the sense of betrayal, and it was that despair that had made him howl and sob, even as the mob beat him.

But now, now it would be different! Now, at last, he had finally met his soulmate, and she had told him how they could be together forever. As this realization gradually engulfed him, his spirit rose, and he hummed as he worked that strange, old song with the sliding minor scales, whose title he could not recall.

Once he had removed all the organs, he thoroughly washed the cavity with a strong disinfectant. As he was waiting for the cavity to dry out somewhat in the arid West Texas heat, he set about disposing of the organs, chopping them into small pieces and dumping them in vats of acid he kept on hand for the purpose of disposing of diseased organs. Her heart he carefully washed in disinfectant before sealing it in a small urn filled with triple-rectified brandy, cinnamon, clove oil, and copal resin, after giving it a lingering kiss.

He took a short break for lunch and drove over to talk to Clyde and Emma about their arrangements for the service. Emma was in a state of numbed shock, her red-raw eyes blinked only sporadically, and she could barely manage monosyllables. Clyde was still wearing a brave front, but his eyes, too, were red from his secret sobbing.

"Allow me to once again tell you how very, very sorry I am for your loss. I am doing the best for her that I can," he said solemnly, and they both nodded slowly. "When would you like the service to happen? Have you spoken with your pastor? I have already made all the arrangements for the interment, but I need to know the day."

"We … we was thinkin' Saturday. That way the others in the congregation can attend and ain't nobody gonna miss work. If, if'n that ain't inconvenient for you, of course," Clyde said, and Emma nodded.

"Saturday, that is in two days. I should have everything ready by then without any difficulty. Shall we say noon? That will give everyone time to assemble without any rush. If that is agreeable, I will make the rest of the arrangements."

Emma stared up at him and mumbled, "Thank you. You been so kind to us. God bless you."

Clyde nodded and put an arm around Emma, "That'll be fine. Thank you." That was all he was capable of getting out without breaking down, and he was not about to do that in front of his wife, or another man.

When he returned from lunch, he carefully rubbed the inside of the cavity with more cinnamon, clove oil, and a variety of other spices and chemicals he had learned of over the years. In another day or so, they would leach out the remaining liquid leaving the cavity comparatively dry, as well as sweetly perfumed. He next filled out the death certificate and everything else required by the state in order for Helen to be interred.

That done, he began going through the closets in search of the special dress he knew he had kept, although at the time he had purloined it, he never imagined the use to which it was now to be put. Nestled in the back of a closet was a trunk where he had cached, carefully wrapped in tissue paper, a spectacular wedding gown of the finest silk, studded about with seed pearls, and complete with a wreath and veil. He grinned as he held it up; it was perfect! It would have to be substantially taken in, but tailoring was one of the many crafts he had picked up along the way. Whistling the odd song again, he carried the finery downstairs and laid it out on the exam table in his clinic.

He spent the rest of the day measuring and cutting and stitching, pausing only to check on the status of Helen's body and once for a brief pause for dinner. He worked far into the night on the wedding gown, checking and re-checking his measurements to ensure a perfect fit. During the trips back to measure Helen, he would coo to her about how beautiful she would look in her wedding gown and speak to her comfortingly. Finally, his eyes and fingers aching, he retired and once again in his dreams he conversed lovingly with Helen, who showered him with expressions of adoration and devotion.

He greeted Helen the next morning. "Good morning, my darling. I hope you rested well and are ready for the final stage of your transformation. Today I will finish making you immortal and dress you for the wedding to come. Be patient my darling, our long wait is nearly over."

He set to work at once, cleaning out the visceral cavity and ensuring it was dry before liberally massaging the interior with more spices and preserving chemicals. When he was satisfied, he began stuffing the cavity with strips of the oiled silk which he dipped in molten paraffin wax to aid their rigidity. He worked carefully, ensuring her body had a natural look and the supple firmness it had possessed in life before finally stitching the body closed with close, careful passes of stout, pale, silken thread.

He gently removed the cloth from her face once he was finally finished so she could see the transformation and be amazed. "There! You look magnificent my dear! No one would even see the closure unless they were looking for it! I've given you my best work, and I have made you immortal as I promised. Now we can be together always. Just a few finishing touches are all that are left. We are nearly done, my love!"

He dug through drawers and cupboards until he came up with a mahogany case with brass fittings. Opening it he removed tray after tray of glass eyes of the finest, most expensive German craftsmanship. "I borrowed these from a colleague in Mexico City a few years ago. They have been very useful! Ah! Here we are!"

he exclaimed removing a pair of pale blue ones. "These should be an almost perfect match!" He carried the glass eyes in a kidney dish over to the embalming table and gently opened her eyelids to compare the color. "It is very close, darling. I don't think we can find anything closer. Now, bear with me, I know this will be unpleasant, but I will work as quickly as I can."

He began humming the old song again as he gently removed each eye, expertly clipping away the muscle and nerve fibers. He filled the gaping sockets with chemicals, then shredded more oiled silk to fill the cavities before expertly inserting the glass eyes. The effect astonished even him.

"Oh my God," he whispered, backing away momentarily. "My love, you … you … dearest love of my heart, you live again, forever!" He crowed triumphantly, clapping distractedly with pure joy.

He washed her down again, carefully drying her then powdering her body with talc to make it easier to put on the undergarments and the dress. Then, having shampooed and dried her hair, he braided it into two French braids which framed her face to perfection, whistling and humming as he worked. He then dressed her and placed her in his finest coffin, completing little finishing touches which added to the illusion Helen was alive and well and ready to be joined to her beloved for all eternity. As a final touch, he gently placed the bridal wreath and veil on her and stood back to admire the effect.

It was astounding. "There, my love! You look divine! Perfect for your wedding day!" He stole a quick kiss and giggled. "Sorry darling, I couldn't wait."

He arose early the next morning and arranged the parlor for the service, dusting and cleaning and polishing the woodwork to make the room worthy of Helen. He then cleaned himself up and dressed in his finest tailcoat and standing collar and was as spruce as a bridegroom could be on his wedding day.

Clyde and Emma arrived first, of course. They had arranged for a sitter for the twin boys because they were too young to know what was happening and were too much of a handful for Emma on this, of all days, to handle.

Salazar exhibited all the gravitas he could muster and greeted them in hushed, reverential tones, bowing obsequiously as he spoke. He led them to the coffin and stood aside to allow them to admire his skill.

"Oh my God! Oh Clyde! What? What … Oh dear lord!" Emma gasped seeing her daughter laid out for a wedding.

"No. Oh God, please, no … no." Clyde muttered, then turned on Salazar. "What have you done, you sonofabitch?" he shouted, his face scarlet with fury, shame and outrage.

Salazar backed away in shock and dismay. "Clyde, Emma, I have done the very best I could do for her, as I promised I would!" he said.

Emma started sobbing uncontrollably, her tiny frame shaking as she gasped and howled. Clyde took two rapid strides toward Salazar; he was going to kill him.

Just then the door opened, and the Pastor arrived with a deputation of six Elders who would serve as pall bearers. Emma shrieked and Clyde turned to see them. He froze in mid-step, unsure whether he was going to just kill Salazar in front of everyone or whether he should break his neck later on.

Emma grabbed his sleeve, "Clyde! No!" she shrieked, struggling to pull him back. More people were entering for the service. Clyde looked at Salazar, then at Emma, and walked back to the coffin, his seething fury barely contained. He gently lowered the lid of the casket and murmured, "I'm sorry honey, I'm so very, very sorry" to Helen as the lid shut. He dug in his pocket and pulled out a keychain tool and screwed the lid down while everyone stared, dumbfounded, Salazar most of all.

The Pastor, who, along with the six Elders, had seen Helen in all her bridal glory immediately understood Clyde's reaction and stepped quickly to the pulpit and addressed the growing, milling throng. "Brothers and sisters, there was a mishap with the embalming. This service will be a closed casket service. Thank you for your understanding."

Salazar was outraged and was stepping forward to protest when one of the Elders, a neckless mountain who was at least three times broader and nearly two feet taller stepped in front of him and whispered, "You best keep yer mouth shut you bastard and leave these people be, else ain't no undertaker in Texas gonna be able to put yer pieces back together or make you look purdy, hear?" He clapped a hand like a cast iron skillet on Salazar's shoulder for emphasis and stood there, blocking him out like an eclipse.

He remained there, keeping Salazar in check while the service was conducted. At the conclusion he, and the other pall bearers lifted the exquisite coffin and carried it out, laying it on a flatbed truck since there was no hearse.

Emma walked up to Salazar and stared at him for moment, then slapped his face hard. "How could you?" she whispered before collapsing against Clyde. Clyde just stared at him and finally said in a low, quiet voice, "There will be a reckoning, there surely will." Then, one arm around Emma they staggered out. The Pastor just shook his head and followed the crowd out.

Suddenly Salazar was all alone. It was like Monterey again, like every other time. He felt the panic rising at the realization these big men, men who could not understand the love he had, the all-consuming passion that fired him, would come back for him and kill him. He rushed frantically upstairs, grabbing luggage and shoving in some clothing, then went through his closets where his treasures were hidden: rings, jewelry, watches, cufflinks, gold and silver coins, a fortune in looted goods, and began stuffing them into bags which he then hid in the luggage. He grabbed everything of value he could easily take and began loading up his car.

"They won't come back until tonight," he told himself as he frantically worked. "Please, God, don't let them come back until tonight!" He looked at his watch, it had been a little over half an hour since they had left, and taken his beloved with them. "Best leave now, just in case," he muttered. He ran back upstairs and grabbed Helen's blood-stained dress and the shift, because he could not bear to leave them. He also grabbed a revolver, just in case and, from the broom closet a shovel.

Loping out to the car, he stashed everything in the spacious trunk, which he closed and locked, then slid into the car, placing the pistol on the passenger's seat before gunning the engine and roaring out of town in a cloud of dust.

He drove for over an hour watching to make sure he had not been followed. He left the main road and circled up and around on some dirt tracks until he was hidden from view. He turned the engine off and then the shaking started, along with the nausea. He opened the door and retched violently until nothing but bitterness was left in him. Then he started to sob uncontrollably, an animal anguish that was past words, he howled and shrieked until there was nothing else left in him, then he opened the trunk and took out a bottle of brandy slugging down almost half the bottle in one go before he leaned against the car and slid to the ground.

He already knew what he had to do; he had known it instinctively from the moment of Clyde's reaction. "No one will keep us apart!" he shouted, raising the bottle skyward before taking another pull at it. "We will be together my love! Forever and always! This will still be our wedding day!"

He waited and waited; the brandy burned itself out at last leaving him parched, while the torrent of emotions finally subsided, leaving him feeling strangely light and delicate. The sun went down in a spectacular golden halo, and Salazar thought of Helen's hair. He dug around in the trunk and changes of clothes, took out a jug of water and some food, and restored himself. The night darkened until the moon rose and by its light Salazar could read his watch, it was almost 10:30. It was time, he decided. He gathered himself up and repacked the trunk, taking the shovel with him he got in and started the car. It was light enough that he could see without using the headlights, and he drove carefully until he had circled the town and was now on the north side of it.

Cautiously, he made his way to the cemetery, parking the car beneath a poplar. He crept carefully along, keeping a keen eye on his surroundings, making sure there was no one in sight. Helen's grave was easy to find as it was the only fresh grave in the lot, and being freshly dug, it was a simple matter for him to excavate it. In less than an hour he had the coffin uncovered. He unscrewed the lid and pulled it back. Helen stared up at him, the glass eyes reflecting the moonlight, and he gasped at her splendor.

"My love! My precious, sweet angel! I have come for you. Now we truly will be together for all time," he gushed as he gently lifted her from the coffin.

Once out of the grave he carried her in his arms back to the car then gently arranged her in the back seat, bundling her with blankets to keep her warm. Returning to the grave he closed the casket, then refilled the hole. No one would be the wiser.

He drove into the night, and for the first time in his life he felt pure joy and happiness. Looking at her nestled in the corner, looking drowsy, he smiled and said simply, "I love you, Helen." After a time, he said, "New Mexico is cool and dry. Let's honeymoon there! Maybe Taos or Santa Fe. The climate will be very good for your condition."

He looked back, and she appeared to nod. He smiled as the contentment of a lifetime slowly oozed and trickled into every empty, aching cavity of his being, and he began to hum again. Suddenly he remembered the name of the tune. "Boda Negra!" he said aloud, "Of course!" and he chuckled.

"IN-A-GADDA-DA-VIDA, ALICE!"

By Ruby Pond

Maeve ran her fingers through her long brown hair. The dirt drive was dark, and the trees towered over her car as she drove down the road to the open field where the movie screen stood. As she pulled up to the speaker, she rolled down the window on her old lavender VW, then pulled a Marlboro out of the glove compartment and pressed the lighter in on the dash. Tapping impatiently on the hard gearshift, she realized the lighter wasn't working. It sometimes did, and it sometimes did not. Tonight, it did not.

"Damn car!"

Annoyed, she rifled through the glove compartment again, looking for anything to light her cigarette. She found a lighter she bought at the art festival last summer with Suz on their road trip.

Suz had been her best friend since childhood. They were together most of the time. They ran away together to Florida last summer, hitchhiking all the way. That was the road trip of a lifetime, until Suz's Daddy sent a police officer (better known to them as a "pig") to hunt them down. All the way from Charlotte, South Carolina to Daytona, Florida. It was a real drag. But deep down, Maeve didn't mind. She was getting tired of sleeping on the cold hard ground or in the sand at the beach. Maeve didn't have a car yet, and Suz didn't even have a driver's license.

Both girls went through a lot of changes that year. From unpopular, straight-A students with unruly hair, to cool chicks with blue eye shadow, black eyeliner, straight silky hair, (thanks to a daily iron across the ironing board), paisley halters, and hip-hugging bell-bottoms. They were cool now and hung with all the cool cats. Maeve was happy with who she was now, though most of the time she stayed in a fog. It was still far-out!

Finally, she came across a matchbook with two matches left. As she lit her cigarette, her nostrils flared, and the pungent odor of leather and smoke painted her throat and lungs, giving her a sense of relief from her frustration. She reached down and traced her finger across the lines of her corduroys. She gently kneaded her thighs, attempting to calm herself down, and reflected on the man at the drive-in's entrance gate. A chill ran up her spine. But it wasn't the ticket taker who unnerved her, even though he was creepy. This anxiety came from something else entirely. As the cartoon noises zipped through the air, and the faint colorful images on the screen darted to and fro, she sat back and let her mind drift through the confusing experiences of the past week.

About a week ago at the beach, she and Suz spent the day tripping with some cool guys they'd met the week before. Juan, Mercedes, Stan, Daisy, and some cat named Fritz. She didn't remember much about the way the day went, except waking up in the bed of a pickup truck and trying to come down from some crazy trip.

That's when she remembered having first seen him. He was just *there*. Long black hair pulled into a ponytail. Kissing the tips of her fingers and laughing. His blue eyes staring through her, all glazed over. Walking around shirtless and showing his hairless chest, he wore a beaded necklace with three tiny skulls hanging from it. His bell-bottoms, with marijuana leaf patches on the knees and a big peace sign patch over one rear pocket, partially covered his dirty bare feet. His unkempt mustache tickled the flesh on her fingers, and she didn't know why, but she loved him. She loved his essence. Her head swam with color, and she tried to sit up.

"Well, right on, Alice!" he said, smiling as he watched her try to get up. "Damn, girl! That was a groovy trip!"

She struggled to get straight and strained to free herself of his spell. All she could take in was his dark skin, blue eyes, and how she was starting to feel about him. She realized there was no coming down any time soon, as she tried to focus on him. He sat beside her and folded his legs beneath him in an "Indian squat." He scratched his beard while he talked. His voice was deep and thick. It sounded like he had cotton in his mouth. She studied his lips as he formed words to speak. "Spooner has s'more acid we can drop … later in the week if you want!" It came out slow, and it was like the words were so heavy they just sat there in the air for her to consider. Then he leaned in and pushed his tongue between her lips.

"Who are you?" she asked, after catching her breath and falling in love.

She tried to sit up again and looked down to find her bikini was still safely secured around her lean, tanned body. But that didn't mean much. There was a blue beach towel underneath her, still covered in sand. She felt the grit on her legs as she attempted to get up.

"I love you!" she said, smiling and amazed at how difficult it was to move her tongue. Then she wondered if she was actually underwater. She didn't feel wet. *Oh well, it didn't matter. It felt wonderful!*

"Who are you?" she asked, with a smile on her face.

"Don't you know?" he asked in a whisper, leaning in close. "Look into my eyes, Alice. Why, I am Satan. You heard me. Satan." He laughed out loud, his voice rising. "Beelzebub! Ha- ha! I'm your dark knight, and you've just fallen off one hell-of-a-ride on my stallion, Alice! You can call me Daddy-O, my little evil Alice in Wonderland!" He traced his finger over her cheek. "And my, but you are an evil one! My Alice!"

His icy eyes danced in the light, and she loved what she was hearing even though she felt scared. She was fascinated by his eyes. So blue! Yet, his pupils were like fire. She thought she saw little red sparks in them. It was wonderful! She wondered who Alice was and why he called her that.

He got up and danced in circles, grabbing the Boone's Farm Apple Wine off the bed of the truck and taking a huge sip. She remembered reaching for the bottle as he danced by, offering it and teasing her. He was trying to lure her out of the truck bed.

"Come on, Alice!" he said. "Come to Daddy! Come to Satan!"

She kept grabbing for the bottle unsuccessfully and giggling, while he danced by her and laughed, teasing her with the wine bottle. *She was so thirsty! Ha, and in love! She wanted to be Alice!*

The next thing she remembered was waking up in her little apartment, and there was no sign of him. She found out later Suz had a bad trip that night, and she went away for a while to stay with her brother in Arizona and get her head on right. But the guy lingered in her mind. She could smell the aromatic cannabis seeping from his skin as though he were right there with her. Every cell of her body levitated a little at the memory of his mustache inching and crawling over her flesh. She longed to see him again. She somehow felt their souls meshed together in some heady psychedelic realm. As the week wore on, it was more and more difficult to focus. Finally, one night, as she was getting off work, she noticed a note left under her windshield wiper with a black rose. "Meet me at the Drive-In at 9 p.m., Alice!" It was written in red ink and signed "S".

She could barely get there fast enough. Now there, she sat waiting. Drawn to a presence stronger than she'd ever felt, (considering her young age) she trembled with fear, but also excitement. She began looking around and noticed her car was the only one at the drive-in, and the screen grew dark. Her sense of excitement was waning, and she started to feel afraid. She had chills, and there was an eerie breeze blowing. She pulled out a rolling paper and her stash from the inside pocket of her purse. Sprinkling a line across the middle of the paper, she carefully rolled it up, then licking the edge of the paper, she wrapped the joint and ran it along the tip of her tongue to be sure it was sealed tight. She pulled a seed from the end, twisted it, then placed it between her lips. Taking her last match, she struck it and took in a deep drag. Holding it as long as she could, she looked around and grew a bit more uneasy as the time went by.

The speaker on her window began to vibrate with a staticky tune she didn't recognize. At first, it played quietly. Then it got louder and louder. The screen came on. Its image was gray and dark. But as the music got louder, the image developed and grew more defined. And she knew the tune now. It was Jefferson Airplane's "White Rabbit." A black and white, but well-detailed image emerged from the screen, and it started moving. It was so familiar, and at first, she thought it was her mother, but then she realized it was herself. Chained to a coffin. She was screaming, yet no sound came out of her mouth. Pills began swarming around her head on the screen, and "White Rabbit" continued to boom from the speakers.

That's when she saw him. Satan! He was on-screen with her. He toked a rolled-up joint and breathed in deeply, then leaned over her body on the screen and exhaled the smoke into her mouth, giving her what was known as a "reefer shotgun." She saw herself breathe in deeply, holding the secondhand smoke in her lungs as long as she could. Then a puff of smoke escaped from her screaming mouth as he walked away from her "screen self" and came toward her. Disoriented now, she realized she was not in her car any longer. He held his hand out to her, and his piercing blue eyes penetrated her fear. She kept reflecting on life and how she used to be a good girl. The lyric "Go ask Alice" faded in the background, playing softly across her imagination as he kept getting closer. Her "screen image" still screaming and struggling to free herself from the coffin, and still muffled like a silent movie. She tried to focus her attention on the image of herself, but she could barely look away from him. He was getting closer and closer. The air was filled with the sweet scent of pot seeping through his skin.

She found herself longing for the days when the weirdest trip she took was on Bobby Jacob's handlebars down to the 7-Eleven to get some SweeTARTS because she helped him with his homework. She made him take the back alley, so no one would see them, and he tried to kiss her and reach his hand under her shirt. She punched him so hard it hurt her hand, and she had trouble writing the rest of the week. She was so afraid he was going to tell somebody. But he never did.

She wished she could have that week of pain and worry back again and trade it for the fear and anticipation she had now. It was so strange. She was terrified, and yet, intrigued. The music got louder again, and she realized he was mouthing the words of the song as he got closer to her. The fear grew inside her, and her "screen self" was gasping for air. She felt the hair on the back of her neck rise, and her tears felt heavy like blood.

That's when she noticed the crown in his hand. A sparkling tiara with spiked daggers protruding from the inner ring. Out of the corner of her eye, she watched her "screen self" die and fall into the coffin. The lid slammed shut, and the crate holding her dead body fell through the earth into a lake of fire and the pits of hell. The lyric "Go ask Alice!" reverberated in that well-known Grace Slick voice. Distracted, she saw he was now only a couple of feet away, holding her crown.

"I love you!" she whispered, mortified.

As he gripped the crown, white-knuckled, and with his blue eyes burning her soul, he formed an "O" with his mouth. "White Rabbit" ended as Iron Butterfly's song "In-A-Gadda-Da-Vida" pounded at the air. She trembled and looked around, realizing she wasn't in the drive-in anymore. "Where are we, Satan?" she asked him.

He thrust the crown down upon her head and looked at her adoringly. As she tried to scream while she lay dying, he said "In-A-Gadda-Da-Vida, Alice!"

GLUTTONY BE THY VICE

By Nicholas Paschall

"You have the right to remain silent," the heavily armored SWAT officer tells me. "Should you show any resistance, we are authorized to use lethal force to maintain peace within the states. Do you understand?" His automatic weapon presses firmly against my left temple, and he has his boot on my back, pinning me to the ground. I truly believe he wants me to resist, so he could put me down.

Asshole.

I hold out my pale hands, palms down, and spread them out on the cool stone floor of my lair. I knew one day they would catch me and drag me from the bowels of my playroom. I just wish they hadn't caught me so soon.

I still have four children left, after all.

The officer grunts, pressing harder on my back with his boot, as another two come up alongside of me, each taking an arm in their firm grip. Carefully, they hoist me up, another four officers aiming their rifles at me the entire time. I smile widely for them.

The smear of red blood dribbling from my mouth makes the one on the left quiver with rage.

The two officers wrestle my arms behind my back, shackling me with a set of heavy silver manacles. The metal stings as it sears into my flesh, but I'm old enough it doesn't send me into hysterics. The officer who'd pinned me to the floor, a heavyset man with weathered features, looks almost disappointed by my lack of reaction. I turn my smile toward him, neck popping several times, as my muscles unlock interlinking vertebrae to allow my head to swivel owlishly.

"Knock that off," he orders, aiming it directly in my face. "Don't give me a reason."

"Wouldn't dream of it, officer," I reply around a mouthful of sharpened teeth, triangular saws arranged in rows. I maintain my staring contest with him, my grin widening as I force him to turn away from my red orbs.

There's still the rumor we can entrance someone with a mere glance.

I love that rumor.

No, we *Nocturnis Sapiens* only have a few distinct advantages over the rest of our mouth-breathing cousins. We have much longer lifespans, for one. I, myself, am well over two hundred years old, and I've met a few of my kind who claim they remember the Roman Empire.

I don't know about that, but they certainly did appear as ancient as the ruins in Italy, so who can say?

We can survive solely on blood, but may also draw sustenance from meat as long as it's fresh. Our organs, for lack of a better term, gain nourishment from blood and tissue, provided it's raw and warm. Our hearts pump only when we have the fluids to do so; without feeding every few weeks, we start to slow down and retreat into hibernation.

Not a pleasant feeling.

Some, like myself, tend to feed more than is required. This is where the vampire myth evolved from, pale figures who move in the darkness and feed on the blood of the living. Mostly true, save for the fact while not dead, I am not biologically alive, either. My heart pumps blood stolen from others, and I have no reproductive urges to speak of.

I simply exist.

We were finally outed in the early sixties, so the government created laws to monitor us. The good little vampires visit clinics to feed on donated blood twice a month, then go about their nights as normally as any human would their days. The naughty vampires like myself, better known as Fangs, get hunted for sport and safety for the public.

I've had hunters come knocking with everything from garlic, crucifixes, bibles, and even crossbows. But those are just myths that bear a shred of truth in them. Garlic does bother our sense of smell, which we use to sniff out blood in the air. Crucifixes, when held by the pious, can harm us and even force us to flee. Bibles are mere books, and crossbows with silver arrowheads spell certain death for an overconfident Fang.

Oh yeah, and the stories about sunlight? Not true! We enter a "death state" during the sunlight hours. For all intents and purposes, we're corpses, bloated with blood. We undergo rigor mortis and gather flies. By the time we awake at dusk, we have an "earthy" smell about us and one helluva backache.

The second set of manacles, linking the ones on my wrists to a metal belt they are fastening to me, makes me wince. Silver is something we're all allergic to, though the older we are, the more we can tolerate.

The older vampires are stronger than the younger ones. The younger ones are those we infect with our lovely condition by transmitting our blood into them through a fun little method called the Kiss of Death.

Yeah, we must lock lips as we bite off a piece of our own tongue, and pump the stolen blood into you, which you must swallow. Takes about three to four pints, so not many can stomach the process.

Heh … stomach it …

I snicker, causing all the officers to flinch and steady their rifles with the sights set on either my heart or face. I hold my hands up as best I can, palms open.

"I'm *good and caught* gentleman, so no need to worry," I say, smiling a lopsided grin as I tilt my head. A curtain of silky black hair swishes across my face. "The big, bad vampire is in chains. You've won."

"Where are the children?" one of them, a black man with a mustache, demands, jostling his weapon closer to me.

"Well, I have four left, if that's what you're asking," I reply, watching as the men look at me in horror. "What?"

"You took an entire kindergarten class!" one of them growls, stepping forward. His beady eyes study me with an unhealthy amount of rage.

"I got hungry."

He lunges forward and bashes me in the side of the head. I topple to the ground. The blood-slickened stone allows for me to slide a few feet, as I laugh at how miserable his pathetic punch is and how infuriated the men must be.

I mean, they stormed my little cave with twenty or so men. There's only seven left.

Between snorts of laughter, I turn to smile at the beady eyed officer. "You best behave, officer, lest I charge you with assault!"

He growls, but he backs off to allow two other officers the chance to scoop me back up. I'm caked in congealed blood, that of the men who'd come charging down into my nest with the hopes of rescuing twenty-eight kids from their fate. I was so gorged on blood and meat their bullets had little effect on me. My body quickly stitched itself back together as they tore into me, allowing for me to tear into them.

Now, having bled nearly dry from the number of rounds spent to take me down, I finally relax and let them have their way. One thing I can say about this great nation I live in (kind of) is the justice system will do what it does best.

It'll mess up.

They haul me up from the depths of my home, tugging at me, as I allow myself to go limp in their hands.

Why make it easier for them?

Outside, half a dozen black vans sit with their doors flung open. I can only imagine how the officers lunged from the vehicles in a silent storm of holy vengeance, ready to storm the dark bastion of my earthen lair. That turned out well enough for them I suppose. But now they'll label me some form of mindless monster, thanks to a high death toll. Rolling my head to the side, I smile as I catch sight of the slight mounds dotting the soft forest floor around my hidden cave.

They have no idea how long I've lurked here, or how high the body count is.

They stop behind one of the vans, hefting me into the back of the vehicle before climbing in themselves. Dragging me towards the wall of the van, they hook my shackles into one of the slots, anchoring me to the vehicle itself. The blood pumping through my veins screams in my ears, stolen from the dozen or so children I'd gorged upon, and the few officers I had the chance to sneak up on. Flexing my arms, I can feel the silvered chains strain, the metal belt they set about my waist clenching around my bones.

I look at one of the officers, smiling. "How are you this evening?"

"Whatever, freak," the officer replied, hopping out of the van to join his comrades. "You're ours now, and you're going down."

His fellow officer moves to sit across from me, rifle resting in his lap and aimed casually at my midsection.

I merely grin as the sacks of meat close the van's double doors, sealing me inside the metal tomb with one of their own. The darkness of the van is soothing, and a spike of fear fills the air. The officer shifts in his seat to turn on the tiny flashlight at the end of his gun. It's bright, but not nearly bright enough to cause a problem.

"So, what's your name, human?" I ask, leaning back against the cool metal of the van. The shredded remains of my shirt are soaked in dried blood, hardly offering me any form of cover. Then again, I hardly care for cover.

"Shut up," he growls, the sweet scent of fear filling the van.

"Your mother must have hated you then," I joke, chuckling darkly as I cross my legs. "Loud as a baby, eh?"

"I said shut up!" he all but shouts, taking up his gun and pointing it in my face.

"I mean, I can see where she got the idea. You're a loud man. I can only imagine what you were like as a baby." I smile as I see his anger rising. *That's it, little man, come a little closer.*

He pokes me in the chest with the barrel of his automatic rifle. "I could shoot you right here freak … claim self-defense. Nobody would say a word. The only reason we fought so hard to take you in alive is to send the rest of your freaky little community a message."

"Oh?" I try to sound interested, but I really couldn't care less. My gaze is locked onto the pulsing vein in his neck. The van rocks and shakes, as a man climbs into the driver's seat. I hear the distant sounds of engines roaring to life in time with the one up front. A light flickers on the ceiling of the van's carrier bay, basking us in a fluorescent glow that makes the officer blink a few times as his eyes adjust.

Now!

I lash out with my crossed legs, one foot connecting with his groin, and the other scissoring to the other side into his hip. This throws him to the floor of the van. He screams in agony, a sound I echo to prevent the driver from thinking something's amiss.

I quickly stomp on his head, just hard enough to knock him out. A gash on his head leaks the officer's glimmering life fluid onto the padded floor of the van.

Looking down at the shackles which have dug their way into my wrists, I flex and pull, straining the metal as I slowly stretch its links.

There it is, I think as one of the links splits apart, freeing my arm from the connection to my waist. It takes less than a minute to free myself of the bothersome shackles, using my long talons to wriggle the metal out from beneath the skin that had already begun to heal over the constricting manacles.

I look down at the body of the officer, who groans low as the van continues to rock and roll down the mountain road. Rubbing my wrists, I smile.

"I said more of you would die before the night was through."

The van bumps along the road, steadily gaining speed. I kneel next to the officer and strip off his vest and armor. I toss his gun to the side and take the time needed to divest myself of the bloody rags and slip on the officer's garb. While it's kind of large on me, the shirt looks and feels much better than the bloody rags I'd been wearing.

Wiping a finger over the gash in his forehead, I drool at the feel of the heady slime dangling from my digit. Leaning forward, I tear into his throat with abandon, pulling at muscles and sinew as his veins burst fluid into the back of my mouth. The delicious, hot life warms my cold body, as I gulp it down in time with his heartbeat.

I spend the next few minutes eating, draining his body of blood and stripping away the juicier chunks of flesh. I pop them into my mouth with glee, chewing thoroughly, around the gristle and fat. The padded floor is now soaked through with blood.

What a shame the loud man had to die like this. If he'd been polite, I would have just knocked him out.

Scooping up the automatic weapon, I pull the magazine out and casually check the remaining ammunition. Full, it would appear.

Slamming the magazine back in, I move up to the wall separating the metal tomb from the cab of the van. The only opening between front and back is a small slit between the two. Putting my ear to the wall, I try to pinpoint where the driver is exactly. I hear his slow heartbeat through the thin sheet metal and press the barrel of the automatic weapon to the wall.

"Knock knock!" I shout before pulling the trigger, letting loose a torrent of bullets into the metal. I angle the gun's barrel back and forth, up and down as I puncture dozens of holes into the van's interior. The van instantly careens as the bullets strike home, punching holes into the driver.

Dropping the gun, I slip my fingers through the holes, pulling and wrenching them apart to gain access to the cab. The driver is dead, or dying. Blood drains from his body like a waterfall, as at least twenty of the bullets appear to have gone through him. The front of the vest is bulletproof and seems to have caught the bullets on their way out of his body.

I smile at the irony.

"Move over," I say. "Your driving days are over." Slipping into the squishy seat, I quickly move to begin driving as safely as possible.

The radio on the dash crackles to life. "Dan, you ok in there? Dan?"

Well shit.

I scoop up the CB, pushing down the flashing red button. "Yeah, I'm fine. Just hit a pothole and heard something in the back. The vamp is still chained up."

The radio goes silent for a few minutes. I drive along the darkened road, my headlights shining on the van in front of me. My side-view mirror shows another van behind mine, boxing me in.

I barely glimpse movement behind the windshield's tinted glass.

"I think they saw me," I mutter under my (lack of) breath. Bullets ping off the side of my vehicle, like rain on a tin roof. "Yes, yes they did."

I spin the wheel to the right, taking a sharp turn off the dirt road and barreling into the forest. A screech of tires alerts me the other van behind mine is moving to follow. Humming to myself as I weave through the tall trees that scrape the sides of the van with loud screeches, I note how unwieldy this vehicle is.

BAM!

A small tree cracks beneath the front bumper of the van as I drive through what was once a young elm. What it lacks in finesse, it more than makes up for in durability! I let out a whoop, testing the shocks of the SWAT van.

"Don't ... stop ... thinking about tomorrow!" I sing merrily as I fishtail, slamming the back of my van into a thick oak before tearing off in a new direction. I can hear the other van struggling to keep up with mine.

The *ratta-ratta-ratta* of automatic fire screams through the night, a couple bullets bouncing off the resilient hide of the van as I speed through the darkened forest. As fun as this is, I truly need to formulate a plan. According to the digital clock on the dash, dawn is but a few hours away, and I can't let myself become trapped out in these woods.

"Huh," I say. "What to do, what to do."

Breaking through the tree line, I come upon a vast expanse of grassy hills and rocky ridges.

"This looks promising," I grin, spinning the steering wheel towards the closest ridgeline. Jumping up and down, the van rolls over the hills, and the shocks do little to soften the bouncy ride. I continue singing along, as I rapidly approach the cliff. If memory serves, this should be a steep drop. Pennsylvania is notorious for hills and ridges, the semi-mountainous terrain making for a beautiful landscape, and, in this case, a great avenue for escape.

The CB radio crackles back to life. "Vampire! Stop now, and we'll go easy on you! There's nowhere for you to run!"

Pulling the CB mic close, I push the button and stare ahead. "I respectfully disagree, good sirs. I told you I'd end up filing against you all for assault. Well, consider this my report."

The van launches off the edge of the cliff, getting a good deal of air and hang time as it hovers, before gravity greedily latches onto the heavy metal box to pull it down.

"Well, got to go," I say. "Have a good night, gentlemen."

I tear the CB radio from the dash and kick open the driver's side door. Before I can leap from the tumbling ton of metal, I hear a low groan from behind me.

Turning, I catch a glimpse of the officer I'd shot up, reaching out and grasping the end of the wet black shirt I'd liberated from my meal in the back.

"Wow, you guys are persistent," I laugh. "And you have terrible luck."

I leap from the spinning vehicle and fly from the van into the brisk night air, to slam into the cliffside.

I scrabble against the stone and the dirt, pulling at stray roots and branches as I struggle to find purchase. I hook my fingers into the cliff, my toes struggling to find purchase beneath me. A distant crash far below, as well as a sudden waft of heat and a flash of light, brings a smile to my face.

That guy truly had horrible luck.

"Wonder how I'm gonna get out of this," I mutter before finding a few loose stones and pulling them out of the cliff face. Digging into the dirt and rock, I slowly carve myself a niche big enough to slide into.

Just as I slither into the crevice I see several powerful beams of light shining down from the top of the ridge. I burrow deeper, worming my way into a tight space where I hope to find peace for a day or so until the coast is clear. Popping my bones out of their sockets, I slither deeper, stumbling out of the crack into a small cave. My eyes quickly adjust, allowing for me to scan the room.

I'm near the ceiling, some fifteen feet from the cavern floor amidst an upturned forest of roots and moss. Looking down, I see various stalagmites and stalactites, along with broad pools of water deep enough for small fish to flit beneath the surface.

A perfect place to sleep off the day.

Slithering down, I flop down to the floor in an unceremonious heap, forcing my joints and bones back into place as I readjust myself back into a humanoid form. After brushing away the dirt and grime, I shed the clothes and rinse my hands in the pool of water.

The blood, sticky and cold from when I was subdued, peels with the shirt like it's a second skin, until I finally have it over my head. Rather than merely rinsing the shirt itself, I decide to slide into the cold water, allowing the dried blood to slowly dissolve into the liquid around me.

The pool is surprisingly deep. I inhale water into my long-dead lungs, sinking my body. I find a comforting darkness that envelops me in watery grave. As the fish swim quickly out of reach, I kick up a cloud of dirt as I finally land at the bottom of the deep pool. Looking around and noting nothing of interest, I burrow into the sandy bottom, forming a shallow hole to rest in.

I can feel the pull of death tugging at my heart. Dawn is approaching. I quickly begin scooping the sand over myself and bury myself as best I can. So long as nobody finds me during the day, I should remain safe.

The pulsing sound of blood fills my ears, lulling me to my nightly death.

Blood.

Warm blood.

I awake to the sounds of two heartbeats. Faint at first, but growing closer. My entire body is cold and dead, stiff with rigor mortis. My joints groan and crack as I bend them. My bones keen and wail as I move. I open my eyes and look around in my watery grave and see thin sheets of ice built up around me. Twisting violently, I break them away; though, not with the same strength I remember having the night before.

Funny, the water didn't seem this cold when I jumped in last night, I think, my mind lagging as I emerge from the sand.

I must have slept for a while to be feeling as drained as I am.

The beating hearts are close, perhaps thirty feet away from me. Are they police? Pushing up and out from my sandy tomb, the water grows thick with detritus. I can see my arms are shriveled and weakened, the muscles mere vines over bones peeking through irritated skin. Looking at my hands, I can easily count the bones in them. My skin is paper thin and paler than I have ever seen it.

Pity, I think. I must have been asleep for months to have fallen into this state. *The cold could have lulled me into a deeper sleep.*

I struggle as I scale the stone walls of the deep pool, my talons longer and far more curved than I remember. My pants, old slacks I'd liberated months before my capture, are now nothing more than icy rags hanging around my legs like a kilt. I cut away the eroded leather belt holding them up.

The heartbeats are closer now, one faster than the other.

Have they detected me somehow? I stop and press myself close to the wall, my hair floating weightlessly around me. They seem to have settled some fifteen feet from the lip of the pool, deeper in the cave than I had explored. I resume my ascension, climbing slowly and painfully as my muscles work for the first time in who knows how long.

Reaching the surface, I peer into the darkness only to be surprised by a sudden brightness.

A campfire is burning twenty feet away. Two people are huddled together in front of it, with their backs to me. I rise a bit more out of the water, slowly pulling myself from the frigid liquid and onto the cold stone.

Slipping across the stone and lowering into a squat, I stare at the two in the cave. They're speaking in hushed tones, laughing every now and again.

"I'm telling you, Rachel," one voice, a rich baritone, says, "these caves are haunted!"

"And I'm telling you I don't believe in that kind of stuff, Jacob," a much higher voice replies, shoving the larger body. "I think you just brought me here to get me good and scared so I'd be all over you."

"Is it working?" Jacob asks. Between the fire and my damaged eyes, I can barely make out his features. Dirty blonde hair with a tanned face. Lean build.

"They say the ghosts of those kids haunt this place," Jacob continues, playfully shoving Rachel and pulling my attention back to their conversation.

"That's messed up, Jacob," Rachel snaps, her tone no longer playful or happy. "There's no reason to make jokes like that! They were just kids!"

"I'm serious! My cousin Trout came in here with a couple of his buddies, and he said the whole place gave him the chills.

Jimbo swore he heard some kids laughing in here last spring, and Laura said she came here with Ronny to, um, hang out. They saw some pale kids with their throats torn out, telling them to leave."

That catches my attention. Most Fangs have a few ghosts lingering around them from their latest kills, as long as the blood of the victim is still within the creature's body. It looks like the group I'd taken over the course of a few nights got some revenge after all, the smug little bastards!

Ghosts, of any sort really, can change the environment in which they haunt. Crops won't grow, animals get scared, and everything gets colder. With twenty some odd kids haunting this cave, they put me on cold storage for who knows how long!

"Now, you're just making things up!" Rachel squeals, looking around the cave with a worried expression. Her eyes sweep past me several times, but the campfire has made her vision weak. I blend in well with the darkness. I take in her appearance, a vibrant young woman with shoulder length blonde hair and delightful azure eyes.

I skulk closer and begin pacing them, following the wall in search of the mouth to my little cave. If I want to remain in any kind of viable condition, I'll need both teens in every way imaginable. Best to cut off their path of escape now, before they realize what I intend to do to them. I slosh about, my innards filled with freezing water.

"So now that you're through trying to scare me, what do you want to do with me?" Rachel asks, a little bit of fire in her tone. She leans back, thrusting her chest out in her tight black shirt.

Jacob clearly understands her meaning and scoots closer to her, one of his arms encircling Rachel's waist.

I need to put a stop to this, if only to save myself from the troubling images of young lovers doing what they do best.

"The ghosts … they're real, you know?" I rasp, surprised at how horrid my once rich voice sounds. I shuffle closer to the fire, allowing a fraction of its light to wash over my emaciated form. Rachel laughs, catching me by surprise, before standing up from the rock she was sitting on.

Laughter is not the reaction I was expecting.

"Really, Jacob?" Rachel drawls, stepping up close to me. "Getting one of your friends to come here and scare me with that cheesy outfit?"

I fold my hands, as she looks me up and down. "God, it looks horrible! Who did this? Trout? Brian?"

Jacob looks on with a mystified expression, shrugging his shoulders at her. He is looking at me with a panicked expression "I have no idea who he is, babe."

That causes her heart to jump, her heartbeat begins to race. She turns to look me over and takes a step back. I edge closer to the fire, savoring the warmth as it starts to thaw the ice in my veins.

"Who are you, then?" she asks, fear evident in her voice.

"Oh, just a weary traveler drawn close by the warmth of your fire," I say in a gravelly voice, squatting down low and letting my talons rake across the stone of the cavern floor. "Would you mind if I stay a while, maybe trade a story or three before I go about my business?"

"I don't know—" Jacob says.

"Jacob! Let the poor man stay for a while. We can get back to what we were doing later!" She turns to me, taking me gently by my emaciated arm. "If this isn't one of your gags, then we have to help this poor man. It's the Christian thing to do."

I chuckle at the very thought. The Christian thing to do would be to preach to me before kicking me away if I don't accept their undead carpenter as my Lord and Savior. I've been around long enough to know what the *real* Christian thing is. It's hardly as pleasant as this young girl is making it out to be.

I shuffle closer to the fire, allowing them to see my nude form. My thighs are thin and sinewy, hips bony. I gaze into the dancing flames while I make a show of holding my hands out to the fire, rubbing them together, as if the heat is of any comfort for me. It's just warm enough to melt the ice lodged in my dead veins. Rachel moves back over to Jacob, sitting down next to him. Both stare at me silently, as I continue my charade in silence.

Playing a game of patience with a vampire is no way to spend your time.

Jacob breaks the silence first, clearing his throat as he moves to toss a few more pieces of broken elm branches onto the flames. "So, what's your name?"

"I have many names truth be told, but I've taken to Smoke as of late," I reply, gurgling as if drowning.

"That's not a name," Rachel says to nobody really, making a point not to look at my bare body.

I chuckle, closing my legs to alleviate some of the girl's discomfort. "What's in a name, child? I merely go by Smoke these days, as those who knew me by my previous name have long since faded into the annals of history."

"Annals of … what do you mean?" Jacob asks, moving an arm around Rachel's waist and pulling her close. I think he can sense the inherent danger I represent, though not necessarily on a conscious level.

"It's a phrase that has gone by the wayside these past few years. If I may ask, what's the date?" I lean forward, my wet hair hanging limply around my gaunt face.

"It's March third, two thousand sixteen," Rachel recites slowly, looking at me as if I have some learning disorder. "My God, how long have you been out of touch with society?"

"Apparently five years, give or take a day," I reply, inwardly cursing the spirits of the damned children.

"So what kind of man calls himself Smoke?" Jacob asks, considering my eyes as he speaks.

"It doesn't matter. What matters is my plan." I reach my hand out and take one of the burning stakes, pulling it from the fire while scowling at Rachel's horrified gasp. The flames lick at my skin, blistering and searing the pale flesh. I pay them no mind. Holding up the burning branch close to my face like a torch, I bare my teeth for them, exposing the rows of reflective fangs hidden behind my lips. "And my plan, for the short term, involves the two of you I'm afraid."

Rachel lets out a tiny shriek as Jacob springs into action. Leaping to his feet, fists balled up at his sides, he moves to stand protectively in front of his girlfriend. "You're a vampire?"

"It would appear so, yes," I answer, tilting my head ever so slightly.

"And this plan of yours … does it involve killing us?" he sniffs, rubbing his nose with his thumb.

I nod. "Eventually, yes."

"And what if I stop you?" he challenges, stepping around the fire with a sense of bravado that reminds me of the men from the days when I had a heartbeat of my very own.

"Then pigs will fly, and hell will freeze over," I drawl. Before he can react, I strain my chest muscles and vomit forth a spray of muddy water, striking him square in the face with the foul-smelling mixture. I aim my spray into the fire, plunging the cave into darkness.

Jacob is shouting, rubbing at his face to clear the gunk from his eyes. I sneak around him and stand to my full height. I throw my weight into it and slam him in the back of the head, dropping him into the smoldering campfire with a groan.

Rachel screams, crab-walking backward into the darkness. Looking at Jacob, I sense he's unconscious.

Good.

I toss the fiery log back into the flame pit atop Jacob, moving to a casual stance on creaking joints.

"Retreating into the darkness?" I ask. "How very clever of you, Rachel. The darkness is a friend to some, and a savior to many more. I can't tell you how many times the darkness has saved me from a fate worse than death."

I stomp on the remaining logs, shattering them into a dazzling display of sparks while simultaneously breaking Jacob's hip. My eyes adjust all the more, and I can see her quivering at the water's edge.

I know she can see my silhouette. I drop back into a crouch and crawl over to Jacob, placing a spidery hand over his mouth. His breathing is slow and rhythmic, the sign of someone who's not in critical condition.

I twist his head until I hear two of his vertebrae crack beneath the pressure. He's not dead, but should he wake, he'll wish he was.

He'd be useless to me if he was.

I lunge across the cavern floor, until I'm practically on top of Rachel. Snapping out with my leg, I catch her across the chest and send her sprawling. I quickly move to straddle her, my withered form far stronger than her mere mortal strength. Pinning her hands above her head, my eyes to flare to life. They cast the area in a dull red glow, just bright enough for the terrified girl to look me over.

She's yet to stop screaming.

I wait until she's screamed herself hoarse. I tilt my head and try to give her the most reassuring smile I can. "Are you done?"

She shivers beneath me, wriggling in my grasp. I bring a long talon up to her throat, instantly halting her movements. "No more trying to run, and for the love of God, no more screaming!"

"What do you want?" she sobs, tears streaming down her cheeks.

I roll my eyes. "Many things, but namely I want information. I heard your boy toy tell a tall tale about some dead kids who haunt this cave. Feel up to telling me a scary story?"

She shivers in obvious discomfort, but I press upon her with my rancid breath rolling over her like a thick fog. She slowly stammers out a story about a serial killer who murdered some kids close by, a total of twenty-eight. Apparently, the serial killer died in a car crash after escaping police custody, and the enraged spirits of the dead now dwell in this cave.

"Well, while that's all well and good, I would hazard a guess and say that doesn't make much sense," I say, drumming my nails on the stone by Rachel's head. "I mean, if this killer died, why would they haunt this cave of all places?"

"I-I don't know," Rachel whispers, still crying. She struggles against my grasp, forcing me to wrestle her back down. She breaks down into mindless sobbing, calling out Jacob's name over and over.

"Anything else worth sharing? Or shall we move on to the main event?"

"No! Please, just let me go!" she begs, shaking her head. "I won't tell anyone you're down here! I swear it!"

I stare at her for a moment before feeling a very distinct pull on my mind, one I haven't felt in quite a while. Deciding her last few moments of life should be educational, I lean in close.

"All right, little girl, here's what we're going to do. As you noted before, I'm a vampire. And not one of the cuddly ones trying to fit into your pathetic little society, like good little boys and girls. No, I'm Old Testament all the way."

Rachel chokes back a sob, staring up at me in utter silence as I continue. "Now, just to prove to me you'll be a good girl and not speak of this, you're going to help me along my road to recovery."

"H-How?" she says with a gasp, looking at me with nothing but utter fear on her face.

I let go of her hands and lean back, holding my arms out wide. "Come on out, kiddies! I can feel you there! No need to hide!"

Slowly, as if emerging from the very shadows themselves, a dozen or so figures encircle us, all wearing the clothes of a prestigious children's academy. Their throats are torn out, eyes uncaring and cold.

"Meet the children I killed, Rachel. At least, what's left of them. And I'd say if I don't eat in the next twelve hours, they'll fade away forever."

At this proclamation, the boys and girls let out plaintive moans and groans of disapproval, some beginning to bawl and cry. Rachel looks at them, confused by their reactions.

I lean in close to her, my lips by her ear. "You see, Rachel, death is truly the end if you don't have a good escape clause, like these good little boys and girls. So long as I feed, they'll continue to exist. Their existence may be pitiful, and it may be full of agony, but it's better than the alternative."

"What's the alternative?" she whispers, her voice gaining strength. "Heaven? Hell?"

"Oh no, nothing as glorious as that. The end is just that. The end. Thanks to my intervention, these children could easily live in this state for another hundred years, before the last vestiges of their blood fades from my body."

"But why would they want that?" Rachel asks, shoving at me.

"Because the unknown of death is far more terrifying than anything I could do to them. Thus, I was able to awaken tonight. They've been steadily growing weaker, and have realized that without me, they're doomed to oblivion."

"Why are you telling me all of this?" Rachel asks.

I chuckle. "If they want to continue to exist, I'll need a fresh source of blood to keep me going."

Any response she could have offered turns into a blood-addled scream as I lunge down upon her tender throat. I tear into it with a hungering fury I have not felt in years. A gush of arterial spray floods past my sharpened teeth, filling my chilled mouth with her delicious warmth.

I gulp it down, suckling at the wound like an infant child at his mother's teat. Feeling the warmth of her life smeared on my face and chin, I look down at her, reading her lips as she mouths the Lord's Prayer.

"You think God will save you?" I look up and around the cave, as if searching for a sign. Looking to the shadowy apparitions, I chuckle. "Children! Let's help her out, shall we?"

The rage and angst from the gathered spirits is palpable, but they obey my request, regardless. In unison, they all begin to sing.

"Jesus loves me, this I know," they chant, their voices whispers on the wind. "Cause the Bible tells me so …"

"Keep singing!" I cry out, as I lean back down to rip into her neck and tear away a new slice of flesh.

I feast for several minutes and through several verses of "Jesus Loves me", consuming her throat and much of her shoulder. I sever her head with ease. Lifting it by her hair, I stare into Rachel's hollow eyes.

Behind me, I can hear her gasp.

"Do you like it, Rachel?" I ask, without looking back at her spirit. "I plan on mounting it on a rock here in the cave for the next pair of horny teenagers to find."

"You're a monster!" she hisses, a gurgling noise escaping from her ravaged throat.

"As are you, by all technicalities. But don't worry. I won't hold that against you."

"Why? Why did you do this to me?" She falls to her knees, the children still singing.

I will her to look at me. "Why? Why not?"

I resume eating, listening to the children sing of the glories of Jesus. I can hear the fear-wracked sobs of the newly made ghost, watching as her body is slowly devoured, piece by piece and drop by drop. By the time I'm done, all that's left are red-rimmed bones and a pool of caked blood along the cavern floor that I'm slowly cleaning with my tongue.

Ah, to be awake once more.

ONE FLESH

By Ezekiel Kincaid

Dreams, life goals, visions. Whatever you want to call it. We all have them. They are the driving force pushing us towards greatness. The things we want to devote our lives to so we can accomplish something significant. The only problem is, for most people, those dreams never become reality. Why is that? Many of us get rather far along the path, then we do one of two things: we quit, or we do something so fucking stupid, the entire thing becomes a dumpster fire. Some of the bad decisions can be overcome, but the others? The dumpster fires? They are colossal fuckups that shipwreck our goal. All we can do is sit back and watch it burn, baby, burn. If you're attentive, you should be picking up on the fact I'm trying to tell you my life took a gargantuan nosedive. Yeah, I'm in the "colossal fuckup" crew. How did I get there? Well, *that's* what this story is all about.

My name's Thom Broussard. I grew up here in Durham, North Carolina. I earned my bachelors and graduated from med school at Duke University. I've wanted to be a surgeon since my sophomore year in high school. It all started with a broken hand.

That year, during a football game, my fingers landed in the face mask of the right offensive tackle. Several bones in my hand snapped. When they operated, the doctor only did a local, which means I got to be awake to see the entire thing. I watched as the scalpel cut my skin and lines of blood started to seep out. Next, they peeled the skin back, pinning it to my hand, exposing the bones. I was taken aback by how white they were. I tried to move my hand, you know, to make the tendons wiggle, but it wasn't happening. I looked on in awe as the doctor screwed my bones back together and sewed my skin. It was during the operation I knew. When the last stitch was snipped, it was already settled in my mind—I wanted to be a surgeon.

I was in my first year of residency at Duke. There were ten of us in my class—six men and four women. The first day, I was checking out the merchandise, if you know what I mean. Two of the girls were bangable. The other two? Meh, maybe if I was desperate. The only problem was Thom Broussard was never desperate. I was a good looking guy. Crystal blue eyes, black wavy hair, olive colored skin, and a chiseled body. Now, if you know anything about women, you know it's not just about the looks with them. If you're going to get them in the sack, you need to learn how to push the right buttons. And I was good at it. I learned early on how to read women. I became more knowledgeable with each different "relationship" on how to get better at giving a girl the affection and admiration she needed.

It was all a game to me. I have an insatiable need for sex. I mean, what guy doesn't, right? In order to meet said need, I realized the typical macho male bullshit wouldn't work. The Tarzan/Jane thing was so outdated. The guy who beats his chest and pressures the girl and talks about how bad he needs her and all that crap—you know what happens to him? He'll stay a virgin the rest of his life and sit home and masturbate, or become so desperate he'll lower his standard to any woman dumb enough to fall for his circus act.

Then there's the guy who knows how to be affectionate, thoughtful, and caring. This poor son of a bitch, however, lacks the balls to make the move. So, you know what happens to him? Same thing that happens to our friend Tarzan.

Then there's me. The guy who, through patience and observation, has figured it out.

You want to know something else? During my undergrad, I made it with twenty-two different girls. These weren't only one-night stands though. Each relationship lasted several months. I'd woo them in, and we'd be going hot and heavy in no time. I used each experience to become more educated about women and how I could, for lack of a better word, manipulate them to get sex. With each girl, the sex would be good for about two months, then I was ready to move on. I don't know, I guess I just got bored. There was something about the thrill of the hunt. Then, as the months go on, the excitement wanes.

I'm not the type who will ever settle down for marriage. I can't see myself having sex with the same woman year after year and staying satisfied. Also, marriage is not the ideal lifestyle for a surgeon. The long hours, the demanding workload. Yeah, not going to happen.

Did I say I couldn't see myself having sex with the same woman for the rest of my life? Well, that was about to change. Like I was saying, during the first day of residency, I was checking out the girls. Of the two hot ones, the girl with the red hair was piquing my interest.

Until *she* walked in.

The head surgeon was Dr. James Kramer. He was a good-looking guy. Light blond hair, dark blue eyes, and rather muscular. He had only been at it for five years but was already making a name for himself. His wife, Rebecca, was one of the surgical nurses. As

Dr. Kramer was standing in the OR, getting ready to kick things off, Rebecca walked in. She strolled past us, her, wavy, shoulder length blonde hair flowing like a golden waterfall. Her eyes were as green as emeralds, and her complexion as clear and smooth as tempered glass.

As she passed me, she ran her hands underneath her hair and pulled it back into a ponytail. I could smell her. Oh dear God, how I could smell her. She smelled fresh. She smelled sweet. She smelled clean. My eyes fell to the rest of her body while her arms were raised. I wanted to grab her right then and there and pull her close. I wanted to feel her plump breasts against me. I wanted to smell her hair. And her lips: I wanted to drink deep from them. They were perfect. A beautiful mixture of sleekness and curves and vibrant, natural looking color.

She walked to the head of the patient bed to stand by her husband, and I watched her perfect body as it passed by. I could see her panty lines through her snug fitting scrub pants. I was already starting to get aroused. I wanted her, and I wanted her bad. And dammit, I was going to get her.

#

Over the next week, I did more observing of Rebecca than listening to Dr. Kramer. I watched Rebecca—no, I researched her. A married woman was new territory for me. For the first time, I was nervous. Nervous about making a mistake. What if she said no? *What if my plan backfires, and she tells her husband? I'm screwed.*

I also felt a tug of guilt. "You can have any girl you want? Why this one? She's taken. Leave her alone," I would tell myself. But I didn't want just any girl. I wanted her. I wanted Rebecca Kramer. My desire for her was beyond any I had ever had for a female. I daydreamed often about what she looked like underneath her scrubs. I fantasized about what our first time would be like, along with all the intricate details of those moments. My thoughts were obsessed with Rebecca. I was so turned on by her, I would go to the one-person restroom down the hall during our breaks and pleasure myself. This was new to me. You don't have to resort to such things when you're having sex every day. For the first time in a long time though, I was in a dry spell, so to speak. I needed her, and I needed her yesterday.

I scrutinized every move she made. From how she held a scalpel, to how she passed a surgical instrument, to how she interacted with people. I watched her eyes and her body language, looking for clues; anything to give me insight or leverage or an opening. There was nothing. My interactions and conversations with her were only related to the subjects and tasks at hand in the OR. I didn't want anyone picking up on my plan.

Then one day, about three weeks into my residency, I saw it. When I did, I knew things weren't all roses and tulips at home. It was a series of body language cues directed towards Dr. Kramer. It was five minutes before we got things kicked off for the day, and a few of us were standing out in the hall chatting it up. Rebecca was there. She was telling us stories about her first year in nursing school and how brutal her teachers were. At one point, when we were all laughing, Rebecca and I locked eyes, neither of us turning away. She *noticed* me. For the first time, she *noticed* me. Her eyes broke away, and she looked down, tucking her hair behind her ear. As she did, Dr. Kramer walked over to our group and placed his hand in the middle of Rebecca's back. She tried to smile. She tried to hide the disgust leaping out of her pores, but I could see it. She pulled away from him. She recoiled as his hand pressed on her back. I grinned, knowing I now had a chance.

I noticed this happen several other times as the rest of the day went on. Dr. Kramer had been illustrating to us the proper procedure for removing an appendix. When he was finished, he walked over to Rebecca, who had her hands on the rail of the patient bed. He greeted her and placed one hand on top of hers. She slid her hand away and walked off. As I watched the scene unfold, I smiled.

I could tell Dr. Kramer was getting agitated with her coldness. He told us all to go ahead and take an early break, but asked Rebecca to wait. I was the last person to leave the room. I left the door cracked and stood out in the hall to eavesdrop.

"Dammit, Rebecca, what the hell is your problem? Why are you being so cold?"

"Well, maybe if you actually treated me like I existed, then …"

They quieted down some, and all I could hear was faint whispering.

"You're never around, James. Even when you are, you aren't."

"Rebecca, you don't understand. Planning for this move has been …"

More whispering.

"You give me nothing, James. No affection, no attention, no appreciation. Except when you want sex. I'm tired of being used. I need a husband, not just someone who pays the bills and throws nice things at me."

More whispering. But I had heard enough. I knew what needed to be done, so I crept off and began to consider my next move. The chess match had begun.

#

I didn't know what happened that night, but the next day … Man, you could tell Dr. Kramer and Rebecca must have had it out. Things were tense between them the entire morning. We could all sense it. At one point, Dr. Kramer got so frustrated he had to step out for about five minutes.

When it was time to break for lunch, I raced down to the cafeteria. I was starving, yes, but it wasn't the reason I was in a hurry. Rebecca was already down there. Today was the day I was going to strike. All I needed was a few minutes alone with her.

I arrived at the cafeteria, walked through the glass doors, and surveyed the room. I saw Rebecca passing through the line with her tray already full and heading to the register. I didn't pay attention to what I got. I just grabbed a bunch of shit and threw it on my tray in a mad frenzy.

I watched her as she paid for her food and wandered around the cafeteria looking for a place to sit. She settled on a table in the back-left corner. She sat with her back facing the room and her front to the wall. Now, to the casual observer, it might not mean much, but it spoke volumes to me. It said she was withdrawing. It said she had been wounded. It said she wanted to be invisible and left alone … but not really. It said it's time for me to make a move. So, I did.

"Hey, Rebecca. Mind if I join you?"

She stirred her glass of tea with her straw and stared at the wall, blank expression on her face.

"Huh?" She woke up from her daze. "Hey, Thom. Sure, take a seat." Her voice sounded flat; tired even.

I set my tray down and walked around to the other side of the gray table. I pulled out a blue chair and sat across from her. She eyed the contents of my tray and snickered. There was a muffin, Twix bar, a bag of Doritos, an apple, banana, and a pack of Skittles.

"That's an interesting meal choice," she said, raising her eyebrows.

"Huh?" I glanced down at my tray. "Oh. Oh yeah. Well, you see, I couldn't decide if I wanted to eat healthy or like a fat kid, so I decided on both."

She rolled her eyes and smiled. "Mmm hmm. Sure." She sipped her tea through her straw. Her voice bounced with a little vibrancy now.

I grabbed my banana and started to peel it. "Tense morning, huh?"

Rebecca let out a sigh weighted down with frustration. "Ah, shit. I know. We try not to bring our personal problems in with us but … planning for this damn move." She kept shaking her head. Her eyes left mine. She turned her head and put her hand over her mouth, then sighed again. "Sorry, Thom. I really am. Look, let's not talk about my relationship issues, okay? I don't want to unload on you. James is a good man. He really is." Her eyes were locked back on mine.

My first thought was, *Who are you trying to convince? Me or yourself?* But I didn't say that. Instead, I said, "Look, Rebecca, I don't know a damn thing about being married, so I couldn't offer any good advice. Now bad advice? I got a shitload of that. So anytime you're in need, hit me up."

She laughed again. Her green eyes started to flicker with life. "I'll do that, Thom."

I put down my banana and opened my Skittles. "In all seriousness though, I was the only boy in a houseful of girls growing up. I know how to just listen and when to shut up. I also learned that even when I'm right, I'm wrong, and that logic has no place when arguing with a female."

For a moment, she thought I was serious. Her face was laden with surprise. When she realized I was being sarcastic, she rolled her eyes at me again. "Oh dear Lord, Thom, just stop before you dig a hole too deep to get out of." She smiled and continued to eat her chicken salad.

"Seriously though—"

Rebecca interrupted me. "Is this seriously like the last time, or are you actually going try and say something meaningful?"

Nice. She was flinging the sarcasm back at me. That's always a good sign.

I gave her a playful glare. "As I was saying, if you need to talk, I'm a good listener. Some people also tell me I'm good for laughs as well."

Rebecca finished off the last bite of her salad and set her fork on her tray. "Thank you, Thom, but I don't think you're very funny." She was trying to put on a serious face.

"I call your bluff. You can't bullshit a bullshitter, Rebecca."

She cracked, and a smile spread across her face.

"Ha!" I pointed at her. "See, you're trying not to laugh now."

She gave in. "Okay, okay, you're funny. Well, maybe just a little."

"Well then, there you go." I held up both hands. We exchanged smiles, and I gave her a wink. It was now time to ease a humor coated compliment in there. "Hey, not to change the subject, but has anyone ever told you your eyes look like the glow of Green Lantern's ring? I mean, I've never seen such green eyes before. Those green scrubs really bring them out."

Now she was cackling. "Thom, you are such a nerd." A lock of her hair had fallen from her ponytail. She brushed it back as she smiled, her eyes still looking into mine. "Okay, goofball, which Green Lantern? Golden Age, Silver Age, or Bronze? Huh? Alan Scott, Hal Jordan, or Guy Gardner? Or maybe you're thinking more Modern Age, say Kyle Rayner?"

My jaw dropped. I hadn't seen that coming. "Nerd? Look who's talking! And there's no question. Hal Jordan. All the rest suck."

She put her hands under the table and leaned forward a tad. "Good answer. He's my favorite as well."

I leaned back in my chair and folded my arms. I eyed her up and down with a look of curiosity. "Huh. Never would have taken you for a comic book girl."

"Oh yeah, why's that?" She sipped her tea.

"I don't know I just—"

She cut me off. "Try and guess my favorite character."

Man, this was going way better than I anticipated. She was starting to feel a connection with me. Take notes, ladies and gentlemen, this is step one of Thom Broussard's *How to Get a Woman Between the Sheets* tutorial.

I pushed my tray to the side, folded my arms and placed them on the table, then leaned forward.

"Come here, you gotta get closer."

"Huh?"

"The eyes are the window to the soul. How am I going to read your mind and find out the answer if I can't look into your eyes?"

She snickered. "Thom, you're a dumbass."

"Just humor me, would you, Green Lantern?"

She shook her head, but complied. She pushed her tray aside, folded her arms, and mimicked my posture. Our eyes met.

I titled my head a little to the side. "Hmmm. Let's see. You're full of surprises, so I know it's not going to be some typical female like Wonder Woman, Jean Grey, or Rogue."

"You're getting warmer. I'll help you out. It's not a woman at all."

"Okay … let me see … I'm going out on a limb here. I'm going to guess what I think are the three most unlikely characters a woman would choose. You ready?"

She nodded and sat up in anticipation. She rubbed her hands and put them in her lap, her gorgeous smile sweeping across her face. For a moment, I forgot about the game we were playing. I wanted to kiss her. I wanted to get out of my chair, walk over to her, yank her up, pull her close, and kiss her long and hard and let my hands go exploring.

"Yo, Thom." She snapped her fingers and waved at me.

"Huh? Oh sorry."

"You spaced out on me there for a sec."

"Okay, here it goes. My guess is Punisher, Ghost Rider, or Constantine."

She placed her hand over her chest and let out a few huffs. "Holy … Crap, Thom. All of them. Those are my three favorites."

Now, let me pause here for a minute and tell you something. No, I'm not a mind reader. I simply got damn lucky. Something like this had never happened before. I was usually good, but not this good. Son of a bitch, I even impressed myself.

"Thom, how the hell did you figure that out?"

Cue smartass comment. "I'm good at reading psycho chicks. Like you, they usually have blonde hair and green eyes. They are disposed to the reading of such violent and morbid characters as the aforementioned."

She threw her napkin at me. "Asshole."

"No, mind reading asshole," I fired back.

"Hey, guys, mind if we join you?" It was Tucker, one of the guys in our class. He was a little on the skinny side, and his curly brown hair had a mind of its own. With him was Mary Kate, the hot redhead.

"Sure," I said. "Come join us. We're talking superheroes."

The two sat down, and we continued our conversation about our favorite comic book characters and superhero movies. When we finished, Rebecca was the last to empty the contents of her tray in the trash. Tucker and Mary Kate were already walking down the hall, so I waited for Rebecca just outside the door to the cafeteria.

"You're gonna be late, then James is gonna rip you a new one."

I pulled out my phone. It was 12:55. "Nah, I still got five minutes. Where you off to?"

She let her hair down and ran her hands through it. "I have a few patients to check on before I have to be back with James."

"Ok, well, I'll see you later then." I turned to walk away.

"Wait. Thom?"

"Yeah?" I spun back towards her, trying not to look to eager.

"Thanks."

"For what?"

"Making me laugh. It's been a rough few days. I needed it."

"Glad I could help." I gave her a wink again.

"Oh, and one more thing."

"What?"

"Has anyone ever told you that your eyes look like King Zarkon's skin?"

This woman was full of surprises. My jaw dropped. "Did you just go all out *Voltron* on me?"

She glanced down at the floor and laughed, then looked back at me. "Yes."

"No. No one has ever said that to me. Ever. You're the first."

"Well, they do."

"Thanks. I guess." I looked at my phone. It was 12:56. "Shit. I gotta go. See you later." She waved, and I took off down the hall, heart racing with excitement.

#

As the days and weeks went on, Rebecca, Tucker, Mary Kate, and I made it a regular thing to sit together in the cafeteria. Rebecca only worked three shifts a week, and I found I wasn't near as engaged in the conversations when she wasn't around. I also tried to get time in with her during our breaks. I was always careful not to be alone with her for too long. As I'd mentioned before, seducing a married woman was new for me. I tried to avoid any hint of suspicion.

I also started to compliment her more. Nothing over the top, simply little comments here and there. I began to leave her little notes as well. I'd slip them in her purse or her planner when she wasn't looking. Some were silly, some were nothing more than "Hey, you're a great nurse. Keep up the good work. You are making a difference," while others were god-awful pictures of superheroes I would come up with. She would reciprocate with the same. She also began to open up with me about her frustration with James. I would simply listen. Sometimes I would respond with comments about how if she were my wife, I wouldn't treat her that way, or something along those lines. I wanted to do anything I could to subvert their marriage. We had made our emotional connection. Now I was trying to figure out how to ease into our first physical one.

\#

I was beginning to see that luring a married woman into an affair was a game of sleekness and stealth. That's what had been so difficult. You have to be like a freaking ninja. If anyone around you picks up on what you're up to, or if you strike at your prey too early, the entire thing will explode like a landmine. This was what had been so hard about first contact. I mean, there'd been a pat on the arm and such, but that shit is child's play. It doesn't count. It had been weeks now, and I hadn't been able to come up with a good scenario. The weapons that work with single women can't be deployed on the married. Nothing I could come up with sounded good. It was either going to come across as intentional or too strong or just downright cheesy.

Then my opportunity came. We were wrapping up our first six weeks, so the class wanted to go to one of the local bars to unwind and celebrate. The plan was to meet up at Pinhook that Friday night. We invited Dr. Kramer, but he declined. We invited Rebecca as well, but she said there was too much to be done before the movers came the next day.

The Thursday before, our little lunch group was having our regular sit-down in the cafeteria. I brought up the idea of all of us coming over Friday when she got off work and helping pack up the rest of their stuff. My hope was she would come hang out with us once we knocked the job out. She was touched and agreed to let us help.

#

We all showed up at Rebecca's house at 7:15 Friday evening. It was me, Tucker, and Lance in my gray Chevy four door pickup. Olivia rode with Mary Kate in her black Altima. The house was right off Cole Mill road in the Stonybrook subdivision. The houses were nice, but per Rebecca, Dr. Kramer wanted something secluded with more land. So, they settled on a house on the outskirts of Durham, almost into Bahama. When we pulled up, Rebecca was just getting out of her car. The house was a large, green two-story with black shutters.

I'm not going to bore you with the details of packing. We knocked it out and were finished in an hour. Rebecca was beyond grateful. She asked us to wait for her while she went up and changed out of her scrubs. When she came down, she was wearing a blue sleeveless blouse. It had rows of thin, layered ruffles on the front. It was modest enough to cover her cleavage, but snug enough to admire her breasts. Her arms were toned and smooth. Her light-colored jeans hugged the curves of her hips. Oh man, she looked so sexy. I was getting turned on, and the night was just getting underway.

Lance had a thing for Olivia. She was the other hot girl in the class, along with Mary Kate. She had jet black hair, blue eyes, and a nice pair. Lance was a pretty suave dude, with dark wavy hair and dark eyes. He wanted to ride alone with her so he could get his game on. I was fine with that. It put me, Rebecca, Mary Kate, and Tucker in my truck. We loaded up and headed to Pinhook. Rebecca texted Dr. Kramer, telling him how we all had come over and helped finish packing, and she would be with us at the bar.

We pulled up to Pinhook around five minutes to nine. It was a faded blue building with red accent work. We walked through the black doors, showed our IDs, and found a table in the back. A band was getting on the stage, and people were gathering on the floor around them.

After we ordered some drinks, I began the small talk with Rebecca. "See, aren't you glad you let us help?"

She nodded. "Yeah, I am." She stared at me for a moment, then smiled. "I'm glad to get out too. I don't do this enough." She looked around the room. "I've never been here."

"Well, that makes two of us."

I was sitting next to her, and she leaned over to me a tad. "Nah-uh. I would've thought you'd be a bar hopper."

"What? Me? No way. I'm too much of a cheapskate. I buy my booze from the store and drink at home."

She laughed and slapped my arm.

After a few drinks, Lance and Olivia went out on the floor to dance, followed by Mary Kate and Tucker. Some more people from class showed up about three minutes later. We said our hellos, then they went out on the floor as well, leaving me and Rebecca by ourselves.

"You much of a dancer?" I asked

She shook her head. "No. Never cared for it."

"Me either. But since we're here, we might as well do something other than just drink."

She took a swig of her beer. "What's wrong with that?"

"Oh, come on. Look, if they play a slow song, you have to dance with me."

"Thom. I'm married."

"Oh, come on, Rebecca, it's just a dance. I promise I won't try and make out with you or grab your butt."

She giggled again. "Okay, fine. Just one dance."

It was 90s night, and the band had been doing covers of Poison and Guns N' Roses. As we were talking, they eased into *November Rain*. Rebecca perked up.

"Ooh, I love this song!"

"Perfect." I popped up out of my chair. "Let's go."

She got up and walked out to the floor. I followed behind her, staring at her ass the entire time. The anticipation was almost too much. I was about to have her close to me. The smell of her hair, my arms around her hips, her breasts being so close ...

She turned around to face me. I walked towards her, reaching my arms out to place them around her hips. Her arms reached my neck first. Upon her touch, I felt every particle in my body come to life, all the way down to the subatomic ones. And when my arms slid around her hips, the feel of her curves as they slid down my arm sparked immediate arousal. We pulled each other close, but not too close. Our bodies didn't touch, but the temptation to bring her in was racing through my veins. Her hair still smelled fresh, even after a long day at the hospital.

"Remember. Watch your hands, buster." Her green eyes were so beautiful. When she smiled, I could still see them sparkle in the dim light of the bar.

"Don't flatter yourself. Old married people don't turn me on."

She started to say something back when a drunk couple came barging in behind her. As they slammed into Rebecca, it put her body flush up against mine. And oh my, was it glorious. I could feel the fullness of her curves and the warmth of her body next to mine.

"Watch it, assholes!" Rebecca turned her head and yelled at them, but they were oblivious. She looked back at me. "Oh my God. Some people. Sorry, Thom." She was still up against me, and I wasn't complaining. "I didn't bump your lip or anything, did I?"

"Meh, just a little. I didn't mind, but if you wanted me to kiss you on the forehead, all you had to do was ask. You didn't need to resort to such violent tactics."

She huffed. "Now who's flattering themselves! In your dreams, pal."

She was still pressed against me. I needed to pull back before the inevitable happened.

"Do you see Mary Kate and Tucker?" I asked.

She stepped back, took one hand off my shoulder, and looked around. Crisis averted.

"No, they're probably doing shots by now." She stepped back in and we resumed our normal distance.

The song ended, so we went back to our table, ordered a few more drinks, and hung out with the rest of our friends. Around ten fifteen, Rebecca was ready to go.

"Thom, I really need to be going. I gotta be ready for the movers in the morning."

I tapped Tucker on the shoulder. "Is it okay if you and Mary Kate bum a ride with Lance and Olivia? Rebecca is wanting to go home, so I'm going to jet out early and take her."

Tucker gave me a thumbs-up.

I looked back at Rebecca. "Sure thing. Let's go."

We walked out to my truck, and I opened the door for her.

"Wow, special treatment huh? I haven't had a car door opened for me in a while."

"Damn shame," I said as I held her hand to help her up.

I walked around to the driver's side, hopped in, and got us moving. She was the first to break the silence.

"Shit. My head is spinning. I drank way too much." She slouched in her seat and rubbed her temples.

I chuckled. "You only had what? Like, four drinks?"

She nodded.

"That's pathetic. You're a lightweight."

She slapped me on the arm. "Just shut up and take me home so I can sleep it off."

"I mean, I had like six, and I'm not feeling a thing."

"Well woopdee-fucking-doo, aren't you special as shit." She gave me a joking scowl.

"You know," I said, eyes still on the road, "you have quite a potty mouth for an attractive lady."

She snickered. "I thought you said I was a gross old married woman?"

I glanced at her. "Oh, that's right. Must be the alcohol talking, sorry."

"Asshole." She slapped me on the arm again and laughed. "No, you're not really. An asshole wouldn't have helped me pack. Thanks again for that."

"Glad to help."

There was silence for a few minutes, then we turned into her neighborhood and pulled in her driveway. Dr. Kramer's black Lexus still wasn't there.

"Where's Dr. Kramer?"

Rebecca was unbuckling. "He texted me, like, half an hour ago. Said he was headed to the new house to take care of a few things before tomorrow. He said he'd be back around midnight. I swear, the man never sleeps." She went to open her door.

"Hold on there, lightweight. Let me help you out so you don't fall on your face."

She rolled her eyes. "You're such a gentleman."

I exited the vehicle and ran around to the passenger side, opened the door, grabbed her hand, and helped her out.

She paused for a second and put her right hand to her forehead. "Give me a sec."

I giggled.

"Shut up." She elbowed me in the side. "Okay, I'm ready."

I put my left arm around her, held her right hand with mine, and guided her up the dark gray stone steps and to the door. I looked at the black door and the green siding. "You know, even your house looks like Green Lantern."

She laughed and put her arms around my neck. I placed mine around her hips and pulled her close. The porch lights were off, and the only illumination was the glow from the stars. Our faces were a mere few inches apart. The moonlight gave her green eyes an enchanting look, seductive even. They were luring me in.

"Thanks for tonight, Thom."

"No, thank you. I had fun with you. You're an awesome lady. One of the best I've ever known."

"You really think so?"

"Yeah, I do. And I'd do anything to see you happy."

"Oh yeah?"

"Yeah."

It was like a magnetic force pulling us together. It just felt right, for both of us. Our lips met, and my God, was it like tasting the delicacies of a goddess. If her lips were this exquisite, I couldn't wait to sample the rest of her.

She pulled back. "Thom, I—"

I didn't let her finish. "Did that make you happy?"

"Yes, but—"

I held her close and kissed her again. This time it was long and passionate. I could feel all of her against me, and she could feel all of me against her.

After a few seconds, she broke it off. "What time is it, Thom?"

I pulled my hand off her hip and grabbed my phone from my pocket. "Ten thirty-five."

"Good, we have time." She winked at me. "Follow me."

We let go of each other, she unlocked the door, and we headed inside. I followed her past the living room and into the bedroom. The walls were a light gray color with a hint of blue. In the middle of the room was a king size bed with white sheets and white comforter. The headboard was a dark oak color, as were the armoire and dresser. To the right was the master bath.

"Hadn't broken the bed down yet I see."

"I was waiting." She gave me one of those playful looks again.

Rebecca guided me by the hand to the bed, where I sat. She came and stood between my legs, then removed her blue blouse. Her lingerie was sky blue lace, and I sat in awe of her.

"What are you waiting for, Thom? Do you like to do it with your clothes on?" She bent over and removed her jeans. I stood up, undressed, and laid down on the bed. She straddled me, and the euphoric experience began.

If kissing her lips was like tasting the delicacies of a goddess, then her breasts were like a long-lost treasure now discovered. I was enraptured by her. I've been with a lot of women, but being with Rebecca for the first time was the most blissful, exultant thing I had ever experienced, and by the sounds she was making, I think she felt the same. The sex was passionate and will go down in history as the most satisfying experience I've ever had. One thing I knew then and there, this was going to last way more than my usual couple of months.

It was 11:05 when we finished. We laid in bed for a moment and simply smiled at each other. We talked about how we were going to come up with a plan to keep seeing each other. She shared with me how she began to fall for me during our lunchtime conversations. I told her I fell for her the first time I laid eyes on her.

We finished our conversation around 11:15 and got dressed. We exchanged cell numbers before I left. She didn't work again until Wednesday, so I told her I would see her soon. We shared another long kiss, then I headed out the door, got in my truck, and drove home. When I arrived, I laid in my own bed and dreamed about Rebecca.

#

Over the next few months, things were going perfect. On the days Dr. Kramer worked late, I'd head over to their new house, and we'd have sex. By the way, the house was fantastic. It seemed twice as big as the old one, complete with a large attic and basement. Dr. Kramer was a musician, so he soundproofed the walls in the basement and made his own little studio. The house itself was rustic looking, like a gigantic log cabin, complete with wrap-around porch and a lake on the edge of the woods. The bedroom had a quaint, rustic feel as well, and it was great for having sex. At least I thought so.

When Dr. Kramer stayed late at the hospital on call, I'd head over there as soon as I got off and stay until around 11:00. We would talk, laugh, hang out, and have sex at least twice. I have to say, though, the most fun was when she and I were at the hospital together. You remember my little bathroom breaks? Well, they were hiked up a notch. We would sneak into that bathroom together and have sex. I would go in the bathroom, then three minutes later she would come, give our little secret knock, and I'd open. I'd leave first, then a few minutes later she would. No one was any wiser.

We would all still do our lunch thing, and we kept the inconspicuous vibe going, but it was hard. We still left each other notes, and when we weren't with each other, we'd be texting, or sexting. It was the greatest few months of my life. We wanted to be together, but we both knew it wasn't possible while I was in my residency. We decided we would keep doing what we were doing until I finished. We were in love, and neither of us had a problem confessing it to each other.

#

We were now halfway through the third month of our affair. Dr. Kramer planned on attending a conference in Charlotte that weekend. He was leaving Friday and wouldn't be back until Sunday evening. Rebecca and I made plans for me to spend the entire weekend with her at the house. We were going to drink, watch movies, and have sex the entire time. It was going to be the most consecutive time we spent together, and we couldn't wait.

Friday night rolled around, and Rebecca came and picked me up. We didn't want my truck sitting at her house all weekend. When we got there, she changed into a red and black flannel shirt and red thong. I was immediately aroused. I made a move on her, but she said she wanted to drink and watch a movie first.

Since it was now the second week in December, we settled on Christmas movies. We started with *Die Hard*. The movie ended, and we had sex. I held her and we watched *Gremlins*, drank some more, had sex again, then passed out.

I woke up around noon. My head was pounding. I sat up in the bed and rubbed my eyes. I could hear Rebecca in the kitchen, so I got up and joined her. The kitchen, like everything else in the house, was big and rustic, with plenty of counter space and cabinets. Before I could speak, she handed me a cup of coffee.

"What do you want to do today?"

I grabbed the cup from her.

"Watch movies and hump like rabbits."

She put her arms around my hips and pulled me close. She had her flannel shirt back on. "What about tonight?"

"See aforementioned."

She gave me a quick kiss. "I can go for that."

And that's just what we did. In between the movie watching and sex, we would talk about our hopes and dreams and what we would do once we could be together openly. Before we went to bed that night, we had one more conversation. We were naked under the covers, holding each other.

"Thom?"

"Yeah?"

"I just want you to know that what I feel for you … I've never felt for anyone before. Not even James."

"That makes two of us. You're the most amazing person I've ever known. I love you, Rebecca. And I mean it when I say it to you. I've never said that to a woman other than my mother." I gave her a little smirk.

"Thom, I want you to know I meant what I wrote in that note. I feel more at one with you than anyone I've ever known. I mean, in marriage you become one flesh with someone. But even though James and I are married, I've never felt that with him. But I feel it with you. I love you, Thom, dear God, how I do."

I held her close, and we fell asleep.

\#

When I started to wake, it felt like I had been asleep for days. Didn't surprise me though. With all the sex and booze, I was in a pleasure coma. I went to move my right arm and roll over, but it didn't comply. Shit. I was sure Rebecca was laying on it. I didn't want to wake her. My left arm was stretched out above my head. I tried to move it, and it stopped short with a clink. It startled me and my eyes popped opened. The first thing I noticed was I wasn't in Rebecca's bedroom anymore. I stared up at the ceiling. There was sunlight shining through from somewhere, trickling across the wall to my left. I looked up again and noticed the row of spotlights. It dawned on me—we were in the basement.

I yanked my left arm and heard the jingling again. I looked up and to my left. My wrist was bolted in a clamp connected to a chain. I couldn't tell where the chain was hooked. I felt the air tickle my legs and my butt sticking to a mattress and knew I was still naked.

"Funny," I mumbled. "I don't remember coming down here and doing any S and M stuff." I jiggled the chain again. "Hey, Rebecca, when …" As I was talking to her, I turned my head to the right. I had to do a double take and blink my eyes several times because there was no way what I was seeing could be real.

My right arm was gone, cut off from the shoulder. Stitched to it with skillful precision was Rebecca's left shoulder. Her left arm was missing. Her head was titled to the right, and she was still out. I looked her over, and her right arm was bolted in a clamp and chained above her head, exactly like my left. The sensation in my right arm (or lack of one) was eerie. It still felt like my arm was there. I even tried to move it. It remined me of the time I had surgery on my hand.

I shook my head and blinked a few more times, but the scenery didn't change. Panic set in. Now, I'm not talking about the type of panic we ascribe as the feeling rushing over us when we realize we've forgotten about a meeting or left the food in the oven too long. No, I'm talking about a sensation of terror and trepidation in the marrow of your bones. Sheer, raw panic.

My breathing picked up, and sweat began to trickle from every part of my body. I spoke between breaths. "Oh motherfuckingshit. Rebecca. Wake up. What the fuck …" I wanted to cry. "Rebecca! Wake up, goddammit!"

A voice came from somewhere in the room. "If I was in your situation, the last thing I would be doing is taking the Lord's name in vain."

I recognized the voice. I had become all too familiar with it over the past semester. It was Dr. Kramer. I gazed around the room, but my position and the low light made it hard for me to see where he was. Then I heard a cranking sound, and the chains began to rattle. I tried to pull my left leg up, but it was chained as well. I tried to move my right leg, but it felt stuck on something. As the sounds continued, I felt a tug on my wrist. The chains were moving, pulling Rebecca and I up to a standing position.

As it lifted us off the mattress, for the first time since I awoke, I stared down at the rest of our bodies. We were both still naked, and the reason my right leg felt stuck was because it was gone, severed from the hip. Connected to my right hip was Rebecca's left. Her leg was missing as well, and the same immaculate stitch job adorning our shoulders was also present on our hips.

I lost it.

I screamed and cried; no, bellowed and sobbed is more like it.

We were now fully erect, and Rebecca's head hung down like a slobbering drunk. In front of us, Dr. Kramer emerged from the shadow of the room. His once white lab coat was stained crimson, his blue scrubs smeared red. Dangling from his left hand was a pair of yellow industrial strength cleaning gloves caked in dried blood. As he approached, a ray of sunlight fell across his face. The look in his dark blue eyes was one of satisfaction, of great pleasure in what one has accomplished.

When he reached us, he didn't say a word to me. He dropped the gloves from his hand and began to pat Rebecca on the cheek. "Rebecca. Rebecca darling, time to get up. Your adulterous days are over, my love."

She rolled her head and moaned, trying to wake up. Dr. Kramer patted her a few more times, and her head swiveled.

"Rebecca honey. Wake. UP!" A load pop rang out as Dr. Kramer slapped the shit out of her.

She woke up from her daze, trying to focus. Dr. Kramer held her cheeks in his hands and looked her in the eyes. When consciousness dawned, she realized it was James's eyes she was looking in and not mine. She shrieked.

Dr. Kramer shook his head and laughed. "That's right, cry it up, bitch. But it's only downhill from here." He let go of her head and submerged into the shadows.

I heard a flicking sound, and the spotlights above beamed over us.

Rebecca turned and looked at me. "Thom?" She was confused. Then she noticed our shoulders. Whatever fairytale or dreamland she thought she was in evaporated. The cold, harsh reality of our circumstances slapped her in the face like Dr. Kramer's hand. She shrieked. "Ohmygodohmygod, Thom, my arm, where is my fucking arm!"

I stared back at her, tears in my eyes and voice shaking. "I don't know, baby. But do me a favor. Keep your eyes up. Don't look down. Whatever you do, don't fucking look down."

She started to convulse with grief, and the sobs leaving her mouth made a chopping sound. She closed her eyes and shook her head. "No!" She shrieked again. "James, you bastard, what did you do? What. Did. You do?" Rebecca opened her eyes and put them back on me. "Thom, I have to look. Please."

I shook my head. "No no no no, please don't, please don't, Rebecca."

"Thom, I have to … I have to!" She was teetering on the edge of hysteria.

As her eyes left mine, I kept pleading with her, but she didn't listen. When she saw her hips, she made the plunge. She tried to slide her right arm out of the chain, and she threw her body forward. When she did, currents of pain dug deep into our shoulders and hip. I winced, and she cried out.

"Ouch! Sonofabitch, don't do that, Rebecca."

"He's right." Dr. Kramer was walking towards us again, holding a metal folding chair. He opened it and sat down about three feet from us. "The metal rod connecting your shoulders and hips might slip loose, then you'll be in a world of hurt."

Hearing his voice caused Rebecca to snap out of her mania. We both stared at him, fear hugging our souls.

"You a religious man, Thom?"

Still breathing heavy, I shook my head.

"No? Well, Rebecca and I are. Bet you didn't know that, did you?"

I shook my head again.

"You see, Thom, I'd expect a heathen like you to do what you did, but Rebecca, she knows better." He looked up at her, and she cried harder. He continued. "Even though you're not a religious man, Thom, I bet you are familiar with the Ten Commandments, huh?"

I nodded, tears forming again at the corner of my eyes.

"You know what the seventh one is?"

I didn't know, but I figured it out. "Do not ... don't commit adultery."

Dr. Kramer tilted his head and nodded. "Good. Good, Thom. You know, Jesus said what God has joined together, let no man separate." He stood up from the chair and started to pace. "You know why adultery is such an egregious sin? No, I'm sure you don't, so I'll tell you. It is the ultimate violation of trust and loyalty. The ultimate betrayal. You see, the husband and wife, when they are joined, are said to be one flesh. Adultery rips the two apart because the adulterer leaves their spouse and becomes one with someone else. The adulterer has defiled themselves and become unclean." He stopped and stood in front of Rebecca.

"Honey, tell me if this sounds familiar. 'And behold, the woman meets him, dressed as a prostitute, wily of heart.' You recognize it yet?"

Rebecca kept crying.

"Let me skip ahead a little. 'She seizes him and kisses him, and with a bold face she says to him, I had to offer sacrifices, and today I have paid my vows; so now I come to meet you, and to seek you eagerly, and I have found you.' No? Still don't? Oh, let me get to my favorite part. 'Come, let us take our fill of love till morning; let us delight ourselves with love. For my husband is not home; he has gone on a long journey.' That's Proverbs seven, my love, and you are that woman."

Dr. Kramer was now standing to my left. He began to whisper in my ear.

"Let me finish the chapter for you, Thom. 'With much seductive speech she persuades him; with her smooth talk she compels him. All at once he follows her, as an ox goes to the slaughter, or as a stag is caught fast till an arrow pierces its liver; as a bird rushes into a snare; he does not know that it will cost him his life.' Did you catch that last part, Thom? It's my favorite. I want you to think about it."

I hung my head, wheezes and sobs flowing from my mouth. After I let out some heavy moans, I composed myself and tried to reason with him. He was still standing to my left, taking pleasure in our suffering. "Doctor … Doctor Kramer, doesn't … doesn't your religion emphasize forgiveness?"

He stepped in front of me. We were almost nose to nose. "Oh yes. I forgive you, Thom. But the Good Book also teaches us there are grave consequences for sin. It's big on justice as well."

I looked away. Rebecca's head was tilted back, and she was groaning. My eyes met Dr. Kramer again. "But isn't … isn't there something about not taking vengeance … and leaving it for God?"

He leaned in. "'For jealousy makes a man furious, and he will not spare when he takes revenge.' Proverbs six thirty-four." Dr. Kramer patted my cheeks, then stepped back a few feet and stood where we both could see him. He produced a folded piece of loose leaf paper from the left front pocket of his lab coat.

"I'm sure you both are curious about how I found out. It was easy really. The phone bill. I noticed that all the sudden, on Rebecca's bill, there were all these texts to this new number. Then, with the help of the internet and paying for a few in-depth searches, I found out the number was yours, Thom. And then I found this." He held up the note with his right hand and shook it like a maraca.

"You know, Thom, you should really be more careful not to drop things in the break room." Dr. Kramer unfolded the note, cleared his throat, and read. "Thom, I feel like we have grown so close over the past few months; like we are truly becoming one. I love you and can't wait to have the entire weekend with you. Love, your sex goddess."

He folded the note back up, rapped it on his palm, and got in Rebecca's face. "Cute, darling. Real cute. Sex goddess." He looked down and laughed. "You dirty cunt. You defiled yourself. You are no good to me. Do you honestly think I would ever go into you again? Huh? After you've had some other man's cock wiggling around inside you? No, your pussy is now just one giant trash heap!" He punched her right across the jaw and stepped away. "Why, Rebecca? Why!"

She screamed, and as she did, blood sprayed out of her mouth like mist. "All I wanted was some affection, James! All I wanted was some attention! You are married to your job, not me! You never change! It's always been this way! Fucking always! You keep saying, oh after this, or when I'm done with this. You just keep giving me your fucking leftovers. I deserve more than leftovers, James! And Thom gave that to me!" She heaved a few breaths out and screamed again.

Dr. Kramer stormed over, grabbed her by the back of the hair, and shoved the note down her throat. Rebecca started to gag. She let out a few violent coughs, and the saliva-soaked paper tumbled to the floor.

"Choke on it, sex goddess. You and Thom want to be together? You and Thom want to be one? Well, I just made that a hell of a lot fucking easier for you two." Dr. Kramer backed away, then went and sat back down in the folding chair. "Now, let me tell you what is going to happen. Listen and listen good, because this is the only time you will hear it. I'm sure you're wondering how I'm going to get away with this, so let me tell you. Today is

Monday. Tomorrow, I am going to call and report Rebecca missing. First thing they'll try and do is ping her phone. I'm going to offer a homeless man a large sum of money to get a room at one of those shady motels in south Durham. He's going to leave both of your phones there. When the police find them, they'll see the texts. They'll probably even figure out that you two had a thing going when they start talking to your friends. What about me? I mean, isn't the jealous husband the first suspect? Sure, but I was out of town at a conference, remember? Now I didn't really go. But I paid for it, and it isn't one of those where there is an elaborate check in to get through the door. As far as everyone knows, I was there and didn't get home until Sunday evening. I was surprised to find my wife gone, even though her car was still here. After a day of trying to reach her, I got concerned. After the police find the phone and figure out the affair, it's noticed that Thom hasn't been in class. His truck is still at his house, so they will assume you used a different vehicle. It'll eventually be a missing person's report that is never solved, or they will decide the two of you were so in love, you left without a trace to be together."

Dr. Kramer stood up. "Now, I'm sure you're also wondering how I'm going to keep you hidden." He walked over to the corner of the room and began to turn a crank. The chains pulled our arms, and we fell to our backs on the mattress. We both hollered as pain radiated through our hips and shoulders. I titled my head up and watched as Dr. Kramer pulled a bookshelf away from the wall. I heard something open, and light appeared from a door-sized opening in the wall.

Dr. Kramer walked back over to us. I heard the chains clanking as he unhooked them and dropped them to the ground. A few seconds later, we were in motion. He was dragging us on the mattress to the door-shaped hole in the wall.

"Panic room." He said in huffs while moving us. "My little secret. Soundproof. Just like the basement. Scream all you want.

No one will hear a damn thing. This will be your new home until things blow over with the police."

The room was a nice size. 15 by 15 foot. It was big, but it was crude. It looked more like a dungeon than a panic room. He dragged us to the middle. I heard some more clanking as he messed with the chains again. After a few more minutes, the cranking noise started, and we were pulled back up to our feet.

Dr. Kramer looked at us.

"Now, as you can see, the room is not finished, but it will do. It's time for the honeymoon."

"The hell? Honeymoon? Dr. Kramer—"

"Oh yes, Thom. Every couple needs that time by themselves. While I go initiate my plan with the police and wait for things to blow over, you two will be left alone here. Left alone to think about the choices you made and how they brought you here. With these choices, your lives will never be the same. I will check on you to lower you back on the mattress and give you food and water."

Rebecca cried, and I asked the obvious question. "What's after the honeymoon?"

Dr. Kramer gave us a sadistic grin. "For a marriage to survive, a couple must learn how to endure suffering together." With that, he stepped out of the room and slammed the door.

We screamed and cursed him. When our voices faded, all we could hear was the humming of the florescent light hanging over our heads.

#

The sick bastard's plan worked. After a few months, the police stopped coming around and said they would be in touch with any new information. Dr. Kramer thanked them and asked if they didn't mind if he still called occasionally to check for updates. They said the calls would be welcomed.

After being locked in that damn panic room for over two months, the day came for us to be let out. Those two months were a psychological mind rape. Locked away, sewn to your lover like you're Siamese twins. Being fed through a straw, and having to sleep in the same room you shit in. You want to know what the worst thing was though? It was not knowing what was coming next. Your mind goes in a million different directions. It comes up with some awful shit. Come to find out, though, all the sick shit I could come up with failed in comparison to what Dr. Kramer had lined up for us.

The first day out of the panic room, he chained us back up in the basement like we were when all this started. Then, he left us there. We were malnourished and dehydrated. I looked over at Rebecca. Her skin was pale, her eyes sunken in. Her lips were cracked and cheeks red.

"Rebecca. I'm gonna get us out of here."

She began with a slow laugh and evolved into a hysterical outburst.

At first, I was pissed. But you know what? As time went on, I realized she was right. This wasn't like the movies. Dr. Kramer had thought of everything. There were no loose ends.

Two days later Dr. Kramer came down to the basement and fed us one hell of a meal.

"You're going to need your strength," he said.

Then he left.

#

The next morning, we awoke to a loud honking noise followed by the cranking of the chains. When we were standing upright, Dr. Kramer was there to greet us, but he wasn't dressed like Dr. Kramer. He was still wearing his white lab coat and blue scrubs, but his face was painted white with black circles around his eyes. His lips were black as well, and they had a dark circle around them. On his head was a green clown wig, bald on top with green hair around the edges. Gripped in his left hand was a rusty and battered red toolbox, and in his right, a bicycle horn.

He honked the horn several more times. "Wakey, wakey. Time for my favorite couple to rise and shine."

Rebecca and I exchanged nervous glances.

"James, what are you doing?" Exasperation coated Rebecca's voice.

"Honeymoon's over." He dropped the toolbox on the ground. The crash caused Rebecca and I to jolt. "But first, we are going to start the day with a little devotion. A little snippet from God's holy word."

I had a sinking feeling this wasn't going to be anywhere close to your grandmother's Sunday School class.

He bent over, opened the toolbox, and pulled out a pocket size New Testament. "Paul says here in first Corinthians six eighteen to flee from sexual immorality. He says every other sin a person commits is outside the body, but the sexually immoral person sins against his own body." He closed the book and pointed at us. "That's you two. You've sinned against your own bodies, so now it's time to reap what you have sown."

I had no idea where this was going, but since he had yet to let us clothe ourselves, I couldn't imagine it would be nice.

"James, why are you dressed that way? You look ridiculous."

He tossed the book to the ground. "Glad you asked." He walked over to the front of the room and wheeled over what looked like one of those rolling antique chalkboards. Instead of a chalkboard, the center was plywood. "All right, assholes, it's time to play a game. What is it? Well, it's a slight adaptation from a kid's favorite party game. I like to call it Pin the Piece on the Adulterer."

He spun the board around. My brain didn't want to accept the information my eyes were sending it. On the board was a boorish, life-sized drawing of a man and a woman. The only way I figured out it was supposed to be of me and Rebecca was because our missing arms and legs were nailed to the board, in the correct spots.

My mind was in overdrive. This couldn't be real. *It's all a nightmare. It's my subconscious warning me I need to break it off with Rebecca. In just a moment, I am going to wake upstairs in bed with her.*

That never happened.

Instead, Rebecca hollered.

"You sick … You fucking sick bastard fuck!"

Dr. Kramer ignored her. "As you can see, I've already begun. Now, the way this works is I am going to guess, in order mind you, which body part began the adultery process, and work my way to the one that consummated it. Sound like fun, kids?"

The boiling panic found its way into my bone marrow again. I was scared shitless. I began to weep. I looked at Rebeca. She was horrified. I could see the dread looming behind her eyes.

Dr. Kramer approached us, clipped the horn to his pants, knelt, and opened the toolbox. He brought forth a pair of pliers and an X-Acto knife.

He stood up and got in my face.

"Okay, Thom. We'll start with you. It's because I know it's never the woman who makes the first move. Always the a-hole dude." He extracted the blade. "Now, let me take one wild of a fucking gander and guess the way this all started was … with your words!"

Neither Rebecca nor I said anything.

"Hot damn, I knew it! Her little whining 'Oh James, you never talk to me or give me affection blah blah blah.' You came in and started talking. Started telling her what she wanted to hear."

I just hung my head.

Dr. Kramer reached down and started honking the horn. "Oh, ladies and gentlemen, am I fucking good, or am I fucking good!" He took the pliers in one hand and the knife in the other. "Open your mouth, Thom, let me look at that tongue of yours."

I was thrown into disarray. I resisted, so he punched me in the jaw over and over. I felt some of my teeth jar loose and spat them to the floor. I was dazed. Too dazed to stop what happened next.

He rammed the pliers in my mouth, pinched down on my tongue, and pulled. Then he dug into it with the X-Acto knife and sliced the tip off.

You ever bit your tongue hard? Like, hard enough your teeth sink into it? That's what it felt like, except with more of a burning sensation. I was unnerved and started to thrash my head and scream, blood pouring from my mouth like a fount.

Dr. Kramer held the tip of my tongue up for further inspection. "No human being can tame the tongue. It is a restless evil, full of deadly poison." He glanced at me. "That's James three eight."

Rebecca lost her shit. "James, you bastard! You're out of your fucking mind!" She kicked her chained leg at him.

With the tip of my tongue in hand, he darted over to her. "Oh no, Rebecca, I am very much in my right fucking mind. It's you two horny dumbasses who are out of your minds thinking you could get away with this."

He left her and went to the toolbox, knelt, and fetched a hammer and nails. He walked over to the drawing and hammered the tip of my tongue to where the mouth should be. "Not bad. We're getting there." He put the hammer and nails in the left pocket of his lab coat and pulled out the X-Acto knife again. He eased his way back to Rebecca, rubbing his chin.

"Your turn, sex goddess. Let me see ... what would have been the first turn on?" Dr. Kramer thought for a minute before he continued. "I got it. It was the way you run your hands through your hair." He gave me a little glance, then looked back at Rebecca. "Oh yeah, I know that's it. It was one of the first things that drove me crazy about you, Rebecca."

Rebecca hung her head. "So what, James? What are you going to do?"

James grabbed a handful of hair and threw her head back. "Oh, nothing much, simply cut your hair."

Relief flooded my soul.

"With the skin still attached."

A lump was building in my throat, and Rebecca's breathing picked up. Before I could even get a scream out of my mouth, Dr. Kramer was scraping the X-Acto knife across the top of Rebecca's brow.

Rebecca cried out in pain. "Thom, oh Jesus, Thom, help me, help me!"

But there was nothing I could do but watch.

After he had made a full circle around her head, he grabbed the hair on top and yanked. There was a ripping and slurping sound as her scalp broke loose from the skull. Rebecca's screams were so deafening, I thought my eardrums were going to burst.

Dr. Kramer retracted the blade and with her scalp in hand, walked over to the board. He nailed it in place and stepped back to admire his work. Satisfied with his artistry, he began to tend to our wounds. Once he was done, he sat back down in the folding chair and educated us on how the rest of this game was going to go.

"Understand how this game works? When you hear the honking of the horn, it means it's time to play. Now, I could come down here at any time, day or night, and honk my little horn."

Neither of us responded. We understood.

Dr. Kramer lowered us back on the mattress and walked out.

\#

Several days passed. Then one night, I was surprised out of my sleep by a honking sound. It was the damn horn, which meant it was time to play the sick bastard's game again.

We were still lying on the mattress. We heard his footsteps descending the stairway, and the honks were getting louder. The lights came on, and Dr. Kramer appeared standing over us. At least he wasn't dressed in the stupid clown getup anymore. Rebecca looked at me and shook her head, which was still bandaged with strands of her blonde hair snaking out the sides.

"Thom, I can't … I can't …"

"What was that?" Dr. Kramer bent over.

"James, baby, please stop. No more. I can't take it."

Dr. Kramer laughed. "You can't take the pain, but you had no problem dishing it out. What you will feel physically is what I feel emotionally and spiritually. Since you have no soul, there is nothing I could do to hurt you. But you have a body. Therefore, it will be the seat of the suffering I inflict."

He sat down in the space between our missing legs and conjoined hips. We both lifted our heads to get a better look at what he was doing. He had a tiny spoon in his hand.

"All right, you heard the horn, so you know what time it is."

All I wanted to do was die. I wanted him to kill us, right then and there. To put us out of our misery and end this psycho circus, but he had no such plans.

I tried to talk, but it just sounded like gibberish.

"Shut up, Thom, you sound like a retard." Dr. Kramer flicked my balls. "Now, I'm ready to make my next guess." He rapped the spoon on his knuckles. "It was the words, then the hair … then it was probably the way you two looked into each other's eyes. Am I right?"

Yes, he was right.

He went for Rebecca first. I couldn't watch, so I turned my head. I don't know if there are words to articulate the sound a person makes when their eyes are being dug out with a spoon. I guess we were fortunate he only took my right eye and her left.

I didn't see him nail our eyes to the board, but it sounded like it didn't go how he wanted. I suspected he tried nailing them through the cornea, and they burst. After a few days of healing up, I got the nerve to look at the board and discovered I was correct. Where our eyes should have been were nothing more than drooping casings.

The game went on. Every few days he would come down and cut something off. Next was our lips. It wasn't as painful as the eye, but it was still brutal. He nailed them to the board and then doctored us up. Another week went by, and our wounds were crusting over. I couldn't see myself, but if I looked half as bad as Rebecca did, I can only imagine.

Her scalp was one giant scab. Her left eyelid was sagging, with blood crusted around the edges. The front of her mouth was only her rows of teeth, with the skin under her nose and above her chin scabbing. She no longer looked like Rebecca, but some grotesque creature from childhood nightmares.

What happened next was hard to watch.

The horn honked, and that gnawing sensation in our guts reared its head. We heard footsteps, then a clank; footsteps, then a clank: again and again. It sounded like Dr. Kramer was dragging something down the stairs. We could hear wheels squeaking once he got to the bottom. When Dr. Kramer came into view, we could see he was wheeling something over to us. It was about waist high and covered in a blue sheet.

"She's got a nice rack, doesn't she, Thom?"

I didn't respond. I couldn't, even if I wanted to.

"I mean, even with her face all messed up, her breasts still look good, don't they?"

He walked over to Rebecca and started to grab and rub her breast. "These were for me, Rebecca. They were mine. But now they're ruined. You've gone and let Thom over here put his mouth and spit all on them."

Dr. Kramer stepped away and threw the sheet off the wheeled object. It took me a second, but when I realized what it was, the churning in my stomach intensified. It was a liposuction machine. The bottom half was metal. On the top were two glass jars with the suction pump in them. Hanging on the side was the hose.

Rebecca torqued her body and screamed. She was saying something, but I couldn't understand. Next thing I knew, Dr. Kramer was ramming the hose into her breast. He flipped on the machine, and it began sucking away.

Dr. Kramer emptied her breasts until they looked like deflated hot air balloons. Rebecca passed out from the pain and psychological distress. The skin of her breasts hung, sagging down past her ribcage.

He removed his yellow gloves and turned his gaze towards me.

"Now, Thom, I can't nail her breasts to the board, now can I?"

I closed my eyes and looked away.

"Thom, tell me. How did you like the taste of her breasts in your mouth? Was it good?"

I still wouldn't look at him.

"Oh, I know it was good." He began to open one of the glass jars from the liposuction machine. "Since you like the taste of her breasts so much, it's only fitting you get to taste all of them." He scooped his hand into the yellowish-orange mush of Rebecca's breasts.

I wagged my head back and forth, grunting and breathing hard. He plopped a big handful on my face where my lips used to be. Some of the mush made it into the back of my throat and under my tongue. I began to vomit in waves. When I stopped, he flung more handfuls at me. It was in my hair, on my face, and inside my mouth.

Dr. Kramer took the remaining breast mush, chucked it across the board where Rebecca's breasts would have been, and left the room. It would be two weeks before we played the game again.

#

Rebecca and I were awoken by the chains hoisting us up to a standing position. Then there was the damn horn again. Dr. Kramer began pulling out the rolling board. He flipped it around so we could see it. The smell was awful. In fact, it was so bad Dr. Kramer had begun wearing a mask when he would come down and check on us. He also started opening the window down there to air out the room.

He sat down in his metal chair and looked at the board. "Now, by process of elimination, you each have only one body part left to deal with. It's the final piece of Pin the Piece on the Adulterer. I'm sure you know what that is for you, Thom."

Yeah, I knew, but I didn't have the strength to fight him. He hadn't fed us in two weeks. Rebecca groaned, so I turned to look at her. Tears were running from her only eye, and I could see the empathy in her gaze. Our moment was interrupted by a loud scraping sound. We looked at Dr. Kramer, and he was sitting in the chair sharpening a pair of garden shears. At his feet was a welding torch.

"Thom, this is what's going to happen. First, I'm going to cut your little thingy off. Then, I'm going to cauterize the wound so you don't bleed out. After that, I'm going to have mercy on you and put you to sleep before I chop your balls off."

He reached down in his toolbox and pulled out a sewing needle and fishing line. "Rebecca, I'm going to sew up that whore hole of yours. It's going to be closed for business."

That's precisely what he did.

I passed out as soon as the shears severed my penis.

When I came to, Dr. Kramer was gone, but we were still hanging upright in the chains. The board was placed only a few feet in front of us. There was my penis, nailed right through the middle. It looked like a Vienna sausage covered in ketchup. My balls were hanging over a nail under it like a pair of earbuds. I tilted my head down and looked between my legs and wept. There was nothing there but pubic hair. I leaned forward and looked down at Rebecca. I could see the indentions from the fishing line in her vagina. He had stitched it tighter than a baseball's skin. She was still passed out, so I hung my head and fell back asleep.

#

Over the next month, Dr. Kramer let us heal. He fed us good food and even started giving us vitamins. Then one day, as we were lying on the mattress, we felt the chains fall from our wrists. I tilted my head back and to the side just in time to see him gathering the chains in a pile. He lifted his hands from the clanking links and came and sat in the empty space on the mattress by our conjoined hips.

"You've spent time together, and you've suffered together. Now it's time for you to learn how to do things together."

Rebecca and I traded bewildered glances.

"Welcome to your new life. You are going to have to re-learn how to do even the most menial task. Like walk and go to the bathroom. You have two weeks to figure it out. At the end of which you will be tested."

With that said, he left and locked the door behind him.

#

Sitting up together off the mattress was the easiest part. Getting to our feet was a challenge. We managed, and after a few tries, could keep our balance. Walking was a bigger issue. I had to swing my attached hip while she stepped forward with her right leg, and vice versa.

In the back of the basement was a bathroom, so it was the next thing we conquered. Once we got good at walking, we attempted to climb the stairs. By the time the two weeks were up, we had a good grip on how to maneuver together. Dr. Kramer was pleased with our progress.

It was now time for the test, and Dr. Kramer led us up the stairs at gunpoint and out of the basement. We were still naked. It was our first time to see the living room since that dreaded weekend. He led us out of the house, across the yard, and to the lake on the edge of the woods. He helped us into the small fishing boat and drove out to the middle of the lake.

As he was leading us to the boat, the familiar churning in our guts picked up. We knew what he had in mind. When we arrived at the middle of the lake, Dr. Kramer killed the engine, then spoke.

"All you have to do is make it one hundred yards. Now stand up."

As we were trying to get to our feet, he kicked us overboard, started the motor back up, and drove ahead one hundred yards.
#

I felt the water gush out of my mouth. I coughed and gasped for air and opened my eyes to see Dr. Kramer standing over me. I took a few more breaths and looked around. We were on the bank of the lake. I fixed my eyes on Rebecca. Her face was a bluish color, and her cheeks were a faded purple. I stared back at Dr. Kramer, my countenance begging for an explanation.

"She didn't make it, Thom. She keeled over about halfway through. You fought hard. You were about ten feet from the boat

158

before you went under. I went ahead and gave it to you, since I'm such a nice guy and everything. Pulled you out and saved your life."

It all hit me. I remembered hearing her cries. I remembered sinking towards the bottom of the lake as she lost her strength. I remembered her face under the water as she drowned.

Dr. Kramer helped me to my feet, put Rebecca's lifeless body around his, and assisted me back down to the basement.
#

A decade has passed since that surreal day. I'm still down here in Dr. Kramer's basement with Rebecca attached to my side. She is now nothing but a skeleton. As I sit here and stare at her skull—the hollow eyes and rounded jawbone—I can barely remember what she looked like. I have watched, day after day, year after year, as her body decomposed next to me. I watched as her skin turned to leather and her remaining hair fell out. I endured the smell of rotting meat and the pieces of dead flesh as they flaked off onto my skin. As her body began to deteriorate, Dr. Kramer had to do another surgery to attach our bones together with wire.

So here we are, still together. So much for death do us part.

The board where Dr. Kramer played his sick little game is still down here. The drawings have faded, and all the parts have decomposed. All that remains are the bones from our arms and legs.

My mind often goes back to all the nights of pleasure Rebecca and I had together, along with all our conversations. It's funny, though I can't remember her face, I can remember every curve of her body. I can recall all the sensations of pleasure she gave to me. I miss hearing her voice. I miss her laugh. I miss losing myself in her green eyes. You want to know what I find to be the most fascinating thing about this entire experience? Even with my manhood gone, I still lust. I would give anything to have one night with Rebecca again. All it will ever be is a desire. Dr. Kramer has taken away my ability to act on that desire. While there is nothing anyone can do to remove the lust from my heart, he made damn sure I could never fulfill it again.

Do I regret what I did? Yes and no. I still cry and grieve Rebecca's passing. She's dead because of me. I mourn because my escapade with her cost me my medical career. I will never get to fulfill my dream of being a surgeon. I wish things would have worked out differently. However, I don't regret being with her. It was good, but it was costly. Was it worth the price? I can't answer that question now. Maybe one day. Would I have still gone after her if I knew what a psycho Dr. Kramer was? The answer is yes. The lust was too strong, and there was not a damn thing I could do other than give in to it.plans are for me. He doesn't keep me chained up anymore, but still makes me stay locked in the basement. It's not like I can really go anywhere. He's kept me around this long, so I don't think he will kill me. But who knows? He's crazy enough to. Who's to say after he's had fun giving me one giant mindscrew, he doesn't off me and throw me in the bottom of the lake? I don't know. One thing I do know is this: As I sit on the mattress and write, with Rebecca at my side, the lust still burns. I've often wondered, if I still had my manhood, would I get desperate enough to engage in necrophilia? Yes, I think I would.

It's getting late, so I am about to stop writing.

After I put my pen down, I am going to give Rebecca a long, passionate kiss, caress her face, pull her close, and fall asleep while gazing into her eyes. I'm going to rub her chest. I'm going to slide my hand down her leg and remember.

Goodnight, my love. I'll see you again when the sun greets us.

INFESTED

By Mike L. Lane

Enraged by the rapid infestation invading his home, Paul charged headlong into the sunlit attic. He bounded the stairs two at a time despite the screaming protests of recent wounds. The hostile takeover had been sudden; the swift transition between a few annoying wasps to a full-fledged outbreak a muddled blur in his mind. The sonsabitches were *everywhere*, swarming the carcass of his dead dog and swooping at his face like kamikaze pilots determined to take him down once and for all. With the spray wand leveled at the hive like a loaded machine gun, blind rage pushed him into the fray. Past the point of no return, he resolved to make his final stand, even if they ate him alive.

He remembered seeing the first wasps back in late July—a sweltering afternoon spent weeding the garden and avoiding his wife—but thought little of it. After all, these creatures thrived in the summer heat. It was like spotting a snake during the first mow of spring or braking for a deer crossing the highway in late September. Startling maybe, but nothing to write home about. Paul was sneaking a well-earned smoke behind the garage when his neighbor, Thomas Lowe, offered him a glass of his mother's sun brewed tea.

"Looks like you've got some squatters, Paul," Thomas said. Ice clinked against the sweating glass as he handed it over and pointed at the overhang. The small, grey hive nestled between the roof and the outer wall hung above them. "Best to swat the sucker down. Ma says if you let 'em roost, they'll breed like rabbits."

"Mrs. Lowe is probably right. I hate those worthless sonsabitches," Paul said. Snatching up a rake, he knocked it loose and crushed the paper-thin nest under heel. A few angry wasps buzzed around in search of their assailant as the men darted for safety. "Those little bastards can breed somewhere else now."

"Well, you know Ma. She can't stand the thought of anyone fornicating," Thomas laughed, shaking his head. The fifty-nine-year-old still lived with his nagging mother, and Paul doubted Thomas would ever flee the safety of Mrs. Lowe's nest. "God forbid anyone enjoy a little hanky-panky, even the damned wasps."

"Sounds like my wife," Paul said. He cast a nervous glance over his shoulder to make sure Charmayne wasn't in earshot.

Thomas bellowed laughter and spent another thirty minutes complaining about his mother's constant henpecking before heading home. Paul went inside, making a mental note to pick up wasp spray on his next trip into town. After scrubbing dog shit from the carpet and enduring Charmayne's own relentless nagging, he forgot all about it.

The first sting happened around mid-August, after he and Charmayne returned from his sister's funeral. Penny's death wasn't a total shock—in many ways he even felt responsible—but the loss hurt him, nonetheless. He and Penny were close until he married Charmayne, but the two women butted heads like rams in the wild, creating a rift in Paul and Penny's relationship. A rift Paul regretted.

"You have to be your own man," Penny warned him early in his marriage. "Mom always said if you let someone walk all over you, you'll forget how to stand and become their rug. Don't be Charmayne's doormat, Paul."

He nodded in agreement because Penny was always right about these things, but by then it was far too late. As much as she hated the way Charmayne dominated him, it was partly Penny's fault for teaching him "The Trick."

Their mother died when Paul was four: a traumatic memory forever burned into his brain. She was taking them to the park, holding his hand in hers while Penny zipped ahead on her bicycle. He remembered being upset because his father wasn't with them, but mom smoothed things over explaining to him when Daddy came home after work, they would all play gotcha in the backyard. A family game his dad invented, gotcha was pretty much tag, but with a jump-out-and-scare-you flair to it. Paul loved gotcha almost as much as he loved his parents. Pleased with his mom's promise, he chased his big sister into the playground with newfound interest.

The park was empty, allowing them free reign on the seesaw and swings. Mom even let him try the big boy slide, a huge feat considering his fear of heights. The first few steps up the daunting ladder were the scariest, but his mom walked beside him with her arms outstretched in case he stumbled. His tiny legs wobbled in nervous excitement, but the gentle reassurance of her hand on his back gave him the confidence to carry on. He was halfway up before he noticed her hand was gone and he was climbing on his own. His heart swelled with pride as he stared down at her from on high, and her smile was brighter than the afternoon sun warming his skin. He looked out across the playground, marveling at how far he could see. Up on his tippy-toes, he spotted the peak of his own house on the far side of Bradbury Hill. This thrilled him to no end. It was like standing on top of the world.

He sat down and scooted his bottom to the slope's edge, anxious adrenaline surging through him. At first, nothing happened, but before he could voice his concern, the surface below him grew slick and his weight plunged forward. His heart leapt into his throat. Like a plane in flight, Paul made a sputtering noise and threw his arms out wide, the descent whipping his hair back and stealing his breath. He hit the ground in a full sprint, cackling like a little madman, circling back to the ladder and climbing up to do it all over again. His mom's laughter was all the encouragement he needed this time, and he slid over and over again, each trip better than the last.

"Let's try the merry-go-round, Pauly. The merry-go-round makes the world a blur. It's magic!" his mom said. She cradled him into her arms and pretended to chew on his belly with a nom-nom sound, sending Paul into hysterics. When she finally allowed him to catch his breath, she motioned for his sister. "Help your brother get on, Penny."

She jumped from her perch on the jungle gym and led him to the center of the merry-go-round. The ride consisted of a large metallic circle painted in an array of reds, yellows, and blues and reminded him of a pinwheel. Iron bars rose up out of the circle in oblong hoops, each bar a different color than the section of the platform it grew from. Since his mom's name was Mary, Paul's four-year-old mind believed the magical structure was called the "Mary-go-round." All these years later, he refused to believe there was anything merry about it.

"Hold on as tight as you can. If it spins fast enough, it'll send you soaring to a whole new world, so don't let go. I wouldn't want you hurtling into space and crash-landing on the moon!"

Soaring to a whole new world meant very little to Paul. To him, landing in the middle of Mrs. Lowe's living room next door would have been a whole new world, but landing on the moon? His mom and sister laughed as he craned his neck and scanned the sky, searching for it behind clouds and wondering how he could get there during the day.

"Commence the countdown, pilot!" his mom commanded in a captain's baritone voice.

"Five, four, two," Paul said, scrunching up his forehead and staring up at the sky. One hand clutched the bar while the other counted down on his fingers. A light bulb went off, and he corrected himself. "THREE, two, one. Blast off!!!"

Mary grabbed an iron support and walked in a circle causing the platform to spin. Paul's eyes widened, and his surprised face cracked into a smile. It was infectious, and Mary's walk became a jog. He made rocket noises and anticipated hovering in the air and zipping out into space. His little hands clutched the bar, and his universe whirled.

"Faster, momma!" Penny cried. Paul was rendered speechless. The fast spin of the merry-go-round sucked the air out of him, a wide grin plastered so far across his face his eyes squinted. Mary ran as fast as she could.

Uncontrollable laughter erupted from Paul, his heart thudding in his chest. If the slide was a plane ride, then the merry-go-round was indeed a rocket to the moon! Mary's smile flashed at him with each turn, and he was mesmerized by the magic ride his mom controlled. The world blurred around him at a dizzy pace. It was like when his dad held him by the arms and spun him in circles, but this was ten times better. His vision struggled to keep up with the turns, fluttering at the edges. Images jumped in and out of focus like flicking through his sister's View-Master. He would see his mom's beaming face for a split second and then she was gone again, melting into the blur. See her broad smile. Then gone again. In an instant, the love, happiness and security he felt was wiped away by his mother's blank stare.

He didn't know what was wrong. The merry-go-round spun at a maddening pace, each quick flicker of his mom's transformation intensifying his fear. Her vacant gaze turned to panic.

Whirl.

Her flushed face contorted into a purple grimace.

Whirl.

She clutched her throat and reached out for the spinning bars.

Whirl.

She stumbled into the merry-go-round, the iron bar striking her head and splattering blood into his eyes. The sickening thud sounded like Paul's rain boots stomping in mud.

Whirl.

Paul's world was tinged in red as she collapsed to the ground, and even though the ride was slowing, his vision still jittered around the edges. Her body lay in an awkward position, her face looking toward him, her torso twisted, and her legs flayed out wide like one of Penny's broken dolls left out in the yard. It scared him for reasons his child's mind couldn't comprehend. Penny leapt off and screamed at her. She shook her like a Christmas present, but their mom just laid there, her glossy eyes aimed at him. He thought for sure she would jump up and scare them by yelling, "gotcha," just like the game they played at home, but she didn't. The longer she lay still, the more frightened he became. His face was wet, and the shaky vision wouldn't stop. Penny said something, her words a jumbled mess of screams and violin strings, but he couldn't understand her. She broke into a run, leaving him and his mom alone. He clutched the iron bar like his mother instructed and waited for the ride to be over, though the merry-go-round stopped long ago.

It was a long time before he understood everything. His mother was dead and for most of his youth, he felt responsible. Mom wanted to send him to the moon and in the end, she died trying. His dad became a different person altogether. He no longer tickled Paul or swung him by his arms. He no longer played "gotcha" with them in the backyard. He explained nothing to Paul about his mother's death, seldom talking to him at all unless it was to scold or whip him. His father became scary in ways Paul never thought possible. Penny protected him when she could, but when Dad was drinking, there was little protection for either of them, and it didn't take much to spark his rage. From talking too loud to forgetting chores, no offense was too small for a beating. Their best defense was to become as small as possible and keep quiet.

"You worthless sonsabitches don't appreciate nothin'!" his old man would yell, slamming down a bottle of Wild Turkey and reaching for the dreaded, leather belt. "You wanna blow smoke, you little bastards? I'll burn your ass 'til you shit fire!"

With his mother gone, Paul wanted to make his father happy but failed to meet the man's fickle satisfaction. If he demanded silence at the dinner table, Paul never breathed a word and chewed his food without sound. This only infuriated the man. He claimed Paul was being a "smartass, worthless sonofabitch" and proceeded to "burn his ass" with a violent lashing. Paul scrubbed the dishes like he was sanding wood, but his father always found a spot on his favorite shot glass or a fork crooked in the drawer, and all hell broke loose. When Paul mowed the lawn, the grass was either not cut low enough or cut so short he accused him of "scalping" it. Either way, it merited an ass whooping. If he left his bike in the yard, his father unbuckled his belt because Paul was killing the grass. If he parked it in the garage, he was whipped because he could have scratched the car. Nothing was ever right, and every incident ended with a sore ass and his father calling him a worthless sonofabitch. In time, Paul's anger became hate. The real "worthless sonofabitch" was his father.

"I'll kill him!" he screamed to Penny in a rambling fit of rage. "Nothing's ever good enough. If Mom were here, she wouldn't stand for this! I know she reached to catch me, but it's not my fault she fell! I wouldn't have gotten on the dumb merry-go-round if I had known it was going to kill her!"

Paul burst into tears, his clenched fists drawing red, half-crescent moons into his palms. His body trembled and his face flushed blood red. He gritted his teeth so hard they threatened to crumble in their sockets. Penny took him in her arms, shaking her head and softly shushing him as he sobbed on her shoulder in gasping heaves.

"It's not your fault," Penny said, leading him to the bed. He cried long and hard and she let him, rubbing his back and hiding a few tears of her own. "Mom didn't fall because she was reaching for you, Pauly. That's not what happened at all. It was the wasps."

"*Wasps?*" Paul exclaimed. "You can't die from wasps! I've been stung before."

"The wasps were only part of it," Penny explained. "She was allergic. There was a nest under the merry-go-round and spinning it stirred them up. Her throat and tongue started swelling, and she couldn't breathe. She panicked, tripped, and struck her head on the bars, cracking her skull. I ran off and found Mr. Lowe, but by the time we got back, mom was dead. It was a freak accident, Pauly."

"I thought she fell trying to grab me. Like she believed I might really float away. Maybe Dad's right. Not only am I worthless, I must be stupid, too."

"You were four," Penny said, squeezing his shoulder. "You couldn't have known. Dad's an ass, but he wasn't always. He loved her, and her death hit him hard."

"Screw him!" Paul snapped, jerking away. He wasn't going to give his father one ounce of sympathy, especially not now. "If I get the chance, I'll show him blowing smoke! I'll torch his bed—set *his* ass on fire! He probably wouldn't even wake up and you know what? That would be just fine by me!"

"Hush!" Penny exclaimed in a harsh whisper. "He's our dad, and he has his faults, but hurting him would make you no better. *Killing* him would make you worse."

"I know," Paul groaned, fresh tears brimming in his eyes. Irritated, he clawed at his scalp trying to put his jumbled thoughts and emotions together in a way his sister might understand. "I get so angry. My vision flickers and everything turns red. My blood boils, and I don't feel comfortable in my skin. Even my bones are knotted so tight, it's like they are shifting and changing. It feels like I'm going to explode."

"Maybe this can help. Have you heard about people who struggle speaking in front of crowds? To help them get through it, they picture everyone in the audience naked."

"I don't want to see Dad naked!" Paul protested, horrified at the idea.

"Me neither, silly. Instead of visualizing him naked, I picture him in a funny outfit when he's in a foul mood. I call it The Trick," she explained. "Instead of seeing him as pissed off Dad, I make believe he's dressed like a monkey or a poodle. Once I even pretended he was Mrs. Lowe with a silver-blue wig, hunched back, and no teeth. I nearly lost my gourd on that one! The Trick works like a charm."

Penny was right. The next time Dad tanned Paul's hide, he gave The Trick a try. He pictured him as his favorite cartoon sailor, with bulging forearms, squinted eyes, and a corncob pipe jutting from his mouth. Dad's voice shifted into the cartoon voice, his rants sounding like a creaky buzz saw. Paul's mind even added the sailor's silly laugh to the end of each utterance for good measure. His dad would say, "You worthless sonofabitch, *ag-ug-ug-ug!*" and Paul would hold his breath to keep from laughing. The convulsing edges of his vision settled, and the world never turned that deep shade of crimson red, warning him his anger was near capacity. It didn't stop Dad from using the belt, but it kept Paul's sanity intact, and he used The Trick whenever his world tilted over into anger. When Mort Carson poked fun of him in school, he visualized the boy as a ballerina, smiled, and moved on without an incident. When his overweight Algebra teacher scolded him for drawing in her class, he pictured her as King Henry the Eighth, stuffing her face with drumsticks, cakes, and pudding. The half-chewed contents spilled from her mouth and onto her gold laced tunic while she ranted in an old English accent. Even when he had misgivings about marrying Charmayne, her overbearing nature rearing its ugly head before, during, and after the ceremony, he visualized her as that year's Miss October and never thought twice about it. With a centerfold's body, he could have said "I do" to just about anyone. Sometimes he wasn't even on the verge of anger to use The Trick. Sometimes he did it for amusement. It always worked just as Penny promised, and he used it at any given opportunity.

But making it work with Charmayne over the years was often a chore. She could be a real bitch at times: a secret thought he kept under tight-lipped lock and key. Because of her harsh, insensitive personality, it didn't matter what centerfold he dreamt up, each time became harder than the last. When Penny was diagnosed with cancer, Charmayne chastised her, stating Penny should have caught the early warning signs. The comment burrowed beneath his skin, but he remained silent, envisioning Charmayne as she morphed into a large, shaggy, abominable snowman. Frost glistened on her white furry lips, and her words turned to unintelligible grunts. His anger passed, no fuss no muss. When Penny wore a wig to Thanksgiving dinner, Charmayne said it made her look like a circus clown. Again, Paul let her insensitive comment pass. Instead, he used it to his advantage. He enjoyed the new over-expressive look—her high arched eyebrows forming a capitol M on her white forehead and the bright red grin grease painted from cheek to cheek—laughing to himself at her round rubber nose and floppy shoes. When Penny made it through the first round of chemo and everyone thought she was out of the woods and on the mend, Charmayne insisted it was only the calm before the storm and even went so far as to guess when Penny would die. In Paul's mind, gibberish fled from his wife's lips like an auctioneer at market.

"All right and ready, there! The life auction's on and how many days you have for Penny; can I get three months, three months now, and two months and a half! Any takers on two—got that two—can we go one? Three weeks now in the back corner, going two? Now two right there, sir—one week to the day for you ma'am? Got it! Going once, going twice, and Penny's gone!" Charmayne's voice barked. She tipped her ten-gallon hat, spat tobacco juice on the floor, and banged the gavel. "Sold 'em right here for a full week!"

The Trick helped him bottle up his feelings, and he held his tongue, though the words cut deep. Her guess was off by a month, but in her twisted way of thinking, she seemed proud she called it. Charmayne always spoke without thinking, and although his pet name for her was Charm, the nickname never rang true.

He forgave her indiscretions time after time, but she put the icing on the cake in the hospital. It was a rough time for him, but Charmayne took no notice. She was almost ecstatic while Penny lay on her deathbed, wasting away. To the outside world, Charm looked like a ray of sunshine, striving to bring hope to a crowd of mourners. Paul knew better. She was only happy because they would finally own their home.

His father died ten years earlier and since then, Paul and Charmayne lived in his boyhood home on Bradbury Hill. People often talk about loved ones dying peacefully in their sleep, but in his dad's case, Paul prayed it wasn't true. He hoped the worthless sonofabitch suffered; his agony lasting for hours on end and far from peaceful. Regardless, the old man's last small kindness was leaving the house to him and Penny. His sister already owned a house of her own and gave the family home to Paul. Never satisfied, Charmayne nagged him to get Penny's name off of the deed. It was one of the rare times he stood up to Charm, but he paid for it from then on.

Now his beloved sister was dying in the worst possible way (the way his *father* should have died), and Charmayne was happier than a pig in shit. To make matters worse, he was Penny's health care proxy. The decision of whether or not to pull the plug tormented Paul. Charmayne was more concerned with the hospital's cuisine.

"The meatloaf in the cafeteria tastes like soggy cardboard," she huffed, scrunching her face up in disgust. "I'd rather drive the forty minutes back home to Malum Rose than eat another meal here."

"Did you not hear me, Charm?" Paul asked in disbelief. His bald head broke into a cold sweat and trolls wrestled in his bulging stomach.

"What is it, honey?" Charmayne asked, feigning concern and taking his hand. "Maybe this is too much for you. Are you ready to leave?"

"Leave?" Paul asked, retracting his hand. "Shit fire, Charm! They're asking me to take Penny off of life support!"

Like he was a complete and utter idiot, she rolled her eyes and said with a laugh, "It's not like you have to actually pull a plug, you blithering idiot. Just go tell them to do it."

Her lack of sensitivity, especially when he needed her the most, pushed his mind to places he didn't want to go. The fire boiled in his veins, and the hospital hallway spun in his vision, his mother's blood tinting the scene. A throbbing ache radiated from his taint as he ground his teeth and his bones shifted beneath his skin. For the briefest moment, The Trick was losing the fight. He wanted to put *her* on life support. He pictured hovering above her, his hands wrapped around her throat. He felt the satisfying crunch of her larynx in his grasp as her face turned from bright red to deep blue. A dark urine stain spread across the crotch of her designer jumpsuit—a preposterous outfit Paul loathed. The outlandish yellow sweats were trimmed in black stripes. "Queen Bee" was bedazzled across her wide ass. The aching anger subsiding, he sighed and shook his head. Charmayne's own ridiculous appearance was enough to bring him down to Earth again.

He left her in the hallway, and after coming to terms with his decision, he gave the doctor the go-ahead. As the machines fell silent, Paul sobbed and waited for the flatline, clutching his big sister's hand. Contrary to what television suggests, it takes a while for the body to finally give in and give up. When thirty minutes passed and Penny still clung to life, Charmayne took her blunt apathy to the next level.

"My God," she sighed. "How long is this going to take?"

Without a word, Paul snatched her by the arm and led her out of the room like a misbehaved toddler. In the empty waiting room, he whipped her around and pressed his face within inches of hers, his bones declaring mutiny against his skin.

"Honey, what's wrong?"

The oblivious, idiotic look in her eyes, and her use of the word "honey," saved her from an out-and-out throttling. In his mind, her yellow jumpsuit swelled into an actual bumblebee costume—something from a low budget children's television series where the characters are larger than life and full of naive innocence. Felt wings sprouted from her back, and her big yellow face stared at him like a dumbfounded emoji. His grip loosened. No matter how dumb she was, he loved her and believed in his heart she didn't realize how badly her words stung. He took a deep breath and let her off of the hook, like always.

"Charm," he said, forcing a smile through gritted teeth, "why don't you go home. I'll handle everything here, okay?"

"I'm taking the car!" she beamed, delighted to leave. She jumped up and down, her swollen bumblebee belly bouncing and the Styrofoam balls of her antennae wobbling on springs. "Me and the girls were going to the movies later tonight anyway. You'll be okay? You were starting to wig me out in there."

"Funny thing to say to a bald man," he sighed, knowing their old inside joke would placate her. "I'll be fine."

Without missing a beat, she kissed his cheek and waddled toward the elevator in a mad dash, her fluffy stinger dissolving into the Queen Bee emblem. By the time he drifted back into the room, Penny was gone.

Her funeral came and went in a haze. For the most part, Charmayne was on her best behavior, standing by his side throughout and accepting condolences from Penny's acquaintances like they were her closest friends. His sister was probably rolling over in her grave, but Paul was relieved Charmayne kept her mouth in check. He was too exhausted to think, much less stress over her uncontrollable nature to say the wrong thing at the wrong time. He wanted his life back to normal, or at least as normal as it could be with the loss of his big sister.

The Friday after the funeral was his first memorable encounter with a wasp. On the internet, Paul made a living writing as a woman on his popular, feel-good blog, *A Joyce to Behold*. His online alter ego was Joyce DeMarco—one of Charmayne's closest friends in real life. Joyce was the embodiment of a single, smart, hardworking, beautiful woman, and Paul used her on his blog not only as his alter ego, but as his own secret muse. Joyce was everything Charmayne couldn't be, and though he knew he never stood a chance with her, he fantasized about Joyce often, especially when he adopted her persona online.

Paul blogged about anything to keep his followers returning. From "*WINCIES! How to Handle the Menzies!*" to "*Separating Mr. Right from Mr. Right Now,*" he found women bought into his articles. They praised his insight, sharing on Facebook and flooding his posts with glowing comments. Due to the nature of *A Joyce to Behold*, his readers would castrate him if they ever found out they were taking life advice from a bald, middle-aged man, but the revenue was phenomenal, and as long as his readers were happy with the content, what difference did it make?

As he struggled with his latest post, Charmayne barged in and sat Zoey at his feet.

"I need you to watch the baby," she said, the statement more order than request. "I'm going to get a Starbucks and a pedicure."

"Charm, you know I'm working," he protested with a defeated sigh. Of course, Charmayne didn't care and always got her way. From the corner of his eye, something darted past the door into the kitchen, but when he turned his head it was gone. "I have to get an article posted by tonight."

"Pretending to be a woman again?" she laughed. "Sometimes you worry me, honey. If I wanted to marry a woman, I would have."

"Might have saved us both the hassle," he mumbled. He imagined Charmayne and Joyce in bed together. The thought of Joyce in all her naked glory was wonderful, but Charmayne's bulging body kept getting in the way, and Zoey's shrill barking killed the fantasy. "I don't have time to take care of your dog. She doesn't even like me."

"She loves her daddy," she replied in a baby tone, stooping down to Zoey and making kissy faces. The excited Pomeranian hopped on her hind legs, trying to reach Charm's face. "She only acts up because she has separation anxiety from Mamma. Don't you, baby?"

Zoey's tail wagged her approval. Paul believed the dog would agree to a lobotomy for another whiff of the stench permeating from Charm's mouth. It amazed him how her breath and Zoey's dogfood were in the same ballpark on the rancid scale.

"You know I can't take her," Charmayne continued. "She'll lick the nail polish off of my toes again and end up squirting all over the carpet tonight. She'll be a good girl. I promise."

Paul looked down at the annoying little dog. He didn't *hate* Zoey, but he often daydreamed what it would be like if he left the front door open. If a passing car happened to hit her in the street, it wouldn't be killing her, per se. Her fragile life left in the hands of fate was something he felt confident he could live with.

"Fine," he submitted. Picking up slick, wet clumps of dog shit was the last thing he wanted. God forbid Charmayne clean up after her own dog. "But get some pictures. Maybe I can do a piece on day spas or something for the blog."

"Sure, I guess," Charmayne sighed in an automatic, uninterested tone. "But you know how weird that is, right? You're always wigging me out with this stuff."

"Funny thing to say to a bald man," he said, completing their worn-out banter with a half-hearted response.

Charmayne covered the dog's face in puckered smooches and baby talk. In return, Zoey bathed her mouth with frantic tongue laps. Paul shuddered. Zoey's tendency to lick her own poop was commonplace. After swapping germs with the dog, she planted a wet kiss on his forehead. He fought the urge to vomit and gave her a weak smile as she rushed out of the room, eager for another adventure with Joyce. If he didn't know better, Paul would have thought the two women *were* having an affair behind his back.

Once the door clicked in place behind her, Paul trotted to the kitchen window with Zoey nipping at his heels. He peeked through the blinds. The car backed out of the driveway, rolled down the street past the playground and disappeared over the crest of Bradbury Hill. With her gone for the day, he poured himself a glass of wine. He didn't need alcohol to get into a writing mood, but it never hurt, and with Charm gone he could enjoy it. He wasn't a heavy drinker like his father—he seldom tapped into the bourbon—but Charmayne didn't need a good reason to nag. She would criticize him for drinking a glass of milk if the mood hit her. Besides, whenever he drank it was difficult to keep his tongue in check. The lack of inhibitions compelled him to put her in her place, and the morning-after backlash was less than desirable, especially with a hangover. He figured he could have a few glasses now, knock out a post, and catch an afternoon nap before she got home.

Before returning to the den, he needed one more thing to set up his ideal writing environment. He rummaged beneath Charm's side of the bed and found what he was looking for. Grinning from ear to ear, he sat back down at his desk, slipped off his loafers, peeled away his socks and slid his bare feet into his wife's fluffy, pink house shoes. He curled his toes and sipped his wine, totally relaxed and ready to wow his readers. Zoey barked at the pink monstrosities on Paul's feet and let out a low growl.

"What? It's not like I'm running around in her panties."

Of course, if Charmayne ever found out, he might as well be wearing them. In her eyes, it made him a full-blown crossdresser decked out in lingerie and lipstick instead of a sensible man who happened to enjoy the comforts of fluffy house shoes. Besides, they relaxed him when he was writing and allowed him to channel his inner Joyce. He kicked at Zoey to shoo her away and set his mind on his blog post.

After years of pretending to be a woman online, coming up with new posts was a chore. It was easy in the beginning. Whenever Charmayne got on the phone with Joyce, he eavesdropped, making notes and researching their problems online for solutions. This simple routine netted him tons of articles, but things changed after one particular conversation. When she thought he wasn't listening, Charm went into great detail about the benefits of her bedroom "toys" and how they pleased her far more than Paul ever could. It was a brutal blow to his ego, but in the name of the blog, he used the information to craft one of his most popular posts to date. The article was a huge success, picking up hundreds of followers and tripling his income. He was delighted, but Charmayne took it personal. Embarrassed, she believed people might somehow find out it was about her. This brought some secret satisfaction to him considering the real shame in the article was his failures in bed. Joyce didn't seem to mind the post at all, but of course, he wasn't married to Joyce. Needless to say, it was reason enough for Charm to cut him off from sex altogether. A sexless marriage wasn't the end of the world for Paul. What hurt was how she became tight-lipped over anything personal from then on. These private insights fueled his blog and without them, he was a man drifting alone in a sea of estrogen. He was at a loss for fresh blog posts capable of retaining his female readership.

Another sip of wine warmed his bulging belly. Charmayne was always at the core of his problems. No matter what he did, she was always right and never satisfied. Why couldn't she see this blog paid for her trips to the day spa? They financed the coffee at Starbucks and the gas she burned parading around town. It wasn't like *she* worked. Yet, no matter what, she was the first to bitch about money. After the service—her moment of good behavior vanishing as soon as the bills came in—she even voiced her thoughts on the cost of Penny's funeral. Her comments came in swarms: sharp pricks of pain digging into his flesh and needling the base of his skull, time and time again.

"You know," she mused, the unemployed accountant in her brain working overtime, "we should have opted for the economy casket instead of the deluxe design you picked out. It's just going to rot away underground, for God's sake! What a waste! We could've saved a bundle!"

Paul groaned at the memory and took another sip, but the echo of Charm's voice ranted on.

"I'll tell you another thing. If all those people would've just given us the money wasted on all the flowers, the funeral wouldn't have cost near as much. Those floral arrangements are just going to die."

He grimaced and poured another glass, trying not to think about Penny's funeral and the ass Charm made of herself at the hospital, but the sting of those memories refused to fade. How could she be so callous? How could she say such cruel, thoughtless things while he grieved the loss of his sister? How could he have married such a self-centered bitch in the first place?

And like that, lightning struck. He shoved the thoughts of Charmayne from his mind and started a post about losing a loved one. Sure, it wasn't gender specific, but anyone could relate to this topic. Inspired, he typed up the title: "When a Sibling Passes."

His fingers glided across the keyboard in a flash, the writer's buzz taking hold and whispering the words in his brain. It was always this way with him. All he needed was a title and a loose idea for guidance. His uncanny ability to inject himself into any given situation—a trait he learned by using The Trick—allowed him to write most anything. The screen filled with words while his vision clouded over, shaping the scene before him in slide show flickers as if he were actually reliving the moments. The sterile hospital air hung thick in his nostrils. His sister's weak smile waned before she passed into a coma. Warm tears streaked his cheeks. The doctor stood before him awaiting his final decision— a life-changer no person should ever have to make. Knots tightened around his vocal cords, and a stone sank to the depths of his stomach. Charmayne was beside him, her mouth gushing absurdities. Fury surged his veins in a slow boil, dissolving all rational thought. His fingernails scraped at his scalp and the odd, throbbing pain pulsated from beneath his balls. The infernal whirl consumed him as a familiar voice whispered in his ear. *Clasp her throat, and squeeze the pompous indifference from her lips.*

A burst of pain shot through his eyelid, snapping him from the writing trance. Howling obscenities, he reeled back in the chair, his hands cupping his face. With the sudden shift in weight, the wheels caught on the area rug behind him, and he toppled over backward onto the floor. Startled from sleep, Zoey yelped and sought shelter behind the door.

"*Sonsabitches!*" Paul exclaimed, getting up slowly. His inflamed eyelid burned and began to swell, impairing his vision.

An angry red wasp buzzed past his face and landed on the soft, white glow of his laptop screen. The insect stared in defiance, staking claim to his workspace. It sauntered down to the keyboard, shifted its wings, and taunted Paul.

"You just signed your death warrant, you worthless sonofabitch," Paul growled, recognizing his father's voice somewhere within his own. He locked eyes on the wasp, eased his hand to his feet, and removed one of Charmayne's slippers. "I don't know how you got in here, but you won't make it back to the hive tonight. Oh, no, my little friend. Tonight, there'll be one vacant slot in the nest."

He struck out in a fluffy, pink flash smacking the keyboard. "Gotcha'!" he cheered.

The laptop squealed in small beeps as he held the shoe firmly down. A flurry of a's, s's, w's and z's raced across the screen, disrupting his article. He raised the slipper and expected a mass of guts and wings embedded in the tread, twitching to the tune of its own death throes, but nothing was there.

"Shit fire!" he yelled. He rummaged through the top of the desk, tossing a stack of papers to the side and almost tipping his wineglass. Somehow the creature escaped unscathed. He swatted at the phantom crawling sensation on his arm and again on the nape of his neck, but nothing was there. He scanned the airspace above his head anticipating another attack, but only dust particles floated down from the ceiling fan. "I know you're here!"

Scrutinizing the room, he realized he might never spot the insect before it struck again. Charmayne—priding herself as the interior decorator extraordinaire—was responsible for the look of his writing den, buying everything in dark red mahogany. He didn't complain at the time because the room's professional vibe made him feel like a successful writer. Now as he searched for a red wasp, the color scheme fought against him as a perfect camouflage. The desk, bookshelves and end tables were all possible hiding spots. The matching desk organizers, paper trays and pencil holder provided refuge, as well. His eyelid pulsed with throbbing heat, closing around his eye and hampering his vision. It was clear he may never find the culprit responsible. For all he knew, the wasp could have flown out of the room. Irritated, he abandoned the search and settled for finding pain relief. He deleted the string of random letters at the end of his post, saved the draft, and gave up for the day. Besides, he needed his pre-Charmayne nap before she came home, now more than ever.

The medicine cabinet only fueled his incensed mood. He stood in front of the mirror, inspecting his wound and gritting his teeth. His eyelid was completely swollen over. A large red welt engulfed the tiny white puncture mark and made his eye droop. He opened the cabinet door and discovered there was no pain medication. No aspirin, no ibuprofen, nothing. The closest thing he found was Charmayne's Pamprin. He popped two in his mouth, polished off the rest of his wine, and hoped it would do the trick. He rummaged through the cabinet for some cream or ointment to put on his eye, but came up short there as well. Torn between skin tag oil and Preparation H, he gave up. Instead, he took an ice cube from the freezer and held it to his throbbing eye. With his medical duties complete, he lay down and welcomed a much needed nap.

The bed was nice and comfortable, begging him to rest his bones, but the inflamed eye robbed his sleep. A headache emerged behind the swollen eye with a pulsating beat of its own. The two pains bounced off the surface of his face like tribal drums. To keep the ice in place, he was forced to lie on his back, a sleeping position he didn't prefer. He always lay on his side at night keeping his back to Charmayne's open mouth (an annoying trait she held both day and night). She snored like a starving bear, blasting his face like a thick, putrid fog if he didn't keep his back turned. If not for the ear plugs he donned as nightly armor, he would never sleep. Sleeping on his side was a habit he formed early in their marriage, and now he couldn't sleep any other way, even by himself. He silently cursed her.

His good eye focused on the ceiling fan, pushing Charmayne from his mind and hoping for a hypnotic effect to ease him into slumber. The blades rotated in a lazy swirl, forming a translucent blur. A slight gap between the base and the ceiling stared back like an eyeless socket. Something moved there in the darkness. Bolting upright, he jerked the chain. The blades slowed to a halt, and he probed the empty space. Nothing stirred. Had something moved there? Was it another wasp? Had the little bastards nested in his attic? What dumbass mounted their ceiling fan cockeyed?

The answer to the last question was simple. There was no doubt his drunken dad was the dumbass who first installed it many moons ago. It would have to be remounted. The gap would bug him until he fixed it, but to do this required professional help because electrical work was well beyond his skill set. Maybe there was a simple solution the collaborative minds of the internet could offer and if so, he could turn it into a Joyce project, along with a full written tutorial. The idea of the real Joyce mounting a step ladder in tight cut-off shorts and a size-too-small halter top as she hoisted the fan in place sounded appealing.

Lost in his fantasy, something moved within the gap again.

The wasp edged its way through the crack. Eyes locked on the red devil, Paul scooted off of the bed and crept to the dresser. He groped across the surface, searching for a weapon. When he landed on Charmayne's hairbrush, he smiled. Like a knight with a broadsword, he prepared for battle, but the fan blades deflated his valor. He could never get a clean swing with them in the way. His eyes never leaving the creature as it played peek-a-boo behind the safety of the fan, he resumed his blind search, knocking over Charm's jewelry box, toppling perfume bottles, and scattering her makeup. Finally, his hand grasped an aerosol can and a simple plan formed. With his left hand clutching the Aquanet, his right hand dug around in his pants pocket and produced his Bic lighter.

The wasp stared at him with a defiance Paul mistook for stupidity. It meandered around the base of the ceiling fan, unaware the odd-looking human intended to roast him. The two combatants circled the fan in a standoff until the wasp stopped and faced him. Its body shook from side to side, and its wings fluttered. Paul raised the can and ignited the impromptu flamethrower.

A stream of fire blazed toward the ceiling with a loud pop. The wasp took flight, zipping to a far corner of the room and seeking refuge on Charmayne's curio cabinet. Paul groaned at the black and brown streak scorched on the ceiling—dreading the inevitable ass chewing to come—but trudged on. He would endure his wife's berating, but only if this sonofabitch got what it deserved. He crept forward, the can leveled at the creature and the lighter ready to strike. The wasp batted its wings in a red frenzy, mocking Paul's pathetic attempt as if it were shaking its ass and taunting, *"Na-nana-boo-boo! You can't get me!"*

"You wanna' blow smoke, you worthless sonofabitch," Paul muttered, spittle flying from his lips. He closed his swollen eye and took aim with the good one this time, hoping to improve his odds. The flame launched across the room in a bright orange stream as Paul kept his finger on the trigger, chasing the beast. The wasp stayed just beyond the reach of the flames, circling the madman in swoops. It dived in, stinging the top of Paul's head.

"Shit fire! Shit fire! *SHIT!*"

"What the hell!" Charmayne screeched. Her shrill voice cut through Paul's lunacy, and he made a startled about-face, dropping the makeshift weapon. A bizarre mixture of anger and panic spread across his face. The skin on his scalp began to crawl and another burning welt erupted.

"There's a wasp!" he exclaimed, picking up his weapons. The metal end of the lighter burned his fingertip and he dropped it, shaking his finger and cursing. Undeterred, he picked it back up, scanned the room, and searched for his nemesis. "I'm going to kill the little bastard."

"*Stop!*" Charmayne yelled. She snatched her hairspray away, and before he could protest, she swatted the top of his injured head. "Have you lost your mind? You've set the drapes on fire, you idiot!"

Snatching up one of his shirts draped over the treadmill, she rushed to the burning drapes to smother the flames. Paul bit his tongue, hate-fueled pressure building up in him like steam as he realized it was his "Real Men Wear Pink" cancer support tee Penny gave him. Charmayne ridiculed him every time he wore it. She hurled comments about it suiting his line of work, but the logo, its color, or his blog weren't her reasons for hating it. Being a gift from Penny was reason enough. Now it lay smoldering on the floor, ruined. Of all the things she could have used, she selected this one out of pure spite. His itching scalp intensified, and he clawed the wound despite the pain.

"Why use a flamethrower?" she asked, bewildered. She tossed his ruined shirt into the wastebasket. "I don't even see a wasp."

"The fan blades were in the way," Paul mumbled, his tone acknowledging how silly his excuse sounded. "I wasn't thinking."

Charmayne spotted burn marks on the ceiling, and her face turned crimson.

"No shit, you blithering moron!" she exclaimed, throwing her hands in the air.

Paul's eyes shifted to the floor. He gnashed his teeth so hard his jaws ached, and he couldn't keep from scratching the persistent itch spreading across the crown of his head. He felt like he was digging a trench into his brain, but couldn't pull his hands away. He shook his head and blinked his eyes to clear the red haze, trying to conjure up an image and let his mind perform The Trick. It was much harder this time. Multiple images projected onto his wife in high shutter speed flickers—a French mime pantomiming mock anger, a giant windsock dancer from the used car dealership on Byars Drive with its arms waving in the breeze, Joyce in her cut-off shorts and halter top pouting, the Malum Rose High mascot yelling through a megaphone and pumping his fist, one of Santa's little elves crossing her arms and scowling—but nothing would stick. With his skin crawling and his bones on the verge of splintering, the sharp pain at the core of Paul's body throbbed through him in waves. In a last-ditch effort, he closed his eyes and reached deep into the back of his brain in desperation before he exploded.

"Look what you've done! The drapes are *melting*!" she shrieked.

When he opened them again, Charmayne transformed. Buried beneath the backdrop of her long black dress and pointy hat, her bright green face beamed. Paul fought back a grin, feeling the pressure subside.

"Is this funny to you? You could have burnt my house down!" she yelled, shaking her straw broom at him.

"I'm sorry, Charm," he said, trying not to laugh. It was hard to shake the mind trick once it stuck. "I was stung by a wasp. See?"

He pointed to his swollen eye first, and then lowered his head to show the welt there as well. He thought a little sympathy would help ease the situation and gave her his most pathetic look. Considering his pain, it wasn't hard to do.

Annoyed, she leaned in and stared down her long, crooked nose for a closer inspection.

"I don't see anything," she said, the wart at the end of her nose wobbling. Sympathy wasn't Charmayne's strong suit, but her hostile tone bumped down a few notches. Paul took what he could get.

"Don't worry about it," he said. The swelling might have subsided, but there was no way she couldn't see his damaged eyelid or the gaping wound pulsing on his head. It was her nature to ignore the obvious if it didn't benefit her in some way, so he let it slide.

"Have you been drinking?" she asked, sniffing him. Her witch face crinkled, and her over-extended nose waggled up and down like a deformed dildo. He giggled. "You know I won't abide you getting wasted in my house!"

"It was only a couple glasses of wine," he shrugged. "It helps me relax when I'm writing."

"I bet. It helped you set our bedroom ablaze, too, you blithering idiot," she huffed, marching into his writing den. In mid-stride something caught her eye. She spun around and Paul almost slammed into her, following on her heels like a scolded puppy. He found himself face to face with the wicked witch and knew her foul breath wasn't a part of his imagination. "Are those my slippers?"

Like a suspect returning to the scene of a crime, he stared at the fuzzy pink evidence and wished he could make it vanish with his mind. He considered making a joke—*Charm, I believe the slippers you're looking for are ruby red*—but thought better of it.

It was difficult to take her seriously with her green skin distracting him.

"Must have been her," he said. Zoey cocked her head to the side as if wondering why he was lying.

"You were supposed to be watching her." She snapped her fingers and pointed to her feet, commanding the dog's attention. Zoey darted across the room, her tail wagging and her little paws prancing. Charm's harsh tone eased into baby talk again. "Did you drag these in here, baby? Did you chew on momma's slippers?"

"If she answers you, I'll eat your hat," Paul said. She stared at him in bewilderment—her puzzled expression seeming to ask *what hat?*—and he couldn't hold back the laughter.

"Don't laugh when I'm scolding her," Charmayne barked. "You'll give her mixed signals. I should be scolding you! It's your fault for not watching her."

"She's not mine," Paul snapped, shocked at his own bold declaration. "Next time, take the mangy mutt with you."

"How dare you be so cruel to our baby," Charmayne gasped. She swept Zoey into her arms and covered her ears, appalled. "I *will* take her with me from now on!"

"Good," he smiled, relishing the victory. The dog would be one less thing to worry about when the wicked witch wasn't around. *I'll fix you yet, Charm, and your little dog, too.*

"You're wigging me out so bad, I don't even know who you are right now," Charmayne said, retreating into their bedroom with the dog in tow. Before slamming the door, she screeched, "You just earned a night on the couch, you heartless asshole!"

Paul didn't mind. Despite the aching throb of his eye and the welt on his head, the small victory invigorated him. He felt like a changed man. He poured more wine and spent the rest of the night wrapping up his blog post in blissful silence. When he finished—a little tipsy, but well relaxed—he curled up on the couch and slept, peaceful for the first time in a long while.

He dreamed of Joyce, and in his golden slumbers she was indeed a Joyce to behold. Like a seductive matador beckoning the frothing bull, her red, semi-transparent negligee fluttered in the breeze, teasing enough soft flesh to spark his imagination and ignite his unbridled lust for her. Billowing in from afar, her steamy curves swayed in a fluid, hypnotic saunter until she was within a whispered breath of him. The warm, soothing scent of vanilla on her velvet skin and the hint of lilac in her long, lustrous curls were intoxicating. Her almond eyes bore into his, and she grinned, biting her lower lip. Joyce was perfect in every way—a level of transcendence his wife could never aspire to—and his heart ached with a forbidden longing impossible to shake. The sexual tension pulsating between them was undeniable, but his mind retreated under the scrutiny of his own insecurities. This couldn't be real. Joyce would never be attracted to a bald, overweight man with nothing to offer and past his prime. He turned away, shamefaced and angry, but the heated desire burning between her thighs drew him back in like a moth to a flame. His neglected penis remembered its purpose, closing the gap between them. With a look of pleasant surprise, she took a step back and wagged her finger. She circled around him and pressed her body to his. Erect nipples caressed his back through the sheer fabric. She slid her hands around to his chest, her delicate fingers tracing the skin in light swirls as they descended over his stomach and down to his crotch. One hand cupped his balls in a gentle squeeze as the other gripped his throbbing penis. An involuntary shudder coursed through him—his temperature rising with every commanding stroke as her creamy lips kissed their way up his neck, her tongue exploring his ear and her teeth nibbling the lobe. Demanding immediate release, he struggled to hold back the urgent pressure mounting deep within his groin, but her strokes grew faster, and her tongue probed deeper in his ear. A relentless gusher raced up his shaft and exploded in a bloodcurdling scream as a sharp pain pierced his eardrum.

"What in the holy hell is going on in here?" Charmayne yelled, rushing into the room with a baseball bat held high over her head and poised to swing. Zoey backed her up, snarling at Paul's screams.

Paul rampaged around the room like a bucking bull, kicking over an end table, toppling a lamp, and tripping over the recliner. He gouged in his ear, digging for the wasp inside. The pain intensified, and he felt its wings beating within his ear canal. An angry buzz consumed all rational thought with deafening sound and white-hot pain. Pulling the lobe down to create a wider exit, he leaned his head sideways and beat at his temple like a high diver tormented by swimmer's ear. The burrowing wasp continued to sting. Blood gushed from his ruptured eardrum and streamed from his palm to his elbow, capturing Charmayne's attention.

"Shit fire! *Shit fire!*" he screeched, pounding his head.

"Stop that!" she demanded. She grabbed his wrist and forced his hand away from the inflamed ear. Blood streamed down his clenched jawline. Still screaming, Paul shoved Charmayne away—propelling her backward into the coffee table and crashing onto her ass—as he made a mad dash to the bathroom.

He ripped through the medicine cabinet, tossing out Band-Aids, pills, razors, and ointments but could not find tweezers. He demolished the bathroom closet, pulling down baskets of towels and washcloths, toilet paper, and shampoo, but the manicure set was nowhere to be found. Panicking, he changed course. If he couldn't pluck the sonofabitch out, he'd drown it. He flipped the nearest sink handle without thinking and plunged his head beneath the stream. Scalding water flooded his ear canal and he jerked his head up, gouging the back of his scalp on the faucet.

With an enraged howl, he threw a pain-fueled tantrum, punching the mirror and cracking the glass. Shards fell into the basin and the impact caused the medicine cabinet door to swing open. He yanked it off of the hinges in a fury, flinging it against the shower door with another shattering crash. He leaned his head above the sink and pounded until stars littered his vision, spittle and curses flying from his mouth. The crushed and mangled body of the wasp fell from its hiding spot and washed down the drain. Relieved, Paul plopped to the ground. The pain was immense, but the culprit was out. With his face in his hands, he wept.

"What the hell is wrong with you?" Charmayne asked, rushing into the room. She stepped over the clutter strewn from the ransacked closet and gaped at the shower's busted door. "Are you stark raving mad?"

"A wasp … in my ear," Paul mumbled through labored gasps. Bewildered and unable to hear him, Charmayne stared at him wide-eyed and threw out her hands in exasperation. Startling her, he yelled, "THERE WAS A WASP IN MY EAR!"

"Bullshit!" she laughed. "You've grown more hair in your ears over the last twenty years than you have on your head. A wasp couldn't penetrate that thick, waxy jungle with a bush hog."

She sighed and her hands motioned around the wreckage of the room, despite his icy glare.

"Was this all some sort of crazy act, Paul?" she continued. "Some twisted ploy for sympathy so I would let you sleep in the bed? Because believe me, you blithering idiot, that shit won't fly with me. I won't abide it."

"*An act?*" Paul snapped. "I gouged my own eardrum until it bled just so I could lie next to *you*? Are you serious?"

"What's all over the crotch of your pajamas?" she demanded. Like spotting a turd at the bottom of a pool, she pointed in astonished horror. "Were you whacking off? Oh my God, Paul! You're pathetic!"

Paul looked away in utter shame, longing for a hole to crawl into. He didn't need to see the evidence of his dreamland encounter with Joyce. He felt the embarrassment drying on his pajamas.

"It was a wet dream," he groaned, his head lowered in defeat. It was a humiliating admission, but on the shame scale, honesty was far better than her accusation. His wounded ego decided it wasn't good enough. "If we had sex every once in a decade, this wouldn't happen."

"You're not touching me, pervert," she said. The revulsion plastered across her face forced him to look away again. "I don't know what kind of sick, ear pain fantasy gets your rocks off, but I'll have no part in it."

"There was a wasp in my ear," he reiterated, pronouncing each syllable slow and deliberate. He snatched up a towel and started to wipe the shame from his pants, but Charmayne hit him across the top of his head. He winced as fresh waves of pain reverberated from the wound.

"Oh, no! Not on my good towels! You can sit in your own filth until hell freezes over for all I care, but you will not soil my towels," she scolded. She started for the door, but whipped back around. "This whole mess is yours to clean and so help me, Paul, it better be back to normal before morning! Acting a blithering fool in the middle of the night to get my attention. You should be ashamed!"

Zoey seconded the notion with a bark as Charmayne stormed out, kicking a shampoo bottle in her way. Deep down inside—somewhere in the dark rift of his rage infested mind—he hated the dog almost as much as her owner. The back of his scalp began to itch again.

The rest of the night was a long, daunting endeavor. After ten minutes of zoning out on the bathroom floor and clawing at the sore, itching welt plaguing his scalp, he hobbled to the kitchen. His ear throbbed with every breath and, not to be outdone, his swollen eye joined in; the two pains alternating beats. If he was going to get everything done to Charmayne's satisfaction—from removing the shards littering the shower, to restoring order in the empty bathroom closet—some serious pain relief would be in order. He cracked the seal on the Wild Turkey and took a shot to dull his agony. Four shots later, the bathroom was as close to right as he could get it. Bottle in hand, he spent the next hour beneath the hot shower. By the time he crashed on the couch, the paranoia of being attacked again robbed him of much needed sleep. He drained the bottle and kept a keen eye on the ceiling. Comfortable in their bed, Charmayne's snores echoed through the house. His hate for her grew.

He must have dozed off at some point, because he was jarred awake by the slamming of the kitchen door. Bolting upright, a rush of pain overtook him—like a skewer shoved into his afflicted ear. He winced in misery, tears streaming from his eyes. A loud, reverberating hum stabbed his brain and agitated the wicked hangover racking his body. Outside, Charmayne started the car and pulled out of the driveway. He was glad. The only cure for his ails was a little hair of the dog. Half asleep, he shuffled to the kitchen.

Somewhere between him and the sweet, mind numbing relief of bourbon, a brown ball of fur tangled his feet and let out a squealing yelp. Paul went sprawling, his chin catching the kitchen counter, slamming his jaws shut and chipping his teeth before crashing onto the linoleum.

"You lying bitch!" Paul yelled, spitting out a mouthful of blood and sandy grit. Electric charges surged up from the roots of his teeth and spread through his split gums as he climbed back to his feet. Not only did he have to suffer through the previous night's injuries—not to mention the fresh hell radiating in his mouth—he would also have to babysit her dog. Again. He grabbed the new bottle, plopped down at the kitchen table and found the note Charmayne left.

Gone to the Malum Rose Music Fest and won't be home until late. I'm still wigged out over last night's incident. Your behavior disturbs me! Wrath? Anger? Sexual perversions? This is not the man I married, and I won't abide surliness, Paul. I couldn't stand to look you in the eye this morning, so I wrote this note instead. Get your act together. We are still partners, and I expect better from you.

Charm

P.S. Keep an eye out for Zoey. Be sure and swap out her water this afternoon. Her little paws bump the bowl, and she hates wet and soggy pet food.

Paul crumpled up the note and tossed it in the trashcan, infuriated. He couldn't believe she refused to acknowledge his pain. Instead of sympathy, she turned the whole series of yesterday's events into him having anger issues! It wasn't like he beat her or strangled the dog. Nor was he a pervert, for God's sake. It was a wet dream. It's not like she caught him with his dick stuck in the vacuum cleaner and a lollipop shoved up his ass. It was natural for a sex-starved man to let off a little pressure in his sleep. If not for the wasp burrowing away into his ear, she wouldn't have even known about it. Who wouldn't go into a fit of hysterical rage with one of those little bastards buzzing around in there? He uncapped the bottle and took a swig.

His actions might have seemed a bit weird to anyone who didn't know him, but twenty years of marriage should have bought him some understanding. He was attacked three times in one day by wasps, the same creatures responsible for killing his own mother, mind you—a fact Charmayne knew all too well. Was it too much to ask for a little concern—some small gesture acknowledging a wasp attack might be a pretty big deal to Paul? Instead, she belittled him. Of course he lashed out. Of course he was angry. Just thinking about it now was causing his blood pressure to rise and his vision to tremor. Sweat poured down his head, and he noticed the front of his shirt was soaked with sweat.

He hobbled into his writing den and turned on the air conditioner, another annoyance he wished he could block out. It was Charmayne's bright idea to install window units instead of central heat and air, claiming it would be a waste of money. She always talked him out of the things he wanted because her word was law, and his opinions didn't matter. Two weeks later, she booked a trip to Hawaii—"just for the girls"—while Paul was left home to care for Zoey. He thought he might get a few pictures of Joyce in a bikini and some writing fuel for his blog. Instead, she tapped his credit card, racking up a bill double the amount central air would have cost. The anger brewing inside of him was like a runaway train, gaining speed with every grievance she ever inflicted on him. He took another drink.

The AC sputtered to life with an awful racket, and he cringed at the thought of how soon it would need replacing. It sounded like Mrs. Lowe—a lifelong chain smoker going on seventy years—struggling to clear her throat. After sputtering for a few minutes, the clogged rattle faded, and the unit blew semi-cool air into the room. Paul sank back in his chair and flipped open his laptop.

Logging into his blog, he noticed an unusually high amount of new comments on the latest post. Anytime there was a spike in traffic to *A Joyce to Behold*, Paul relished it. Comments and traffic equaled cash in this business. Intrigued and eager for a pain distraction, he read through them. His blood boiled as the repugnant title leapt from the page.

Women Are Stupid People!

Paul read the title over again in utter disbelief, the realization of being hacked dawning on him at once. He was mortified to find his name—*Paul Toliver* instead of Joyce

DeMarco—in the byline, accompanied by his own broad, goofy smile. The ridiculous picture winked back at him with the smuggest, shit-eating grin. His cocky air screamed, "Gotcha' suckers!" The photograph was taken on his birthday at the Howdy Club two years ago, one of the rare occasions his wife allowed him to drink without too much fuss. He was fuzzy on the details—the drunken buffoon waving back at him undeniable proof of his intoxication—but only Charmayne or Joyce could have taken the picture, he was certain of it. He kicked back another shot and read the article.

It was a complete expose outing him as the author behind all of Joyce's posts. Written in the most callous male chauvinistic tone, it blasted his followers for being gullible enough to buy into the act, using the most derogatory words to describe them. He cringed with every venom-filled sentence as the post revealed the entire charade, but the comments sunk a lead ball in the pit of his stomach. An angry mob lashed out across the internet and seized him by the throat, torches and pitchforks at the ready. His regular supporters, women who praised him for his gardening tips and dating pointers, were now foaming at the mouth to castrate him in the most creative ways. *A Joyce to Behold* was over. Furious, he slammed his fist down hard enough to rattle the window pane and scratched at his head, digging fingernails into an itch beyond reach. Clawing away at his scalp, the title caught his attention again.

Women Are Stupid People!

The words leapt out at him. Not because it was the most ignorant statement ever written, but because of the clue resting within those four words. Women Are Stupid People—W.A.S.P.

A horrible idea formed in his mind and Paul jumped up from his chair. Bolting for the kitchen, a burning acquisition circled his mind like vultures spotting fresh roadkill. He dug the note out of the trash and smoothed the crinkled piece of paper on the kitchen table.

Gone to the Malum Rose Music Fest and won't be home until late. I'm still wigged out over last night's incident. Your behavior disturbs me! Wrath? Anger? Sexual perversions? This is not the man I married, and I won't abide surliness, Paul. I couldn't stand to look you in the eye this morning, so I wrote this note instead. Get your act together. We are still partners and I expect better from you.

Charm

P.S. Keep an eye out for Zoey. Be sure and swap out her water this afternoon. Her little paws bump the bowl and she hates wet and soggy pet food.

Charmayne used the acronym in her note, not once, but four times. The first was easy. *Wrath? Anger? Sexual perversions?!* W.A.S.P. If not for the bombardment of aches and pains, he might have noticed when he first read it, but now the use of the word was obvious. *Won't abide surliness, Paul.* W.A.S.P. *We are still partners.* W.A.S.P. *Wet and soggy pet.* W.A.S.P. He couldn't believe it, but there it was in Charmayne's handwriting, bold as you please!

He re-read the note, scrutinizing every detail. Besides the acronyms, there were a couple of taunting anagrams as well. "Swap" and "paws" used the same letters as wasp. Even her mention of looking him "in the eye" and "keep an eye out" seemed like jabs at his swollen eye. She was laughing at him. The unmistakable feeling was taking hold, quivering the edge of his vision and coating the room in a translucent red. The same anguish he felt when his mother died. The same red-hot fury he felt every time his father reached for the belt. The deep pain throbbed below his ass like bones shifting through his skin. He couldn't contain it.

The air conditioner coughed and gargled in his den, but Paul ignored it. His eyes burnt a hole in the note, and his mind raced, the pieces fitting into place. Charmayne destroyed his blog. There was no doubt she was hateful enough. Not only did she sabotage his blog, she was *taunting* him. The note was proof. The only question remaining was what would he do about it? Like a shaken soda, years upon years of bottled anger bubbled up inside him, threatening to burst through the loose cap of his sanity and explode. The air conditioner spewed, sputtered and died, redirecting his wrath.

Paul charged the den like a lunatic, cursing the unit as the source of all his misery, raking fingernails into his cranium and ripping the wound. He flipped the power switch—oblivious to the red smear he left behind—but nothing happened. In a mad frenzy, he toggled the switch back and forth, over and over again. When it refused cooperate, he punched the vents as hard as he could. Pain surged from his fist all the way up his elbow. Clutching his bruised and busted hand, he plopped back down in his chair defeated.

The unit kicked on with a horrible groaning, bucking against the window frame in spasms. A swarm of wasps erupted from the vents en masse, pelting his chest, arms, and face like a fleet of tiny planes on a bombing run. He reeled backward, tipping his chair and toppling to the floor behind him. With a furious buzz, insects flowed from the air conditioner and blanketed the room in a crimson haze, their wings batting wildly. Welts raised on his skin as a bombardment of needles pierced his face, neck, and arms. He scrambled on all fours, searching for shelter he couldn't find. The air was heavy with wasps, and the group buzzing sounded like a symphony of rambunctious kindergarteners raking bows across violin strings, reverberating into Paul's punctured ear and traveling up and down his spinal cord. They dive-bombed him in waves while others crawled across his skin, itching and stinging their way to newfound, unsullied areas beneath his shirt and burrowing underneath his waistband. With hysterical alarm, Paul ripped off his shirt and shucked his pants, swatting at his assailants with wild abandon. Their bodies crunched and contorted beneath his blows, but the angry outnumbered the wounded, and each attacker left their mark. No flesh was left unharmed, and the most sensitive areas flared the worst—like pulling his dick from an ant bed. He danced around the den kicking, screaming, and cupping his exposed privates. The surging anguish was so immense his brain couldn't process it all at once. Struggling to maintain consciousness, he collapsed into a quivering ball on the floor.

In the dying light of his fluttered vision, he watched in horror as the swarm fled the room as one, funneling through a growing fissure in the ceiling—a gaping, crumbling chasm spanning the length of the room, never present before. Busted plank edges lined the hole, and he could see the storage boxes and stowed away furniture collecting dust in the upstairs attic. Charm's old, antique mirror glared down at him; a silent sentry standing guard over the forgotten accumulations of their marriage. Like a speeding train entering a tunnel, the darkness swallowed him whole in one large gasp, and the world ceased to exist.

When he came to, his battered body shook with fever, puffed and inflamed. The slightest movements rippled shockwaves throughout his system. His stomach lurched, and a stream of bourbon-soaked vomit hit the floor, splattering his nude body in slimy chunks of undigested food. Bile followed soon after, as well as several violent dry heave convulsions he fought to rein in. Below the illness and fatigue, somewhere deep within the dark abyss dividing his mind, his strongest emotion thrived—a juggernaut of pure, unstoppable rage. Wiping his mouth with an aching forearm, he glared up at the ceiling crack and a mad grin spread across his bumpy, swollen face. This was war.

Like the wasp from the day before, there was something in the attic these creatures were drawn to. Whatever the reason, the worthless sonsabitches congregated up there, and he wasn't waiting for another attack. It was time to go on the offensive. His meddling wife's betrayal was bad enough—*if she wanted to blow smoke, he'd burn her ass until she shit fire, by God*—but he wouldn't cower to a swarm of insects in his own home. He snatched the Wild Turkey and upturned the bottle, chugging large gulps like water on a sun-drenched afternoon in the Sahara. The deep gold bourbon burned his gullet in a liquid blaze, but he didn't care. Rushing down his throat faster than he could drink, the alcohol seeped from the sides of his mouth and down his chest, rivulets forming below his man-breasts and traveling down the bumpy terrain to his bare, festered crotch in tributaries. He pulled the bottle away and gasped for breath. With a scorching belch, he sprayed a fine mist into the air like a dragon bellowing steam. He closed his eyes, and the satisfying warmth of the whiskey spread throughout his body, dulling the pain of a thousand wasp stings. He slammed the half empty bottle down on the table. A golden ring of alcohol stained Charmayne's note, and he marched outside.

Paul stormed across his lawn and flung open the garage, naked as the day he was born. Hunched over her rose garden, Mrs. Lowe lifted her head as he passed and dropped the pruners in shock. He was sure he looked like a half-crazed, feral animal, but he didn't care. She barked something at Paul—a wailing rant about fornication and perverts doomed to burn in a lake of fire—but her protests were white noise in his focused mind. He rummaged through the garage, flipping over boxes and storage totes with one specific item in mind. Nestled away beneath a cabinet and hiding behind the leaf blower, he found what he needed—a four gallon backpack sprayer.

He purchased the sprayer last spring when researching better ways to spread liquid fertilizer around the oak trees at the edge of his property. He didn't care so much about the trees, but it made for a great article. The post netted him a lot of affiliate sales for this particular sprayer—highlighting the ease of use, the adjustable nozzle, and the sturdy backpack straps—but he never figured he would use it again. He twisted off the cap, grabbed the mower's gas can, and filled the tank with unleaded. He slung the straps over his shoulders and marched back into the yard. Mrs. Lowe was shaking a gnarled finger at him and shouting into her cellphone, and in passing, a snippet of her conversation broke through his one-track mind.

"There are impressionable children in this neighborhood, for God's sake!" she screeched. "I will not tolerate him parading around naked, Charmayne!"

In a phallic gesture, he aimed the nozzle at the old crone and sprayed a stream of gas at her. Aghast, she reeled back out of reach as it splattered like piss on her floral muumuu. She scurried into her house, the door lock clicking behind her.

Back inside, Paul took another long swig and drained the bottle. He wiped the dripping residue from his lips, dumped out a kitchen drawer, and pulled the barbecue lighter from the pile. On the lighter's long metallic wand, his crazed reflection grinned back at him.

"I'm coming, you worthless sonsabitches," he said, his gaze shifting from the lighter to the ceiling above. "I gotcha now."

In the hallway, he pulled down the drawstring for the attic hatch, unfolded the ladder, and made his ascent, each step creaking beneath his bare feet. Sunlight filtered through the attic vents and lit the triangular shaped room as Paul eased into the opening, armed and alert. The giant fissure running the length of his den's ceiling should have been visible, but it wasn't. Boxes filled with discarded clothes, forgotten breakables wrapped in newspapers, and family heirlooms were stored here, as well as the Christmas tree and holiday decorations. Abandoned picture frames, chairs, and end tables were stacked together in one corner collecting cobwebs— the old antique mirror still at his post. He ventured further into the attic—certain he would see the chasm wide enough to expose his den below—but the gaping hole wasn't there.

"Impossible," he muttered, clenching his teeth and digging at his scalp with the pointed end of the barbecue lighter. "I could *see* the mirror."

The enclosed, dusty space was dank, and a strong whiff of dead, rotten fish lurking somewhere behind the wall of boxes stopped him in his tracks. He wasn't sure what it was, but the odor didn't sit well on his stomach, and he wasn't ready for another round of barfing. Assaulting his nostrils, the putrid scent grew stronger, and he buried his nose in the crook of his arm, turning away. His eyes landed on a new horror.

"Shit fire!" he stammered, moving away from Zoey's stiff body. She lay on her side with her paws kicked out, never to bark at his odd behavior or tangle in his feet again. Her glazed eyes bulged with accusations, and for a moment Paul felt a tinge of guilt. He often daydreamed about her demise, but they were harmless fantasies. He never really wanted her dead—*did he?* He couldn't fathom how she got up here in the first place. A horrifying thought took hold, but the idea was insane. How many wasps did it take to drag a small dog up into an attic? A *closed* attic.

Zoey's skin rippled as something shifted inside her. Her belly inflated up and outward. Random cracking noises emitted from the dog as if her bones were splintering. Her stomach deflated with a gargled groan, then swelled up again. Paul took a nervous step back. It collapsed with another wet moan and extended again, each fluctuation stretching the flesh like a thin balloon. He aimed the sprayer's wand at the expanding corpse, his mind in petrified disbelief.

Two things happened at once, burning the memory into Paul's brain for the rest of his life. Zoey's eyes popped from their sockets, and her bloated stomach burst. A swarm of angry red wasps erupted from within, circling the crowded space of the attic. Paul turned to run, the full tank on his back sloshing with every step. He smacked into a low hanging beam, dropped to all fours, and scrambled over the Christmas tree in retreat to the attic's far corner. The wasps attacked, stinging his head, shoulders, and legs. He swatted at them and pedaled forward in a blind rage. The rotten fish smell grew stronger, and when he lifted his face up to its source, he screamed.

The back half of his attic was filled from floor to rafters with a massive wasp hive. Millions of hexagonal holes glared back at him like Zoey's empty eye sockets, brimming with a multitude of wasps emerging in an angry, humming rush. Slimy, pale green larvae squirmed and wiggled inside. Piles of dead wasps littered the foot of the hive, but the living carried on with their hateful lives like it was no bother. The screeching violin howl radiated from the nest's center, and Paul's mind screeched in return, begging for mercy. His fingers plowed into the back of his head, ripping flesh from the irritated wound in chunks. Blood spewed down his face, but he couldn't stop. The infuriating itch commanded him to remove the source, digging for bone if need be. A terrifying thought crossed his delirious mind. Last night's wasp—the sonofabitch that burrowed into his ear—must have laid eggs. Struck with the vision of Zoey's body blowing up like a balloon and exploding from the inside out, he could feel the bastards squirming beneath his skin. Blood streamed from his ears and eyes as his mind raced. *Are thousands of larvae—maybe even millions—hatching inside me?* His shattered mind believed it.

The hive roared to life in an enraged force. The riotous buzzing was a resounding thunderclap, vibrating the walls with earthquake force. Paul couldn't hear himself think. For a moment, all of his anxious fears—his split scalp, aching body, and the horde of babies incubating somewhere inside his brain—crumbled beneath the atmospheric pressure and the horror creating it. Ripping the hive's paper-thin walls to shreds, an immense red haze erupted from the nest and directed their full attention on him in unison. He braced for another round of pelting, fear and sweat rolling down his naked flesh in the attic's heat. The multitude hovered toward him like an angry red cloud, slow and calculating, a mindboggling swarm of epic proportions. The mass was so dense it obscured the tattered nest behind them. Every living wasp in the room fell into line and toward him on a mission. He awaited death, his sprayer loaded and his lighter at the ready. He wasn't going out without a fight.

In a fluid motion the colony swept forward and engulfed him in the eye of the storm. Horrified, he let out a scream of rage and prepared to burn himself alive, but to his astonishment, he was left untouched. The noise was maddening, but no wing grazed him and no stinger pierced his skin. They avoided him. He turned to watch the mass pass by and hover over what remained of Zoey's lifeless corpse. They covered her body, lifted her from the floor and floated her carcass back to the nest. Like a living wood chipper, they shredded the dog into pieces. Bits of bone, tufts of fur, and tiny morsels of meat pulled and separated from Zoey's suspended body. The swarm whittled her away into nothing over the course of a few minutes, patching the shredded nest and tucking morsels away in the hexagonal holes so the larvae could feed. Before he knew it, Zoey was gone.

His vision palpitated in rapid, disjointed flutters, and the familiar red haze coated his sight. The shifting in his bones snapped and popped like breakfast cereal, and he gritted his chipped teeth until he felt them crack, his inflamed mind never acknowledging the pain. The mounting rage seethed past his capacity to hold it in. He didn't have a wasp problem. *He was completely infested.* Zoey's fate made it clear. His house was overrun—if he didn't wipe them out now, they would feast on him, too. He primed the sprayer's pump, adjusted the nozzle to full force, and aimed.

"I gotcha now, you worthless sonsabitches!" he screamed, yelling at the top of his lungs and soaking the nest. Drenched wasps struggled to fly and took swirling dives to the floor, kicking and twitching their limbs in an effort to survive. Those fortunate enough to avoid the liquid darted at him and stung, assaulting in waves. In his rage, Paul could no longer feel their efforts. He doused himself from head to toe, bathing in gasoline and fumes. His crazed eyes gleaming in the chrome reflection, he held the lighter before him like an enchanted talisman holding all life's answers within the trigger. As he started to squeeze, her voice— the only voice capable of giving him pause—cut into his lunacy.

"Oh my God, Paul!" Joyce exclaimed, standing at the top of the ladder. Her frightened concern compelled him to look back at her, and she moved toward him, her hands reaching for him. "What the hell are you doing?"

"Get back!" he gasped, shooing her away. At the sight of her, the red haze lifted, and his anger subsided long enough to show genuine concern for her safety. His eyes darting all over the room, he flailed his arms and urged her to leave before the red swarm attacked her. "Run away! Get out of the house as fast as you can before they see you! They're everywhere!"

"Who are *they*?" she asked, puzzled. She took a cautious step forward, shaded her eyes from the blinding sunlight filtering through the vents, and quickly turned away, repulsed. "Why in God's name are you *naked*, Paul?"

Embarrassed rage flushed over him, his vision shaking, the red tint coating the room like blood from a severed artery. Joyce's words stung. Memories flashed through the jittering reel-to-reel of his mind, and one still clicked into place—Joyce laughing and snapping the Howdy Club picture of him drunk off his ass, the shit-eating grin plastered across his face. The picture she used to destroy his blog—his only true escape from Charmayne's clutches. They were both out to humiliate him.

"Why are you here? To gloat?" he snapped.

"I heard you screaming," she said, still refusing to look at him. "It smells like a gas station in—"

"You don't like me very much, do you?" he growled, moving toward her like a caged tiger. "Why do you find me so repulsive? Look at me, dammit!"

He lashed out and grabbed her wrist, whirling her round.

"You're wigging me out, Paul," Joyce gasped, pulling toward the open hatch. His grip tightened, and he jerked her back.

"Funny thing to say to a bald man," he returned, his reply automatic. His words felt jumbled, and his jaw ached. Breaking cracks ransacked his bones to the marrow, and coursed from his toes all the way to his eye sockets—a tectonic shift splintering his skeleton and shuffling the broken parts colliding inside him. "Tell the truth. Wrecking my blog was hilarious, wasn't it? I bet you two busted a gut typing it up—ruining my life!"

"You're not making sense," she exclaimed, her voice taking on a fever pitch as he dragged her through the attic. "What's wrong with you?"

"I loved you, you know? I knew I couldn't have you—hell, I'm not delusional, and I'm not the worthless sonofabitch you think I am—but that blog was my way of being close to you. It wasn't harmful, and I never pushed myself onto you in any way. So why do it? To make *her* happy? You can't begin to fathom the ball-busting, life-sucking misery I endure here!"

"I did *what* to make *who* happy? I don't know what the hell you're talking about!" she yelled, struggling to break free from his grip. He shoved her forward with all his strength, and she fell at the foot of the nest, sprawling. The wasps hovered around her, waiting for their moment to strike in eager anticipation. She moved to get up and he advanced, the wand aimed at her face. "Let me out, Paul!"

"Oh, no. You're staying right here with me," Paul said, the eerie sound of his father's voice mingling with his own. A deranged grin spread over his face. "You've caused more than your fair share of grief. I'm thinking I'll return the favor."

Joyce scrambled on hands and knees to get past him, fleeing toward the open hatch.

He could feel the widening smile split his skin all the way across his jawline, pushing his mangled mouth and crumbling teeth forward. Searing pain ripped along his shoulder blades, breaking free from his crawling flesh in a rush of wind around his ears. Lunging, he wrapped an arm around Joyce's throat, snatched her back in what could only be described as an odd, floating glide, and caught a glimpse of her terrified reflection in the old antique mirror, struggling in the clutches of a horrific creature his mind couldn't comprehend.

The horrid face was an alien combination of peeling human flesh and a protruding mandible. Antennae sprouted from a gashed, bald head and curled around to the front like horns. Transparent wings shimmered behind its back, and warped legs and feet hung below a swollen, bulging belly. One splintered forearm thrust Joyce against the nest and retrieved the dangling wand; the other clamped a deformed claw around a barbecue lighter.

"Are you insane? I won't abide this, you blithering idiot!" Joyce shouted at him. The sound of her voice agitated the constant pain radiating from his taint, surging through him like a swift, hard kick to the balls. Through the red haze, he stared at the bubbled over eyes glaring back at him in the mirror—*his eyes*, he acknowledged with fascinated horror—and his vision vibrated out of control. "You're hurting me, Paul!"

The final pain, the one he knew he couldn't avoid, erupted between his anus and his scrotum in an excruciating rip. The stinger formed; he knew it was time to use it.

"You hurt *me*, you hateful bitch!" he yelled, no longer able to hold back the fury bursting from his body. He wished he could rely on Penny's trick to contain his wrath. The desperate plea circled his draining mind and begged it to project any random fantasy to quell this loathe-filled anger, but it was far too late. He held the wasps responsible, the hateful little bastards breeding and infesting everything—infesting *him*. They would get their just desserts as well, but Joyce—she deserved to feel his wrath more than anyone. She was as responsible as the wasps in his newly formed eyes. Despite her wailing protests, he sprayed her down with the wand, wishing Charmayne was here to get hers.

"You wanna' blow smoke?" he said, holding the lighter out between them and applying pressure on the trigger. "I'll burn your ass 'til you shit fire, Joyce!"

"*WHO IS JOYCE?!*" Charmayne screamed at the top of her lungs before the attic exploded in flames.

KAIROS CHAMBER

By Feind Gottes

They passed the weather worn sign, with its paint flaking and falling off, boldly pronouncing their entrance to "The Drive-in of the Damned." It didn't appear particularly ominous, but Al's hand was still chilled from the operator's touch. Emily giggled at the sign, placing her hand atop Al's on the shifter of his brand new Ford Mustang, one of only a few V289s released in its initial run. A shiver went up his arm at the soft touch of his lovely date for the evening, but he still couldn't shake the chill the operator had given him.

"That cat was a real snap case. Did you get a load of him?" Al asked his date.

Emily looked at him with a coy smile, "Don't sweat that flake, Daddy-O! Let's get down to the passion pit!" She gave him a wink to emphasize her enthusiasm.

"Right on!" Al revved the Mustang's engine, as Emily revved his.

Al steered his new ride around a bend in the path, giving them a view down into the quarry. Neither of them had ever seen anything like it before. Several screens were arranged in a circle at the bottom of the quarry. There were so many that neither of them could tell how many there were. It seemed anyone coming there had a screen all to themselves.

"Now that's a real passion pit!" Al exclaimed. "Looks like no one is going to be bothering us. That's for sure!"

"Should we make out, or bug out?" Emily asked, with a smile and a wink.

"Let me clue you in, baby. Albert Laskey doesn't bug out … unless the fuzz shows up." He shot her a wink of his own.

"Bad Al Laskey? I think I like that." Emily giggled, giving his hand a squeeze. "Do you think we'll be able to see the Blood Moon from down here? I don't wanna miss that."

"The paper said, and I quote, 'For June, 24th 1964 the lunar eclipse will be visible from 9:06 p.m. to approximately 10 p.m.'. It's June 24th so I guess we'll know in about an hour. I don't know how good our view will be once we're down there, baby. I didn't know that kind of thing was your bag. Very cool." He shot her another wink and a smile.

"I go ape for rarities like the Blood Moon. You have no idea!"

"If we can't see it we'll bug out to a better spot! Can't disappoint my baby on our first real date."

The Mustang rounded the final curve to their screen for the evening, coming to a stop just far enough back so the couple didn't have to strain their necks to see. Neither of them expected to see much of the flick other than the first few opening scenes, but Al saw no need to get a sore neck for a few minutes of some anonymous flick. He set the transmission in first gear, set the parking brake, then turned the engine off. He had to admit he immediately missed the purr of the two-hundred-ten horses powering the 289 V8 of his new ride. Al was a *sosh,* not a dirty greaser, so, of course, Al Laskey Sr. had actually bought the car for him.

"What movie are we supposed to be seeing anyway?" Emily asked.

"I dun know. This place is a little weird. Probably some cheap Vincent Price flick at best."

"Ooh, I love scary movies!" Emily squealed.

"You are one far-out chick, aren't ya? Blood Moons? Scary flicks? Next you'll tell me you're a female vampire!" Al laughed.

She looked at him with deadly seriousness then said, "I vant to suck your …" Emily paused with a sly smile, "von eye trouser snake. Ha! Ha! Ha!"

They burst out laughing. The sun was just beginning to dip in the late June sky, only a few days removed from the summer solstice. They still had about an hour before it would be dark enough for the movie to begin, which would coincide with the lunar eclipse creating the Blood Moon Emily insisted they not miss.

"I'm bored," Emily said, still wiping the tears of laughter from her eyes. "Why don't ya' hit the music machine, sugar."

"Sure thing, baby."

Al twisted the radio knob, bringing it to life. Immediately the sound of The Beach Boys "I Get Around" filled the air. Al started bobbing his head to the beat while Emily tapped her foot.

"So, are you one of those Beatlemaniacs or a little surfer girl?" Al asked.

"I like a little bit of everything as long as you can tap your foot along to the beat. I'm not one of those chicks screaming at the airport for the Fab Four if that's what you're asking. I don't get those people at all. It's a band! Get over yourselves! Now send that cutie, Ricky Nelson, my way, and maybe I'll make him scream!"

"You are one bad baby!" Al smiled.

"Oh, come on! Who's your fantasy girl? Let me guess. Hmmm. I think you look like a Brigitte Bardot kinda' guy, or maybe Marilyn Monroe?"

"I wouldn't kick either of them out of bed for eatin' crackers, that's for sure! But if you're gonna make me pick just one, I'll take Bettie Page every day of the week and twice on Sunday! She's one hot momma!" Al smiled.

"If I let you pick two?"

"Now you got me in the hot seat. Do I go with two brunettes, or do I pick a blond to complement the brunette? Tough one, but since we're in pure fantasyland I'd have to go with Audrey Hepburn. Maybe they'd pull a little bad cop, *very* bad cop on me!" He winked at his date.

"Well now. Who's the real bad one now?" She returned his wink with one of her own.

The radio faded from The Beach Boys to "Needles and Pins" by The Searchers, before the DJ interrupted for a commercial break. Al and Emily continued their small talk as advertisements for things they didn't care about played through the speakers. Their banter seemed more like that of two old friends than a couple out on their first date, a fact which wasn't lost on either of them. Their friendly flirting was the only thing giving lie to that fact.

Commercials faded to the serious voice of the news announcer: "The search continues for three civil rights workers who disappeared on Sunday night after their release from a Mississippi jail. The three young men, Michael H. Schwerner, Andrew Goodman, and James E. Chane, failed to check in upon their release, which is considered standard procedure. Federal authorities are now heading up the search amidst fears the three may have become victims of foul play."

"I'd hate to see those boys turn up dead," Al stated, sternly, "but they did go poking their noses in where they didn't belong."

"That you or your daddy talking?" Emily raised an eyebrow at him.

"Don't get me wrong. Black folks down there should be allowed to vote and just plain be treated like actual human beings. I'm just sayin' they kinda' went lookin' for trouble, and it looks like they found it. I don't really doubt they'll find 'em hanging from a tree somewhere in the swamp, especially the black kid. I'm not racist, I'm just sayin' down there in Mississippi, *they* are. There's no sugar coatin' that fact." Al's eyes seemed to plead his case as much as his eyes.

"I know you're probably right but it ain't right. Those kids are younger than we are, and they don't deserve to die because they were trying to do some good in this world!" Emily began to tear up, "Black, white, whatever. We're all just people!"

"I'm just glad we don't live down there. Tonawanda, New York may not be perfect, but it ain't the backwards backwoods swamp of the Mississippi!"

"Amen, brother!" Emily said, lifting her hands to heaven.

"I don't think I'm the preacher type, darlin'! However, if you feel the need to get on your knees and give … uhhh … confession, then be my pretty little guest!" He wagged his eyebrows, expecting to be slapped.

"Only priests take confession, Daddy-O, so you're preaching to the wrong choir. Too bad!" She sneered, sarcastically. "I was starting to like you."

"Consider me converted, baby!" Al shouted. "Hallelujah!"

This time Emily greeted his words with a slap, albeit a light one. The couple shared one laugh after another while waiting for the sun to set and the Blood Moon to rise. As they waited the sexual tension between them filled the cabin of the Mustang to overflowing. They flirted back and forth, each with their own plan on how they wanted the evening to proceed. Al seemed to Emily as though he were holding back slightly, while Al couldn't understand why Emily was so anxious to see the Blood Moon.

Finally, the sun sank along the horizon, its last dying rays creating a halo. Emily's dark brown eyes stared with excitement into the bright blue rings of her companion. Al stroked her dark brown locks gently as he leaned forward, hoping her ruby red lips would meet his for their first kiss of the night. Emily didn't disappoint, reaching up to grab a handful of Al's short blond hair and pulling him roughly to her. Their lips met, closed to start, before parting as the passion of their kiss turned into a soft dance of tongues.

Emily pulled back from the kiss, squealing in delight and confusing her date for a moment. "It's starting!" She exclaimed. "Yay, Blood Moon!"

"Oh, cool!" Al feigned excitement, following his date's gaze to a spot in the sky behind him.

"I'm so glad we can see it! Ooh, and look!" She pointed to the movie screen. "Our movie is starting too. Hope it's something good!"

"Or boring," Al said, smiling. "That way we won't feel bad about missing it." He winked at Emily who smiled in return.

Names of actors and actresses popped on the screen that neither recognized, but they assumed they were about to see some low budget horror film at best, given the name of the place. The screen faded to black before the title blazed onto the screen in red scratchy letters, announcing the movie as *Kairos Chamber*. Neither of them had any clue what that even meant.

"Is that a name or a place?" Emily asked, scrunching up her face.

"Not a clue. I hope it's not subtitled. I hate reading a movie."

"Can't read, huh?" Emily giggled.

"'To the moon, Alice!'" Al shouted the infamous Ralph Kramden retort, followed by laughter.

"Please do! Look! It's about half-red now." Emily could hardly contain her excitement.

"You certainly are fascinated by this thing. May I ask why?" Al lifted an eyebrow.

"Monsters come out to play when there's a Blood Moon! Maybe we'll see a werewolf!"

"Are you from outer space? If I see a werewolf, I'm laying rubber!"

"I didn't take you for a candy-ass. Perhaps I need to reconsider this date." She gave Al a stern, motherly look.

"Your loss, sweetheart." He winked at her. "Plus, it's a long walk home."

"You'd make a helpless little girl, one *this* sexy, walk home alone in the dark?" She batted her eyes at him.

"Well …"

"Oh damn! Look!" Emily squealed out suddenly.

"What?"

"That actor. He—" She looked from the screen to her date, then back again, "—looks just like you. That's either super cool or super creepy. You didn't tell me I was dating a movie star!"

Al looked to the screen, unable to believe the resemblance, "Good golly Miss Molly! Would you look at that."

Al's jaw dropped open as the pair sat staring at the screen. The resemblance took them both aback. Emily was smiling fascinated by the coincidence, while Al seemed to be almost horrified by what he was seeing after the initial pleasant shock. As he stared at the screen, his grip tightened on the steering wheel. He wriggled in his seat. Both were mesmerized for the moment by what they were seeing.

The actor on the screen appeared to be having a date over to his place for a cocktail before the pair went to dinner. Al's acting doppelganger seemed to be a young and affluent man, not unlike the "real life" Albert Laskey, Jr., with his eyes glued to the screen. The young man stood at a small bar making small talk with his date, while he made a cosmopolitan for her and poured two fingers of scotch on the rocks for himself. Their banter wasn't anything out of the ordinary. In fact, it was rather droll and labored, but the actor wasn't exactly Cary Grant or, Emily thought, that hottie James Dean who was taken too soon. The pair on-screen finished their drinks, continuing their banality with Al's twin suggesting one more cocktail before they left for the evening.

Emily looked over at her date, still stunned by the resemblance. Al was practically white-knuckling his grip on the steering wheel, and perspiration was visible on his brow. He appeared either to be extremely uncomfortable or ill to Emily's eye.

"Are you okay, Al?" she asked, with genuine concern.

Emily's voice coaxed Al from his wide-eyed stare at the screen. "Yeah, yeah. It's—it's just odd, I guess. It's like watching myself." He feigned a smile, but he was clearly discomfited.

Emily leaned across the short space between the bucket seats to rub his thigh. She wrapped an arm around his, resting her head on his shoulder as they continued to watch his twin on the screen. Al's twin was at the bar making another drink for the young couple, though he glanced nervously back over his shoulder to see if his young date was watching him. She wasn't. Al's doppelganger pulled a piece of red lace from his pocket, wrapping the ends tightly around each hand. Emily held her breath as the man crept up behind his date, took a deep breath, then swung the red lace bound between his hands, over her head, and around her throat. The man's eyes went wide as he smiled insanely, pulling the red lace tight around his would-be date's neck. The woman kicked out in her struggle as Al's twin strangled her from behind. The woman reached up, struggling to free herself or to scratch her attacker before slowly slumping over in the high-backed Victorian chair she was seated in. As they watched, Al tried to close his eyes or look away, while Emily stared at the screen with a smile on her face, apparently amused by the spectacle.

"You are a real bad daddy, aren't ya?" Emily lightly slapped Al's thigh, "Do I need to check your pockets, mister?" She giggled.

"Uh … no." Al stuttered. "Of course not."

"Ooh, look! The Blood Moon is full now!" Emily tried to change the subject, seeing that her date was shaken from the scene they had just watched.

"That is very cool." Al tried to act enthused, but he was still shaken by what he had just seen.

Emily slid her hand to his crotch, giving him a gentle squeeze while whispering, "Need a little cheering up?"

Al turned back to her with a smile, catching the movie screen in the process. "Oh shit!" he shouted.

"That wasn't the response I was hoping for, sugar."

"No! Look! Now it's you!" Al was shaking, pointing up at the screen.

The scene of the movie had switched to some sort of flashback. A young man walked along a dirt road in what appeared to be ancient Greece, though Al wasn't entirely sure. As he walked, a young woman popped out of the trees along the side of the road. The actress was a dead ringer for his date, only with longer, curlier hair. Al couldn't help feeling a stir in his groin as the woman, like his date, was beautiful. Only her twin on the big screen was completely naked. Her long, dark hair hung nearly to her supple backside.

The tables had turned. Al was enthralled by the image of his date's doppelganger on the big screen. Emily was seemingly uncomfortable with seeing herself. The young Greek, like any young man, was instantly mesmerized by the woman's alluringly beautiful nudity. He asked the woman if she was a temptress sent to test him, to which she replied that she was merely lost in the woods, having lost her dress in a thicket of briars. He asked the woman to step back out of sight while he procured her a new garment to cover herself. A short time later, he returned with a dress he had borrowed off a drying line and handed it to Emily's beautifully naked twin. Al couldn't help but be thoroughly aroused, while Emily stared in wide-eyed terror at her doppelganger. as he had a few moments before at his own.

"Are you alright, baby? Shocking seeing yourself on a movie screen, isn't it?"

"I—uh—it's weird," Emily said. "It's like—um—seeing myself in a past life or something. It's freaky."

"We can always bug out if you want. I didn't like seeing myself up there either. This whole place is a regular creep show."

"Umm … I don't think we can. It's creeping me out, but I think we have to stay. I don't think we can leave. Not yet, anyway."

"If Al Laskey wants to leave, ain't nobody gonna stop him, baby," Al said, as if it was a fact written in stone.

"Then there's no harm staying a little longer. I'm fascinated how they knew … I mean … how authentic this seems. It's uncanny— the resemblance—that choker guy was to you, and now this hot momma looks like my twin. Helluva coincidence if you ask me. It's creepy and fascinating at the same time."

"I guess you're right. Besides, we can always make out if it gets too creepy." Al winked at her.

Emily slapped him, playfully. "Ewww! Looks like the creep is in *here*! Now shush, so I can watch! The Blood Moon is about over anyway."

"Yes, ma'am." Al said, with a smile.

They returned their eyes to the screen and Emily's doppelganger. The young couple on-screen soon arrived back in the home village of the young man, whose name is Menippus. Soon after, they made plans to marry. The young woman, Empusae, showered Menippus with gold and silver. Many servants appeared to come out of nowhere, though he was too blinded by her beauty to question any of it.

"What a dummy!" Al cried. "Can't he see she's evil or something?"

"Think if I stripped down naked right here and now, you'd stop to see how evil I am?"

"Well … that's different."

"Really? How? Because you didn't pick me up naked on the side of the road? I could be the devil in the flesh, Daddy-O and you'd miss it, because you're a man, and you think with the wrong head." She winked at him, while giving his crotch a squeeze.

"Well, if you put it that way …" He smiled at her. "But if you started showering me with gold and silver, I think I'd get a bit suspicious right quick."

"You might be surprised." She winked at him again. "Now shush, and watch what happens."

The scene shifted to the day of Menippus and Empusae's wedding. After the ceremony, a grand reception ensued with a table heaped with food and wine, along with minstrels playing as their guests made merry. Menippus introduced his new bride to his best friend, Apollonius, who seemed strangely skeptical of the bride, eyeing her with caution, though he greets the woman with a smile. While Empusae consorted with her many servants, Apollonius insisted Menippus take a private walk with him. Once out in the courtyard and away from the guests noise and Menippus' new bride, Apollonius cautioned his friend against his choice of a bride. Of course, Menippus took offense as any man would, and grew angry with his lifelong friend. Apollonius told his friend something about Empusae wasn't right, and he believed he could see through her disguise. Menippus grew even angrier. Apollonius pleaded with Menippus to listen, telling him he believed his friend's new bride was nothing more than a demon in disguise. He told Menippus he believed Empusae was some sort of succubus that will devour him. Empusae, who had secretly followed the pair, stepped out, demanding Apollonius leave and never return. Menippus pulled his sword on his best friend, putting an exclamation point on the demand. Apollonius reluctantly left, though his seed of doubt had been planted in Menippus, who then looked at his bride with new eyes.

Empusae took Menippus' arm but could see Apollonius had planted doubt in her husband's mind. They rejoined their guests to feast and dance, though Menippus began to brood. As the sun sank slowly in the sky, the guests filtered out, with the exception of the few who had imbibed too much wine and passed out along the bench seats of the many tables. A few of them had fallen against the wall in various places. One young Greek was passed out cold on top of a table and facedown in a plate of grapes, which would likely stain his face for days to come. Empusae led Menippus to their bed chamber, though her hold over him had become drastically reduced by Apollonius' words. Once alone, Menippus confronted his new bride about Apollonius' accusation. She resisted, but doubt had broken the veil hiding her true nature. Through the chamber's window, Menippus watched a Blood Moon rise behind his bride, shedding the veil even further. No longer did he see the beautiful woman he had met on the road. Beneath the illusion, she was something altogether different.

Menippus demanded his bride tell him who she really was. Empusae fell to her knees, begging Menippus not to force her to confess, but he commanded her to do so. Tears streamed from her eyes. Empusae stood before her bridegroom, while her servants screamed in terror. The gold and silver she had showered upon Menippus vanished, along with her servants, as their screams echoed through the chamber. In the red light from the Blood Moon, Menippus finally saw his bride in her true form. His eyes went wide with terror as the gorgeous woman he met on the road transformed before his eyes. Empusae now had a mechanical left leg made of brass, while the other seemed to be that of an ass complete with cloven hoof. His eyes scanned up in horror as her torso turned to one of a serpent with her soft, supple breasts now sheathed beneath dark yellow scales. A forked tongue shot out from a face turned ancient and haggard. The soft, smooth skin of her arms remained, but now led to hands that stretched out into sharp talons that looked as deadly as the fangs now poking out from her once full lips.

"Damn!" Al cried. "That's worse than finding out your new wife has a dick!"

"Shhhh!"

"Sorry, sorry."

Menippus cried out "Why me?" from the drive-in speaker hooked on the Mustang's window.

Al watched, fascinated, as his date's evil twin explained to Menippus she always chose the young and beautiful, because draining them granted her eternal youth. Al couldn't help to flinch as the monster on the screen shot forward, ripping Menippus in half with her clawed hands and spraying blood everywhere, before shoving her face into the cavity and sucking him dry. Empusae finished with a slurp, licking her lips as the camera zoomed in on her blood soaked face until it is focused on her bright, burning yellow eyes before fading to black.

"Damn!" Al shouted, with a smile plastered to his face. "I don't know what the hell this flick is supposed to be about, but it's a real trip!"

"Like that, did ya?"

"I don't know if I'd say *like,* but did you see the way she ripped him apart? That was cool! Glad she only looked like you! You're not secretly a Hollywood starlet are you?" Al joked.

"Maybe, maybe not. There was a Blood Moon tonight, so maybe you should be careful." She looked up winking at him.

"Well, at least I know that wasn't actually you, unless you're about … what? Four or five thousand years old?"

"I'm much older than that, sugar." Emily said, slyly, "Better watch out! Maybe I only agreed to a date with you so I can drink your blood in order to keep this fantastic figure. Bettie Page ain't got nothin' on me, Daddy-O."

"*Now* who's the creep?" He cringed back from her, playfully, "Oh crap! Looks like I'm back up."

"Oh sweet! Who you gonna strangle this time? Are you from Boston and didn't tell me?"

"I never strangle and tell." Al blew her a kiss.

"Careful now! You saw what I just did to that Greek kid."

They both laughed.

Back on the screen, Al Laskey's double drove slowly around a small town that looked eerily similar to one not far from where they sat. Al squirmed in his seat, discomforted by the image. Emily couldn't understand why seeing an actor that looked like him made him so uncomfortable, though she had growing suspicions after seeing her own twin up on the big screen. Al's evil twin rolled slowly down the town's main drag, in a car that also seemed eerily similar to the Mustang they were sitting in. He was ogling young, teen girls as they made their way home from school. Wet leaves clung to the curb, showing it must be late spring, just as it had been a couple of weeks ago. Al's twin came to a stop as a group of cheerleaders bopped into a malt shop. He sat there silent, staring and then reaching down to rub his privates through his jeans as he watched the young girls through the window.

"Ooh, you are a real bad daddy," Emily said, squeezing his arm tighter while running her hand up and down the inside of her date's thigh. "So tense," she turned and whispered in his ear. "Want me to help you relax?"

Al was frozen, his eyes glued to the screen, as though he were under a spell not even the suggestion of oral sex could break.

On the screen, his twin continued rubbing and squeezing his privates while watching the teenage cheerleaders through the picture window of the malt shop. He watched until the girls had their orders filled and moved out of sight. He breathed a sigh of relief as his twin restarted his car and moved on. The relief was only momentary, as the camera zoomed in on the actor's keychain. A single shell casing with the initials "APL" carved into it, exactly like the war souvenir his father had given him. It dangled from his keyring, slowly rocking back and forth. Al stiffened, praying that his date had missed it.

Emily looked from the screen to the key chain hanging from the Mustang's ignition in utter disbelief. She could sense Al holding his breath as she turned the shell casing in her fingers, revealing those same initials, APL. She let it go as if it were red hot.

"What's the deal, Al?" Emily asked, as she retreated to the passenger side of the car again.

Al was sweating, not sure how to reply. "I—I—I don't know. This is crazy!"

"Crazy, because it's true?" Emily demanded.

"How … how could it be true? That's insane!"

"He looks exactly like you and has your same exact keychain! Tell me you aren't the sicko I'm seeing up there!"

"Of course not! Are you telling me you're really some blood-sucking demon that has survived thousands of years?" Al thought his only hope was to take her focus off what they had just seen.

Emily was silent a moment. "Empty your pockets."

"No! Why?" Al asked, confused again. "You didn't answer me! Are you some ancient succubus or not?"

"Just empty your pockets, Al! If you don't have a piece of red lace hiding in there, then we'll bug out. But if you do, you're gonna be sorry you ever met me." There was fire in Emily's eyes as well as her words.

"Now hang on a second, damn it! I ain't doing nothin' until you answer me. Go on! Lay it on me! Let's hear some lingo, or you can beat feet home, girl!"

Emily turned away, unable to look the man she now suspected of being a murderer in the eyes. *Breathe and just think*, she thought to herself. So she had picked a date with a deep dark secret! Didn't she have many deep, dark secrets of her own? While she sat trying to decide her next move, she glanced back to the movie, still playing on the screen. Al was onscreen, larger than life, but she recognized this scene. It was the moment they had met two weeks prior to this night. She watched as her twin approached the brand new, bright red Mustang, with the blond hunk sitting behind the wheel. She tapped on the window to get his attention. Al had been staring across the street when the tap snapped his head around. He looked up startled, expecting to see some local fuzz but swiftly but swiftly changed to a hundred-watt smile, seeing the dark-haired beauty peering through his passenger window. She now had no doubt about who her date was, but her own veil had been broken too.

"I guess there's no point in continuing the charade any longer." Emily said, softly.

While Emily was distracted by the screen, Al had pulled the red lace from his front pocket, wrapping it firmly around both hands, ready to choke the life from her as he had so many others before her. He leaned in, about to wrap the lace around her pretty neck when she turned back to him with her veil of deception removed. A thin, forked tongue shot from between her supple lips as she spoke, accentuating her S's into hisses. Even though he had seen her transformation a few moments before, it was another shock altogether to see her true form just inches away. Emily stared at him with her snake-like hypnotizing yellow eyes that held him as still as the dead.

"What are you?"

"I've had many names, in many places, in many times. The Greeks called me and my sisters *empusa,* which seems as good a name as any. I am a daughter of Lilith, the true first woman. We are the cursed, the outcast. And you? You're dinner." Emily's disdain for man, especially Al, dripped from every syllable she spoke.

The red lace dropped from Al's hands as the empusa's clawed hand punched into his chest. His jaw dropped as she held his still beating heart up before eyes that didn't know they were already dead. Al's body slumped against the driver's seat as she gulped his heart down with a hard swallow. Before his blood went cold, she dove face first into the gaping hole in his chest, sucking up every last drop. The demoness sat back, savoring the last of Albert Laskey Jr.'s essence in her mouth, and suddenly burst out laughing at the thought his blood wasn't the fluid he had hoped she'd be slurping down tonight.

She leaned back in the passenger seat, wondering if the screen would show her anything after this night. She contemplated how stupid mankind was. She and her sisters had sent souls to their father in hell since the dawn of time, and yet they were nothing more than forgotten stories of myth now. *At least early men had feared the Blood Moon*, she thought, *though they knew not why.* They fed at will, but under the power of a Blood Moon, they always fed. She burst out in laughter once again, finally remembering the film's title, *Kairos Chamber*. Seeing Menippus again after all these years should have jogged her memory sooner, but the insignificant are easily forgotten. She suddenly remembered that *kairos* was a Greek term meaning "something akin to a perfect or opportune moment."

"*Kairos Chamber*! We were sitting in it the whole time!" She laughed until tears rolled from her eyes.

THE BEAST WITH TWO BACKS

By John Dover

"That bitch!"

"Frank, you gotta calm down."

"I don't gotta do nothin'. She wants to run around behind my back like that? Fine! But I don't gotta calm down about it."

Frank drowned his fifth shot of Wild Turkey, paying no heed to the uncomfortable eavesdroppers disturbed by his belligerence. His audience flinched as he hammered his glass to the table, signaling the assassination of another round of his brain cells.

It was four o'clock on a Thursday afternoon. Too early for most to be one or two shots in, much less a half bottle, but Frank was pissed. Jimmy sat across from him, shrugging and silently apologizing for his companion's behavior. Sorry, not sorry. Jimmy had just delivered the news Frank's wife of three years was stepping out on him with the pre-med student renting a room down the block from his own house.

"Fuckin' bitch!" Another sloppy toast to the cheating gods, and Frank sent a sixth hearty pour down his gullet. The rickety table he and Jimmy were commiserating at shook with the heft of Frank's heavy fist. His husky frame carried more weight than the battered table was used to taking from its regular customers.

"Come on, man, you gotta calm down a bit. We're gonna get kicked out."

"You think I care what these lowlifes think? I've busted half'a them for drunken, disorderly, and disturbing the peace. They can suck it." He went to fill his glass again but missed his target, christening the table with half the liquid that was meant for his chalice of misery.

"Even worse. Piss 'em off too much, and they know exactly who to call the local patrol down on. I don't feel like calling in the favors and dealing with paperwork that'll cause, so let's settle down a bit."

Frank grimaced, staring into the pool of bourbon gathered on the table, wishing he could shrink and dive into the silky liquid and inhale its biting essence into his lungs, drowning in a literal pool of alcohol. He would have to settle for the slow route.

"Whatever, Jimmy." He swiped the spill off the table and steadied his aim for another pour. He drank but slowed his vigor and only took in half the generous shot, letting the warmth of the previous hits settle into his bloodstream and cart him off to a place with softer edges.

"I'm really sorry, man. Who'd have thought I'd be right for once? I figured she was taking up a pottery class, not working someone else's clay." Jimmy consoled as Frank pouted. He fidgeted with his glass; his fingers dampened from the gathering sweat on the outside of the untouched Fuzzy Navel he was obliged to order in solidarity with his partners misery.

Walking the beat as partners the past ten years was the most committed relationship for either of them, Frank's marriage to

Tawny being a close second. Jimmy was proud of his moniker as a lifelong bachelor. He carried less girth but was quick and wiry, making them a balanced duo. Jimmy would chase the perps down, and Frank would hold them and provide a quieting blow if necessary. They were a good team.

"What do I do now, Jimmy?"

"Run in the jackass for pedophilia and get him marked as a sex criminal?"

Frank smirked at the idea. "Tempting."

"Have you thought about confronting her, man? Maybe I got it all wrong. It wouldn't be the first time, you know."

Frank's eyes hardened at the thought of being all worked up for no reason. "If you got something like this wrong, I'll run *you* in for pedophilia, you dick. You don't just throw this accusation out there without proof." He slugged down the last of his bourbon and set the glass on the table.

"Well I'm pretty sure, like eighty-nine percent sure, about what I saw and heard."

"Eighty-nine percent? You can't even lie yourself into an A? What the fuck, Jimmy?"

"Like I said, I heard from Stan down in processing that he was pretty sure he saw a chick that looked a lot like your girl getting handsy with some kid, walking into the Lamplighter Motel down on Sycamore."

"No, you said you saw Tawny getting handsy with the college kid down the block. That's not a he-said-she-said possibility. That's a statement of fact, jack hole." Red crept up Frank's neck with his frustration at the dissemination of information from his partner. He ignored the foggy warmth of inebriation setting in, poured another brimming shot of bourbon, and gulped it down.

"Well, I figured it was how it went down. You said Tawny hasn't been very attentive lately."

Frank's glass smacked down on the table, startling Jimmy and drawing attention to them once again.

"Take it back, Jimmy." Frank's grip tightened on the shot glass.

Jimmy licked spilled Fuzzy Navel from his fingertips. He gave Frank a sheepish look. "I'm sorry, man. You know I love you both to death, but you have to admit, she gets a bit familiar with other guys sometimes. And to be fair, it's not like you haven't strayed before."

Frank grimaced. His indiscretions were not the point. He chose to ignore his own bad behavior and expected his partner to as well.

"I'm not the one on trial here. Besides, she's a people person," Frank said, gritting his teeth through his half-hearted defense of Tawny's behavior.

"She likes attention, that's all I'm getting at. Now loosen up on that glass before you shatter it into your hand."

Frank knew Jimmy was right. Tawny's fingers would linger a bit too long during greetings, or she'd flirt with the bag boy at the Sac-n-Save a bit too convincingly. She possessed an amorous nature, but he ignored it for the most part. When they were first together, she tested the waters of his jealousy a few times, seeing if he would fight for her, which he did, or stand up to any bitchy comments sent her way when she would wear too short of a skirt, which he also did. He was a noble, if not always faithful, territorial type, and she liked that. But if *she* was straying, that was too far. He could handle being the overbearing husband. He could not handle being a cuckold.

"Fine, she likes attention. That don't mean she's steppin' out on me with some punk kid."

"Ok, but, and I mean this with all due respect, do you really want to take that chance?" Jimmy picked up his drink and took a long, smooth sip.

"No. But that brings me back to my question of what do I do? There's no proof, just some pencil pusher's possible account of some chick who looks like my Tawny, being a little handsy with some random kid. I can't throw that accusation at her and not expect her to deny it and think I'm an over-possessive lunatic."

"I don't know, man. All I do know is that we have patrol in about six hours, and if we're not gonna go throw some kid to an alligator, you best slow down and get some coffee or a burger in you."

Frank looked down at the blurring shot glass between his thick fingers. Even with his heavy build, the booze was wrapping around him like a cozy blanket, sparks of heat flashing across his ears as it took hold.

"You're probably right. Do they have food at this place?"

"Maybe, but I'm pretty sure you need a tetanus shot before they'll let you order anything." Jimmy took one last drink and signaled the bartender for the tab. "Let's get you out of here," he said to Frank and began to shuffle his partner out to their unmarked cruiser.

As Jimmy propped Frank up against the dull brown paint of their vehicle, Frank took his partner's face between his massive paws. "You're still a dick, man. But I love you."

Jimmy waved away the gust of bourbon-tainted breath that wafted from Frank.

"I love you too you, big bear. Now let's get you out of here."

Chapter 2

The next day, Frank coasted through the morning briefing in a daze, splashing coffee down his throat hoping to scald away the lingering poison of his hangover.

Walking past the holding pen on his way to his desk, a smoky, familiar voice called out. "Late night, sugar?"

Frank turned to see Kami. Her six-inch heels gave the illusion of height to her latte-skinned, slight frame. Her teased-out afro added to the image and reminded Frank of his childhood, sneaking into the afternoon matinee of Pam Greer double features. Kami's technicolor fishnets and thin tube top completed the caricature of the retro street walker she portrayed each night.

"I thought you quit the life, Kami. What are you doin' in there?"

"It was a misunderstanding. I was just asking for directions." Her innocent tone and batting eyes were deceived by her coquettish smile.

"Yeah, sure. Tell it to someone who doesn't know any better."

"Why you gotta be such a dick, Franky?"

"It's my nature, Kami."

Frank walked on and fell into his seat, unhappy with the prospect of sifting through the day's mangle of paperwork, torturing his bloodshot eyes with the small print and fluorescent lights buzzing away above.

"How ya doin' this mornin', partner?" Jimmy said, lowering a Styrofoam cup of coffee over Frank's shoulder.

"Be doin' better if I had something other than this sludge to drink down. Who's in charge of brewing this morning? They know they're allowed to freshen the grounds at least once a week, right?" He rescued the cup from Jimmy's grasp and took in a scalding sip, wincing at the bitter liquid as it bit at his taste buds.

"I think it's the newbie partner that Roscoe just picked up. She ain't as bad as the last guy. Remember? You could stand a spoon up in whatever it was he brewed."

"At least that would cut through a hangover. This piss barely passes *as* piss."

"I didn't know you were into water sports, big guy." Jimmy cocked a sarcastic eyebrow in Frank's direction.

The two partners joked and chipped away at the pile of paperwork heaped among their joined desks. Frank could not focus. His blank stares bore into the same page as the morning passed by. He shook off his daze around eleven and turned to Jimmy.

"I'm useless," he leaned back and sighed. "I'm gonna go down to the diner and get something to soak up some of last night."

"No worries. I'll hold down the fort unless you want some company."

"Nah. Someone has to toe the line."

"Go get your head on then. I'll catch up with you this afternoon."

Frank nodded and was off.

Down the street from the police station stood The Swing Shift diner. Decked out with booths upholstered in weathered red pleather and a counter with chrome-trimmed cushioned stools, the grease-filled air greeted the blue-collar workers and police that buzzed around the neighborhood on their way on and off shift. Twenty some years before, the owners served their patrons with pride. Once the reality of owning a five-dollar-a-plate restaurant hit them, they shifted to counting the days when some developer would swoop in and offer to buy up their broken dream at pennies on the dollar, freeing them from their self-induced prison of debt and sweat.

It was too early for the lunch crowd, so Frank was able to procure one of the many weathered booths. He wanted to get lost in the daily crossword and soak up the latent alcohol in his bloodstream with a plate of bacon and copious amounts of burnt coffee. He wrestled with his paper while Trudy slumped over to his table to take his order.

"Whatcha havin' today, hon?" she asked, chomping on an overused piece of gum.

"Gimme a double order of bacon and some coffee, black."

"You look like shit. You okay?"

"I'll be fine, just need to soak up last night. Thanks."

The haggard waitress shrugged and was off to get his order of grease and caffeine. The squeak of her battered orthopedic shoes chased her to the kitchen.

Frank didn't like being hung over and definitely didn't like the uncertainty that he felt towards Tawny. He was sure he was right about her stepping out, but he needed proof before he was willing to go toe-to-toe with her. Last thing he needed was to feel the crack of her gin bottle upside his head for his rash conclusion, and then she might leave him.

Frank scavenged through the limp newsprint for his crossword. The jingle at the door announced another customer escaping the streets to the greasy spoon's sanctum. He didn't take notice until the other customer's footsteps came to his table and stopped. Frank looked up. The aura from the fluorescent lights of the café reflected off the neon accents that brandished Kami's working girl regalia. He squinted.

"Want some company, sugar?"

"I'm really not great company today, Kami."

"You never are, but nobody likes to sit and eat alone. Better to sit at the same table and ignore each other rather than act like we don't even know the other."

"We don't know each other."

"Well we know *about* each other at least. Maybe we can remedy the other part." She gave him a smile and slid into the booth opposite Frank. He grimaced and returned to his hunt for the missing crossword.

"So, what's good here?"

"Nothin."

"Quite the corporate spokesman, aren't you?"

Frank crumpled his paper and looked at Kami, exasperated at having to feign conversation. "It's a fucking greasy spoon. It's not supposed to be good. It's supposed to be fast and filling."

"Sounds like my last client." She winked at him.

He couldn't help but chuckle. "You mean alleged client."

"I mean alleged penis. At least give me something to pretend to react to. I swear, I have a sign on my ass that says, must be no more than two inches to ride."

"Charming."

The waitress came back with a hot cup of coffee, sloshing some on the table as she set it down in front of Frank.

"Hon, you can't be turning tricks in here," she said, scowling down at Kami. A loose shock of red curls escaped the haggard bun held in place by a lone bobby pin.

"And you can't be servin' up healthy doses of salmonella with the tuna surprise, but you seem to be doing okay."

"Cool it." Frank broke in. "My acquaintance is joining me for some breakfast. So just take her order, and we'll be on our way when we're done eating." He mopped up the spilled coffee with a napkin rescued from the rusty dispenser on the table.

"We're on lunch now."

"Then make it a burger and fries. Rare." Kami beamed her mischievous innocence up at the sullen waitress.

"Fine. Anything to drink?" Her hands were on her hips, daring Kami to be smart again.

"I'd love a beer, but I'll settle for a cup of that stale coffee."

The waitress spun and huffed off to the kitchen to place the order and most likely spit in the coffee before returning.

"Sorry about that," Frank apologized.

"No worries. Being in the service industry, I deal with that kind of crap all the time. It's a hazard of the trade."

A cup of coffee was dropped onto the table with little flourish or acknowledgment, and the waitress was off again.

"So why you in here and not doing your usual slog of paperwork, Frank?"

"It was a long night last night."

"What happened?"

"Trouble on the home front. I'm sure it's nothin' though."

"It usually is." She sipped her coffee. "But sometimes it's not."

Frank raised an eyebrow and clenched his jaw.

"I'm really not in the mood to discuss this, Kami."

"Why not. Maybe I can help give a fresh perspective. Could either help you clear your conscience or confirm your suspicions. What do ya say?"

Frank considered his options as Trudy returned with his plate of bacon. She skid his plate down in front of him and spirited off to check on the burger and fries.

He took up a piece of charred swine and sunk his teeth in. The flavors of the past twenty-four hours of an uncleaned grill clung to the fatty meat, and its healing relief slowly took hold as he dove into his story of Tawny's distance the past few weeks.

As he gnashed away at his bacon it all rushed in on him at once. Hidden text conversations while they cuddled on the couch. Her rushing out the door at odd hours for "forgotten" appointments. Cryptic messages he would catch a glimpse of on her phone, but then when he would snoop further, like the paranoid cop he was, he would find no such conversations in her history. The random excursions and classes Tawny was signing up for but never talking about.

Aside from that, he noticed the same car that usually parked in front of a house two blocks away, parked out front of their house when he would come home off a night shift. Once or twice he swore he heard it tear off just after he entered his house.

Kami's burger arrived, and she tore into the overcooked meat and crispy fries as he continued.

He'd seen the signs so many times when brawling couples were brought into the station house, their limits finally pushed too far, and their forgotten passion shifted to passionate rage, manifesting in sinking a knife into the leg of their one-time lover, or worse.

Kami swallowed a large bite of ketchup doused burger. "Hell, honey sounds like you got all the proof you need. Why not just confront her or kick her to the curb?"

"We've been together a long time. I know what the signs say, but I still have a hard time believing that she would do that to us."

"I don't see an *us* in your story. She's screwing *you* over."

"I feel gutted." His fire from the night before was tamped to a smolder by the self-pity weighing him down. He sulked over his tepid cup of coffee wishing he could sink into the deep recesses of the aged restaurant booth.

"Shit, Frank. You ain't gonna do yourself any good you keep whining like a bitch. Eventually you're gonna have to man up and act on this. One way or another."

"Yeah, but if I go off the handle on her, and she isn't even bangin' this guy, then I just shot myself in the head."

"Sometimes you have to fuck up to show you're still alive."

Kami surveyed the damage in front of her. A morsel of bun lay defeated on the side of the plate. She swiped up the remnants of a pool of ketchup with a lone limp fry. She downed the last of her coffee, stood, and swiped Frank's final strip of bacon from his grease laden plate.

"Maybe if you decide to be a man about this, you'll look me up. I have a way with situations of this nature." Kami winked, spun and sashayed her neon clad figure out of the diner, the bounce of her afro waving goodbye to Frank.

Chapter 3

The rest of Frank's day floated past in a fog. The bacon helped settle his stomach, but his brain wouldn't focus. He called it a day around 2:30 on the guise there was a canary with a tip for him across town. He really just wanted to sit down to a bucket of chicken and a six pack and watch the sun stroll across the horizon while the neighbor kids played in the street.

He entered the two-bedroom ranch style house knowing it would be too early for Tawny to have made it home from work yet. The dentist office where she worked never cut her loose before six, leaving the unkempt house alone and quiet.

Their home's hushed emptiness always unnerved him. He powered up the TV to provide some background noise as company. The sportscasters buzzed on, recounting the previous night's hockey exploits. Frank paid no attention and proceeded to the kitchen to unload his heavy arms.

The six-pack of cheap IPA clinked on the stone counter, followed by the cardboard clunk of the half-empty bucket of chicken. He rescued a bottle of the beer, and with a smooth motion from the bottle opener on his key chain, flicked the cap off. Frank raised the fizzing brew to his lips and dropped the keys on the counter. Beer in hand, he opened the porch door, and a waft of warm air washed over him as he stepped out onto the screened patio that overlooked the woods below their neighborhood. A small creek peeked through the leaves, gurgling softly as it wove among the trees. Frank breathed in the humid air and watched as a hornet collided with the screen that impeded its desire to join him for a drink.

The bitter sting of the IPA soaked into him as it mingled with the chicken digesting in his stomach. He plunked down onto a cushioned wicker chair and breathed in the cleansing world around him. He wished away the events of the night before and hoped that he was just being a paranoid ass about this entire scenario.

Dogs barked their greetings around him, and the birds from the woods sang their response. Frank sipped his beer and slowly drifted off in the comfortable warmth of his sanctuary.

Chapter 4

Grotesque images contrasted by the sensual assault of two lovers surrounded by a haze of smoke flashed across his eyelids. Naked bodies pressed together. Kami's glistening lip gloss saturated smile stretched across a sharpened row of teeth. A knife slashing across a hand, splashing blood across some animal's rotting carcass. A room spinning out of control with a fireplace blazing up the wall, licking at its wooden planks as if to burn it all down but never following through. Kami's sweat-drenched body writhed in front of him, her nipples taut with excitement. The surreal world of his nightmare swirled around and spun with the brutal images of flesh, smoke, and an ungodly concoction bubbling in a cauldron.

The yips and yelps of the neighbor's dogs in the waking world were transformed into freakish shrieks in his muted hellscape. The figures convulsed and passed in and out of one another. Frank stood staring at them in his dream, first as if he were disconnected from the moment, then he was there, holding the bloodied knife, the fire's flames lapping at his nude body as the writhing figures howled in a mass of flesh and bone that dripped to the floor like a puddle of spilled, sweaty compote.

He wanted to scream, but his throat was barren, unable to manifest his own terror at the coagulated mess that oozed, bubbled, and grew in front of him. He stood frozen in fear as the sloppy mound rose up and formed an abstract vision of a body. Its misshapen limbs dripped with sores that seeped with the sickly-sweet stench of rot, infusing the air around him. He gagged for breath that was not tainted with the musty taste of roadkill and vomit that putrefied the ether. At the top of the blob-like figure, a malformed globe rose up and perched on a too thin branch of a festering neck. It swayed back and forth as the eyeless head split into a sinister vertical smile from top to bottom, its slash of a mouth quivering open, viscous jelly dripping from the jagged flesh with multiple rows of teeth being revealed in the dim, flickering light of the fire. The gaping mouth rippled with a perverse pleasure as two black orbs opened on either side, reflecting Frank back at himself with focused and hungry intent. It leaned forward, and Frank's head was enveloped in the sharp mass of dripping teeth and all he smelled was the rancid hot breath of the creature that crunched down into the bone of his skull.

Frank woke with a start, spilling the remnants of his beer down his leg, Tawny's lithe fingers squeezing his shoulder.

"Whoa, baby," she said. "You okay?"

Frank breathed heavy and scanned the room, still caught up in the surreal imagery that licked at the back of his brain.

"Yeah. I'm fine. Just dozed off I guess." He brushed the cold beer from his pant leg, speckling it across the floor of the porch.

"Well you must've had quite the dream, big guy."

"Something like that. What time is it?"

"It's about eight thirty. I tried to call and tell you the girls wanted to grab dinner, but you didn't pick up."

"Shit, I left my phone in the car. Sorry, baby. How was work?"

"It was work. Nothing too exciting today," she turned to go back to the kitchen to get a beer for herself and called over her shoulder, "How about you?"

"I ducked out early. Felt like shit all day."

"I bet. I didn't even hear you come in last night." She returned and handed Frank a fresh beer. She pulled up a second aged wicker chair that cracked under her and sat facing him.

"Yeah, I got a bit too far into the bottle. Just flopped out on Jimmy's couch because I didn't want to wake you up, then hit the road pretty early to get a jump on things at the precinct."

"Well, I would have appreciated a heads-up. I know you work weird hours, but I still worry about you, ya know."

"I know. Sorry about that. So, what did you get up to last night anyway?"

"I let the neighbor kids tag team me in the back yard. Usual Thursday shit."

Frank grimaced and choked down his drink of beer.

"You know I don't find that funny."

Tawny giggled and took a drink of her beer. "Lighten up, Franky. It was only *one* of the neighbor kids."

He tensed up, and his agitation grew with her taunting. He was not in the state of mind to deal with her jokes about sleeping around.

"That's not funny, Tawny."

"Man, look who woke up a Grumpy Gus. Never mind then." Her mood shifted from bubbly to sullen. She gave a huff and uprooted herself from the crackling of the wicker chair, retreating to the television to escape her husband's sour mood.

"Come on, Tawny. Ugghh. I'm sorry." Frank wrestled himself from his chair, giving chase.

"Forget it, Frank. I'm not in the mood for your jealousy shit tonight. Just leave me alone."

"Dammit, Tawny, settle down."

"Don't tell me to settle down. You've been absolutely foul lately, and you haven't even said you like my new haircut."

"New haircut? When did you get that?"

"Two weeks ago, you prick."

Frank slapped his palm onto the center of his face, dragging it slowly down, stretching his features in a sharp tug, breathing hard to tamp down the growing heat in his belly. "Jesus, Tawny. I'm sorry about the hair."

"Sorry about it? What, is it awful?" She spun on him, twisting his words and intent to her advantage.

She liked to see him wriggle and squirm. She was smarter than he was and able to maneuver through their spats with acrobatic ease, and they both knew it. A malicious glint flicked in her eyes.

He knew he wouldn't win. He never did. "Nope. Not tonight." Frank turned and headed back out the door, busting through the loosely hanging screen door, almost knocking the fine mesh out of its precarious roost. He walked off the porch, patting himself down to check for his wallet and keys before storming off too far.

"Where the fuck do you think you're going?" Tawny shouted in close pursuit.

"To the bar. I can at least drink in peace there and not worry about the bartender's latest fashion choices."

"You're such an asshole!"

"You ain't wrong, baby, but you ain't exactly Mother Teresa yourself."

His temper was off the chain, and he knew he needed to get out of there before one of them went too far. His suspicion of her flings was driving him further away, but he was unable to face the possible truth. He was either wrong and deserved every bit of shit that she threw his way or he was right, and he could not face the fact he was too little of a man to walk away and let her be.

He got to the car first but not by much. He opened the door, and Tawny kicked it shut, almost catching his fingers in the gap.

"Jesus. You almost took my hand off!" Frank spun and bore down on her. He never hit her, but he was worried one day he might snap, and that was a line he did not want to see himself cross.

"Where do you think you're going? We have to finish this!" She put both hands on his chest and pushed him hard against the beat-up car. She gave his cheek a hard slap but followed it with grabbing him between both palms and smashing her lips to his, pressing her will onto him, pinning him to the car. The heat of their fight ignited passion the two hadn't felt between the sheets for some time.

He tasted Tawny's breath; the warm fumes of her beer mingled with saliva twisting with his own. Her soft tongue gripped at the inside of his teeth, pulling his mouth in closer, searching for a dance partner. He pressed back, the sweat of the summer day lubricating their bare arms as they wrestled for dominance. His grip wrapped around her wrists and he pushed her away, their lips ripping apart with a gasp.

"No!" Frank pushed her back firmly, and she stumbled backwards but kept herself upright, panting and glaring at his insolent response to her impassioned advance.

"What do you mean, no?"

"I don't work like that!"

"You sure as hell do, asshole!"

"Not today I don't." He wiped the wet from their kiss off with the back of his hand and looked down in defeat. He pushed himself back up and opened his car door, dropping himself into his seat, his erection sending a shot of sharp pain through him as it grazed the steering wheel on his way to the seat.

"You can't just go!" Tawny's anger was palpable.

"Watch me." He turned the key, and the car fired up. "Don't wait up." He slammed the gear rod into reverse and sputtered out of the gravel driveway, a plume of dust replacing where he stood just seconds ago.

Tawny stamped in the driveway, kicking loose rocks in his direction then turning and screaming herself back into the house while a couple of neighbors unsuccessfully pretended to ignore their skirmish and then went on with their evenings, dinner table conversations fueled with the exploits of their crazy neighbors.

Chapter 5

The sticky heat of the summer night stoked his temper as he drove towards downtown. He had no destination other than to drink and quench the embers of his anger. He didn't know if his paranoia was warranted or just the unchecked aggression from the dark world he walked around in while patrolling the streets. He dealt with so much dysfunction and sadness, it was difficult to compartmentalize it all. Once in a while his feelings for the lowlifes in his job leaked out into his daily life, and he didn't like it.

The sun ducked low, warming the sky with the purple haze of dusk, coloring the streets in murky silhouettes. The town took on a sharpness. Razor edged shadows stalked along the ground able to cut a vein open if you crossed them.

Even as early as it was, Frank recognized the workers who staked their territory to take advantage of the evening traffic. Their high heels, too short skirts, and revealing tops draped in leather and fur. The pretty boys in tight jeans and t-shirts cooed at the coy family men who pretended not to take a second glance. They were easy to distinguish from the merchants and pedestrians who were making their way home after a hard day's work. It was their turn to work the streets and milk the businessmen for their hard-earned dollars.

The sky darkened, and the street lamps popped on, lighting Frank's way through the evening as he wound through the slippery heat on his way to nowhere in particular.

A traffic signal blinked red, and he slowed to a stop. As he sat waiting his turn, a slender figure passed in front of his headlights, and a hint of recognition went through him. The stylish afro and confident gait of the familiar street walker waggled to the far corner, paying him no heed. Frank hesitated as the light turned green. Then, he cranked his wheel and pulled around to the opposite corner. He threw the car into park and rolled down his window.

"Hey! Kami!"

The caramel-skinned girl turned at the recognition of her name, then beamed a bright smile at Frank. She checked the street and sauntered over to the side of his car.

"Hey, Frank. Whatchu doin' out here tonight?"

The smell of peppermint-glazed breath chased by the sweet scent of cotton candy perfume filled Frank's car, and he felt warm and stupid at the thoughts that crowded his frazzled brain.

"Just out for a drive and a drink. You stayin' out of trouble?"

"Baby, I don't know what trouble is." She winked, and her wide smile confirmed she really didn't.

"You just coming on shift?" he asked.

"I don't know what you're insinuating, since all I did was crawl out of my crib to see what's going on tonight."

"Sure." He smiled, and they exchanged a knowing glance. "You hungry or want a drink before the crowds roll in?"

"You trying to entrap me, sweetie?"

"Not a bit. Could just use some company."

"You buyin'?"

"You know I am."

Kami, still leaning over into his window, craned her neck around to see if there was any other traffic or unmarked vice units waiting to pounce. Frank took in the smooth, long neck that led to a shadowed grouping of cleavage. His mouth watered. She returned her attention to him, satisfied that this was a friendly offer and not a set up.

"I wouldn't mind a swig to loosen up a bit." She stood straight and made her way around to the passenger side. She got in and settled into the seat infusing the cabin with her sweet scent. Frank hoped the smell would linger after she left. It was much more inviting than the stale cigarettes and sweat that currently welcomed riders into his decrepit chariot.

"Where do ya' like?" he asked.

"Let's go down to the Cauldron Lounge. It's usually good for some company later in the night."

"Sounds good."

Frank dropped the car into drive, and the loud engine rumbled.

The all but empty Cauldron Lounge sat under the Bayside Bridge, a beacon to the dock workers and blue-collar day shifters looking for cheap beer and loud crowds on game nights. The lack of pretension carried its own flavor of territorial charm. If you were not a regular, you were sure to turn the heads of the scraggly-toothed mainstays who occupied the weathered barstools. The jukebox played a select loop of 70s power ballads and hard rock with a smattering of 80s hits that colored the room in nostalgia.

Frank pulled into the small parking lot and nestled his car into a spot overlooking the river. The two exited his rickety ride and headed towards the faded red door of the Cauldron. The bar patrons knew Kami but not Frank. Even without his badge brandished on his belt the bartender marked him as Five-O the second he followed Kami into the room.

"What can I get you, Officer?" The gruff bartender asked, announcing to his surlier patrons they best be on their better behavior for a while.

Frank smirked. "Cute trick." He gave a cursory look to the meek selection of cheap booze and even cheaper drafts. He motioned to Kami. "What's your poison, Kami?"

The bartender gave a sarcastic scoff.

She paid no heed to the unwelcome gesture. "Jack and Coke."

The bartender stood still, arms crossed, in no hurry to serve her.

Frank snapped his fingers to bring the bartender's attention back to him. "Hey, Skippy! Get the lady a Jack and Coke and a Wild Turkey on the rocks for me." He pulled out a twenty dollar bill and slapped it on the sticky bar. The bartender looked annoyed but swiped up the cash and slid the appropriate change back to Frank before getting the drinks together.

Frank grabbed their drinks and change, leaving a lone dollar tip in exchange for the gruff service. They headed off to a back, corner booth away from the judgmental looks and the technicolor lights of the small bank of rigged gambling machines that chirped and twittered against the far wall.

The two chatted about nothing of importance through their first drink, and Frank kept the booze rolling for another couple rounds as they cut through the idle banter and allowed their guarded personalities to show past the contrived veneer they both clung to for protection in their daily lives.

"So, what's the real deal with you and your girl, Frank?" Kami asked, and then looked hard into his falling face as she took a sultry sip of her drink. The ice cubes danced off her lips, and her tongue pushed back the fizz as she sipped.

Frank gulped and took a hard pull on his Wild Turkey. His fingers and toes were tingling with the lightness of inebriation. He cleared his throat. "We're not in a good place."

"Well that's obvious" She sniggered as she took another sip.

"And here I thought I was hiding it well." He smiled back.

"Not so much."

"I have the feeling she's stepping out on me, but I can't prove it, and the longer it goes on, the more I come off as a buffoon."

"Don't worry. You're a buffoon without this to define you." She gave Frank a wink and a flirty smile across her drink.

"You're a real help."

The two shared a booth and volleyed banter for the next couple hours. One drink pouring into two, three, and four. Frank's senses dulled until the world spun away, and he was unaware of the acrid powder Kami slipped into his final round masked by the alcohol it swam in.

Chapter 6

Frank sat bolt upright, a thin sheet scarcely covering his lower half. Sweat drenched his hair and the bed he found himself in. He looked around the room, lit only by the stubborn shafts of daylight that squeezed through the ventilating cracks in the wooden walls of the acrid smelling shack.

He kicked his feet over the side of the bed. He stood to test his legs, but they were jelly, and he dropped back down.

His vision was hazy from the fog that rolled around in his head. He wrestled with the images that haunted him from the last evening's nap. They dodged in and out of the thick muck of consciousness. His skull pounded, and the monsters that clung to him from his dreamscape teased him in sharp flashes, fighting with the blur of reality he fought to pull himself back into.

The painful, vibrant flashes quickened as the room around him spun into focus, and he gripped his head with a low groan. The phantoms roared and were gone as quickly as they appeared, leaving him in the quiet of the musty room, panting, his hands slipping through his sweat drenched hair.

Another sound wove through his breathing. A female voice humming. It was not a familiar tune, but it soothed him and calmed the fading headache. His heart slowed, and he felt the blood and strength return to his legs. He grabbed hold of the sheet around his naked waist and stood to survey the dim room's spartan surroundings.

The bed was encased in mosquito netting. He passed through the opaque curtain and his dim surroundings came into focus. The room was outlined by rough, splintered wood walls. A table coated in melted candle wax was near the dormant potbelly stove in the corner, and a trunk made of iron and oily wood sat in the middle of the room.

He squinted and located a pitted iron doorknob off to his right, a seam of daylight cutting a ragged rectangle in the wall, signaling the exit. Frank clomped across the room, the long bed-sheet trailing in his path. Every step prickled with sharp sensation under his feet. The dust covered floor offering up its splinters if he got too hapless with his footing. At the door, he wrapped his thick feeling hand around the cold knob. The latch gave way with a scrape, and the door fell open to the outside, bumping against the wall as it swung wide. Frank shielded his eyes from the onslaught of sharp streaming light that bade him welcome to the day.

Just off to the right he saw the source of the morning song. Kami stood under a camping shower, light shimmering off her round curves, washing away the exploits of the past day as she crooned her improvised tune. Her hair, that last night stood tall and proud as a well-coifed afro, draped down her back, guiding the water on its path across her shining buttocks on its way to the rusty drain she stood over.

Frank's mouth dropped open at the sight of the dripping beauty. He always found her to be attractive but kept their relationship professional, as he never was quite sure if he would have to bring her in or answer a call about her untimely death one day. His eyes burned with the fresh etching of her figure as she communed with the water that traced erratic paths down her smooth, shimmering body.

She turned her head his way, a coy smile painted across her face, her eyes blinking away the cleansing water.

"Good morning, sunshine!" she called to him.

He fumbled his sheet in surprise and in the stammering knowledge he was caught peeping like a school boy.

"H … huh … hey." He rescued his makeshift sari; although, the erection that surfaced would have held the heavy sheet in place just fine. "Good morning."

Kami giggled at the blushing man. She turned towards him, giving him an even better look at her toned body, her nipples taut in the morning chill and her defined stomach muscles leading down to a well-groomed landing strip that Frank had a sneaking suspicion he visited quite voraciously the night before.

"Did I wake you, sugar?" She asked, relishing in the gentle waterfall of her shower, teasing his eyes for a while longer before pulling a chord that cut off the flow from the large reservoir housed on the roof of her shack.

"Don't think so. Had a weird dream."

"That's a shame. You seemed like you were sleeping the sleep of the dead." She wrung out the excess water from her hair and flung it back over her shoulder, grabbing up a towel to mop up the rest of the water from her body, still showing no real effort to hide herself from his wide, unblinking eyes.

"Hey, so what happened last night?" Frank asked, working to reel in his adolescent urges and get a handle on where they were and recall their activities from the night before.

"Nothing you should be ashamed of, lover." Kami winked, wrapped her hair in the damp towel and knotted it into a loose turban as she strode toward him.

She came up alongside him. Her height was a good six to eight inches below his, so she stood on her tiptoes, pecked him on his cheek, and laid her hand on his chest.

"You certainly know how to take care of a lady." She pecked him on the cheek again with a smile behind her lips and then gave a gentle pat to his cheek before moving past him into the dark room.

Frank hung his head in shame. "Fuck," he said under his breath.

Kami padded softly into the shack, her naked body drying in the stale air. She went to the stove and retrieved a candelabra and a box of matches Frank would have sworn were not there before. She placed them on the wax laden table and lit the lot, illuminating the room with a soft yellow glow.

"Listen, Kami. I don't remember what we did last night, but I know it–"

"Oh, relax big guy. Remember what I do for a living?" she asked facing him, lit by the candles' dancing shadows. "Last night was fun, but I sure as hell ain't looking for no beau, let alone one that has as much baggage as you're carrying around right now." She pulled her turban down, dropping her hair, still a bit damp, to rest on her shoulders.

"I didn't mean to," Frank stammered, again wrestling with the sheet at his waist to maintain some sense of decorum, even though he was pretty sure she was privy to the full show the night before.

Kami took up her towel, gave it a quick twist and snapped the wet whip at him, raising a small red mark on his chest. "Don't be such a bitch," she said.

"Ow." Frank rubbed at the red mark, nursing the sting of the towel and his own embarrassment.

"We both needed something last night," Kami said, walking over to her chest near the bed and retrieving a thong, beginning the ritual of hiding herself from the prying eyes of the public. "You gave me a much-needed night off and an even more needed *getting off*," she said, pulling on a white cotton half shirt. "And in return," she pointed to the table with the candelabra on it.

Frank gaped at a small, corked glass bottle glistening next to the candelabra, positive he didn't see it there before. He was also aware that his eyes were clearing up as the haze of his stupor lifted, and the viewport he observed the world through was less foggy by the second.

"What is that?" he asked as he cautiously moved to retrieve his prize.

"That is nothing more than my heartfelt thank you, Frank. It'll clear up your wonders and fears about your wife's suspected affairs." She paused while she tugged on a tight pair of faded jeans, her round curves protesting then relinquishing the right of way to the shape defining garment. "And if there is nothing to reveal, then you'll know that too."

Frank reached the table and leaned over to take a closer look at the opalescent green bottle. The milky liquid inside revealed nothing, and there were no instructions labeled along its side; although, he almost expected to see a shaky skull and crossbones scrawled across its front.

"I don't get it." He stood and turned to Kami. "What exactly is it?"

She smiled and walked over to him, keeping his eyes in her stare. She stopped in front of him and presented the bottle, breaking their connection as it raised between their gaze.

"There's nothing to it. Just pour it into her drink."

"Is it poison or something?"

"It's not poison. She won't even know that she's drinking it. It has no taste, no odor, and once it goes into a drink, it disperses, and you can't even see it."

She grabbed Frank's hand, lifted it up and placed his fingers around the glass bottle. "No need to thank me."

"But—"

Kami kissed him hard on the lips. He inhaled her sweet breath, and as quickly as he felt her tongue lick at the inside of his lip, he was alone in the humid hut, the musty smell of mold and dust all around him.

He spun and searched, but there was no evidence of Kami. The candles had burned out and gone cold, the day shifted from morning brilliance to hot afternoon sun, beating down on the tin roof of the decrepit shack.

He stood clothed and, in his hand, felt the cold weight of the green glass.

"*Just put it in her drink. She won't even know it's there ... it's there ... it's there ...*"

Frank shook his head with the fading words and spun towards the door, running out and diving into his car. He fired up the engine and tore out of the abandoned homestead. He fought to figure out if his night with Kami was real or not. As he sped down the unattended dirt road towards the highway, he kept telling himself it was all a bourbon induced, paranoia-soaked dream. Then he looked over at the green bottle that sloshed in the passenger seat next to him.

"*It'll clear up your wonders and fears about your wife's suspected affairs.*"

A loud horn of an oncoming vehicle screamed at Frank. He hammered down on his brakes in time to avoid being torn in half by the speeding car. He didn't know how long he was careening down the dirt road in his trance.

A cloud of dust enveloped him, and he breathed hard as the adrenaline from the near miss washed through his system. As he caught his breath, he lifted the bottle to study the viscous milky concoction inside.

His breathing slowed with the ebbing rush of adrenaline. Hunger rumbled in his stomach and screamed for a loaded breakfast burrito with extra hot sauce. He looked up and down the quiet country road to make sure he was not going to cause another accident and headed back towards town.

Chapter 7

Instead of dealing with the fallout of not coming home two nights in a row, Frank went straight to the police station where he kept a spare change of clothes in the locker room.

"What the fuck happened to you last night, man?" Jimmy asked, "Your lady texted me all night asking where you were." He gawked at Frank demolishing a double-sized burrito.

Frank worked a massive bite, shifting the contents of his mouth enough to talk past the mound of mush with minimal splatter. "Don't worry about it." He went back to chewing.

"Don't worry about it? Jesus, man. Are you fucking around on her again?"

Frank raised a middle finger at his partner instead of even trying to work words past the food that filled his cheeks to near breaking point.

"Oh man, you are." Jimmy sat back in his chair, a sarcastic grin creasing his face from cheek-to-cheek. "It better've been worth it is all I'll say."

Frank mashed the final squishy bits of food down his throat, holding Jimmy's gaze in his own. He opened his mouth as if to say something, then filled it with another massive bite, and followed up with another dismissive hand gesture.

"Fine. Whatever. I ain't your mama."

"You're right. You're not," Frank mumbled and continued to dismantle the rest of the burrito.

The rest of their day was marked with paperwork, an ass chewing by the captain for Frank's tardiness, and then door knocking and following up on leads to clean up some loose ends on a few of their open cases.

At quitting time, they parted after a quick drink, giving Jimmy another chance to pull out of Frank what happened the night before. But they left it with a few choice biting insults that didn't mean anything personal and headed their own ways.

Frank had no idea what he was going to tell Tawny. He knew she would be pissed. He was not known for staying out all night except for when he was on the job, and she knew he was not on shift so that would not fly if he tried that angle. This was not the first time he stepped out on Tawny. His guilt about messing around was usually tied up in his anger after one of their rows, so last night fit his pattern.

All day he wondered about the words Kami used when talking about the liquid in the vial. How he would be shown about Tawny's affairs? He told himself it was silly, and he would just pour the bottle out once he got home. Who knew what type of shit Kami was trying to get him to pour into his wife? It was ridiculous to even entertain the thought that somehow, she'd concocted something that would reveal his wife's deception.

The sun dipped down behind the horizon, and the street lamps were blinking on with their sporadic coded hellos. Frank chuckled at himself and how he didn't even think anything happened between him and Kami. He was sure he was too drunk. She must have just taken him home and dropped him unconscious on the bed, and the rest was her messing with him.

Yeah, that was it. She was messing with him.

His mood grew warm as he thought about apologizing for blowing out of the house last night and for crashing on Jimmy's couch because he was too embarrassed to come home. Yeah, he was sure that would go over. It was as close to the truth as he could remember anyway.

He pulled into his driveway. The tires crunched to a halt on the gravel, and his faithful steed, rumbled to sleep as he clicked off the key.

He got out of his car and saw the small glow from a cigarette burning red in the shade of the porch where Tawny sat in wait. He exhaled to gather his courage and headed to his reckoning.

Chapter 8

Fortunately, the bottle Tawny threw missed Frank's head. He only received a spark of pain from a ricocheting shard of glass as it glanced off the door frame behind him instead of a concussion from a direct hit.

"Settle down, Tawny," Frank said, holding his hands up in surrender and in defense of any further projectiles.

"Don't tell me to settle down!" She stood and reloaded with another near-empty beer bottle, winding up for a toss. "Where do you get off staying out all night? Again!"

"Baby, I—" He ducked under the second bottle. This one broke with a sharp splash, coating the door and ground with backwash, beer, and the bright sparkle of shattered glass. "God dammit! Hold on! I'm sorry! I should've called." He edged closer to her in hopes of wresting any further projectiles from her grip before she littered their porch any further with multicolored glass bits.

Tawny readied a third bottle, threatening him with a direct hit now that he was edging into close range.

"Sorry? Fuck you! You're a cop, you son-of-a-bitch! I worry about you when I *know* where you're at, and now you speed off and stay out all night and day without even a text!"

Tawny wound up for a third throw. Frank took advantage of the moment before she could release her weapon, and he rushed her, grabbing her and holding tight to the hand that held the bottle. Instead of throwing the bottle, the warm fizzy contents dumped down on top of the two as she struggled to get free. Covered in the fermented foam of the beer's remains, Frank squeezed her wrist and shook her wielding arm. The bottle released and landed with a bounce on the cushion of the chair behind her. Disarmed, she stumbled backward and thumped into the wall. She slid down to the floor, exasperated and sputtering beer.

Frank wiped the sticky liquid down his face, spitting out a fine, sour mist and blinked the remnants from his eyes.

Tawny sat on the ground, wiping beer from her eyes and flicking her long bangs out of her face. With a swish, a light splattering of IPA and hairspray speckled the wall behind her. They gave a mutual laugh as the tension ripped open, and their emotions dripped down their cheeks.

"I'm sorry," he said, "I should have called."

Tawny chuckled. A lump rose in her throat, and the laughter shifted to a sob. "I thought you were dead." She brought her knees up and cradled her face between them, crying and screaming away her anger.

Frank moved next to her, lowered himself down and draped his arm around her heaving shoulders. "I know, baby. I'm sorry."

They sat there, rocking back and forth, the beer drying to a sour, sticky coating until the tears were gone and their silence was reflected back by the evening's sounds overtaking the chaos of their violent exchange.

"You're an asshole, you know that?" Tawny asked, raising her head from her knees and looking into Frank's shimmering face.

"You're not wrong, baby. But we're switching you to cans," Frank said and gestured to the pile of broken glass.

They laughed and stood up to survey the damage.

"I'm glad you're all right."

"And I'm sorry for picking that stupid fight. I just needed to get out of here for a while and ended up too drunk to drive home. Jimmy dragged me to his house to sleep it off, again."

"That makes sense. But you still should have texted or called today," she said and gave him a soft hit to the chest to show she was getting over it, but he was still not fully forgiven.

"Fair enough. Why don't we go get cleaned up, then I'll take care of this mess?"

Tawny nodded her head, her lower lip still pushed out in a soft pout. Frank took up her chin between his thumb and fingers, raised her face up to his and kissed her tenderly. The fear and anger of the moment melted away as the two made their way to the shower.

"You want the first one?" Frank said.

"No. I want to feel your skin against mine. Would you join me?"

"You sure?"

She answered by fastening her fingers into the top of his jeans, leading him along the hallway to the shower. As the water heated, they kicked off their clothes and stole soft, inviting touches in the process.

The sharp needling heat from the shower was chased across their bodies by roaming fingertips mapping out the lovers' bodies. Their fingers were lubricated by the slick water and the familiar touch of longtime lovers who still knew how to ignite the passion of the other. The small shower was overtaken by the harmonious wrestling match of the two passionate warriors who'd succumbed to each other's will. Kisses mixed with the hot spray quenched their thirsts as they thrust upon each other until the water ran cold, and they were left panting and clutching at each other for the fading heat of the moment.

The chill finally took over, and they separated, a warm smile shared between them as they switched off the frigid downpour and retreated to the lingering steam that hung in the bathroom.

As they dried, their almost forgotten familiarity and appreciation floated in the room, mingling with the shower's steam. Frank liked this. He always loved the look and the feel of his lean lover. He let his glances linger and appreciate her movements as she stood naked in front of the mirror drying her hair, the gentle curve of the small of her back rolling into the subtle round curve of her buttocks that rounded into her nicely muscled legs. She always stayed fit, and the years that added inches to his stomach cultivated Tawny's beauty. His hand lifted and landed on his once toned belly that hovered just above his belt line.

"You are a beautiful woman, you know," he said, a hint of melancholy coloring his tender tone.

Tawny stopped her drying, letting the towel drift down to the floor revealing her hairless frame. She smiled at the compliment and blew a playful kiss. "Careful, lover. I might make you go another round." She winked and retrieved her towel. "Now get dressed. I'm hungry and want you to take me out for a burger."

Frank smiled. He grasped his towel around his waist and left her to her own in the bathroom. The door closed as he moved into the bedroom to dry and get dressed himself.

As if to announce his arrival, Tawny's phone buzzed an alert of a received message. He moved over to the dresser where her phone sat, the screen still lit from the message notification. It was a text with an image attached, but the image was too small to see, and he did not recognize the sender before the screen went dark.

Frank looked around to make sure she was still in the bathroom. His cop curiosity tended to get the best of him on occasion, even when he knew it shouldn't. Why did he want to jeopardize their reconciliation? He didn't know, but even as he questioned his own paranoia, he felt himself lifting up the phone and touching the screen to bring it back to life. The smartphone awoke with the notification and request of a password to fully open and reveal its content. He thought for a moment. He didn't know her password. Not for sure. They'd known each other a long time but at least to an extent they respected the privacy of the other. Until now.

He swiped to reveal the password screen. He knew he would only get two shots to open the phone or it would lock, and he would get caught snooping. He bit his lip, thinking of what she would use. He went for the obvious first, her birthday. The screen shook its disapproval and prompted him to try again. One more chance left. The only other number he could think of that might mean anything to her was their wedding date. He started to put it in, then hesitated. It wasn't the wedding date that she would use. It was their first date anniversary. The date they fell for each other and the date they celebrate every year. For all the missed birthdays, botched Valentine dates, and near-forgotten wedding anniversaries, they both always remembered that first date night. It was a night that established the tone of their relationship. All the chemistry, excitement, tension, and explosive passion that defined them was wrapped up in that date. That had to be it.

He hit the delete key, erasing the numbers he was about to submit and replaced them with the anniversary date. He held his breath and hit enter. The screen flashed a welcome, and he was in. He opened her messaging app and saw the unfamiliar number untagged with any name or avatar. He swiped it open, and his heart sank.

The screen filled with a prolific stream of flirts, pics, and random conversations that went back months and came in at all hours. He skimmed through and tried to detach from the building anger at every self-indulgent selfie that sped past his eyes. He scrolled back to the most recent. The message was short. "Guess I won't be mowing the lawn shirtless for a few days." The accompanying photo brought a sick, dry taste to his mouth. It was a shot of a back that was marred by red streaks highlighted by a couple of overzealous ones that broke the skin. The muscled back of the boy down the block slapped Frank across the face, and the proud sneer of the boy looking over his own shoulder as he took his picture in the mirror taunted him with mirthful glee, mocking his blindness and revelation, showing Frank that he was right about everything he needed to be wrong about.

He fought the urge to snap the phone in two. Instead he closed the app, put the phone back to sleep, and gently set it down on the dresser. He stood for a moment in silence, soaking in the horror of what he just discovered.

"Hey, baby. You okay?" Tawny said from behind him.

Frank was startled back to reality. His towel dropped away without the support of his free hand to hold it in place. He was embarrassed and scrambled to retrieve it and hide his shame.

"Sorry, must've dazed off for a sec."

"I guess. Not that I mind the view, handsome." Tawny walked past him. She gave his bare ass a slap as she went to her dresser to finish getting ready.

Frank winced at the playful sharp smack and felt it to his core. A slap to his pride. But he needed to play it cool.

"Where you wanna go to, Tawny?" He cleared his throat and retrieved some fresh clothes.

"The Suds Zone always has the best fries," she said with rapacious zeal.

"Can do, babe." Frank pulled on a black T-shirt and jeans. "Hey. You want a beer while you get ready."

"You read my mind, lover. Thanks"

"Okay. Be right back."

Frank went to the kitchen. He retrieved two cold beers from the fridge. His hands shook as he wrestled the tops off. He set the bottles on the counter, and the rage overtook him. His silent scream resonated inside his skull. He fought the urge to rip the counter top up from its roost. Tears gathered at the edge of his eyelids, clinging until they dropped to the ground, wetting the grime of the floor away with the betrayal his ignored hypocrisy generated.

Then, as if called, he looked over to see the small bottle from Kami's place sitting on the counter just out of reach, beckoning him. He could not explain how it got there. He didn't care either. His hands shook as he reached for the cold bottle. Its smooth, handblown craftsmanship soothed his fury-heated skin. The milky liquid hypnotized him.

"Just put it in her drink. She won't even know it's there ... it's there ... it's there ..." Kami's words echoed and faded away in his head.

As Kami's voice stroked his emotional bruises, he noticed that he was pouring Tawny's beer into a glass and chasing it with the uncorked concoction. The two liquids danced in the glass as the potion swirled and shifted from milky to a hazy film, to fully incorporated into the fizzy beer. Frank could not smell any acrid addition to the brew, just the hoppy, grain laced scent of the cheap beer.

"Whatcha doing, baby?" Tawny came up behind him as he observed the potion's incorporation.

Frank started at her entrance but managed to keep the beer from splashing across the floor.

"Whoa, you sure are jumpy this evening," Tawny chuckled at his startled look.

"Yeah, I'm fine. You know, just feeling a bit dazed still. You took a lot outta me, Baby." He managed a smile and offered up the beer to her.

"I'll say. Someone needed a bit of a release." She took the beer and gave him a mischievous, knowing grin.

She lifted the drink to her lips, taking in a hearty gulp.

He made to tell her something as the beer washed across her lips, but stopped himself, joining her with his own and a growing sense of curiosity as to what that stuff would do to his cheating wife, but also, where did the bottle go? He could swear it was in his hand when she entered, but now it was nowhere, not on the counter, not in his hand, not even stashed in his pocket.

Whatever.

Whatever Kami set in motion Tawny had coming to her.

Chapter 9

They spent the rest of the evening eating and drinking with the other regulars at the Suds Zone as if all the bad juju from the past few days was melted away. They joked, they flirted, they came off as a normal couple with nothing wrong in their lives.

Around nine o' clock they headed back to the house and started their evening ritual to prepare for bed. At ten o' clock, Frank got a call from his partner there was a dead body in the low-rent district and the captain needed them to go down and write off the incident as either a murder or a suicide.

"Damn it, Jimmy. Can you take care of this on your own?" Frank growled at his partner on the other end of the phone.

"Nope. Sorry, man. I'm on my way and will be at your place in ten to pick you up."

They hung up, and Frank went to break the news of the late-night shift to Tawny.

"No worries, baby. I'm pretty beat anyway. I'll just finish off another beer and crash out with some trashy TV. Don't worry, I'll be here when you get back," she said and then cradled his face between her soft, sweet-smelling hands and kissed him goodbye as Jimmy pulled up to retrieve him.

Frank enveloped her in a hug, feeling her body fall into the softness of his embrace.

"I'll try not to wake you when I get back," he said and kissed her goodbye on the top of her brow. He headed out, grabbed his leather jacket, gun and badge and was off with Jimmy to kill the next few hours with the unsavory task of determining the death of a likely junkie who gave in and blew his hidden wad of cash on some bad drugs.

Chapter 10

Frank's suspicions of the crime scene proved correct. The guy was riddled with needle marks and sores. His emaciated face was pulled back in a grotesque death masque of dopamine induced elation. A stream of vomit leaked from the corner of his mouth. His bile-bloated lungs, suffocating him. He died alone, his body illuminated by the buzzing red neon glow from a nearby market streaming in his window. It took about an hour to clear the scene and declare the junkie pushed the plunger on the syringe himself with no evidence of outside assistance.

After filling out the requisite reports and blowing off some steam with a couple shots, Jimmy drove Frank home. He entered the quiet house, the TV left on when Tawny stumbled off to bed. The night was thick with the summer heat, and he already sweat through his t-shirt and was in need of freshening up. He didn't feel up for a full scrub down but jumped into the shower to cool off and wash away the oily sickness of his toxic evening. He needed to confront Tawny about the little shit down the block, but now was not good. He needed to get some sleep.

He finished up in the shower, did a cursory drying, wrapped his towel around his waist, and went to his bedroom to throw on a fresh t-shirt and boxers before bed. He stepped into the dark room and was accosted by the smell of burnt flesh and sick. He choked back his own vomit and fought to breathe through the toxic fumes that engulfed the bedroom. A haze hung in the room, coating the air with a mist that stung his eyes and clogged his nose and throat with the acrid smell of death.

"Tawny! What the fuck is going on? Are you in here?" He coughed and choked, searching the moist fog for any sign of Tawny.

He heard a rustle and saw a shape shift in the bed.

"Tawny, we gotta get outta here!" He reached toward the figure, wanting to grab it and run from the abrasive air.

The shape shifted and rose. His teared-up eyes could barely make out the outline of Tawny through the burning haze. Something was wrong. Tawny was small and lithe, and what moved towards him was awkward and bulbous. There seemed to be too much there. Not that it was a fat figure, it was just too much. He thought his eyes must be screwing with him. It was as if there were more arms, legs and everything than there should have been.

"Tawny? Is that you?" He squinted, and his voice grew frantic as he realized whatever was moving towards him could not be Tawny.

"What the fuck? Who's there? Tawny?" He held his hands out to ward off the oncoming shape.

He spun and ran from the room, his towel dropped free in the hallway, his belly and manhood flapped free as he ricocheted off the walls, his eyes still not clear of the film from the gaseous air in the bedroom. He stumbled and tripped on a shoe as he fell into the living room, his head glancing off the coffee table opening a gash and ringing his bell just enough for him to take a beat on the floor, grasping at his throbbing skull.

Heavy footsteps reverberated through the thin floor of the old house. Frank lifted himself up on all fours. He fought the pain in his head struggling to get his bearings in the cluttered living room. He searched for his service revolver, but it was in the kitchen. He scrambled to get up as the footsteps rounded the doorway, a cloud of thick stench wafted around the corner following the figure like a cape.

Frank pushed himself back against the couch wiping at his eyes to get a clearer look at the intruder.

In front of him stood an abomination he could not have ever imagined would exist in nature let alone be standing over him in his living room. He flashed back to his nightmares, of the swirling vision of Tawny and her lover entangled as one, and when reality ripped back into his vision he was faced with the horror of Tawny spliced and intermingled into the flesh of the neighbor boy. They were a tangle of lewd seduction entwined by melted flesh. Where their skin touched was fused in a gelatinous incorporation of the other. His penis melted into her vagina, her legs still wrapped around him and molded to his waist, her breasts mashed into the boy's hairless, muscled chest. Their heads melted together, her forehead pressed into his cheek, her once vibrant hair now matted with mucus and blood as their bodies meshed together. The beast that towered over Frank gurgled and bubbled as if still in transition to its final form.

"What the Fuck! Tawny, no!" Frank screamed as the beast with two backs lurched towards him, the hands of the fused lovers beckoning him to join them in their macabre embrace.

Frank was frozen. Screams of terror and disbelief roared in his head, only to be drowned out when the beast spoke.

"Hello, lover. We were gonna surprise you." The sound that exited the beast was Tawny's and the boy's speaking in near unison, the upper tones of hers mingling with his, generating a rattling chorus of pain, fear, and succulent sexual permanence.

"What?!" Frank's terror shook him. His voice quivered with the vision in front of him.

The creature knelt down over Frank, straddling him, dripping the morose concoction of fluids and congealed skin across the floor and over his legs. It sizzled and burned as it landed on him. He winced as the pain raced through his body.

The creature leaned in, its entwined faces next to his.

"You always said you wanted a threesome. You still game?" The two faces leered and licked at their lips. Frank's screams were drowned out as the two mouths enveloped his, their tongues lashing out to melt with his in a deep and bonding kiss that entwined the three in a bubbling mess of melted flesh. Frank's adrenaline-induced erection was consumed by the monsters undulating mass with slippery ease as its weight settled down on him.

Frank wanted to scream, vomit, fight, break free all at the same time. He was helpless under the weight of the beast that pulled him further inside with every second. His nightmares came true, and the only one to blame was himself. It didn't stop him from screaming in his own chest the words that started this whole scenario, "That bitch!" The words rang in his head as their writhing bodies melted into one pulsating mass until all that was left was a pool of milky liquid that swirled and bubbled until settling to a still, translucent puddle on the cluttered floor.

The liquid slithered through the obstacles of the room, weaving past clothes, discarded beer bottles, the coffee table legs, and other refuse on its way to the kitchen. It climbed the counter on a route towards the small green glass bottle that sat in wait. The liquid slithered into the mouth of the bottle until every last drop of the melted lovers was recovered. The bottle righted itself, and a weathered cork jumped into the air and landed with a squeak, securing the contents away before the bottle vanished, reappearing in the dim light of the candelabra on the rickety table inside the musty shack Kami called home.

HOT PREMIERE

By David Clark

"Hey Joe, is it safe to go in there yet?"

Fifty-three-year-old Fire Chief Joe Mitchell walked toward Detective Mike Wilson. Mike has been at the scene for the last several hours waiting to enter and start his investigation.

"Mike, it will still be a while. There are several hot spots I am still worried about, and there may still be gas in those cars. We just don't know." Mike looked back at the telltale signs of white and gray smoke rising just beyond the fence behind them.

"Thanks, how is our survivor? Is he able to talk?" Mike was referring to sixteen-year-old Matthew Reynolds, who fire crews pulled from the apocalyptic scene moments after they arrived. He was huddled in the bathroom with flames approaching. Somehow he avoided being burnt by the flames, but soot covered every inch of him, and he suffered smoke inhalation.

"Yeah, he can talk. Follow me." Mike followed Joe over to a line of five Cadillac Miller-Meteor Ambulances, parked waiting to transport victims. So far only one had any activity.

"Robert, Mike wants to talk to the kid," Joe called over to the ambulance driver. Robert opened the back door, exposing the cramped work area. Matthew was lying in the bed with an oxygen mask over his nose, a paramedic hunched over him. Joe asked the paramedic to step out for a minute to let the detective talk to Matthew. Mike took off his tan sport coat, folded it in half and laid it on the top of the ambulance. He removed his houndstooth fedora and put it on top of the folded sports coat. Stepping up on the bumper, he contorted his six-foot four-inch thin frame to fit in the cramped space next to the gurney.

"Hi Matthew, I am Detective Mike Wilson. I need to know what happened tonight. What do you remember?" The kid stared up at him with his eyes wide open; the whites contrasted against his soot covered face. He was in shock, and Mike knew it. Who wouldn't be, considering what he survived?

"Matthew, can you hear me?"

Matthew turned his head and nodded. Mike reached up and pulled the oxygen mask down below his mouth. "I need to know what happened here. I know it's hard, but can you tell me what you remember?"

Matthew spoke with a scratchy voice as he recalled the events of Friday evening. "We were so excited. Everyone was talking about the grand opening of the Third Street Drive-in all day at school. Robbie, Dale, and I went together in my brother's Chevelle. I begged him for weeks to let me borrow it. He agreed at the last moment. We got to the drive-in around seven. It wasn't open yet, so we sat there in line with a lot of other cars. There were banners and balloons announcing the grand opening hanging from everywhere. Everything was so new and clean. Even the driveway in and down the rows was clean, white rock."

Matthew coughed and took a few deep breaths through the oxygen mask before continuing. "After twenty minutes, old man Richardson opened the gate and let cars in one at a time. We pulled up and paid five dollars. We drove in through the gate, past the concession stands, and turned down the center toward the front. The rows filled up from the front first. I think we ended up on the second row. We could smell the fragrance of melted butter wafting in the breeze while we were waiting outside; it made Dale hungry. We went to the concessions for food; he had to have popcorn. By the time we started back, the entire place was full. The movie hadn't started yet, but it was dark. The only light sources were from the concession stand in the back, the bathrooms up front, and the torches lining the fence in the back and on both sides."

Matthew calmed down, but Mike could tell some thoughts still hit an emotional nerve. His voice grew stronger, but from time to time he coughed and needed to take a drag on the oxygen.

"The previews started, and the torch light lowered to next to nothing. There was a big cheer, and a few cars honked; then it became dead quiet. You could hear nothing but the sound of crickets and wind under the volume of the preview coming through the speakers hanging on our windows. Then *Attack of the Ancient Zombie* started. It was great. I've never seen a movie on a screen so big before." Another cough and a quick wipe of some new tears. "It was about halfway through the movie when Allison Leary came and knocked on our back window and waved. She wanted me to walk with her to the concession stands. I didn't want to miss the movie, but there was no way I would refuse a chance to spend time with her. I got out, and Dale jumped up to the driver's seat."

Matthew propped himself up on his elbows and moved around on the gurney trying to get comfortable. "Detective, can I sit up? Everything is so cramped in here, and it's getting warm."

"Do you feel well enough to get out?"

"Yes, sir."

Mike scooted out of the back and stood up, stretching. "Hey Robert, Matthew is feeling a little claustrophobic; any objections if we get him out?"

Without a word, Robert rolled the gurney to the edge of the bumper. Easing it over he allowed the first set of wheels to fall to the ground. He locked them in place and pulled until just the front edge was left in the ambulance for support. He unstrapped Matthew and helped sit him up.

"Is that better?"

"Yes, sir, it is. Thanks," Matthew looked more comfortable, but still stared straight ahead.

"I will leave the oxygen mask right here for now in case you need it. If you start feeling bad, you call me, okay?"

"Yes, sir."

With that, Robert left so Matthew and Detective Wilson could continue talking.

"So, Allison Leary came by your car?"

"Yes, we walked to the concession stand. We stood and talked while in line."

"Up to this point did you see anything suspicious?"

"Suspicious?"

"Yes, was anyone acting odd, anything seem out of place or get your attention?"

Matthew paused for a second to think.

"It was dark. Most were watching the movie, but a few were walking around. I'm not sure I could describe any of them though. I'm sorry."

"It's okay. Go ahead from the concession stand." Mike retrieved a three-inch notepad from his shirt pocket.

"I think we were in line for maybe ten minutes. I offered to help carry the food back to her car. It was parked on the opposite side of the lot from us. We were halfway there when I heard a loud metal crash behind us. I looked back and saw the gate had closed. A lot of folks were looking too."

"Could the wind have blown it closed? Was there a big gust or something?"

"There was a small breeze, and the gate was corrugated metal panels, so I guess the wind could have blown it closed."

Mike made note of the gate closing, his first lead that may aid the investigation

"After a few seconds, everyone's attention went back to the movie. A minute or so later everything seemed brighter. The torches on the fence were burning higher than before. I thought it was just a mistake, and they would turn them down soon." Matthew's voice cracked a little, and for the first time he looked back over his shoulder at the smoke hovering over the drive-in and stared.

Matthew's eyes refocused back on the detective. "We hadn't reached her car before we heard the first screams. At first, I thought they were part of the movie or someone messing around, but then they continued. I turned toward the screams and saw the torches on the fence tilted inward shooting flames toward the cars like a blow torch." Matthew's body shuddered. Mike put a fatherly hand on his shoulder. "Take a breath and go slow."

"I saw … I saw one girl running across the lot. She was a big ball of fire, with flames streaming behind her. She came from the back row of cars, which were now ablaze. Those trapped inside were thrashing around trying to get free, but couldn't. Everyone was panicking. Some started their cars to leave while others ran to help. The torches grew stronger creating a wall of dancing flame, catching anyone or anything within thirty feet of the fence. Everywhere I looked, I saw cars in flames, people running ablaze."

Matthew looked toward the fence in the distance. "Some tried to make a run for safety and leave, but couldn't. The gate was locked. A few cars rammed it, but they didn't break through. The line at the gate grew longer. They tried to climb over, but it was too tall. As they tried to escape, the fire spread from car to car and along the ground. Detective, it only took minutes for the flames to cut the lot in half. It trapped those by the gate in the back where the fire was faster. It moved from car to car pushing people into the back corner with no escape. Everyone was screaming and yelling. I kept watching to see if anyone would open the gate or pull down a piece of the metal fence, but nothing. There was nothing any of us could do. I stood there and watched. The screams were horrifying. I saw no one escape from back there." Matthew's eyes pleaded with the detective. "There was nothing we could do to help them. We were cut off from them. I tried to think of a way, but there was nothing. Honestly, sir, we couldn't help them."

"We know. But there is something you can do now. You can tell me everything you know, and I can try to find out what happened and why. Can you help me?"

"Yes, sir. I grabbed Allison's hand, and we ran back to my brother's car. We felt the heat burning our skin from a distance. Dale and Robbie were standing outside our car. I yelled at them to get in. They jumped in the back. Allison and I got in the front. I saw Joseph Marts' F-250 Camper Special speeding through the flames for the fence. I followed, thinking he would break through, and we could follow him out. When he hit the fence, it held, and a large fireball shot straight back at us. The flash of heat caught everything in the car on fire. I looked up, and flames were rolling across the headliner. The heat was suffocating, and smoke was filling around us. Robbie and Dale tried to climb out over the top of me to escape. I fought them off while trying to get to the door handle. I found it, pulled, and fell on the ground. They fell out on top of me. Flames consumed Robbie's shirt, and he took off running. I looked back in the car for Allison. She was screaming and trying to push the flames away with her hands. I called to her, trying to get her out of the car, but she didn't hear me. Before I could reach in and grab her, the whole car was consumed in an inferno of intense heat, white hot flames, and smoke. I saw her sitting there limp. Her skin was melting off of her face."

Matthew stared off into space. His body was there with Detective Wilson, but his mind was a million miles away, trapped in the horror of what he just witnessed. His voice became as void of emotion as the stare in his eyes.

"I stood up and looked around and saw nowhere to go. There was screaming and shrieking. Bodies lying everywhere, smoldering. Thick black smoke obscured my vision and caused my eyes to water as I tried to find a way out. The combined smell of burning flesh, gasoline, oil, and plastic made me nauseous and dizzy. The sounds of the screaming, crackling of the fire, and the occasional pop of melting tires came from everywhere. There was no way out. I saw the bathrooms and ran there and tried to climb up the outside, but couldn't reach. I went in to see if there was a way to the roof there and saw a small vent, but I had no way to reach it either. When I tried to leave, it was too late. The flames were already licking at the door and coming through the gaps in the door frame. I hid in the back corner as far away from the door as I could. The entire room filled with smoke, and I could feel the heat from the fire coming through the door and radiating through the back wall. That is the last thing I remember."

"Thanks, Matthew. You sit here and relax. If you can think of anything else, you let me know." Detective Wilson put his pad back in his pocket.

Mike walked around and searched for the Fire Chief. He needed answers, ones he believed he could only find inside the fenced off drive-in.

"Hey Joe, can we go inside yet? I am thinking this is a crime scene now."

"Yeah, you and I agree on that, Mike. Come look at this." Mike followed Joe over to the main gate and pointed, but he didn't need to. Mike already noticed the lock on the outside.

"So, someone locked it from the outside?"

"Oh, that's not all." The two of them squeezed through a small gap the fire crews cut in the fence. They stepped from a recognizable landscape into the foreign fury of hell. Mike looked around and saw nothing but shells of cars, burnt ground, and mounds of debris. He could determine which were coupes, four doors, or trucks, but not the model or the color. They were metal smoking hulls now. He continued his survey of the devastation as Joe called to him from across the way. "Mike, come over here."

Joe stood by one of the torches pointing ominously inward. "See these pipes? They go back to a central propane tank behind the concession stand. From there you can adjust the flame, but do you see this elbow here and the chain?"

Mike stepped closer to examine what Joe was trying to show him. Each torch was connected to a threaded-T pipe. The connection was still loose. A detail that struck Mike as odd. If you were doing this for gas, you would never leave it loose. The slack in the joint lets it rotate ninety degrees from straight up to straight out horizontal. Joe pulled on the chain he pointed out, and the pipe moved.

"Are you telling me this chain lets someone move the torches?"

"You can follow the chain all the way back from torch to torch, across gears attached to the pipe. It ends back behind the concession stands."

"That is not normal." Detective Wilson felt confused. The questions of *why* and *what for* flooded his mind. He struggled to accept the growing probability this was intentional, not just a horrible accident. None of this made sense. He looked around while trying to process what he just learned. There is no patch of ground unburnt. Smoke rose from everywhere.

He saw smoldering dark mounds of debris along the fences. He walked toward one of the piles. There was something sparkling in it. Shock overtook his brain when it realized it was a ring on the finger of a burnt girl protruding from the mound. The mound itself was a mass of burnt humanity. Other bodies hung on the fence, continuing the struggle to get out, even in death. Each body was either burnt to a blackened crisp or overcooked by the intense heat to the point of falling off the bones. Faces were scalded to the extent of not being identifiable or even resembling anything human.

The detective stumbled backward and landed on his backside. "You okay?" Joe asked as he approached with an extended hand to help him up. Mike realized he tripped over another teenager whose swollen skin resembled a slab of barbecued meat. He stammered and crawled backwards until Joe helped him to his feet. "Easy there, take a minute."

"Joe, are all those—"

"Yes, each of those piles are burnt victims. They were trying to get out at those points. The one back there by the gate is three times as large as the others. They never had a chance."

Mike surveyed the entire scene. Rammed up against the fence he saw what he believed was an F-250 with what looked like the hull of a Chevelle behind it. That had to be the car Matthew was in. The pipe between the fence and the truck was broken. A ruptured gas line explained the fireball. He took a few steps closer to the truck and observed two partially cremated skeletons in the front seat. There was not an ounce of flesh, hair, or fabric left on them. His thoughts moved to Matthew's Chevelle just a few feet behind it, but he couldn't make himself look. He knew inside that charred metal hull were Allison Leary's burnt remains.

"How did Matthew manage to survive?"

"He was lucky. When we got to him, the floor was covered in water. The best we can figure is the heat from the fire caused the pipe to burst covering him and the entire building."

"Lucky kid. Any signs of the owner, Henry Richardson?"

"It will take days to sort through this, and even then, we will not be able to identify everyone. My guess is we are looking at over two hundred victims here, but ..." Joe paused with a concerned look on his face. "There is a parking space outside the fence labeled Owner; his truck is still there. You need to follow me."

Mike followed Joe behind the concessions. Waiting to greet both of them was a devilish skeleton perched over the gas pipes inside a chain-link box. It still had one hand on the crank attached to the chains they noticed earlier. "I think it's Henry. Mike, he locked himself in to keep anyone from stopping him."

ALL BOYS TOGETHER

By Richard Farren Barber

Once a month Dad would load us kids into the car and drive north. It wasn't an easy drive. Jimmy or Sophie would spend the journey complaining, and Julie would always be sick before we got back home, but we made the journey nonetheless.

Mum stayed at home and made Sunday dinner or battled a pile of ironing. Once, I got up the courage to ask her why she never came with us. She told me it didn't concern her. I tried to argue it didn't concern me either, but each month I was still expected to go.

The radio was always turned off on those trips. It wasn't like driving to Rufford Park, where Dad would listen to football or obscure sports channels. Maybe that was why I disliked those drives so much; they felt wrong from the moment we left the house.

I always knew where we were headed as soon as Dad said, "Fancy a car ride?" Normally, I would track our route on the large AA roadmap Dad kept in the back of the car, but on those trips, I stared through the windscreen and stayed silent. I knew the route anyway, past the old cinema and out of town. I had landmarks to watch for: the petrol station with no pumps, the cemetery, and the burned-out pub. I didn't need a map.

After about twenty minutes, Dad would turn off the road onto a rutted track that probably never saw any traffic other than our car. The car bucked on the uneven road, and if Julie was going to be sick, that was usually when it happened. On either side of the track, thick hedgerows clawed at the car panels. They scratched at the windows like they were trying to get inside, and during that part of the trip, even Jimmy would be quiet.

Dad would get out of the car and march up the overgrown path. At the height of summer, the grasses and nettles reached up to my knees, and some winters the snow got inside my shoes, and it took weeks for my feet to dry out.

Dad marched with his head bowed, glaring at the ground, while the others and I ran to keep up with him. There were trees on both sides of the path and houses hidden beyond the branches. Broken houses with smashed windows and fallen walls where no one had lived for at least a hundred years. In summer, when everything was green, I couldn't see those other houses, but I still knew they were there. I could feel them behind the trees, watching as I ran to keep up with Dad.

He would stop in front of the rotting wooden gate and rest his hands on the top bar. For a long time, he would just stand there. Over the years, I learned to stand beside him and keep quiet. I think Dad appreciated that. He never spoke to me about it, but I think my silence meant a lot to him.

Finally, he would sigh and say, "That should be ours."

He would speak without taking his eyes off the house. "That should be *yours*."

I never knew how to reply. Apart from the time spent hanging over the gate and staring at the old house, my dad never mentioned it. Some history I learned from Mum, but most I got from my Uncle Frank during the week he came to stay with us.

I was fourteen, old enough to understand he was apt to tell me something he shouldn't, but too young to point it out. We sat in the back garden as the daylight faded. Uncle Frank had taken possession of one of the deck chairs from the garage, and I sat on the scuff of ground at his feet and looked up at him. I adored Uncle Frank. He frightened me, but maybe that was part of the attraction. He was everything my father was not. Where Dad was soft spoken and introspective, Frank was loud. Where my father spoke in slow, considered sentences, Uncle Frank quickly passed judgement on everything. As the week progressed, I heard him contradicting statements he had made only a few days earlier. I came to understand it was *just Uncle Frank*. There was Drunk Frank, Sober Frank, and Hungover Frank. Each had their own personalities. Each had their own challenges.

Drunk Uncle Frank was the one I liked the best. I know that isn't such a great thing to say, but Drunk Uncle Frank told me things no one else would, like how to ask a girl out on a date and how to get over it when that same girl rejected me. Drunk Uncle Frank was the fount of all teenage knowledge. I sat with my back against the crooked leg of the deck chair, surrounded by crushed cans from the lager my uncle consumed. Each night, before I went to bed, I took the cans, hid them in my bag, and dropped them in a bin on the way to school the following day. I knew if my dad saw how much Frank was drinking, his stay would be cut short. I couldn't afford for that to happen. There was still so much about the world I needed to learn.

The last night Uncle Frank stayed with us in July, the air remained warm even after the sun faded. I sat outside, tasting summer on my tongue and listening to birdsong and music from a party a few houses over. I heard my mother and father arguing inside. I think Dad was anxious about Frank. He seemed to find fault with everything his brother said or did.

"You know what they're arguing about?" Uncle Frank asked me.

"You?"

He shrugged and took a slug from the can he was holding. "Maybe that's what they *think* they're arguing about."

He held out the can, like he had done every night, but this time I took the drink from his hand. It tasted of old socks. I tried not to cough and handed the lager back to him without saying a word.

"No, you're best off out of it," he said. He held up the can like it was an offering to some unseen God. "It's probably caused more arguments than money, religion, and race put together; yet, we still can't do without it." I recognised the maudlin tone, although I thought it was still a little early for Drunk Frank.

"Your dad doesn't like me," he said. Before I could open my mouth to protest, he shushed me and carried on. "Don't say anything. You don't need to defend your father. That's not how it works. Your parents are there to protect you, and they do a good job of that."

I said nothing. Uncle Frank's words were too close to something I had overheard between my mum and dad that morning, about how Uncle Frank was a bad influence.

I nodded. It felt wrong to lie to Uncle Frank, even when lying felt like the right thing to do. I was fourteen, still trying to understand the difference between good lies and bad lies.

"They aren't arguing about me. They're arguing about The House." He looked at me. "You know about The House?"

"Dad takes us up there sometimes."

Uncle Frank raised an eyebrow. "So you *know* about The House?"

"No. He drives us out there some Sundays, and after we've spent a little while staring at it, he brings us back. He doesn't speak about it, though."

"What's it like?" Uncle Frank asked. I was flattered, I admit. I found it hard to believe there was anything on earth I could know more about than Uncle Frank.

"It's …" I stopped. I didn't have the words to capture the feeling it prompted in me. It was dread; yet, I knew part of me enjoyed going—when we drove out to the house, it almost felt like I was taking part in a sacred ceremony. Or maybe a duty. Yeah, that was what it was—our visits to the house were a duty.

Uncle Frank nodded, as if I had managed to communicate more about the old house by what I had not said than by any description I could give.

"Yeah, it does that to you," he said.

He looked at the back window. I followed his gaze and almost expected to see the silhouettes of my parents, but, of course, the only thing I saw was the brown curtains with the yellow light seeping out around the edges.

Uncle Frank lowered his voice. "Have you ever been there at night?"

"No!"

I had seen the house during the day, and I knew how terrible it was. I imagined travelling that old country road in the dark and stillness of night, and the idea turned my skin cold.

Uncle Frank looked again at the window. My parents' voices grew louder, building up to the sort of argument I had only ever witnessed once or twice before, when the house was silent as winter for days afterwards.

"Where does your dad keep the car keys?"

"In the drawer by the telephone."

"Could you get them?"

I nodded. My mouth was too dry for words. I wanted to tell Uncle Frank although I knew where the keys were, I didn't want to get them. I didn't want to sit beside him in silence, as we bounced along that country road in the dark. I didn't want to stand outside the house and see those blind windows without even the sun's reflection to distract me.

Uncle Frank drained his can and stood up. I thought he would sway and maybe stagger when he walked, the way he did most nights when it was time to go inside, but there was a graceful fluidity to his movement.

"Well, go on then," he told me. If I'd been older, I would have been able to say no, and if I'd been younger, he wouldn't have dared to do anything, but I was fourteen, and that's a magical age. My sisters and brother were inside the house, and it occurred to me this was something that might never happen again—not only the chance to go out in the car with Uncle Frank, but to sit out in the garden listening to him spin tales about hitchhiking through France and Germany or working in a bar in Mexico.

I eased open the back door and was struck by the sound of my parents' shouting. I tiptoed past the closed kitchen door to the front of the house. The drawer squeaked as I opened it. I froze and listened to the rhythm of my parents' argument, expecting them to pause and investigate the noise. When they didn't, I wrapped my fingers tight around the car keys to prevent them from clinking together.

Uncle Frank waited for me at the back door. He held out his hand, and when I gave him the keys, he stood there for a moment. "It's for your own good," he said. "It's part of you." He paused to search for the right word. "It's part of your heritage."

We walked along the side of the house. He unlatched the gate, eased it open, and closed it behind me once we were both through.

Yellow streetlights poured down on us. I felt like someone in one of the houses would shout, "Uncle Frank and Mickie are sneaking out!" But we made it to my dad's car without being stopped. Uncle Frank fumbled with the keys, and I took them from his hands. When he breathed out, I could taste the stale lager on his breath, but when I'd unlocked the door I held the car key out, and he opened the driver's side. I slipped into the passenger seat and turned to buckle my safety belt. Uncle Frank watched what I was doing and shrugged, then he pulled his own belt around him.

The radio was on when he turned the key in the ignition, but he silenced it with a flick of his wrist. "Can't stand that crap."

"Me neither," I said, and Uncle Frank laughed.

He steered between the rows of parked cars. I'd watched my dad do the same thing hundreds of times before, but this time I was utterly fixated. I didn't breathe again until we were on the main road. We passed the old cinema and the cemetery. Uncle Frank didn't speak until the streetlights had been replaced by open fields of ink-black night.

"You know where it is?" he asked.

"I think so."

"Good, because I haven't a clue."

I looked over at him. Most of his features were hidden in the dark, so it was impossible to tell what he was thinking.

"Why are you doing this?"

"It needs to be done." He fell silent, and I thought that was all the explanation I was going to get. Then, he started to speak once more. "You need to know, and your dad is never going to tell you. But you're the eldest boy, the next in line, and you need to know."

"Turn here," I said. Uncle Frank was slow to respond, and we almost overshot the junction before he put on the brakes. Uncle Frank battled with the steering wheel and cursed under his breath until we were back on the left-hand side with the hedgerows pressing against my window.

"Next time, try and give me a little more warning."

"Sorry."

I saw the next turn coming up, but I was tempted to let Uncle Frank drive straight past. Maybe we could carry on, and he would give up and turn back home. Except I was terrified. I imagined Uncle Frank in a bar in Mexico with his hands pulled into fists as he stood his ground or covered in grease and sweat on an oil rig with blood oozing from cuts across his arms. I didn't think he would hurt me (not really), but I knew I didn't want to see Angry Uncle Frank.

"Turn right up ahead," I said. "It's a sharp corner, almost hidden."

He grunted and slowed the car down, until it would have been quicker for me to get out and walk. He found the turn-in, a gap in the hedge where even the rutted wheel tracks were overgrown.

I stared out the window. Occasionally, I saw a light where a house sat among the dead trees.

A pale face stared out from between the dark branches. I jerked back in my seat. By the time I realised what I had seen, the face was only a stain on my memory.

"What is it?" Uncle Frank asked, but I said nothing. If I didn't acknowledge the boy, he might not really exist.

Trees pressed in on both sides. Branches stretched out and brushed the windscreen, scraping against the glass like fingernails. I played with the door handle but didn't try to open it. Uncle Frank said nothing; he simply peered through the dirty windscreen. A couple of times he squirted water onto the glass and tried to clear it, but that merely turned the dirt into mud.

I made a point of staring at the plastic grey interior of the car, because that meant I wouldn't see anything outside. I wouldn't see the boy's face peering through the bushes, lit up by an eerie pale light. I wouldn't see the ghost houses out in the middle of the woods with the broken down walls and large stones, overgrown with moss. I wouldn't have to look at the house as we got closer and closer, until finally Uncle Frank stood on the brakes, and they squealed like a child's scream.

"Here we are," he said.

I looked out through the windscreen.

That's not so bad, I thought. *It's not really any different from how it looks during the day.*

The house was lit by the twin beams of the car's headlights, like scenery on a stage. The broken window glass reflected the light. I wondered if kids came out here to throw stones at the windows, and then I thought of the long walk up that narrow track, and the way the branches clawed at you as you passed. I thought about the boy's face I'd seen peering through the trees as we passed, the dead boy with pasty white flesh and eyes black and hollow, and I was sure no one came up here. No one but my family.

The wall was pitted and uneven. Some bricks had crumbled into dust. There were tiles missing from the roof. I imagined the walls inside would have decorative paper speckled with mould. The bare floorboards would be warped.

Uncle Frank drummed his fingers on the steering wheel. Once I noticed it, the noise began to irritate me.

Uncle Frank stopped, and silence washed through the car. He didn't look at me. He simply stared at the house. I tried to decide if he loved it or hated it. Maybe it was a bit of both.

He pulled at the door handle and missed it. I wanted to laugh, but somehow it didn't feel right. He tried again, and this time he seized the catch with his fingers. When he pushed the door open, the car rocked on its springs.

The door slammed shut behind him with a violence I found terrifying. I sank into my seat, hoping to disappear between the folds of soft blue material. *He's found it,* I thought. *He can have a look around for a few minutes, and then we'll head back home.*

As he walked in front of the car, the light flared across his lower body. He put both his hands on the car bonnet and stared through the windscreen. "Come on!"

I shook my head.

A look crossed Uncle Frank's features. It was too fleeting for me to truly understand what it meant, but it scared me. It scared me more than his erratic drive out to that place. It scared me more than the boy's pale face amongst the trees. My mind created a vision in which Angry Uncle Frank shouted and cursed and wrenched open the door to drag me out of the car.

The look passed, and it was only my Uncle Frank staring in through the car windscreen once more. I fumbled for the handle and tumbled out onto the ground.

Uncle Frank laughed at my exit and hurried to help me up. My hands and knees were covered in dead leaves, and he started to brush them off me, even though each time he did it felt like I was being beaten.

"That's better," he said and pulled me to my feet. He put a hand on my shoulder, a thick and meaty hand more familiar with handling wrenches and hammers. His knuckles were grazed from punching drunk men. It was a hand completely unlike my father's. He steered me forward, pressing down on my shoulder until it ached. He drove until we stopped at the rickety fence marking the edge of the property.

"Look," he told me. "No, not at me. Look at that." He nodded in the direction of the house.

"That should be your dad's," he said. He thought about that statement for a moment before modifying it. "It should probably be yours now, oldest boy in the family and all that."

"I don't want it."

I thought Uncle Frank was going to hit me. He lifted his hand from my shoulder. His breathing became faster. Ragged. When he put his hand back down, I felt each finger press into my muscle.

"We used to come out here as children. Your grandfather didn't have a car, so we'd get a bus and walk from the village. We'd stand here outside the gate, and he'd tell us about the house. There was still a family living in the house then, and if they saw us, they'd come out and shoo us away. Like they were ashamed to see us because they knew they were squatters."

I tried to imagine people living in the house. A mother, father, and a couple kids playing in the garden. There was nothing to suggest the house had been occupied for years, maybe decades. But Uncle Frank was old, so when he said there had been people living in the house when he was a child, I believed him.

"Come on, then," Uncle Frank said.

I turned back toward the car, but I'd only taken one step when Uncle Frank grabbed me by the elbow.

"Where are you going?"

"Back to the car."

He laughed. "Not yet. We can't come all this way and not go inside."

Inside?

He opened the garden gate with his free hand. The bottom of the gate scraped along the ground, drawing an arc in the dirt. Uncle Frank stepped onto the path. An uneven line of broken red bricks jutted from the ground like crooked teeth. The edges pressed against the soles of my shoes as Uncle Frank dragged me along the path.

This close, I discovered the house had a smell. It made me think of a dead cat I once found. The fur was white and matted with blood. Ants crawled across its hair and around its mouth. It smelled almost sweet.

The house was like that, almost sweet. Like a birthday cake. I swallowed, and I could feel the stink burning down my throat. I imagined small black ants skittering into my lungs.

Little of the door remained. Two wooden panels were missing, and the others were cracked. I could see straight into the hallway beyond, where shadows shifted in the dark. I'm sure I saw the silver reflection of the car's headlights in a pair of eyes burrowed deep inside the house. The glint was gone a moment later, as if it had only ever been my imagination, or the creature chose that moment to close its eyes.

Uncle Frank bullied his way into the house. The door collapsed into a pile of rotten wood, which crunched beneath his shoes as he stepped into the hallway.

I looked behind me, from the house to the forest surrounding the property. Beyond the glare of the headlights, I saw the boy peering at me from between the trees.

I turned to follow Uncle Frank, and after staring into the beam of the car's headlights, the hallway looked to be in total darkness. "Uncle Frank!" I called. My voice echoed off the walls.

"Don't dawdle," he muttered.

I looked in the direction of his voice, and the sheet of pure black separated so I could make out my uncle's silhouette. As I stared into the grainy darkness, my sight returned. Now, I could see the carpet and the pattern on the wallpaper. There were pictures on the walls. It was still possible to make out some grey images of children wrapped in formal clothing and posed in awkward family groups.

Uncle Frank swiped at a picture, and it crashed to the floor, breaking the glass. "Don't look at them. They don't belong here." He lifted his foot and crushed the heel of his shoe into the middle of the photograph. "This is our house. Ours!"

He moved further into the house without waiting for me. I stared down at the photograph and managed to see the face of a small child. There was a strong resemblance between the photograph and the boy who had peered at me from the bushes.

"Your grandfather lived in this house, and his father before him. There's been a McCullough living on this land for the past eight generations." Uncle Frank's voice rippled out from the room. I found him standing in a room where most of the far wall was stained with black patches, as if the plaster was infected with a disease.

"It will always be ours. As long as we remember."

I thought of our small house in the middle of our ordinary little street, with walls so thin I could hear the couple next door screaming whenever they had a fight. I didn't want to live here in the woods. I didn't want to lie in my bed upstairs, waiting for the boy from the forest to creep into my room.

"Can we go now, Uncle Frank?"

"Go?"

I shuddered at his voice. I understood why drunks at a bar in Nebraska would do whatever they were told when Uncle Frank shouted at them.

"I don't like it here," I told him.

His fingers tightened their grip on my shoulder.

"You're hurting me."

The fingers got tighter, and I couldn't tell if he hadn't heard me or didn't care. I wanted to cry, except I thought Uncle Frank might be the sort to dismiss tears by saying, "Big boys don't cry."

He took his hand from my shoulder, but even after it had gone, the pressure remained like a phantom. "I'm sorry," he said, "but you've got to understand. I'm not doing this for me or your dad. Not even for your brother or your sisters. I'm doing it for you. This is where you belong."

"But I don't want it." My voice trembled, and I worried this would make Uncle Frank even angrier. "I just want to be back at home."

Uncle Frank knelt, so he was able to look me in the eyes. "You *have* to want it."

There was a loud crash from the second floor of the house. The sound ripped through the silence, and immediately the air in the room filled with dust.

"They're still here," Uncle Frank said. He ran from the room, his footsteps thundering up the stairs.

Who? I wanted to ask, but my mouth was too dry for speech. The first thought that came to mind was the white face of the boy. I looked around the room, as if I might find him standing behind me.

Darkness hung from the corners.

From upstairs, there came a soft scraping sound. It stopped, as if it knew it had been heard, and then, a moment later, it started again. It came from almost exactly above my head, and I looked up, but all I saw was the water-stained plaster of the room's ceiling. I lowered my eyes and looked around the room.

The boy's face peered in at me through the window.

I screamed.

His skin glowed. It reminded me of the moon. Pale white, almost sickly.

Then he was in the room with me. The chill flowed from him in thick waves pressing against my skin and stealing the heat from my body until I was pale and cold as the small boy.

I screamed again. The boy opened his mouth to mimic me, but no sound emerged from his throat.

There was another loud crash from the room upstairs. Once more, the air filled with dust. Uncle Frank screamed. Up until then, I'd never heard a grown-up scream; even when my dad had broken his arm, he hadn't made a noise, only grown whiter and whiter, before the doctors took him into the bowels of the hospital to fix it. Hearing Uncle Frank scream was somehow worse than the white-faced boy staring at me.

Upstairs, there was another crash and then a loud clear crack of wood snapping. It seemed the whole house shook.

The boy took a step toward me. I held my ground, although my legs were so weak, I felt they might melt away beneath me. "You don't scare me," I told him.

He took another step. It was like standing in front of an open freezer. I felt the cold on my skin and on my lips. "You don't scare me. This is my house." I shouted at him, as if the words held a magic charm. As if saying them might make them true.

Silence swept down from upstairs. Uncle Frank stood at the top of the stairwell. Blood ran from a gash on the side of his head and dripped from his chin.

The boy looked from me to Uncle Frank, and there was no mistaking the terror on his face. If I hadn't been so afraid of the child, I might have felt sorry for him. It would be a lie if I didn't admit there was, at least, a small part of me that enjoyed the fear on his face. I wanted him to feel some of my terror.

Uncle Frank stepped down the stairs to meet me, and I took a step closer to the boy.

"My house," I told him.

The boy shook his head. *No.*

"My house," I said.

Uncle Frank stepped closer. The staircase shuddered beneath him, and I heard the wood creak and groan.

The boy disappeared.

Uncle Frank ran down the remaining steps. His cheeks were red, and his breathing was laboured, like he'd just run a cross-country race. He stopped short, as if he wanted to reach out and hug me, but something prevented him. Some sense it was not the proper thing to do.

His hands hung in the air before him. He looked awkward. "Has your father ever … touched you?"

I looked at him, and there was something about the awkward way he spoke that told me he wasn't simply asking about whether Dad had beaten me for breaking the kitchen window.

"Touched me?"

Uncle Frank's hand burned against my head. It was at once soft, and yet I felt the full weight against my skin. It burned. I wanted to ask him to take it off, but I was too afraid. If I had acknowledged his hand, then I wouldn't know how to respond if my father ever asked, "Did Uncle Frank … touch you?"

I smelled the sweat from Uncle Frank's body and the meaty stink of his breath. He leaned in close, so when he spoke, his words were warm against my cheek. "Has he ever done anything that made you feel uncomfortable?"

"No," I said. I could see in Uncle Frank's face I had spoken too quickly. He stared at me, his vision burrowing into my soul. It was almost a hunger. I felt like an insect trapped under a glass.

"Never," I said. "Dad wouldn't do that."

"I know," Uncle Frank said, and this time it was the speed of *his* reply that betrayed the lie.

"Why would he do that?"

Uncle Frank shrugged. "It's what he knows. It's what all of us know."

"Your Dad?" I asked, without being able to finish the question.

Uncle Frank nodded, and his eyes were bright with tears. I wanted to say something to make it better, but I didn't have the words.

His hand was heavy on my head. I tried to wriggle away, but when I started to move, he pulled me closer to him, and the smell of his body grew stronger. I thought of the pale-faced boy. *Had he struggled? Is that what happened to him? Is that why he was still around?* I thought about my great-grandpa, a man I'd never met, and a man we never talked about, even when my dad brought us out here to his house. I desperately wanted to ask Uncle Frank what happened to him and how he lost the house. But even more than that, I understood I didn't want to know.

I tried to pull away from Uncle Frank, and this time, there was no way to ignore his hand locked around my arm, stopping me from escaping.

"Uncle Frank, that hurts!"

"Ssh," he said. His big, flat hand pressed against the side of my face. My stomach lurched.

"Please, Uncle Frank!"

He stroked my face with his hand. The rough skin scratched against my cheek.

"Ssh."

I stared past Uncle Frank. Through the window, I could see the screaming face of the pale boy.

A thumping sound came from upstairs. I screamed, and as I looked across the room, I was no longer sure if the image I saw in the glass was the pale boy or my own reflection.

I pulled free from Uncle Frank and lurched across the room. It took him a fraction of a second to respond, but by then I had reached the hall. I hit the stairs, two at a time. I looked no further than the next step, until I got to the top of the stairs. Presented with three doors, I picked the only one already open.

I ran into the room, but before I had a chance to turn and slam the door behind me, Uncle Frank was there too.

"Please," I whimpered.

I backed away, dragging my feet across bare floorboards. I looked around for a weapon, but there was nothing. The room was perfectly empty, only bare floorboards and bare walls. The window was intact and looked out upon ragged trees. The thin sliver of the moon peered down on me, the only witness.

I felt my heel catch against something, and my shoulders pressed against the wall behind me. Nowhere left to go. The smile that crept across Uncle Frank's face was almost feral.

He took a step closer.

From the corner of my eye, I saw a slash of silver at the window. The boy's face peered in, his mouth stretched in a silent scream.

Uncle Frank stopped in the middle of the floor and followed my gaze. It was the boy. It was the only explanation. The boy made him think twice. It was like Uncle Frank had been replaced by a monster, but now the monster had gone. Uncle Frank stood alone in the centre of the room, like he had woken from a dream.

He looked away from the window, and I knew the monster was still in the room with me.

I screamed.

Uncle Frank surged toward me.

A loud crack sounded. Uncle Frank stopped and looked down. His foot disappeared between the floorboards. When he tried to pull his leg from the hole, he screamed, and I could see blood, black in the moonlight, staining the jagged edge of the broken floorboard. He looked over at me. "Mickie, you need to help me!"

I pressed my back further against the wall.

"Mickie!" he shouted.

I shuddered at the sound of his voice.

I shuffled to the right, until I reached the corner of the room. Uncle Frank twisted his body to follow me. His face was pale and sweat rose on his brow. "Mickie! Help me, Mickie!"

With my back pressed against the wall, I shuffled, until I reached the doorway. As I fled the house, I heard his voice trail behind me. "Don't leave me!"

I pulled open the car door and locked it behind me. Through the windscreen, I saw the house washed in pale light. Although it had to be my imagination, I still heard Uncle Frank screaming for me to come and set him free.

They found me five days later.

TRENCH MONKEYS

By Carl Barker

Bent double, like old men stumbling beneath heavy sacks, the relief unit slowly picked its way into number five trench beneath an indifferent moon and collapsed exhausted against rotting sandbags. The incumbents silently watched them unload equipment, a brief clattering of shovels and duckboards accompanying the cacophony of wheezes as the new arrivals sucked in a lungful of air. Many immediately regretted it, nearly choking on the fetid odour of the trench. Bodies lay everywhere, piled almost as high as the sandbags, and the smell of cordite and death hung heavy in the still night air. Several of the fresh recruits parked a custard at once, heaving up what little food they had managed to stomach before commencing the long arduous trudge through the maze of trenches. Pale, timid faces gazed about in uncertainty, but for the men already in place the new arrivals were nothing more than a respite from the usual boredom of sentry duty.

Owens crouched alongside the dark edifice of Brookes' thickset frame, chewing nervously on his fingernails and noting without surprise not one of the veteran soldiers around them stirred to assist the replacements. Only the sick and the wounded were being sent back for the moment, and resentment was plain to see upon the face of every man who watched the lucky ones leave. The outfit had been hollowed out by heavy losses, and the tattered remainder leant untidily against the walls of the trench; gaunt bodies hung like badly placed marionettes as they envied the dead and the dying.

Private Siegfried shot himself in the foot only yesterday, the poor fool's mind having finally snapped, and as his stretcher passed by, several of the men cursed him for yellow. Momentarily wishing it was him laid out on that stretcher, Owens kicked out sullenly at a passing trench rabbit, sending the mangy black rat scurrying away. Courage was an unbearable weight pinned to his chest, and only the reminder of his father's low opinion of cowardice kept his place on the line. He watched one of the new draftees clamber eagerly up onto the fire step and poke his head above the lip of the trench. His reward was the solitary crack of a rifle, some coal-faced sniper out in no-man's land chalking up his first of the night. Flung back into the trench, the youth lay sprawled across the boots of his comrades, blood ebbing from the fresh hole in his helmet like a leaky tin boat.

Already hardened to the sight of death, Owens ignored the cries of horror from the new recruits and dejectedly launched a dark gob of spit after the retreating rat, as a burly shout came from further down the trench.

"Reckon that's another shilling you owe me, Charlie, cos that one there's my horse."

The realisation that bets were being wagered on their lives dawned on some of the newcomers, and a chorus of mouths hinged dully open in shock, muted by the lack of compassion.

A murmured chuckle stole through the trench, before a low grunt came in reply.

"Put it on my tab will you, mate, and we'll settle up after."

Nobody laughed at that one though, the sudden thought of home too much to bear. As men wiped away muddied tears, Captain Lawrence emerged from his bunker and did his best to comfort the men.

"Now come on, lads" he chided, removing his cap to smooth back an errant, reddish-brown fringe. "That's no way to greet new arrivals."

Turning to the relief unit, he straightened slightly and firmly replaced the cap before barking orders.

"You men, there! Get those fresh duckboards laid out on the double! I want a full equipment inspection in fifteen minutes, and I expect everything to be A-1!"

An explosion of activity followed, and satisfied, the Captain turned his attention to the maintenance of his service revolver.

Owens gazed solemnly at his superior officer, observing the man's unerring attention to detail, as Lawrence withdrew a seemingly endlessly folded handkerchief from his breast pocket and began industriously wiping the barrel of his gun. The steady, sweeping motion of his hand was like that of a man shaving, a contradiction given the captain was unable to grow even the most rudimentary of moustaches. Despite this, though, the captain's barren top lip had somehow endeared him to his men, marking him out as subtly different from his fellow officers and giving him an air of calm indefatigability. *Did he even see the fear all around him?* Owens wondered. Or was it simply the captain politely refused to become better acquainted with death? Either way, he had decided Lawrence was the best sort of officer to follow: unflappable and overtly centred (as his class and upbringing belied) but caring enough of those men in his charge he engendered a dedication to duty. Definitely the sort of man of whom his father would have approved. Together with the oversized Brookes and the ashen-faced Stokes, Owens had found himself a trio of companions with whom to see out the war.

As each man stiffly rose and drew his bayonet ready for morning inspection, Owens couldn't help but think of Dumas—a troop of fearless swordsmen brandishing blades. In Stokes, Brookes, and their fearless captain, he found his Three Musketeers, and with himself cast in the role of the dashing D'Artagnan, he reckoned the four of them might just well fight their way into Paris.

*

After morning register and inspection, the usual meagre ration of Bully was handed out, and the men returned to sentry duty with still half-empty bellies. Out here in the endless fields of holes, there was no cockerel to commence the dawn, and instead, Owens listened to the high-pitched whine of enemy mortars in the distance. Their voices were like angry birds, filling the air with a high-pitched whistle before each shell fell to earth, and the dull pitter-patter of shrapnel following like rain on dry ground. Creeping barrages were a daily occurrence, the German guns seeking out their targets by the blanket approach, and Owens thanked his lucky stars their position was not currently in the Hun line of fire.

The new recruits clustered close together in the bed of the trench, their blank, staring faces an indication of the dull terror slowly creeping upon them. Owens remembered his first day on the frontline, when he had been saved from a potato masher by his pal, Tommy Boyle. Throwing himself on top of Owens at the last moment, Tommy had taken the full force of the grenade in the small of his back, the blast turning his insides to outsides on the surrounding walls. Afterwards, with his ears still ringing, Owens spent hours frantically pulling blood and scraps of torn flesh from his uniform, as they carried what was left of Tommy away. Unlike his three companions, he'd not yet charged the enemy in battle, but having already stared death full in the face, he was in no hurry to go over the top.

Few of the pale-faced additions looked old enough to be here, he mused, but then he himself had signed up long before his eighteenth birthday. Owens' older brother Frank joined the artillery at the start of the war and had been only too happy to put in a good word for his brother. He could have gotten into the gunnery range—been a powder monkey running shells and the like—but Owens had wanted to be in the thick of it.

*

Around noon, the breeze stiffened, and word came down to be on the lookout for gas. The men took turns at the periscope, scouring no-man's land for any sign of approaching fog, whilst the rest perched tensely on the fire step, clutching their smoke helmets. Owens had never been caught in a gas attack, but he had heard the horror stories from some of the others and found himself staring nervously into the glass eyeholes of his mask. He scrunched the chemically treated cloth of the hood like a child hugging its blanket. *How could so monstrous a thing be the difference between life and death for a man?* he wondered, as the soulless lenses stared up at him. Between the thick flannel folds, he could feel the snake-like outline of thick rubber tubing within, waiting to invade his throat should he be forced to don the mask, a coiled viper waiting in sackcloth.

Suddenly, a yell came from the nearest watcher, and alarms rang out on empty shell cases all along the trench wall. A crazed fumbling followed, each man scrambling to remove his tin hat and pull the thick cloth of his mask down around his face before the fog reached the trenches.

Yanking his own mask down, Owens took the foul-tasting respirator tube between his teeth and swallowed hard, sucking it as far down his throat as he dared without choking. He breathed in sharply through his nose and then out through the tube, as they'd shown them in training. Already, the air he inhaled was beyond foul, having passed through the chemically treated exterior, and he came close to vomiting at once. Vision was limited, and Owens peered out through dirty panes, struggling to make out the shapes of his comrades, the frantic sound of his breathing now a hurricane in his ears. Someone nudged him roughly and looking up, he saw the first tendrils of mist begin to wrap themselves over the lip of the trench.

Heavier than air, the Hun gas crested the wall like the sea washing over an ineffectual defence of sandcastles and sinking down into the dank muddy corridors beneath. It lay coiled at their feet to start, coalescing into a turbid soup around each man's ankles before slowly ascending their legs. From somewhere close by, an officer yelled for the men to prepare for attack and trying desperately to ignore the sensation of slow drowning, Owens affixed his bayonet to the end of his rifle and placed one foot on the fire step, brandishing the thin sliver of steel towards the enemy.

Time seemed to slow, marked only by the gradual, clinging progress of the gas as it hungrily climbed their bodies, and in the queer silence that followed, Owens noticed something odd. The fog was not greenish-yellow as had been described to him by those who had seen it, but a vibrant blue instead, which seemed to pulse as it moved. The colours were hypnotic, the gas neither coalescing nor dissipating, as it steadily inched up their torsos. *What new Hun devilry was this?* he wondered. Glancing down, he glimpsed rats, usually the first to desert their posts before an attack, continuing to scurry underfoot in search of food amongst the hastily discarded packs, seemingly unaffected by the gas. When no attack came, the men began to exchange worried glances, and it was then the first screams began.

Further down the line, a young private fell to his knees, writhing and clawing at his mask. Within rapidly-clouding blue sink-holes, his terrified eyes stared out at his comrades, the smoke having somehow penetrated his mask, and as further screams lent their voices in chorus, Owens saw the first wisps of blue gas rise to encase his own face in smoke. His first thought was to rip off the mask and climb up to safety, but a chorus of rifle cracks sent those men who had already thought of this tumbling back into the trench, and he realised there was nowhere to run. Collapsing on all fours, the men crawled desperately in the brume, floundering as though engulfed in fire or lime, their senses charred by slow terror, voices whimpering like those of boot-beaten curs. The carpet of hungry rats surged through this forest of limbs, but still death would not come for them. So they crouched, trapped in this nightmare of dank earth, steadily breathing in the blue smoke of the Hun, each man silently wondering to himself whether he was already dead. Owens watched his friends silently drowning for over an hour, until at last, a change in the wind tugged the remaining porridge aloft, and their trench was once again clear.

Knock-kneed and trembling, men numbly removed their hoods and clambered to their feet, uncertain as to what had transpired. With no sign of a German advance, they could only assume this new form of gas was ineffectual. That night though, not one of them slept. Each man lay awake in the darkness, wondering whether the blue spectre of death still roamed the corridors of his chest and might yet re-emerge from froth-corrupted lungs to steal his breath.

*

The dawn returned the normality of yet another cold day, and the mood in the trench seemed to lighten. The morning "stand to" coaxed movement from wearied limbs, and after a meagre breakfast, the men returned to their positions, some writing letters to home or cleaning equipment. Still more asleep than awake, Owens slumped on the fire step and stared foggily into sullied palms, his cold-numbed fingertips clumsily tracing the two lines which now crisscrossed where once there had been three.

Glancing to his right, he saw Brookes had removed his tin hat and sat, cradling it lovingly in his arms, and whispering within. Owens had discovered some weeks ago Brookes carried a faded photograph of his fiancée tucked into his helmet and between duties would often strike up a conversation with his sweetheart, crooning softly to her and reassuring her that he would see her again. Many of the men took Brookes for a simpleton and treated him unkindly as such, but Captain Lawrence had chosen to take the man under his wing, realising the man was no more fool than the rest of them.

"You chattin' up that pretty young lady of yours again, Corporal?" one of the men called sarcastically, from further along the cramped trench. "Telling her you'll be home soon, I expect?"

"He's got as much chance of presenting her with the matrimonial peacemaker as I have," another called, and the two men set about laughing, their raucous hooting tugging others from slumber.

The teeth, which Brookes bared fiercely in response, were long-bloodied by trench mouth—dark, ulcerous gums protruding untidily from beneath cracked lips, as he glared down the trench. An animalistic tension seemed to envelop them all, and exchanging alarmed glances, Owens and Stokes placed their rifles quickly to one side, grabbing hold of Brookes' shoulders, as he made to throw his considerable weight in the direction of his tormentors. A loud bellow of rage sounded from deep within his barrel chest, the thick muscles of his brow straining as he howled, and they did their best to pin him against the sodden trench wall.

Seeing his opponent restrained, the smaller of the two loudmouths plucked up what little courage he possessed and came sauntering along the trench, his gangly arms gripping the wall planks, as he swung leisurely from side to side. Coming to a halt no more than three feet away, he scratched furiously at his groin before holding up both fists in mock readiness.

"Come on then, you big burly bastard," he taunted. "We may have all gone west by tomorrow, but I'll put you right on your arse, so I will. Then maybe I'll go visit that pretty girl of yours."

Brookes roared even louder at that, throwing off the fours arms that held him and dropping forward onto two mammoth, clenched fists in the dirt. The faintest wisp of blue smoke escaped his nostrils, as he grunted and padded slowly forward on all fours, thickened knuckles planted firmly in the river of mud at their feet.

"Yeah right, Neville!" one of the men called out with a grin, "and my prick's a bloater."

"He'll be galloping his maggot like the rest of us, more like," another gibbered, and that fearful hooting began again, the regiment screeching in animalistic unison.

"Bloody no chance, either way," a third finished, "cos Neville's got no chance of a stiffy with that knob rot of his."

Embarrassed by the mention of his lice born affliction, Neville rounded on his erstwhile supporters, launching himself into their midst. As the four descended into a wild scuffle, Owens did his best to calm Brookes down.

"Leave him, sir" he pleaded, desperately locking both arms around the older man's midriff. "Neville's not worth the trouble. Hoof and mouth disease is his trouble, is all."

Brookes eyed him warily, the bestial rage in his eyes beginning to subside. Grunting, he slumped both shoulders in resigned defeat and hid his face in his hands.

Owens retrieved his rifle and slung it over one shoulder, watching as Stokes plucked Brookes' helmet from a puddle and handed it to him. The corporal sullenly nodded in thanks and laid a hand briefly across Stokes' bony shoulder.

"I just can't stand to hear the voices, Stokesy" he whimpered, hugging the hat to his chest.

Despite his immense size, Owens saw Brookes was just as scared as the rest of them, and he found himself wondering just how many more dying screams their gentle giant would stand before he lost it completely.

*

The afternoon brought an ominous grey cloud, hanging belligerently over the trenches like a stampede of elephants threatening to tear up the sky. Owens listened to the familiar 'ack-ack' of British anti-aircraft guns, as they sent a squadron of encroaching Fokkers scuttling back behind enemy lines. The steady whir of propellers subsided, and an eerie silence replaced it, the air still, as though waiting.

Owens clutched his rifle firmly to prevent his hands from shaking.

"What's it like out there, Stokesy?" he muttered, straining to keep the tremble from his voice. "Out in no-man's land, I mean?"

Stokes regarded him with a stoic expression, having never uttered a word in all the time Owens had known him, but those milky grey eyes held the remnants of unimaginable horror. Owens turned away, stomach churning.

The storm clouds blackened, a first barrage of water falling from the dreary sky. Owens listened to the tuneless tinkle of raindrops upon tin hats, the rain soon becoming a deluge.

"We ain't gonna make it, are we, Stokesy?" he whispered at one point, but the only reply was silence.

*

The downpour continued unabated for the next two hours, no doubt compounding misery on both sides of the trenches by filling up shell-holes and soaking through sandbags. With it came a further influx of rats; brown ones this time, the larger and infinitely more feared cousin of the usual black ones. Attracted by the smell of fresh meat, they swarmed over the now half-submerged bodies, gorging themselves on the blanched flesh. As he watched them fight greedily over the contents of eye sockets, Owens realised his father was wrong. There was no glory in this.

Reaching into his pocket, he withdrew the lucky charm his mother had given him on the day he enlisted: a silver key ring adorned with three tiny monkeys, each one crouched into a different pose. The metal felt ice-cold against his skin, but it was a link to home nonetheless, and he grasped it tight in his fist, praying for deliverance.

*

Dusk brought with it a brief respite from the weather, and after dinner was served, another fight broke out further down the line with two small groups coming to blows over an accusation of stolen food. Owens sleepily watched the smallest member of the losing party huddle against his comrade in a corner afterwards, both nursing a fresh set of bruises. In the failing light, it appeared as though the scrawny runt was industriously pulling lice from the other man's hair and popping each one into his mouth, but he dismissed this as nonsense, drifting back into sleep.

His dreams were filled with strange visions of men hooting fearfully at a night sky, lit up by artillery fire. Driven wild by the incessant pounding of the guns, they tore the uniforms from their backs, revealing layers of coarse black hair beneath, each man's flesh now hidden beneath a thick hide of fur ...

Owens awoke with a jerk, his body caked with a thick layer of sweat which gave off an odd, musky odour. Glancing around, he found several pairs of wide eyes staring back at him and realised he was not the only one plagued by bad dreams.

*

As dawn broke, Brookes was the first to spot the messenger boy carefully picking his way along the water-logged trench.

Drawing level with their position, the youth stooped to catch his breath for a moment before asking as to the whereabouts of their commanding officer.

"He's gone for a shit with a blanket wrapped round him" came the usual sardonic reply, but already soaked to the skin and benumbed with cold, the lad took little humour from the joke.

Emerging from his bunker, Captain Lawrence knocked out his pipe on the wood of the doorframe and considered it for a moment, as though he had no idea as to its purpose. Looking up, he noticed the messenger boy and scratched thoughtfully at the long, fleshy protuberances which had appeared on either side of his forehead. His once tidy fringe dangled from the edge of his cap, hanging loose down the saggy flesh of his face, and he reached out to the boy with one hair-covered palm, pursing slightly bulbous lips.

The youth deposited a sealed envelope into the captain's outstretched paw and saluted briefly before darting away. Owens stared after the boy's retreating figure, trying to remember a time when he'd ever felt that young.

The three of them waited anxiously as the captain struggled to tear open the orders. When he did finally look up from the paper, Lawrence's weak smile was of a man with no choice but to accept the impossibility of the task laid out before him.

"Well, lads," he muttered, smacking those oversized lips together again, "looks like the brass hats have finally made up their minds. They're giving us another chance to give Fritz a bloody nose, because we're going over the top."

The captain moved on down the trench, passing the message to the rest of the unit. Owens stared blankly into the sodden earth at his feet as Stokes and Brookes shuffled numbly back to their seats. It was then it occurred to him Lawrence's face had been entirely covered with a fine down of hair.

Huddled in a corner, barely warmed by the bodies of his trembling comrades, Owens turned his mother's charm slowly over and over in his own fur-covered hands, eyes drawn to the dull glint of besmirched silver. The charm's tarried surface mirrored the muddied state of his own thoughts. His once stainless intentions of fighting for King and country were now sullied by the dark realities of war. There was no adventure to be found here, no daring missions of unbridled heroism to take home to his father. Here, waited only death and an endless river of mud. His terrified whimper went unnoticed amongst the sobs and grunts of his comrades.

*

One hour later, Captain Lawrence got stiffly to his feet and lumbered along the trench, instructing each man to check his equipment. A final register coaxed a ragged collection of guttural acknowledgements from the throats of men who had spent some time crying. When the order to fix bayonets came, it was so far removed from the fierce call to arms intended that several of the men just stared blankly at each other in terror, having quite forgotten their wits. The officers made their way through the ranks again, doing their best to hearten the men.

"Chin up, boys," one muttered, to those who still heard him. "This time tomorrow, we'll all be drinking champagne on the streets of Ypres."

"I don't think I have it in me to kill a man, sir" wept one of the new recruits, fumbling clumsily with his bayonet.

The officer stared at him, forlornly.

"War makes beasts of us all, lad," he whispered.

As the sun slowly rose over no-man's land, Lawrence stooped between Owens and Stokes, with Corporal Brookes to his left as both men took their revolvers club-like in oversized fists. The stench of fresh piss wafted through the ranks as men took hold of rickety ladders and made peace with their god.

Reaching into his pocket one last time, Owens withdrew his mother's key ring and hung it on his rifle for luck. The three tiny primates hung from the hilt of his bayonet, their tiny silver faces contorted into expressions which he now knew so well.

Captain Lawrence was the blind one, incapable of seeing the atrocities taking place all around, both paws clasped firmly over his eyes. The deaf ape was Brookes, unable to stand so much as a word from his comrades as to the true nature of evil without becoming enraged, and finally there was poor Stokesy: struck dumb by the horrors of war.

As whistles sounded all along the trench and terrified primates began pounding up ladders into the paths of waiting machine guns, Owens kissed his mother's key ring for luck and wondered if any of them would ever live to be wise.

BACK SEAT MAN

By Wolfgang Potterhouse

The condescending car salesman in Oklahoma City said the "o-fficial" name of the color was Mars Grey. He had hair jelly crusted in the top fold of his ear, which is a weird thing to remember, but right now you'll take what you can get. Concentrating, you can picture the guy in detail: uneven sideburns, gaudy turquoise pinky ring, nubby charcoal teeth where he chomped his pipe, porcupine eyebrows—these are not the clues to your past you are looking for, so you try to think of something, anything, to push them out. You wonder; maybe Mars is one of the twinkling stars you see mirrored on the shiny hood. "Mars ain't a star, dummy, it's a planet, and it ain't grey either, it's red." All this is out loud in your syrupy Texas twang. Where you're from no one is ever in a hurry to say anything. *Great, now I'm talking to myself.* You pop a Lucky Strike halfway from its pack and use your lips to pull it the rest of the way out. A quick pat down of the pockets, no matches. You turn the cigarette under your nose to breathe in as much tobacco aroma as you can, then slip the cigarette over your ear with a disappointed sigh. It's strange you're able to remember details like the factory name of the Chevy's paint and the sloppy grooming of a guy you only met once, while you are incapable of remembering any other details or experiences. The motel in your mind where you thought your memories stayed seems vacant. In fact, it seems those memories have all checked out, without leaving a note of explanation or a forwarding address.

This car appears to be the exception; you remember everything about her. Your pride and joy, she's a 1939 Chevrolet Master 85: low, smooth, and sleek like a grey panther. You can recall a tiny flaw in the chrome on the hood ornament, you know the trunk squeaks when you open it and outright squeals when you close it, and without looking, you remember the clock is broken and stuck at fourteen past five. You're trying to regain access to the closed off back rooms of your brain, but you don't know how to pull back the curtain. It's more than a little alarming to not know who you are, but there are no shadows, no shapes, no hints or traces of anything in those memory banks. *Patience*, you coach yourself. *Drive, breathe easy; it will all come back.*

Maybe this is a dream swirling in your subconscious like a thick fog on a warm morning, and you should relax and enjoy it. Something from your childhood bubbles to the surface; the sun rising over the rolling meadows behind the homestead, golden rays highlighting the pinks and pewters drifting in the lazy morning mist while the cornfield next to the house whispers its secrets in the soft breeze. The memory is pleasant, but it doesn't help you figure out *what's going on right now.* How did you get here? You don't remember getting in the car. Shoot, you don't remember coming home from the Navy. Something strange is happening. You're not losing your cool yet, but this feels wrong, unnatural.

The moonlight plays on the polished black metal of the dashboard, snapping to the rhythm of the road. Momma Moon taps her foot to the same beat as she watches you from the side view mirror. Not a lot of guys wax the dashboard, but hell, you wax and buff everything. By hand. Even the windshield.

"Now hold up," you say out loud to the moon in the mirror. "Somehow, I know I polish the dashboard and the windshield, but I don't remember how I got back in town?" How can you know that and almost nothing else? *Why* do you know that and nothing else? What can you do to rebuild the context of your life?

Maybe these memories will pick up more snow as they roll downhill, gaining mass and momentum until this makes a little more sense.

Driving.

Cruising.

You know this road, Route 21, but everyone calls it Center Street. You are heading out of town, into the country. *Okay,* you say to yourself, *it's coming back now, bit by bit. Patience. You unfold a map one section at a time, right?*

Only one reason to drive all this way; only one thing on this road—out this far anyway.

The drive-in down in the old quarry.

The Broken Hearts Drive-in Auto Amphitheater. A huge place. Six screens set in a massive circle around a city block sized granite chasm half filled with water. People pay their money then pick the path which corresponds to their movie and drive down.

You've been there a million times. First cigarette, first beer, first kiss, first awkward hand inside the bra—groping, trembling, sweating. *Do I push her bra up, pull it down, unclasp the back?* You remember these moments like they happened yesterday, but what are you doing here *now*?

You see the sign. "Broken Hearts" it says, the rest of the words unlit; a somber beacon in crimson neon. You slow as you approach the space in the tree line that serves as the entrance, braking without downshifting. Something you can't quite put your finger on, a shadowy, dark curiosity, is pulling you, luring you.

You turn the car and roll in, extra slow to savor the sound of gravel crunching under your tires. A familiar, almost haunting sound; you relate it to anticipation, longing, desire.

The ticket booth stands waiting on the left, a wood and glass sentinel guarding the fun from the uninitiated, the unpaid, the undeserving. No lights appear to be on inside the booth, but you think you see beams from headlights reflecting through the trees down in the quarry. They must be open for business, so you steer the Chevy up to the booth.

You stop. Saying the lights were not on wasn't accurate. A faint, flickering, orange-red is glowing from below the window line, dancing in the shadows as if the floor was on fire. You roll your window down. Silence. No heat, no smoke, only the dull shimmering glow, like someone was turning a ruby in front of a flashlight beam as the battery wore out. You roll the window back up.

The eerie feeling of the night mingles with the familiar pleasures of your car and the moonlit drive-in, and you are aware of how weary you are. "I think I'm going to park up here for a while and see if I can't find some matches in that glove box and have me a smoke or two. Maybe get a bit of shuteye, maybe take in a free picture—I got to have some time to think and see if I can make some sense of all this, or wake up from whatever this dream is." Even though she's no longer in your mirror, you assume the moon has no reaction to this announcement.

You aren't sure if you fell asleep, or if you were—or are—dreaming; honestly, you aren't sure about anything at the moment. You regain awareness like the radio in your mind is taking its time to warm up. There is a movie playing on the drive-in screen in front of you, but you don't remember driving down one of the paths. You missed the title and the opening, but what you see provokes a flood of memories.

Flickering on the screen in black and white is an aircraft carrier, pounding through the waves in the open ocean.

You sit up fast in the car, shaking off the hazy, groggy feeling. The aircraft carrier has a huge "6" painted on the flight deck. Your ship! The Enterprise! There she is, steaming into Pearl after the attack, thick black smoke still billowing all around her from burning hulks on land and in the sea. You were on that ship—right there, right then, that ship sailing through hell. You've got to be dreaming. This is not a good feeling.

The scene shifts to sailors eating oatmeal and bread off metal trays with no plates, drinking black coffee from small, dingy white mugs, and flapping their jaws about this and that. An officer rushes into the mess hall, his bearing hurried and intense.

Buddy Lee Childress was in the mess hall when the news came down about the Japanese attack on Pearl Harbor, 7 December, 1941. This was Lee's birthday as well as his one year anniversary in the Navy. He joined, like so many other boys he knew back home, and so many others he had gotten to know, to fight. He chose the Navy with the specific intention to hunt Nazi subs, which had been terrorizing everything that floated on the Atlantic. He ended up here in the Pacific though, the wrong ocean and the wrong enemy. In reality, there was no enemy, although the Japanese appeared to be spoiling for a big fight. Lee was disappointed to be so far from the action, but his job flying in dive bombers made up for it.

The news of the attack on America, with almost catastrophic losses to its fighting fleet and horrifying death toll, was like a baseball bat to the stomach—but now they were in the war! Now *he* was in the war! No one in the mess hall cheered the news, but everywhere there were excited yet hushed proclamations and predictions, and more than a few fists pounded on tables. Lee couldn't wait to join the fray.

Although he flew in planes, Lee was neither a pilot nor an officer. He was an Aviation Radioman Second Class; in common vernacular, a radio gunner, rear gunner, or back seat man. He preferred back seat man, because the other titles sounded limited. Yes, he operated the radio and defended the plane with the rear facing machine gun, but he also oversaw a full set of controls to fly the plane in an emergency. He thought it was a pretty important and dangerous job, and like most young men, he enjoyed an underlying assumption of immortality.

He sat back-to-back behind his pilot, Ensign Jeff Baker, in a Douglas Dauntless SBD-2 dive bomber. Lee was trying to think of a name for her; he loved this powder blue angel of death. Some of the pilots said SBD stood for "Slow But Deadly," and it made Lee smile when he heard it. *Slow? Not in a seventy-degree dive, she ain't!*

Ensign Baker was a black-haired Irishman from Quincy, Massachusetts, with a voice like nails and gasoline. He was dead serious about his job, and everything else—one look in his dark eyes told you all you needed to know about his patience for other people's nonsense. Baker and Lee were friendly, but not friends. Although they would need to rely on each other in life and death situations, none of the pilots and gunners had much occasion to intermingle below decks. "Brown Shoes and Blue Jackets don't mix," everyone said—not because of any tension or strife, but the officers were their superiors at all times. Baker was a Naval Academy graduate, green and "gung-ho." Their squadron's emblem was a charging ram, and Baker featured it as a tattoo on his forearm. Lee wanted to get one too, but he didn't have the guts to go under the needle.

Their ship, the carrier USS Enterprise (which they referred to as "The Big E") delivered a squadron of Marine fighter planes to Wake Island, and was heading back to Pearl Harbor when they heard the news of the attack. They witnessed firsthand the devastation and carnage.

A memory emerges; you're flying a training mission in the Dauntless, waiting for your turn to practice with the rear mount machine guns. A dark blue Grumman Wildcat fighter plane pulls beside you, towing a large black windsock, the target which you are meant to shoot at. You do so, without an ounce of success. One pass was all you got, and there it was, your rear gunner practice. There was no promise or even indication you would be provided other opportunities to hone your skills.

As if prompted by this memory, there you are on the screen, talking to your friend from Texas, Carl Shumaker, after the gunnery exercise. Your Texas drawl sounds different coming through the drive-in speaker than it does inside your head.

"That thirty cal is about useless, man. Even with two barrels, I might as well take out my forty-five and shoot it at the Japs. I can't lead the target enough—the wind whips them bullets back like I'm throwin' cotton balls out the car window, and I gotta aim so far above the target to compensate for the bullet falling that I'm guessing where it's gonna go. It's like spitballs in a straw, Carl. I tell you what. Spitballs in a straw."

You stare at the drive-in speaker. It is hooked over your half-down driver's side window, like it has been many times before. Did you put it on there? You grip the wheel and pull yourself forward. What is going on?

June 1942. Coded radio intercepts have been deciphered, the American fleet has been dispatched, and the Japanese fleet is expected near Midway Island. Lee's Dauntless was one of hundreds of planes sent out on search-and-destroy. He was in his seat, facing backward, scanning the horizon for enemy planes, and the ocean for ships. They were looking for a major Japanese task force, whose detection would trigger a massive attack. Fighters, torpedo bombers, and dive bombers dotted the sky. Squadrons from Enterprise, Hornet, and Yorktown were in the air, spread out for stealth and safety. Radio silence was mandatory, so right now, Lee was a lookout.

Two problems plagued him. One: when they scrambled to take off at 0400, he forgot his coat—Baker, in his Boston accent, called it a pah-ker—and his winter boots. At 13,000 angels—their slang for feet—it started getting cold. At 19,000, it was freezing. Lee was stomping his feet and clapping his hands to try to maintain circulation. Problem two: nature was calling. He was going to have to either wet himself, or writhe around to try to get several layers unzipped and unstrapped, all the while maintaining his views of the horizon and the ocean. He figured a Jap gunner would let loose without thinking about it, but he was an American. A civilized human being.

Sitting in the car, watching these events play out on the screen, you remember how hard it was to unbuckle your belts, unzip your flight suit and uniform pants, and aim off to the side with no feeling in your frozen fingertips.

This mini flood of memories seems like a good thing, but you are forced to confront the fact you are watching your own life, your own past, on the screen, which makes less than no sense. It sure doesn't feel like the past, though. This is off the charts on the bizarre-o-meter. Are you dead? Is this heaven? Hell? Something in between? Are you on God's layaway plan? The Devil's?

"What the fuck is going on?" You are not a man given to cursing, but your head is getting swimmy. This is too much. You have strong urges to either force this through some filter so it adds up or run away and get away from it. You look around outside. There is a black Buick parked a few slots over to the left, a middle-aged woman—is that *your mother?*—looking at you with disgust, shaking her head.

"NO!" You shut your eyes and drop your head, trying to collect yourself. Calming your breathing, you slowly look back. No Buick. No Joan Childress and her Christian condemnation.

"What the FUCK?"

The next time you look up, it is back at the pale glow of the movie screen.

The Dauntless rolled a bit to port but stayed its course as Ensign Baker strained to see through the clouds to the surface of the sea. He needed to get more than a fleeting glimpse of what he thought he saw. Baker leveled the plane in an instant with a disquieting, uncharacteristic jerk. This got Lee's attention, then Baker started yelling over the in-plane radio. "Port side! Port side! Multiple wakes in the water, multiple enemies spotted!" Baker was the first in the group to see them. He throttled up to pull alongside another SBD, the one flown by the squadron commander. Jeff used hand signals. The commander broke radio silence, and the attack was on.

The Dauntless formations started to glide down to 12,000 feet while the Devastators pressed the attack. One torpedo hit was enough to cripple—sometimes sink—an enemy ship, but on this day *no* hits would be scored by any American torpedo bombers. The Japanese Zero fighters and anti-aircraft gunners on the enemy ships focused their fire on those slow, unprotected, outdated planes, and they shredded them. Lee could see tracers and fires and explosions and splashes. He waited for his turn to die.

I guess this is what I deserve he thought, and his mind stopped cold. Why was he thinking he deserved to die? What had he done? People below him were dying in a slaughter. This was no time for cold feet, conscience, regrets, or any feelings at all. *Do your job!* Lee thought in a scolding tone, trying to clear his mind. He and Baker readied for their bombing run.

This hits you like a slap. In the movie, you thought dying was what you *deserved*. You know your memories are short circuiting, but you had not done anything to warrant that kind of self-condemnation. You suffered from a well-earned case of pre-battle jitters; that was all it was.

Wait—is this real? Did you *hear* what you *thought* in the movie? You are starting to get spooked. Clear thoughts. Deep breaths, no panic.

Something moves in the darkness in front of your car. You freeze—eyes squinting to see, but there's nothing. You feel that unmistakable feeling of someone watching you. With a quick gasp, you realize the Buick is back. This time it's not your mother sitting at the wheel. This time it's Betty. She's glaring, and you can feel the icy disapproval. Deep breath. This can't be real. Head down, chin pressed to your chest, eyes shut. Calm down.

Betty, your girl. Sweet Betty. Not the kind of girl for groping at the drive-in. The kind of girl who kept her legs shut. The marrying type. She is worth waiting for, and you depend on her. She writes to you every week. When did you last write to her? Back when you were a boy, not a man. Not a killer.

Slow down—who did you kill? You had not entered the battle yet! Some elusive, evasive memory is hiding in the dark. Waiting. Watching you.

Eyes open again. No Buick.

This is a dream. This is your mind playing tricks. Remember. REMEMBER! NOW! Did the Japanese shoot you down? Were you wounded? Killed? *Oh my God. Oh my God. Calm. Calm. Easy. Stop shaking. Concentrate on your breathing. Face front. Deal with this. Be a man.*

The movie holds the clues.

Baker held at 12,000 feet as the American torpedo attack and Japanese resistance raged beneath them. Lee was moving his machine guns back and forth, sweeping the sky with his eyes, but he saw no fighters coming to greet them. The first SBDs started to peel off into their dives, and still there was no sign of a single enemy approaching the entire formation. They were either going to get picked apart during their attack, or the enemy was too preoccupied with the torpedo planes to notice the SBDs. Lee heard the dive brakes crank open, and felt the airplane slow, then roll. In ten seconds, Baker, Lee, and their Dauntless were pointed almost straight down, right at an enemy carrier. Pilot and gunner both kept their canopies open, and the wind screamed their battle cry.

Lee intended to hold his defensive position, but there were no Japanese planes in sight, so he pivoted his seat and faced front, looking into the dive. He was not supposed to do this. He couldn't help it.

You don't remember this as much as you *feel* it happening. Your mind is racing as you turn in the gunner seat. Jeff is a better-than-decent pilot, but he is one *hell* of a bombardier. The best in the outfit. You are going to score a hit, right through the flight deck. You can feel it. Pushing 200 knots now, shrieking through the air. The Japanese carrier is already on fire—finish her off! 4,000 feet, 3,000 feet, 2,000. Drop it Jeff! 1,500 feet, 1,200 feet, you feel it in your back before you hear it; the swing releases and slings the massive bomb under the propeller as the Dauntless strains to pull out of the dive. 900 feet, 600 feet. Spinning on your seat, you see your shell, black with yellow stripes, enter the flight deck. Two beats—no explosion. Was it a dud? On a direct hit? 400 feet. You are almost in the ocean. Your aircraft is shaking and shuddering. Is this where you die?

The flight deck of the Japanese carrier explodes like a hundred suns at once. Pieces of who-knows-what bounce off the Dauntless. Click, thud, whack. Pieces of the flight deck, pieces of ammunition and supplies from the ship that blew up, and pieces of the hundreds of enemy sailors incinerated in the blast. Jeff pins you in the seat as he climbs out of the dive.

You are reliving this as you are watching it on the screen. You are baffled, terrified, thrilled—it may be even more intense than when it happened live.

Lee pulled his guns back up to the ready position. He needed to calm down and be prepared to perform his job. Anti-aircraft shells were bursting all around them; each concussion shook the plane with a jolt. Holes from the shrapnel started appearing in the rear fuselage of the plane. There were quarter sized holes here and there, and a couple fist sized ones. *That can't be good*, Lee thought, but at least there aren't any holes in me. He knocked on the wooden stock of his machine guns as the enemy carrier exploded again. They were still low enough so he could see men, some of them on fire, jumping into the sea. The ship was blazing; he was sure it was a goner.

"That carrier is done! Ensign Baker, you sunk her!" Jeff didn't look back, but held the stick between his knees and pumped his arms into the wind. It was the first emotion Lee had ever seen from Baker, so he pumped his arms up as well, and added a "yee-haw" at maximum volume.

Their elation was short-lived. A Japanese fighter dropped out of the sun's glare into a perfect killing position behind them. Lee didn't wait. He opened up with his twin guns into the nose of the enemy plane. Fire leaped from the barrels of Lee's machine guns, empty brass casings streaming into the sky. He could see the guns on the Zero flashing, he could hear bullets cracking and whistling over his head, but he had not been hit, and his plane was still flying. The Zero pulled up a bit to change his aiming angle, and Lee poured a few bursts into the plane's belly. When part of the engine cowling blew off in a cloud of oil and fire, the Zero's nose lurched down, and it started to roll over. Lee could see the frantic look on the pilot's face as he fought the plane nosing down. The Japanese pilot lost the fight and hurtled towards the sea. He did not bail out.

Lee, the back seat man from Texas, shot down an enemy plane in his first combat experience. He killed a man. "You okay?" It was Baker on the comms.

"Yeah." Lee said, all of a sudden exhausted. He turned and banged on the pilot's shoulder, and when Jeff twisted around to look at him, Jeff smiled and gave a thumbs up.

You did that, you remember, because you needed to *see* Jeff was all right; you needed to see he could fly you back to The Big E safely. No, neither of those were right. To be truthful, you needed to *see* he wasn't covered in blood. Why? This was triggering something, something right behind a black lace veil you couldn't quite see through. Something backlit you weren't able to see the shape of, no matter how much you squinted.

Covered in blood.

Baker said he was fine; Baker looked fine. Combat produces terror and emotional chaos; were you coming down from those temporary highs? Descending through the vapor of bravado to the chilly reality of your human weakness? The reality of being a killer, or that people were trying to kill you? You killed a man yourself, and many more on the ship you hit. Were you on sensory overload? No. There was something. Some memory, out of your grasp, at least for now.

Calm down. Breathe. Think. Remember.

On the movie screen, American sailors pushing, refueling, repairing, and re-arming planes to go back into battle. Flagmen waving in wounded fighters and dive bombers. A close-up of your plane landing, the arrestor hook catching the first cable and yanking it to a stop. Ensign Baker standing on the wing with his arm around you, not smiling this time, but raising a fist to salute your victory. Excited, passionate conversations below decks, Brown Shoes and Blue Jackets all venting, lamenting, boasting, and rehashing.

Tears of passion, pride, and frustration wet your cheeks. You took part in something huge. Important. You can feel it, but there are so many things you can't remember, and somehow you know they are not good. Why is part of your life story playing out on this screen here in the woods? Dreaming. The only explanation, so relax. *Collect yourself. Come back down.* Close your eyes, and open your mind. Solutions, or explanations at least, must be in there, and you've got to uncover one thing at a time. Like a puzzle. One piece at a time.

What else had you done? What couldn't you access? What couldn't you remember?

What—or who—was covered in blood?

Close your eyes. Better. Thinking calmly. Still, nothing's clear, but at least your mind stopped machine gunning into the dark.

Thud. Something hits the trunk of the Chevy. You don't move, you shut your eyes even tighter.

Go away.

Thud. Harder, louder.

You glance in the rearview. A fluttering form, like a sky-blue sheet on a clothesline in a June breeze. You twist around, craning to see. A figure walking around the back to the passenger side, a woman, taking her time. Blonde. A light blue dress. You hold your breath, motionless, waiting. The door opens.

She sits down next to you in gentle silence and shuts the door, staring straight out the windshield, hands folded in her lap, looking pretty, as always. You know her, or *knew* her. She should not be here.

"Lee," she says, her voice guarded and methodical with a dose of sharpness. She turns to look at you. Her blue eyes hold no emotion, convey no intent.

You take a deep breath for strength. "April." Your fingertips could only brush against these memories a minute ago; now you hold a few in your palms. You turn your hands over and look.

Her name was April May. Cute name, cute girl. Nice, quiet, harmless. She did have a reputation though, for being a "sharecropper"—easy, slutty. Rumors said she went all the way with at least five guys in high school, and went down on several more. She was not in your circle of friends, and wouldn't have been in your circle of anything if you hadn't joined the Navy.

After finalizing your paperwork, you were forced to wait three months until you shipped out. A frustrating delay, but the Navy wanted men who could type for their radio school, and you had taken a typing class junior year, so they volun-*told* you that you were going to radio school.

Betty was your girl for junior and senior years, and you knew she was the one. You knew she would wait for you while you fought for your country. You knew she would be by your side forever. She was perfect. A perfect, pretty, proper Christian girl.

You hated her so much. You hate her now.

She was the *right thing* to do, not what you *wanted* to do, and you resented her.

April slowly looks back toward the screen. You do as well. The movie appears to be showing a flashback. Several boys are springing out of a yellow Ford convertible parked in front of Miller's Dairy Bar. You are jumping out of the back seat, not using the door even though it is open.

Lee and four of his friends vaulted into the soda shop and crashed at the counter, making as much noise, and gathering as much attention, as they could. "Pete, my man, what do you say to some Cokes on the house for five future national heroes? We have all enlisted to defend this glorious democracy we all hold so dear." This was Eddie Moncrief talking, and he was doing his horrible, nasal FDR accent.

"Is that right?" Pete said with a wide smile. They act like they know Pete pretty well. It is clear he likes them. "Maybe I could do half price? I can't let y'all get me fired, 'cause then I'd have to join the Army too!"

You remember this; a few months later, Pete didn't have a choice as to whether to join or not, and a couple years later, the lower half of his body was blown off by a Japanese mortar shell on Iwo Jima. You remember who you met at the fountain that day, too.

"They were old enough to die for their country, but not yet old enough to buy a beer, so they stopped at the soda fountain to celebrate." A narrator has been added to the film. You are too uneasy and confused to notice.

"We got me and Jimmy going into the Army," Eddie again, running the show, this time with his normal Texas cadence. He's pointing at each boy as he talks about them, and a few customers clap. "We got Lee and Slim going into the Navy, and Stanley here has messed up and joined the Marine Corps. We're gonna give 'em hell on both sides of the globe!"

The entire patronage of the soda shop stood and gave the young men a standing ovation. It was electrifying. Lee blushed, first because of the applause, but then because he noticed who was standing next to him. *Dang, is she beautiful!* Sitting down now, nervous and unsure of what to do with his hands. He didn't look straight at her until she spoke to him. "Congratulations, Lee." Soft. Sweet. That smile. It was April May. He wondered if the whole soda shop could hear his heart pounding as he gathered some composure and smiled at her.

"You knew of her from school, but this was your first ever conversation," added the narrator.

Did the narrator say "you" and "your?" You look at April sitting next to you in the car. None of this is real. Her hands are still folded, watching the film. *She should not be here.* You can feel madness tickling the back of your brain, and tears are streaming down your face. Why?

Are you losing your mind? Is it already gone?

"Thanks, April," Lee says with a faux confident smile. April smiles back. Lee and the boys have a few sodas; Lee spends the whole time talking to April. The boys tease him about telling Betty he's "taaalk-iiing to Aaa-priiiil." She would never believe it if they did tell her. April's hand finds Lee's thigh as she laughs at his teenage jokes.

Lee stays behind when his friends leave. April is making him feel lighter than air. Every time she looks at him, every time she smiles, he forgets how to breathe. He holds her hand and almost passes out. They make a plan to meet again tomorrow, without the extra cast members.

Betty believes Lee's lie about doing calisthenics to get ready for boot camp. "I can't come over for family lunch. I need to run and workout every day. I gotta be in fighting shape when I get there."

They don't order sodas this time; Lee grabs April by the hand and leads her out to his car. He opens the door for her, and she kisses him on the cheek as she sits down. Lee is beaming as he walks around to his side, thinking this is the happiest he has ever been. Being near April is the most alive he has ever felt; the anticipation of touching and kissing her is so intoxicating that Lee can't think of anything else. He can't wait to get in the car and let her blue eyes start melting him again. Nothing else in the world exists. He slides in next to her. "God, you smell good," he says, reaching out to touch her hair. "You're so beautiful," he whispers, leaning in, brushing her cheek with the back of his fingers. She pulls him in and kisses him, soft at first, then with an intensity and passion that he did not know existed. April slides her hand up his thigh and doesn't stop. Time stands still.

Lee knows he wants to marry Betty. He also knows he might get killed or maimed in the war, and he does not want to die a boy, a virgin. With these thoughts marinating, Lee takes April out to the drive-in, where there is no movie playing at one-thirty in the afternoon.

Lee and April kiss and touch until she breaks contact, then slips out her door. Lee is a little confused until April pushes her seat forward and glides into the backseat. "Come on," she says, unbuttoning her dress.

The movie shows everything from their backseat tryst.

It was only once. Not that big of a deal.

Betty never knew, and you never saw April again.

Right?

None of *this* is real, but what you are remembering is real enough.

Oh God. *What the fuck is all this?*

You look over at April, her frosty blue eyes now locked on yours. Her face at once expressionless but angry, blank but hurting. She's sending chills down your spine. Your arms are gooseflesh. She moves her hands off her lap, holding them out to you as if to beckon for an embrace. "Don't touch me!" You look down in horror. Dark red blood is spreading across her lap and dripping over her legs, more blood than you have ever seen.

Almost.

More memories. You are not seeking them anymore—they are hunting you.

April came to you the week before you were scheduled to ship out, and she told you. Your baby was inside her. She was getting rid of it and wanted you to help. No, to be accurate, she said *you* needed to *do it*. No doctors would help her for less than five hundred dollars, and her parents would kick her out of the house if they knew. She begged you, desperate and sobbing. It had to be done now.

You drove her out to the drive-in again, because you knew you could be by yourselves to talk about this, deal with it, get it figured out. You both sat on the grass next to the car. You were embarrassed by the situation, and you didn't know the right thing to say or do, but your main thought was this: why couldn't you love her? Did what people thought or said matter? You doted on and intended to marry a girl you hated; you used, then cast aside, this wonderful girl. Did this make one lick of sense? Are you so shallow, so weak? You were angry, but not at April. You were disgusted with yourself.

You remember what happened next.

Through her sobs, she pleaded for your help. She brought out a long thick wire, like an open clothes hanger, and she showed you what to do.

You wouldn't do *that*! You couldn't, but you also could *not* have a baby right now, and not *ever* with her.

It was a confusing and overwhelming situation, and you cared about April, but you needed this to go away.

She would leave, she promised; you would never see her again.

April pulled her plaid skirt up; she wore nothing underneath. She gently pushed you to lie down on your back, then climbed up, straddling you. Her anguish and torment did not suppress your obvious arousal; she opened your pants and slid her body up until you became one with her again. Her desperation somehow made her more desirable, her tears somehow made her more beautiful. You *did* love her, and you told her so.

When it was over, she lay next to you, tranquil now, and again asked for your help. She reaffirmed it would be the last you ever saw of her, and explained again what you needed to do.

You did it.

You did what she told you to do, what she begged you to do, but something went wrong. There was blood, so much blood, and it wouldn't stop. At first, she tried to keep you both calm, but panic set in when the bleeding did not slow down. She needed to go to the hospital, or she was going to die. You both knew this. April begged for help again—this time begging for her life.

A few minutes ago, you told her you loved her.

Now, you knew you were not going to take her to the hospital. You were not going to lose Betty, and your reputation, and your honor, and your future.

No.

April stopped moving. She stopped talking. She stopped breathing.

It started to rain. You stood up and looked down at her. She was *covered in blood*. The bottom half of her dress was saturated. Her hands were wet with blood from her attempts to stop it, to save herself, and everything she touched was smudged and plastered with gruesome scarlet, including her hair and face, and your arms, shirt, and pants.

You grabbed her wrists and started to pull her across the grass and gravel. You hauled her like a sack of garbage over to the woods and dumped her. You covered her body with rocks, branches, and leaves so it would rot there undetected.

So April and your baby would rot.

You left. You left the drive-in, you left town, and you left your old life. You became a back seat man in the Navy, and you forgot about being a back seat boy in Texas.

You forgot, until now.

A quick glance next to you, and April is gone. You are not surprised. She was only here to prompt the memories of what happened, and now you remember. You look out to the woods where you dumped her body, nothing. Rearview mirror, nothing.

Your eyes find the movie screen the same moment a scream rips from the speaker hanging on the window. Your scream.

Jeff Baker was hit in the arm, but he was level-headed and still doing his job. Lee Childress was screaming. There was a camera shot of his ankle, and it was a mess. He was bleeding in a flow, not a drip, and the unnatural angle of his foot showed how mangled his ankle was.

It was August of 1942. They were flying a mission over Guadalcanal, and were confronted by Japanese fighters. Lee and Baker turned to run—the Dauntless was not a dogfighter—but they were outnumbered and pursued by the much faster airplanes, leaving them no choice. Baker used some clever flying to down a Zero with the front facing .50 cal machine guns, but not before the Japanese pilot wounded them both. The SBD-2 did not have a self-sealing fuel tank, and Lee could smell and see the leaking fuel, which wouldn't matter if they got shot to death, but if they wanted to live, they needed to get out of there now.

Another Japanese fighter closed in on their six o'clock, and Lee emptied his thirties at the gleaming green plane with the bright red circles on the wings. He could not confirm any hits on the Zero, but it stopped firing as well. *He must be out of ammo too*, Lee thought. The Zero flew next to them, and Lee and the Japanese pilot stared at each other. The pilot was unshaven and young, with shimmering dark eyes that betrayed how much he was enjoying himself, in spite of his attempt at a bloodthirsty warrior face. He wore a leather helmet with white fur lining, but no goggles. The Japanese pilot broke character, smiled, and pointed behind them. Lee turned in time to see another Zero bearing down on them. Flashes on its wings and over its engine indicated this one was not out of ammunition. Lee ducked down.

Bullets pierced and gashed the Dauntless. Smoke poured from the engine, and the plane dipped to port and began to lose altitude. Lee saw the Zero banking around to make another pass from behind. He turned to check on Ensign Baker. Jeff was dead. Most of his head was gone; chunks of hair, skull, and brain were a bloody mess all over the inside of the cockpit.

No.

Lee was furious—not scared, not nervous. Growling, through clenched teeth, he swiveled his seat to the front and took out his auxiliary control stick. He shipped it into place and righted the plane. The wings leveled out, but the nose did not want to come up. He couldn't work the rudder pedals, at least not with his right foot, because it was shot to hell. Maybe he could push them one at a time with his left foot. Airspeed was dropping. The plane was starting the inevitable process of falling out of the sky.

Lee was in big trouble but still not panicking. He swung his head around to track the killer Zero, and there was the first one, the out-of-ammo Zero, still flying next to him off the starboard wing. The Japanese pilot was still smiling, and gave him a salute. Lee looked to his six o'clock; the not-out-of-ammo Zero was closing in. Lee was facing forward since he was now the pilot, but he was determined to keep fighting the enemy, and to keep the Dauntless in the air. He had never before displayed courage, bravery, or even tenacity, but his inner gladiator was now calling the shots. He wasn't thinking about anything other than his next move to survive. He pulled his .45, and reached back with the pistol in his right hand while holding the stick with his left. Searing pain engulfed his ankle.

He opened fire with his pistol, the Zero opened fire with its two cannons and two machine guns. The sound of bullets hitting metal was louder than the howling wind, and oil sprayed from the engine. Black smoke joined the white smoke filling the cockpit, stinging his lungs. The Zero flew over the Dauntless with a snarl and a hiss, and began to bank around for a front assault. He was going three times faster than the Dauntless, and Lee knew he was a dead man. No hope, no escape.

Lee aimed the plane's nose into a shallow dive, hoping against hope the Zero would miss him again, or run out of ammo, and with luck, he might be able to ditch in the sea. He looked to starboard, where he received another smile and a wave from the Japanese pilot. Lee threw his empty .45 at him. The Pilot's eyes widened with mock fear, and he offered Lee a slight bow before he peeled off. Sayonara.

The other Zero bore down. Straight in, twelve o'clock high. Lee ducked down.

He could hear and feel bits of metal and canopy glass flying around, mixed with the smell of oil and spatters of blood and flesh. Pieces of his own plane hitting him. Pieces of Ensign Baker.

He sat back up.

You sit back up.

On the screen, the Zero is closing in, the black and white images still enough to rage in your mind with shock and anger, forcing you to relive this horror.

The car windshield cracks and shatters in a staccato percussion of violence and hate. Broken shards and slivers implode into the car. Several holes appear in the glass in front of you, and a thick spray of dark red covers most of the car's interior. On the screen, the Zero thunders overhead. You swear you hear its engine behind your car as you try to see how bad your wounds are. Your chest has exploded, your Mae West life vest hanging in tatters of yellow and red. The pain is beyond human capacity; you can't breathe.

Metal grinds as you find reverse and pop the clutch. There's no time to turn the car around, so you slam the gas pedal down with your left foot and try to steer up the hill and out of the drive-in backwards. Gravel sprays and nicks off the car. The engine is wailing, matching your desperation. You get up the hill, blinking and struggling to see through the blood streaming down your face, and the blood splattered all over the back windscreen. The thin steering wheel is hard to grip, slippery with blood splashed and sprayed from your ruined chest. You accelerate with a lurch once you reach level ground; your grip on the wheel fails, and you veer hard right, still in reverse. The front wheels jump off the ground as the Chevy slams backwards into a maple tree.

Leaves and whirlybirds fall in slow motion as you manage to work the latch and fall out of the car. You've got to get out of here. If you can escape this drive-in, this purgatory, this hellscape, maybe the curse can be lifted. Maybe life can make sense again. You get to your feet.

No.

You scream and collapse. The smashed ankle will carry no weight. Crawling is your only option, so you get to it. Elbows and knees. Blood is streaming from your mouth, your lungs are heavy and dense, but you are moving. Get your bearings. Heading to the woods, the bad place. The ticket booth is fifty feet away; maybe you can make it, keep moving.

Is that screaming noise the ghost Zero coming back to finish you? Can't be.

You are hunched over, forehead scraping the ground. You fall. No strength. You belly crawl a few more feet. So much blood. The Zero's guns open up. Gravel kicks up around you, and a rock or bullet fragment blasts through your eye. You barely flinch. Fuck it. *Keep going.* Twenty feet, ten, you're there. No one is manning the booth, but as you look up to the ticket window with your remaining eye, you see that glowing orange light.

The Zero's guns open up again. Sparks and splinters are flying; you reach up and open the door and pull yourself in.

Hellfire. White hot. You collapse. Blind. Numb. Can't move. "You cannot cross until you accept your deeds." The narrator again. You notice the sound of moving water as your body is spread on something cold, flat. A bony hand cradles and lifts the back of your head as two pieces of cold metal are placed on your useless, unseeing eyes. "For the boatman," you say, or hear, or something, or anything, or nothing.

MERCY

By W.J. Renehan

Edwin lay awake in the dark listening to the house. The night wind whipped without whistling in the eaves making the old boards creak. He rubbed his eyes wearily and turned on his side. His dreams had been troubled as of late, and even though he was exhausted he still found himself resisting the black waters of sleep. Moonlight slanted through the small window, bathing all with a cold sheen.

Mercy cried out in her sleep from across the room, a quiet whimper. Perhaps she was having bad dreams as well. He pulled his covers off and swung his legs over the side of the bed. The wooden boards were cold under his stocking feet. They squealed as he pulled on his coat and boots.

The cold bit at his cheeks as the snow mottled landscape yawned to greet him. He walked to the outhouse. After he'd relieved himself, he started back toward the warmth, but he stopped abruptly, struck by the uneasy, heightened feeling that someone or something was watching him.

An owl called from the branch of a nearby tree, a short, baleful hoot. Edwin smiled and was about to turn toward the house when out of the corner of his eye he saw something strange. There was a figure standing in the middle of the western field, staring at him. It was lank, unnaturally tall and thin. It held its hands level with its chest, long, slender fingers splayed out. Its skin looked bone white in the moonlight as it stared, unmoving.

A vagrant, Edwin thought. Perhaps he'd become lost. At length he motioned to it. In response, the figure cocked its head and raised a long, pale finger to its lips.

Edwin turned to the house, wondering if he should wake Father, but when he looked back the figure had vanished. He watched the field for several minutes before returning to the house, cursing his imagination for playing tricks on him.

Edwin woke before sunrise. He hauled water up from the well and left it by the stove for Mother. He then went to the barn to see to the livestock. He set out hay for the horses, filled the pigs' trough, then went to check on Gretta.

The cow was dead, slumped over in her stall.

"Damnation," he cursed under his breath.

Pa would take it hard, money being as tight as it was.

He puzzled over what had killed her. She was young, had been in good health, well cared for.

"Goodbye, Gret," he said, laying a hand on the poor creature.

For a moment he thought of the man in the field. Maybe he hadn't been a mere figment of imagination. Had he come nearer the house—the barn? But there was no sign of foul play. Still the thought troubled him.

He laid an old blanket over the cow and went back to the house.

The smells of coffee, frying eggs and potatoes wafted in the air. Mary Brown was over the stove, George Brown sitting at the dining table. Edwin hung his coat by the door.

"Gretta's died in the night, Pa."

George Brown looked up from his plate.

"You're joking?"

"Afraid not."

"Poor thing," Mary said.

"We can't afford this," George cursed, and banged his fist on the table.

"It'll be all right, Pa," Edwin assured. "Jonas Fournier tells me there's work to be had on his father's property. I could take him up on it, make some extra money."

George shook his head. "No, I can't spare you. There's too much to be done around here."

"I meant in my spare time."

"That's few and far between. I don't want you running yourself down. Then you'll be of no use to anyone."

Edwin heard a soft thud upstairs and the sound of Mercy's angelic voice, singing "I'll Fly Away."

"Another county heard from," Mary pronounced as the girl bounced down the stairs.

"Good morning!" Mercy exclaimed, as though it would be one through her merely saying so.

"Not so good, Sis," Edwin replied. "Gretta passed last night."

"Oh no!" Mercy cried, crestfallen. "Poor Gretta!"

"I don't think she suffered."

"She was a good cow."

Edwin smiled. The girl was sensitive when it came to animals. She had been nearly inconsolable when their collie Annabelle died.

"What you got on today, Son?" George asked.

Edwin took a cup of coffee from the stove and sipped at it.

"We need more firewood. Been burning through it fast this year. Thought I'd head up past the north field and cut some timber."

George nodded. "And I'll go into town. We're low on supplies. Hitch up the wagon for me, Son, when you're done with breakfast."

Mercy jumped with excitement.

"Can I go into town with you, Pa? Oh, please say yes."

"No, no," George replied. "You've got your chores and helping your mother."

"No fair!" the girl pouted.

"Oh, come now," Edwin said, putting an arm around her. "Finish your chores early, and you can come out to help me gather wood."

Mercy hugged him, beaming.

His breath plumed ghostly in the crisp air, the frosted grass crackling beneath his boots. Axe swung over his shoulder, Edwin whistled as he walked along, following the rock wall that skirted the north field. The sun was higher now, cutting through the pale blue like a knife.

He worried, but hid it well. The fall harvest had been meager, and finances had been tight. It wore on father most, though he did his best to share the burden. But things would turn, God willing. He resolved then and there the next growing season would be their most fruitful yet.

He set to work with a renewed vigor, and soon had a large pile of fresh cut timber. It was warmer now, the midday sun bearing down, and he removed his heavy jacket, hanging it from the branch of a nearby tree.

Outside was where men were meant to work, not cooped up in some store or musty office in town. He couldn't imagine living like that. No—he was his father's son. Salt of the earth, born of the land.

He took a deep breath of the fresh, pine scented air and turned back to the task at hand.

After a time, he heard the sweet sound of Mercy's singing approaching, and then she was there by his side.

Her beauty struck him, as it was known to do on occasion. Her features were delicate, green eyes set in her angelic face, her skin fair and freckled. She was the portrait of innocence, unblemished by worldly cares.

She carried her frayed old poppet with her, cradled in the crook of her arm. Elizabeth, she called it.

"And how are you ladies today?" Edwin asked.

"Cold," Mercy replied and rubbed her gloved hands together.

Edwin grinned. "Well you could keep warm by gathering some kindling."

He watched as she scampered off into the woods, and was about to turn back to his work when he heard her cry.

"Edwin! Come and see! Come and see!"

He dropped his axe and ran toward the sound of her voice. She was about twenty yards up ahead of him, staring up at something among the trees.

He jumped over an ancient stump and ducked under a low hanging limb. "What is it?"

"I don't know!"

He reached her side and looked up where she was pointing.

"There," she said.

And he saw.

Among the tree limbs was a large wreath of woven briars hung on a length of rope.

"Why would someone hang it up there?" she asked.

"I'm not sure."

There was something off about it that he didn't like.

"Come on," he said eventually. "Let's go back. I don't want you going so deep into the woods without me."

"No fun," she replied, turning back in the direction they'd come from.

Edwin watched the wreath sway in the wind for a minute, then headed back himself.

Shadows danced as tree branches scraped across the side of the house like skeletal fingers. Edwin slept; his dreams fevered.

In sleep he saw the bedroom door creak open a few inches, long pale fingers wrapping around it, easing it gently. Slowly the door opened onto the dark hall, but he could make out a shadowy form on the threshold, just shy of the moonshine spilling through the window. The figure cocked its head, raised a finger to its lips, and stepped into the room, into the light.

The man from the field, Edwin thought, panicked.

The figure moved to Edwin's bed, its long-nailed fingers clicking impatiently on the footboard. Its black lips pulled back over a set of gleaming fangs, and there was a slight, rasping hiss.

Then, quick as lightening, it was at Mercy's bedside, bending over her little body. It brushed the hair out of her eyes with its foul hand—

Edwin woke gasping.

"Mercy!" he cried, turning to her, but her bed was empty— the girl missing.

He sprang to his feet, pulling on his boots. He raced down the stairs, and seeing that she was not in the house, he opened the door and stepped out into the night.

He circled the house and barn, not finding her, then started to call her name. "Mercy! Mercy!"

George and Mary were coming out of the house.

"Edwin, what's happening?"

"I can't find Mercy!"

"Dear God!" Mary cried.

"Now calm down," George said. "She couldn't have made it far."

They lit lanterns and set out into the cold and blustery night.

Morning dawned bright and clear, and with no sign of the girl. They had returned to the house and were sitting around the dining table eating the little breakfast they could manage, each sick with worry.

Mary broke down in tears.

"We'll find her, Ma," Edwin soothed.

He moved to the front window overlooking the yard, and looked out. "My God!" he cried, rushing to the door. Throwing it open he was confronted by Nathanael Freemont, a neighbor. He held Mercy's small body in his arms, pale and unmoving. "Get her inside," Freemont cried. "Lord, she's cold as ice!"

Inside they laid Mercy in bed, covering her with heavy blankets. Mary stayed with the girl, Edwin and George leading Freemont downstairs, sitting down at the table.

"God save her—I pray I wasn't too late!"

"Calm yourself, Nathanael," George said, placing a hot cup of coffee down before him. "Take your time, tell us what happened."

Freemont took a sip of coffee and tried to settle himself.

"I was hunting in the woods off the western edge of your property when I came upon the Old Snake stream that cuts through there. That's when I saw her, laying on the bank, skin as white as snow. Thought she was dead at first, but when I approached, I could see the rise and fall of her chest. So, I dropped my gun, wrapped her up in my coat and run her here as fast as I could."

"Thank God you were there, Nathanael," Edwin said, placing a hand on the man's shoulder. "Bless you."

Freemont turned to him. "Why was she out there, and in nothing but bedclothes?"

"She disappeared from the house," Edwin replied. "We searched for her all night."

The men were silent for a few minutes, the only sounds those of the wind outside, and the low fevered moans of Mercy from the upstairs room.

At length Mary came down the stairs, looking haggard and worried.

"Her breathing is steady, but there is a fever on her the likes of which I've never seen. We need to fetch Doc Warren."

"I'll go immediately," George said.

Freemont stood. "I'll accompany you."

"Thank you, Nathanael."

After they'd left, Edwin tiptoed up to the bedroom and looked in. Mercy moaned softly in her sleep, shivering underneath the many blankets. Sweat beaded on her flushed forehead.

Edwin knelt and offered up a silent prayer.

Night fell, and with it the fever continued to burn.

Doctor Spence Warren placed the back of his hand against Mercy's forehead. She radiated heat.

"And she's not woken?" Warren asked, turning to Mary.

She shook her head. "She stirs from time to time, but never opens her eyes."

"I see," he pulled the blankets down to uncover her chest, placing his stethoscope over her heart. "Her pulse is faint. I fear she's fading."

"Please, Doctor," Edwin pleaded. "There must be something you can do."

"I'm sorry," Warren replied, removing the stethoscope and placing it in his bag. "She is beyond my skill."

He stood and moved to the door, George stepping aside. "All we can do now is to make her as comfortable as possible. Keep a cool cloth on her head for the fever, and massage her arms and legs to keep the blood circulating. She's in God's hands now."

He placed a reassuring hand on George's shoulder. "Talk to her—all of you. Let her hear your voices. She's still here."

"I'll see you out, Spence," George said, leading him down the stairs. Edwin listened to the creak of their footfalls before turning back to Mercy.

Mary held her little hands.

"Oh, my child … my little child …"

She began to weep.

Edwin comforted her. "Strength, Ma, we need to be strong for her."

For a long time, they were quiet, listening to the sound of Mercy's shallow breathing. Around midnight her body convulsed, her head lifting from the pillow, her face a fevered map of agony. Her eyes shot open and she cried out, crazed, fever delirious—seeing but not seeing—on the precipice of some terrible black gulf. She let out a blood curdling shriek, then fell limp, expelling her last breath.

Her eyes glazed and she fell still.

"She's away," Edwin cried. "She's away …"

Mary collapsed on the bed; arms wrapped about the lifeless child.

"Oh no," George whispered. "No, no, no …"

Outside, the night wind wailed.

Mary dressed her daughter in white. She had always looked best in white—but now, in death, the color only magnified the ghostly, frozen paleness of her fair skin.

The sun fell on her through the high windows of the church.

The entire congregation was present, the silent mourners lining the pews in solemn observance.

The small pine coffin lay at the head of the aisle, directly before the pulpit.

The only sound as the Reverend Northup approached was that of Mary Brown choking back tears.

The Sullivans were there—Robert and Emily, and their two young sons, William and Peter.

Old man Watkins was present, leaning against the back wall beside Stewart Markley and Marcus Bremmer. He still had a ball in his leg from the war, and that day it was aching him something awful.

Young Sara Whitman only had eyes for Edwin, though he took no notice of it, his mind far away.

Samuel Townes stifled a yawn, looked about to see if anyone had noticed.

The Reverend situated himself, then looked up.

"We gather this day to see off one of our flock—one of the brighter lights that shone among us—a gentle, temperate soul who touched each of our lives in a special way. I speak of course of Mercy Brown, youngest child of Brother George and Sister Mary, sibling of Brother Edwin. May God shine his light upon them during this trying time."

He paused, then continued.

"Death, as the good book teaches us, is a return. A reunification with God the Father. The culmination of our mortal being, and a liberation of the immortal soul. Do not pity the girl, for she now walks the majestic halls of the Father's house. Peace is hers, beyond all suffering. Let us pray:

"Yea, though I walk through the valley of the shadow of death, I will fear no evil: for thou art with me; thy rod and thy staff they comfort me ..."

Edwin put an arm around his mother, her body racked with sobs. George stared ahead, eyes brimming with tears.

At length the service concluded, the members taking turns in offering their sympathies, before exiting out into the February cold. The sky was grey and overcast, as though nature herself mourned.

Mercy was to be kept in an aboveground vault until spring, the ground being frozen.

Edwin felt weak in the knees as they closed it up, and his mother collapsed in his arms.

"It's all right, Ma," he whispered in her ear. "It will be all right. We still have each other ..."

It was the truth, and it would have to be enough.

As they departed it began to snow.

Time drew out slowly in the following weeks, under the oppressive, dull hiatus of winter. Pain smoldered like undying embers in their souls, their dreary work made all the drearier. Mary kept to the house even though Edwin encouraged her to venture out. George, for his lot, took to the bottle for the first time since his youth. It came more naturally than he thought it would.

Edwin found himself taking longer and longer walks each day. There was something in it which gave him peace. The bustle of town came to be more attractive to him, and he found himself spending more and more time there.

He took a job with Jonas Fournier on his father's land, and began to stay there instead of returning home. A month passed.

"I appreciate your help," Jonas said one morning, picking up errant pieces of split wood. "And I don't mind having you stay, but don't you worry about your family? When was the last time you saw them?"

Edwin brought his axe down with a grunt, splitting a thick log. "I can't stand it there. It is an unending funeral."

"They have been in my prayers. You should see them, my friend. I will go with you if you wish."

"Thank you, Jonas. But that won't be necessary. I will go to them tomorrow." Closing his eyes, Edwin turned his face up to the sun, letting it warm him.

He stood outside the farmhouse, watching small wisps of smoke rise from the stovepipe. It was freezing out, but he waited a long time to go in, summoning himself. Finally, he walked up to the door and pulled it open.

No lamps had been lit, and with the late afternoon sun retreating in the west the shadows ruled.

Mary sat at the dining table alone.

"Hello, Edwin," she said without looking up. She was knitting something.

"Mother," Edwin acknowledged. "Where is Pa?"

"Oh, he's lying down. He's been sleeping during the day lately. Only wakes at night."

Edwin looked around. Empty liquor bottles were strewn about the room.

The old man was sleeping one off.

Edwin walked into the kitchen and looked in the pantry. The shelves and cupboards were empty.

"Ma," he said, "When was the last time you ate something?"

"Oh, I haven't been hungry," she replied, cheerfully.

She looked pale and haggard, her hair dirty and unkempt. She stank.

How long had she been sitting there? Edwin wondered.

"Has anyone been looking after the livestock?"

She didn't answer, focused on her work.

"Ma, you need to take care of yourself—"

She looked up then. "Have you seen Mercy, Edwin?"

He stared at her, confused.

"What do you mean, Ma?"

"Just what I said; have you seen your sister?"

"Mercy is dead."

"No, she's not, silly," she replied laughing, as if that were the most absurd idea she'd ever heard.

"Mercy is dead, Ma. She's up at Chestnut Hill. Remember?"

"That's nonsense. I saw her just last night. She comes to me."

Edwin stared, bewildered. She'd lost her senses, truly.

"Ma—"

"I'm making her a sweater." She cut him off. "It gets so very cold at night. And to think of her out in that cemetery, it chills me to the very bone."

What could he do? He would have to move back now. He couldn't leave them like this. They wouldn't last a month.

He pulled his coat tighter about him and ran a hand through his hair. He would build the fire up first, then he would check the animals. He hoped to God they were alive.

The real work would begin after that.

"What's this?" George slurred from the bedroom doorway. "Oh, Edwin, I'm glad to see you."

"There's to be no more drinking under this roof," Edwin said sternly. "You've lost your way, Pa."

"You don't get to tell me that," George countered. "I own this house. I'll do what I want in it."

"Not if you don't want my fist in your face, old man."

This gave him pause.

"How could you let Ma get like this?" Edwin demanded, motioning to Mary. "What kind of a man are you?"

George hung his head with no reply.

"Things are changing around here," Edwin declared. "And it starts right now. Pa, you get some wood for the stove, it's freezing in here. I'm going to check on the animals. First thing tomorrow I'll go into town. We need food."

He looked at Mary, then back to George, neither meeting his eyes.

"Damn it all," Edwin cursed, stepping out into the night.

He couldn't sleep, the night drawing out endlessly before him. Every time he closed his eyes all he could see was Mercy staring back at him. Mercy in her frozen vault, eyes open, her gaze cutting into his soul.

He missed her almost more than he could bear—but giving up was not an option. He was the man of the house now, and he would live up to his responsibilities.

A strong gust of wind rattled the old tree outside, branches scratching at the side of the house. He pulled his blankets tighter and tried his best to settle his mind—a futile effort.

Midnight passed without a whisper, and still he lay awake. But then he heard something. Soft at first, from the downstairs.

"I'm coming ..." Mary's voice. "Hold on, darling ..."

She's talking in her sleep, Edwin thought. He'd heard her do so from time to time. What was she dreaming, he wondered.

It was quiet for a time, but then he heard the low creak of the floorboards as someone made their way from the bedroom, down the hall, into the front room.

"Wait, darling ... Wait for Mother ..."

He heard the front door unlatch and the small candle on his night table guttered. He jumped up and rushed to the window, looking down into the yard.

Mary knelt, staring into the western field, arms outstretched as if in embrace. She was saying something, but Edwin couldn't make out what it was over the night wind.

He pulled on his shoes and jacket and ran down the stairs to the ground floor. The doorway yawned before him. Exiting the house, he found Mary, still on her knees, head cocked to the side at an unnatural angle. As he cleared the distance to her, she collapsed in the dirt.

"Ma!" he cried, cradling her head.

She looked at him, dazed, seeming to search for her words. Then her eyes widened.

"Edwin, oh Edwin … Mercy was here …"

"Pa!" Edwin shouted back toward the house. "Pa, get out here!"

George came stumbling out of the house in his pajamas. "Mary! What's the matter? What's happening?"

"Help me get her in the house," Edwin commanded.

Supporting her limp body under each arm they made their way back, her stocking feet dragging.

Inside they laid her on the bed, covering her with blankets. She was pale and shaking with chill. They did their best to warm her.

George paced frantically, unable to calm himself.

"I'll not lose her. I'll not lose my wife as well."

"Pa, calm down," Edwin said. "You're of no use to her like this. Now quick, fetch some hot water."

George stood staring at Mary, not comprehending.

"Now you, old fool!" Edwin shouted.

This shook the man from his stupor.

It was while George was out of the room that Edwin noticed them. On the right side of Mary's neck just above the collarbone there were two small puncture wounds. They ran with a slight trickle of blood. He dabbed at them with a handkerchief until the bleeding ceased.

When George returned Edwin applied a warm washcloth to her forehead, brushing the hair out of her eyes.

"Hold on, Ma," Edwin whispered. "Just you hold on."

The midmorning sun spilled through the bedroom window as Doc Warren leaned over Mary to examine her.

"She rages with fever, just as with Mercy—her heartbeat is rapid, her breaths shallow. Her skin is like milk and is cracked and swollen about the mouth. If I didn't know any better, I'd say these are all symptoms of acute anemia. But you say it came on quite suddenly?"

"Yes," Edwin replied.

"I'm not sure what to make of it."

"What of the wounds on her throat?" Edwin asked.

"Wounds?"

Edwin looked closely—the two small marks had disappeared, the skin smooth and unscarred.

"But there were—"

"You're exhausted," Warren said, standing and putting a hand on his shoulder. "You need rest."

"I can't leave her—"

"Doctor's orders," Warren cut him off.

George stepped into the doorway.

"I'll be with her, son; get some sleep."

Edwin nodded after a moment, went upstairs, and was asleep before his head hit the pillow.

When he woke it was dark; he reached over to his bedside table and checked his pocket watch.

Just after midnight.

The house was quiet, and for a while he lay awake staring into the darkness. He was about to doze off when he heard Mary's voice from her bedroom—a soft whimper.

Edwin got up and went downstairs.

The first thing he noticed was that the front door was wide open. Then he saw his father was asleep at the dining table, his head resting beside an empty bottle.

Edwin turned and rushed to the bedroom, to his mother's side. Her lifeless eyes stared upward, wide with abject horror, her mouth gaping in a silent scream.

The wounds on her neck had reopened, and blood soaked through the pillow and mattress, pooling on the floor beside the bed.

"Ma," he cried.

The sound of childish laughter sounded from outside, and Edwin sprang to his feet, rushing to the front door and out into the night.

A small, ghostly white figure was walking into the western field.

"Stop!" Edwin shouted.

The figure stilled on command.

"Show yourself," he said, moving closer.

The figure took a slow turn, and that was when everything stopped for Edwin.

Her angelic face—her lovely brown braided hair—the dress in which she had been interred, now stained with splashes of dark blood.

"Mercy?" he half whispered, heart pounding in his chest.

"Hello, brother," she sang, her voice like chimes in a soft wind.

"But you're—you're—"

"Dead?" she giggled. "No, brother, I'm so much more than that."

He was silent for a moment.

"Did you kill Ma?"

She smiled, revealing a set of jagged fangs.

"That's how it starts. That's what he told me. It starts with the family."

"How what starts? Who are you talking about?"

"All will be revealed in time, Edwin."

She began to walk away, stopped after a few paces and turned back. "Give Pa my regards."

She disappeared into the field, leaving Edwin breathless and shivering.

He buried his mother under the twisted, ancient elm they liked to picnic under during the warmer weather, the ground having thawed some.

His first memory was of her—her rocking him in her arms, singing, lulling him to sleep. She had taught him to read, taught him about nature, taught him about faith. Father had always been mercurial, distant—but she, she had been everything to him. How was it that the world kept turning?

He had just finished smoothing out the dirt when he noticed how quiet everything was. No birdcall, no wind through the trees, no sound from the house.

"Pa?" he called. No response.

He went into the house. "Pa?" Nothing.

He went to check for him in the barn, and it was there that he found him.

Edwin cut the rope with his boot knife, the old man dropping to the hay-strewn floor with a dull thud.

He stepped down from the ladder, sat on a bale of hay and watched for a while.

He could have picked a higher beam and tried to break his neck, but no—his father had gone the slow way. And maybe that's what he'd intended.

Edwin put his head in his hands and wept bitterly.

It was mid-afternoon when he began to dig a second grave.

His throat burned as he took another pull from the bottle, emptying it. Father had at least left him with an ample supply. He tossed the bottle against the far wall, sending bits of glass flying. Laughing, he pulled another from the pantry, unscrewing the cap manically, taking another long drink.

She'd be back tonight. He was somehow sure of it.

Placing the bottle down on the table he moved to the wall at the head of the dining table and reached high up to where his father's Winchester hung. He then retrieved the box of shells from the back of one of the high kitchen cabinets. Father had always worried about Mercy reaching them. Edwin laughed at the thought and began to load the weapon.

When she showed tonight, he'd blow a hole through her face. A simple enough plan.

His hands were shaking. He took another long pull from the bottle and sat down in his father's old rocker with the rifle laid across his lap.

The sun still shone in the west, bathing all in an otherworldly, mauveish half-light.

The liquor was working its way, and he felt his nerves smoothing out. He urged on the night, and whatever it might bring.

Mercy's pallid face greeted him as he woke.

She smiled, lips pulling back over gleaming fangs.

He groped for the rifle, only to find it was missing.

"You won't be needing that," she giggled.

She took a little turn about the room. "Just look at this place. Aren't you sick of it, Edwin? So dank and sad."

"This is our home!" he shouted.

"Was," she corrected. "There's nothing left to it now. Just some old rotted boards and the silence."

"Thanks to you."

She turned to him, eyes shining in the candlelight. "Yes."

"Why?" he demanded.

"Why does the beetle nourish the lark? Because it is the way of things. The natural order."

"There's nothing natural about what you've done."

She shook her head, disappointed. "How blind you are, brother. But I will open your eyes—"

In a flittering instant she was before him, hands wrapped about his head, drawing his gaze into her own.

"Look at me, Edwin—look at me."

Her eyes stared, black and glassy, like those of a doll, but there was something within them, something alluring, seductive. He found himself falling into them, dark waters immersing his mind, washing away all fear, all doubt. And there was a sound, in the depths of the void, it throbbed and hummed and wound about him—like—like the summer! Yes, that's what it was: the summer, singing in his head—the calls of birds, a chorus of insects, the whispers of breezes, flooding his senses. And through it all came the sound of Mercy's sweet voice.

"You love me, don't you Edwin?"

"Yes," he replied in a whisper.

"You would do anything for me?"

"I would ..."

She laughed, but it was a cold and hollow sound.

"Then you must listen carefully ..."

And he did.

It was midmorning by the time Robert Sullivan finished loading up the wagon for his trip into town. William and Peter were running about the yard engaged in a game of tag. Robert stood for a moment admiring his children before calling them over.

"Boys! Come here!"

They did as they were told.

"Now boys, you can play for a little while longer, but then I want you to get to your chores. I want a good report from your mother when I get back."

"Yes, Father," they replied in unison.

"Good."

They stood and watched as the wagon worked its way down the road until disappearing around the bend.

William shoved his brother. "You're it!"

He then sprinted off into the large hayfield.

"I'm gonna get you!" Peter howled, giving chase.

William ran and ran, the winter air cold in his lungs. Eventually he reached the rock wall that marked the northern end of their property. He jumped over it and ran deep into the woods, taking cover behind a dense thicket. He could see Peter approaching the wall, not too far off now.

Then came the sound of crunching leaves from behind.

William spun around to meet a tall figure emerging from the dense woods.

"Hello, William," the figure said, the glare of the sun skewing the boy's view.

"Edwin Brown? Is that you?"

"Yes," Edwin replied, before punching the boy in the face. William fell to the ground in a heap, unconscious.

Edwin moved to scoop the boy up, but as he did so he caught a glimpse of something among the trees.

Peter stared, a confused expression over his face.

Edwin started for him, and the boy turned to run. The chase lasted only a minute before Edwin closed on him, knocking him to the ground.

He dropped a knee on the boy's back and pulled a jackknife from his boot.

"Please!" Peter cried, but Edwin had already plunged the blade into the boy's back. Hot blood splashed his face as he stabbed the boy over and over again—until his soft cries gurgled to a shallow halt.

Edwin wiped the blade clean on the boy's sleeve and tucked it back into his boot.

He turned and went to collect what he had come for.

Emily Sullivan was dropping a bucket down the well when she was startled by a short cry.

She turned to see her youngest son stumble out of the hayfield, blood running from his mouth and down his shirtfront.

She ran to him, the boy falling into her arms.

"Peter! What happened? Dear God, who did this to you?"

He coughed up a spray of blood and spittle, fighting for breath. His skin was pale and frozen. Finally, he was able to form the words:

"Edwin … Brown …"

He expired in his mother's arms.

It was near sunset as Edwin reached the farm, the boy hoisted over his shoulder. He'd avoided the roads, sticking to the woods so as not to be seen, and he was now cold and weary.

But Mercy would be pleased.

He smiled to think of her—she who was all he had left in the world. She was his responsibility now, and he would bear that weight no matter what it might entail, no matter how black the deed.

The boy stirred, and Edwin quickened pace.

He bound William to one of the barn's support beams, then set about lighting lanterns, as dark had fallen.

"Momma," the child murmured, eyes squinting under the brightness of the lanterns, slowly coming to his senses. "Momma, what's happening?"

"I'm sorry, William," Edwin said. "Your mother's not here."

"But I am," a voice sounded from the doorway. Edwin turned, and there she was—radiant, divine. Her snow white skin almost seemed to glow. Edwin thought that was how angels must look.

Her purple lips pulled back over elongated, jagged canines, wet and shining.

Seeing her, the boy began to scream, struggling against his bonds. Edwin shoved a balled-up rag into his mouth.

"Oh, William," she said, walking toward him slowly, deliberately, "surely you know that it's no use crying. There's no one for miles, and no one knows you're here."

She stroked the boy's cheek with a pale finger.

"My bountiful wine press for a while …"

Edwin stood back in the shadows, watching the dance.

He didn't approve of how she toyed with the boy. Was that truly necessary, the act grim enough as it was? But what was he to say? He feared her. She had shown him beauty, yes—but could she not also show him horror? He did not wish to find out.

"You're part of something beautiful," she whispered to the boy. "You're the beginning of something wondrous …"

She grabbed the boy's head by the hair and pulled it to the side, exposing the neck. "So fine," she whispered in his ear, as a lover might— and in one fluid movement she latched onto his throat, lips sucking at the torn flesh.

The boy squealed, eyes gaping wide and panicked.

Edwin's stomach turned, and he fought to keep his gorge down.

After a few minutes Mercy pulled back from the boy, her crimson lips smacking wetly. She basked in the warm, invigorating rush, the boy's blood flowing through her—nourishing, rejuvenating.

"What now?" Edwin asked, stirring her from her ecstasy. She turned.

"He must rest. Bring him to the house. When he has regained his strength, I shall return, and by then the infection will be well along its way—"

"And then?"

"He will change. Become as I am.

Edwin was quiet for a moment.

"Why did ma not change?"

"Because she did not drink of my essence. I must give him my blood to affect the metamorphosis. That's what Malcolm told me."

"Who is Malcolm?"

"The one who made me."

"Why make more of you? Why the boy?"

She sighed. "Because it is only natural—the most natural thing in the world—to spread. The old world has been drained of its vitality, but the new, the lifeblood of the new world runs pure, untapped. A new arcadia, flush with life—"

"MY GOD!" came a shout from the doorway.

They turned to face a group of men with torches and rifles. Robert Sullivan was at their head, Samuel Townes, Stewart Markley, and Marcus Bremmer behind him.

Sullivan stepped forward; shotgun raised.

"William!" He turned the gun on Edwin. "What have you done, you son of a bitch?!"

Mercy hissed, bearing her fangs.

Sullivan shrank back, trembling.

"Dear God—that's Mercy Brown!"

"She's dead, you fool," Samuel Townes replied.

"No," Sullivan said, turning the gun on Mercy now. "That's her, plain as God damn day!"

The men murmured.

"Monster!" Sullivan cried and fired.

The blast hit her square in the chest, ripping through her dress, but she did not flinch, unharmed.

"DAEMON!"

The others began to aim their weapons, zeroing in on Mercy. But with preternatural speed she flew past them, knocking Townes and Markley to the ground, disappearing into the night.

Regaining their feet, the two men rushed at Edwin, restraining him. They bound his hands behind his back and gave him a few swift punches to the gut. He doubled over, gasping.

Sullivan rushed to his son, untying the boy and laying him down on the hay-strewn floor. "It's all right, William. Papa's here, no one will hurt you …"

Sullivan pounded on the heavy oak door.

"Reverend! Please answer!"

After a minute the door unlatched and swung open, Reverend Northup stepping out into the frozen night. "Robert, what are you doing out at this hour?"

"God's work, Reverend. I've seen it with my own eyes; we all have—Edwin Brown has been communing with devils. He's raised his sister from the grave— she walks this very night! They killed my youngest, Peter, and assaulted William. He lies at home unable to wake."

"Good God," Northup replied. He turned to Edwin, who was restrained and under guard. "Edwin, is this the truth? Are you in league with Satan?"

Edwin looked up. "You don't understand. None of you—"

Steward Markley struck him in the gut with the stock of his rifle. "Save your excuses, you filth. You'll hang for what you've done."

"What of the monster, Reverend?" Sullivan asked.

"In God's name she must be destroyed."

"But she had disappeared, slipped into the night."

"Worry not. There is but one place she can turn."

A light rain began, mist rising from the snow mottled ground, hanging ghostly over the Chestnut Hill graveyard. Reverend Hale led the party, hissing torch held before him, passing between graves and tombs.

Edwin was silent as he trudged along, the occasional shove forcing him to quicken pace. Samuel Townes leaned in close, smiling.

"Gonna hang you in the morning. You'll be in Hell before noon."

Edwin turned, his dead stare meeting the man's. There was nothing, no trace of emotion there. Samuel's smile disappeared, and he stepped back, averting his gaze.

They arrived before the vault, blazing torchlight illuminating its iron face.

"Satan must be given no quarter," Reverend Northup pronounced. "It is God's will that the daemon be destroyed."

He turned to face the men. "She will appear but a child, but do not be fooled; the evil which animates her is older than our world. Do not listen to her words, for she may poison you against one another. Do not meet her eyes, or she will influence your senses. Heed my words, men."

Stewart Markley and Marcus Bremmer pulled the iron door open with a harsh grating sound, then thrust their torches into the darkness.

Inside, the coffin lay intact—unopened.

The men came forward and lifted it, carrying it out into the night. Placing it down on the earth, they proceeded to remove the nails. This accomplished, Robert Sullivan opened the lid, revealing what lay beneath. The men gathered around, staring with wary, morbid curiosity.

Mercy lay within, with all the appearance of death—save for a slight blush to her cheeks.

"We must pierce her heart," Northup said, holding out a long wooden stake. It is the only way to be certain."

He motioned to Samuel Townes. "Young Samuel," he slipped the stake into the man's hand. "The heart."

"Yes, Reverend."

He moved to stand over the body, running his eyes over the girl, gathering his courage. Her face looked so placid, so innocent, but the scene at the barn returned to him: her fanged mouth running with blood, her eyes as black as bottomless pools.

Those eyes were open now—it hadn't registered in his mind, but he was already lost in them. His sweaty hand gripped the stake, and he raised it over his head.

"Die, monster!"

And with that he spun and drove the stake through Stewart Markley's neck. A drowned scream bubbled up from his throat with a gout of dark blood

"Dear God!" Northup cried.

Marcus Bremmer rushed at Mercy with an axe raised over his head.

But her black gaze washed over him, and he planted the axe in Reverend Northup's gut. He doubled over moaning, his bowels sloshing out, steaming on the ground beneath him.

Seeing opportunity, Edwin began to struggle with his bonds.

Townes pulled the stake from Markley's neck and turned on Robert Sullivan. Sullivan raised his rifle and blew a hole in Townes's shoulder. The man collapsed to the ground. Sullivan scrambled to pick up the stake, then turned on Mercy.

He dropped to his knees and, closing his eyes, began to stab wildly at her. He struck her several times in the abdomen before finally connecting with her ribs, then, using all his strength, he punched through them, piercing her heart.

"No!" Edwin cried, falling to the ground.

Sullivan opened his eyes just as the change began.

A great geyser of blood rushed from her mouth. Her skin blackened and shriveled up to the bones, crackling and peeling like burning paper. Her eyes burst, white mucous splashing Sullivan's face. Her limbs began to writhe and convulse, smoke rising from bubbling, blistering boils, before the body crumbled to dust.

"My God," Bremmer cried, standing over Hale's lifeless body. "Did I … Did I …?"

"It wasn't your fault," Townes spoke, clutching his wounded shoulder. "She bewitched us, just as the Reverend said she would."

Sullivan stood and turned to Edwin.

"It's just you now, you bastard."

Moonlight shone through the barred windows of the cell, casting Edwin in striped shadow. He would hang on the morrow, but he wasn't afraid.

He'd be with Ma and Pa again.

Maybe even with Mercy.

Surely God would not punish a child, if he were truly just.

The creak of an opening door sounded down the hall, and Edwin assumed it was the night guard again, come to jeer at him. He looked up as two snow white hands with long, jagged nails wrapped about the cell bars. Then the face appeared between them; the face from his dreams, from that night in the field.

"Hello, Edwin," came the soft hiss of a voice.

Edwin cocked his head. "Malcolm is it?"

A smile split the face. "Indeed."

"What do you want?"

"You, Edwin. I came for you."

"What do you mean?"

The monster sighed. "It was all for you. Mercy, your parents, the Sullivan boys—all a test. A test you passed, Edwin."

The cell door unlatched and groaned open, the figure spreading its arms in embrace.

Edwin slid back against the wall, eyes wide, trembling.

"Don't be afraid, Edwin," the monster soothed. "Take my yoke upon you and learn from me, for my yoke is easy, my burden light."

Edwin met its ancient eyes, and instead of fear he felt relief, for he could hear the summer coming back, humming in his head like a hive—and Mercy's voice was there too, calling him home.

AWAKENING

By Tara Bennett

Make it stop!

My senses are on overload. The constant tick of the clock is piercing my brain. A shiver dances along my skin. Though it is the middle of July, I can't get warm. A thick odor lingers in the room. It smells like skunk. The taste in my mouth is awful, like I've been chewing on a pipe. I don't understand this. The light is almost too bright. I can see indistinct shapes. My head is in a fog, and I feel like I've been unconscious for days. Where am I? What's going on? Why can't I remember what happened?

Think!

I feel like I've been through hell. Pain has taken over my body, particularly the right side of my head. I struggle to move. Something cold and hard is beneath me. A sticky, wet substance pulls from my cheek as I push myself up, not quite onto my knees. Am I in a room? Yes, that must be it. There's a faint outline in the distance. A sleeping bag?

Turning my head is difficult, but I manage. It must be morning. Light shines through the window blinds, and yes, I am in a room. There's a rectangular shape along one wall–a TV? And something long across from it, a couch maybe? It dawns on me then. I'm not just in any room, but in a living room. I still don't know how I got here. If I can just move, maybe I can figure it out.

The smell is so strong I think I'm going to vomit. What *is* it? Maybe it's not just a skunk, but a dead one.

Wherever I am, I hope the heat kicks on soon, it's freezing in here. No. That's not going to happen. It's summertime. Maybe the air conditioning is on, and that is why I am so cold. Wait! The sleeping bag. If I can reach it, I can warm up. At least I can cover my nose with it and get some relief from this gawd awful smell.

These people are pigs. There is trash on the floor. Bottles and cups and … was there a party here? Was I at a party and passed out? Maybe … They shouldn't have left this mess. They need to clean this place. Or hire a maid. Ooh, a maid! If they have a maid, maybe she'll find me and help me. Maybe she'll tell me what is going on and why I feel so bad, like someone struck me in the head with a hammer several times. *Please* have a maid.

No. That makes no sense. There's no maid. If they had a maid, this place wouldn't be trashed and wouldn't smell like someone died here.

Like someone *died?* Is that what I smell? Not a dead skunk, but a dead …

What if someone *did* die in here? The scent is horrific. That must be it. I could be in here with a dead body! Someone could find me *and* the body. What if I get blamed for killing someone? I could get arrested for murder. There is no doubt they would pin it on me. Someone is dead, and I'm here. Case closed. Even if I don't remember anything—and I don't—I'm going to get the blame. I'm going to go to jail. I can't go to jail. I'll never survive jail.

I need to get out of here. Move, damn it! Why can't I move my legs? I'll never get out of here if I can only move my head and arms.

My nose itches. Ewww ... my face feels sticky. The left side screams when I touch it. I must have been in a fight. But I can't remember any of it. I hope I got some good ones in before my beating, because that is what it had to be, a beating. That would explain why my head hurts. One mystery solved! Now, how I'm going to get out of here? Maybe I can slide my way around until my legs decide they're going to work. I honestly don't think that will happen. Something has happened to my legs, and I think the beating I received had something to do with it.

At least my eyes are clearing. It's getting easier to see. I think I see a door. It's on the other side of the couch, near the television. I have to get to it. I have to. I can do this. I am getting out of here. There's no way I'm sticking around this place. Here we go, one arm in front of the other, right? It would be much easier if it wasn't so damn cold though. Moving will warm me up. Perhaps it will get my legs moving too and get me out of here faster. I can hope, right?

Almost to the couch. I feel like a baseball announcer. *He's rounding second on his way to the couch. He's nearing the sleeping bag at third, and on his way to the edge of the couch, home plate just beyond it!* There's no smell of popcorn or hotdogs here though. Just the odor and it's getting worse. I am *so* using that sleeping bag to cover my face. I need a break from this stench.

Whew! I finally made it to the couch. Cheers for me! Break time. I'll just lean here for a second or two, just long enough to catch my breath. The sun must be up all the way now, but I'm still having trouble seeing. It's like someone put gauze in my eyes after hitting me in the head repeatedly.

I need to hurry. Someone will show up eventually. Then I'm toast.

The smell is worse as I try to round the couch. It could be something outside, something I have to get by in order to escape this nightmare. Almost there; I see the sleeping bag clearer now. Wait. There's *something* else. *That's* not a sleeping bag. Is it a pile of clothes? I can't quite make it out yet. I have to get closer.

My vision clears as I near the pile.

Is that a foot?

Is that a pair of jeans?

Is that a sweatshirt?

Is that blood? Yes! Lots of blood.

Is that m*y* foot? Are those *my* jeans? Is that *my* sweatshirt? Is that … *my body*?

That's *me*.

I … I don't understand. How … how can I be there, and be *here*? That can't be … that can't be *my* body. I'm not …

Dead.

I touch the side of my head. I haven't been struck by a hammer or bat or a pipe. The left side of my head is missing. I can feel sharp fragments of bone—my skull. I taste blood. I feel the pain.

I'm dead.

I'm dead.

I don't know how I got here or what happened to me. All I know is I'm *never* getting out of here.

ABOUT THE AUTHORS

NICHOLAS PASCHALL has been writing professionally since 2011, with over twenty anthologies and magazine pieces under his name. His first published novel, *the Father of Flesh*, came out through Darkwater Syndicate in 2017. The sequel, *Travails for Teyuna*, came out the following year. Nicholas was a recurring columnist for *Dark Eclipse Magazine* for two years and has been a recurring writer for the London Horror Society since 2016.

Nicholas maintains a website that he updates with new stories, serials, and novel tie-ins every Monday, Wednesday, Friday. He can be found on Facebook and Twitter, and would love to hear what you think of his work.

Twitter: @Nelfeshne
Facebook: @NickPaschallHorror
Website: https://www.nickronomicon.com/

MIKE L. LANE writes horror fiction and loathes writing bios because lies are far more entertaining than the truth. He was born and raised in El Dorado, Arkansas, but rest assured there is no gold there. He longs to live in the collective mind of horror fans everywhere, burning character driven nightmares into their subconscious with a blowtorch. Currently, he resides in the shadows, crafting dark, twisted tales and anxiously awaiting the day he will plunge the world into darkness! *Mwahahahaha*! He enjoys screams, madness, nightfall, cemeteries and My Little Pony. You can follow Mike's path of destruction through the links below.

Facebook- https://www.facebook.com/MikeLLaneAuthor
Web- http://mikellane.com/
Amazon- https://www.amazon.com/author/mikelane

RUBY POND is an author, creative prose and poetry writer who lives in Florida with her husband and two children. She has had a passion for writing since childhood but, was steered toward a career in the medical laboratory field after one term in the US ARMY. Her writing accomplishments include: poetry and short story publications in Rhetoric Askew Anthologies, Volume 3 and 4, two other anthologies due to be released in the summer of 2018 and she is currently working on a novel and a children's book. You can find some of her work on her website at

https://www.rubypondallthatiswriterly.com and also on theprose.com.

W.J. RENEHAN published his first novella, Night's Harbor, in 2015. This was followed by volumes one and two of his short story collection Shades and Divinations. He had previously published a well-received horror fiction study in 2013, The Art of Darkness: Meditations on the Effect of Horror Fiction. Renehan is as well a respected horror reviewer and serves as editor-in-chief and publisher at Dark Hall Press, home to Shane Stadler's critically acclaimed Exoskeleton and other high regarded works by a range of authors.

EZEKIEL KINCAID resides in Baton Rouge, Louisiana, with his wife, four children, and two dogs. When he's not working, writing horror, or doting on his family, he likes to train in martial arts. The only other language he is fluent in is sarcasm. For fun, Zeke enjoys watching people get in socially awkward circumstances. He hates cat videos but loves watching wrestling promos from the 80's.

DAVID CLARK is the author of multiple horror novels and anthologies, and has been featured in other published anthologies. His writing focuses on the suspense, horror, and sci-fi genres with a writing style based on reality, and developing characters the reader can connect with and pull for. He sends the reader on a roller-coaster journey the best fortune teller cannot predict. He feels his job is done if the reader has a visceral reaction to his tales.

https://www.facebook.com/DavidClarkHorror/
https://www.amazon.com/author/david_t_clark

Hailing from the not so frozen wilds of Northern England, CARL BARKER is the author of numerous horror short stories, his work having been published in a variety of magazines and anthologies including The Alchemy Press Book of Urban Mythic 2, Shadow Masters – An Anthology from The Horror Zine, and Paul Finch's Terror Tales series. Carl's debut collection, 'Parlour Tricks', was published by Parallel Universe Publications in the summer of 2017 to positive reviews. He is currently working on what he hopes will be the first of a trilogy of linked novellas set in the late nineteenth century.

Carl currently lives and works in the North East, where it's really not as grim as people make out, and is a member of both The Horror Writers Association and The British Fantasy Society.

For more information about his work, please visit www.holeinthepage.co.uk

WOLFGANG POTTERHOUSE is a prematurely grey, occasional vegetarian, middle school teaching, non-native Texan. He has four children and a beautiful wife, all of whom think he is a pretty okay dude. He is a Cancer and is not afraid to tear up when someone gets voted off Master Chef. He has several stories published in an accordion file in his den; this is his second story to get legitimately published.

PETER MOLNAR is an author, singer-songwriter, musician, educator, and editor. His short stories have appeared in City Slab: Urban Tales of the Grotesque, Necrotic Shorts, Hydrophobia: A Charity Anthology to Benefit Hurricane Harvey Victims, and the upcoming Tenebrous Tales Anthology. His blog, "As the Shadow Stirs", is a mashup of music, movies, horror, and superheroes and can be found on his home webpage. Broken Birds is his debut novel. He lives and works in Southeastern Pennsylvania with his wife, daughter, and two cats. Currently, he is at work on his next book and a slew of new short entries. Visit Peter at the following sites:

www.petermolnarauthor.com
www.facebook.petermolnarauthor.com

www.PMolnarAuthor/twitter
www.instagram.com/pmolnar423